THE ROAD TO THE OPEN

THE ROAD TO
THE OPEN   BY
ARTHUR SCHNITZLER

AUTHORISED TRANSLATION
BY HORACE SAMUEL

NEW YORK · ALFRED A. KNOPF MCMXXIII

GEORGE VON WERGENTHIN sat at table quite alone to-day. His elder brother Felician had chosen to dine out with friends for the first time after a longish interval. But George felt no particular inclination to renew his acquaintance with Ralph Skelton, Count Schönstein or any of the other young people, whose gossip usually afforded him so much pleasure ; for the time being he did not feel in the mood for any kind of society.

The servant cleared away and disappeared. George lit a cigarette and then in accordance with his habit walked up and down the big three-windowed rather low room, while he wondered how it was that this very room which had for many weeks seemed to him so gloomy was now gradually beginning to regain its former air of cheerfulness. He could not help letting his glance linger on the empty chair at the top end of the table, over which the September sun was streaming through the open window in the centre. He felt as though he had seen his father, who had died two months ago, sit there only an hour back, as he visualised with great clearness the very slightest mannerisms of the dead man, even down to his trick of pushing his coffee-cup away, adjusting his pince-nez or turning over the leaves of a pamphlet.

George thought of one of his last conversations with his father which had occurred in the late spring before they had moved to the villa on the Veldeser Lake. George had just then come back from Sicily, where he had spent April with Grace on a melancholy and somewhat boring farewell tour before his mistress's final return to America. He had done no real work for six months or more, and had not even copied out the plaintive adagio which he had heard in the plashing of the waves on a windy morning in Palermo as he walked along the beach. George had played over the theme to his father and improvised on it with an exaggerated wealth of harmonies which almost swamped the original melody, and when he had launched into a wildly modulated variation, his father had smilingly asked him from the other end of the piano—" Whither away, whither away ? " George had felt abashed and allowed the swell of the notes to subside, and his father had begun a discussion about his son's future with all his usual affection, but with rather more than his usual seriousness. This conversation ran through his mind to-day as though it had been pregnant with presage. He stood at the window and looked out. The park outside was fairly empty. An old woman wearing an old-fashioned cloak with glass beads sat on a seat. A nursemaid walked past holding one child by the hand while another, a little boy, in a hussar uniform, with a buckled-on sabre and a pistol in his belt, ran past, looked haughtily round and saluted a veteran who came down the path smoking. Further down the grounds were a few people sitting round the kiosk, drinking coffee and reading the papers. The foliage was still fairly thick, and the park looked depressed and dusty and altogether far more summer-like than usual for late September.

George rested his arms on the window-sill, leant forwards and looked at the sky. He had not left Vienna since his father's death, though he had had many opportunities of so doing. He could have gone with Felician to the Schönstein estate ; Frau Ehrenberg had written him a charming letter inviting him to come to Auhof ; he could easily have found a companion for that long-planned cycle-tour through Carinthia and the Tyrol, which he had not the energy to undertake alone. But he preferred to stay in Vienna and occupy his time with perusing and putting in order the old family papers. He found archives which went as far back as his great-grandfather Anastasius von Wergenthin, who haled from the Rhine district and had by his marriage with a Fräulein Recco become possessed of an old castle near Bozen which had been uninhabitable for a long period. There were also documents dealing with the history of George's grandfather, a major of artillery who had fallen before Chlum in the year 1866.

The major's son, the father of Felician and himself, had devoted himself to scientific studies, principally botany, and had taken at Innsbruck the degree of Doctor of Philosophy. At the age of twenty-four he had made the acquaintance of a young girl of an old family of Austrian officials, who had brought her up to be a singer, more with a view to rendering her independent of the limited, not to say impoverished, resources of the household, than because she had any real vocation. Baron von Wergenthin saw and heard her for the first time at a concert-performance of the Missa Solemnis and in the following May she became his wife. Three years later the health of the Baroness began to fail, and she was ordered South by the doctors. She did not recover as soon as was anticipated, with the result that the house in Vienna was given up, and the Baron and his family lived for several years a kind of hotel-life, as they travelled from one place to another. His business and studies frequently summoned the Baron to Vienna, but the sons never left their mother. The family lived in Sicily, Rome, Tunis, Corfu, Athens, Malta, Meran, the Riviera, and finally in Florence ; never in very great style, but fairly well nevertheless, and without curtailing their expenditure sufficiently to prevent a substantial part of the Baron's fortune being gradually eaten up. George was eighteen when his mother died. Nine years had passed since then, but the memory of that spring evening

was still as vivid as ever, when his father and brother had
happened to be out, and he had stood alone and helpless
by his mother's death-bed, while the talk and laughter of
the passers-by had flowed in with the spring air through
the hastily opened windows with all the jar of its unwelcome
noise.

The survivors took their mother's body back to Vienna.
The Baron devoted himself to his studies with new and
desperate zeal.   He had formerly enjoyed the reputation of
an aristocratic dilettante, but he now began to be taken
quite seriously even in academic circles, and when he was
elected honorary president of the Botanical Society he
owed that distinction to something more than the accident
of a noble name.   Felician and George entered themselves
as law students.   But after some time their father himself
encouraged the boys to abandon their university studies,
and go in for a more general education and one more in
accordance with their musical tendencies.   George felt
thankful and relieved at this new departure.   But even in
this sphere which he had chosen himself, he was by no
means industrious, and he would often occupy himself
for weeks on end with all manner of things that had nothing
at all to do with his musical career.

It was this same trait of dilettantism which made him
now go through the old family documents as seriously as
though he were investigating some important secrets of
the past.   He spent many hours busying himself with
letters which his parents had exchanged in years gone by,
wistful letters and superficial letters, melancholy letters
and placid letters, which brought back again to life not
merely the departed ones themselves but other men and
women half sunk in oblivion.   His German tutor now
appeared to him again with his sad pale forehead just
as he used to declaim his Horace to him on their long
walks, there floated up in his mind the wild brown boyish
face of Prince Alexander of Macedon in whose company

George had had his first riding lessons in Rome ; and then the Pyramids of Cestius limned as though in a dream with black lines on a pale blue horizon reared their peaks, just as George had seen them once in the twilight as he came home from his first ride in the Campagna. And as he abandoned himself still more to his reverie there appeared sea-shores, gardens and streets, though he had no know- ledge of the landscape or the town that had furnished them to his memory ; images of human beings swept past him ; some of these, whom he had met casually on some trivial occasion, were very clear, others again, with whom he might at some time or other have passed many days, were shadowy and distant.

When George had finished inspecting the old letters and was putting his own papers in order, he found in an old green case some musical jottings of his boyhood, whose very existence had so completely vanished from his memory, that if they had been put before him as the records of some one else he would not have known the difference. Some affected him with a kind of pleasant pain, for they seemed to him to contain promises which he was perhaps never to fulfil. And yet he had been feeling lately that something had been hatching within him. He saw his development as a mysterious but definite line which showed the way from those first promising notes in the green case to quite new ideas, and this much he knew—the two songs out of the " Westöstliche Divan " which he had set to music this summer on a sultry afternoon, while Felician lay in his hammock and his father worked in his armchair on the cool terrace, could not have been composed by your ordinary person.

George moved back a step from the window as though surprised by an absolutely unexpected thought. He had never before realised with such clearness that there had been an absolute break in his life since his father's death down to to-day. During the whole time he had not given a single thought to Anna Rosner to whom he had sent the songs in manuscript. And he felt pleasurably thrilled at the thought that he could hear her melodious melancholy voice again and accompany her singing on that somewhat heavy piano, as soon as he wished. And he remembered the old house in the Paulanergasse, with its low door and badly lighted stairs which he had not been up more than three or four times, in the mood in which a man thinks of something which he has known very long and held very dear.

A slight soughing traversed the leaves in the park out-side. Thin clouds appeared over the spire of the Stephan Tower, which stood directly opposite the window, on the other side of the park, and over a largish part of the town. George was faced with a long afternoon without any engage-ments. It seemed to him as though all his former friend-ships during the two months of mourning had dissolved or broken up. He thought of the past spring and winter with all their complications and mad whirl of gaiety, and all kinds of images came back into his memory—the ride with Frau Marianne in the closed fiacre through the snow-covered forest. The masked ball at Ehrenberg's with Else's subtly-naive remarks about " Hedda Gabler " with whom she insisted she felt a certain affinity, and with Sissy's hasty kiss from under the black lace of her mask. A mountain expedition in the snow from Edlach up to the Rax with Count Schönstein and Oskar Ehrenberg, who, though very far from being a born mountaineer, had jumped at the opportunity of tacking himself on to two blue-blooded gentlemen. The evening at Ronacher's with Grace and young Labinski, who had shot himself four days afterwards either on account of Grace, debts, satiety, or as a sheer piece of affectation. The strange hot and cold conversation with Grace in the cemetery in the melting February snow two days after Labinski's funeral. The evening in the hot lofty fencing-room where Felician's sword had crossed the dangerous blade of the Italian master. The walk at night after the Paderewski concert when his father had spoken to him more intimately than ever before of that long-past evening on which his dead mother had sung in the Missa Solemnis in the very hall which they had just come out of. And finally Anna Rosner's tall quiet figure appeared to him, leaning on the piano, with the score in her hand, and her smiling blue eyes turned towards the keys, and he even heard her voice reverberating in his soul.

While he stood like this at the window and looked down at the park which was gradually becoming animated, he felt a certain consolation in the fact that he had no close ties with any human being, and that there were so many people to whom he could attach himself once more and whose set he could enter again as soon as the fancy took him. He felt at the same time wonderfully rested and more in the vein for work and happiness than he had ever been. He was full of great bold resolutions and joyfully conscious of his youth and independence. He no doubt felt a certain shame at the thought that at any rate at the present moment his grief for his dead father was much alleviated ; but he found a relief for this indifference of his in the thought of his dear father's painless end. He had been walking up and down the garden chatting with his two sons, had suddenly looked round him as though he heard voices in the distance, had then looked up towards the sky and had suddenly dropped down dead on the sward, without a cry of pain or even a twitching of the lips.

George went back into the room, got ready to go out and left the house. He intended to walk about for a couple of hours wherever chance might take him, and in the evening to work again at his quintette, for which he now felt in the right mood. He crossed the street and went into the park. The sultriness had passed. The old woman in the cloak still sat on the seat and stared in front of her. Children were playing on the sandy playground round the trees. All the chairs round the kiosk were taken. A clean-shaven gentleman sat in the summer-house whom George knew by sight and who had impressed him by his likeness to the elder Grillparzer. By the pond George met a governess with two well-dressed children and received a flashing glance. When he got out of the Park into the Ringstrasse he met Willy Eissler who was wearing a long autumn overcoat with dark stripes and began to speak to him.

" Good afternoon, Baron, so you've come back to Vienna again."

" I've been back a long time," answered George. " I didn't leave Vienna again after my father's death."

" Yes, yes, quite so. . . . Allow me, once again. . . ." And Willy shook hands with George.

" And what have you been doing this summer ? " asked George.

" All kinds of things. Played tennis, and painted, rotted about, had some amusing times and a lot of boring ones. . . ." Willy spoke extremely quickly, with a deliberate though slight hoarseness, briskly and yet nonchalantly with a combination of the Hungarian, French, Viennese and Jewish accents. " Anyway, I came early to-day, just as you see me now, from Przemysl," he continued.

" Drill ? "

" Yes, the last one. I'm sorry to say so. Though I'm nearly an old man, I've always found it a joke to trot about with my yellow epaulettes, clanking my spurs, dragging my sabre along, spreading an atmosphere of impending peril, and being taken by incompetent Lavaters for a noble count." They walked along by the side of the railing of the Stadtpark.

" Going to Ehrenbergs' by any chance ? " asked Willy.

" No, I never thought of it."

" Because this is the way. I say, have you heard, Fräulein Else is supposed to be engaged ? "

" Really ? " queried George slowly. " And whom to ? "

" Guess, Baron."

" Come, Hofrat Wilt ? "

" Great heavens ! " cried Willy, " I'm sure it's never entered his head ! Becoming S. Ehrenberg's son-in-law might result in prejudicing his government career—nowadays."

George went on guessing. " Rittmeister Ladisc ? "

" Oh no, Fräulein Else is far too clever to be taken in by him."

George then remembered that Willy had fought a duel with Ladisc a few years back. Willy felt George's look, twirled somewhat nervously his blonde moustache which drooped in the Polish fashion and began to speak quickly and offhandedly.

" The fact that Rittmeister Ladisc and myself once had a difference cannot prevent me from loyally recognising the fact that he is, and always has been, a drunken swine. I have an invincible repulsion, which even blood cannot wash out, against those people who gorge themselves sick at Jewish houses and then start slanging the Jews as soon as they get on the door-steps. They ought to be able to wait till they got to the café. But don't exert yourself any more by guessing. Heinrich Bermann is the lucky man."

" Impossible," said George.

" Why ? " asked Eissler. " It had to be some one sooner or later. Bermann is no Adonis, I agree, but he's a coming man, and Else's official ideal of a mixture of gentleman-rider and athlete will never turn up. Meanwhile she has reached twenty-four, and she must have had enough by now of Salomon's tactless remarks and Salomon's jokes."

" Salomon ?—oh, yes—Ehrenberg."

" You only know him by the initial S ? S of course

stands for Salomon . . . and as for only S standing on the door, that is simply a concession he made to his family. If he could follow his own fancy he would prefer to turn up at the parties Madame Ehrenberg gives in a caftan and side-curls."

" Do you think so ?   He's not so very strict ? "

" Strict ? . . . Really now !   It's nothing at all to do with strictness.   It is only cussedness, particularly against his son Oskar with his feudal ideals."

" Really," said George with a smile, " wasn't Oskar baptised long ago ?   Why, he's a reserve officer in the dragoons."

" That's why . . . well, I've not been baptised and nevertheless . . . yes . . . there are always exceptions . . . with good will. . . ."   He laughed and went on.   " As for Oskar, he would personally prefer to be a Catholic.   But he thought for the time being he would have to pay too dearly for the pleasure of being able to go to confession. There's sure to be a provision in the will to take care that Oskar doesn't 'vert over."

°   They had arrived in front of the Café Imperial.   Willy remained standing.   " I've got an appointment here with Demeter Stanzides."

" Please remember me to him."

" Thanks very much.   Won't you come in and have an ice ? "

" Thanks, I'll prowl about a little more."

" You like solitude ? "

" It's hard to give an answer to so general a question," replied George.

" Of course," said Willy, suddenly grew serious and lifted his hat.   " Good afternoon, Baron."

George held out his hand.   He felt that Willy was a man who was continually defending a position though there was no pressing necessity for him to do so.

" Au revoir," he said with real sincerity.   He felt now

as he had often done before, that it was almost extraordinary that Willy should be a Jew. Why, old Eissler, Willy's father, who composed charming Viennese waltzes and songs, was a connoisseur and collector, and sometimes a seller of antiquities, and objets d'art, and had passed in his day for the most celebrated boxer in Vienna, was, what with his long grey beard and his monocle, far more like a Hungarian magnate than a Jewish patriarch. Besides, Willy's own temperament, his deliberate cultivation of it and his iron will had made him into the deceptive counterpart of a feudal gentleman bred and born. What, however, distinguished him from other young people of similar race and ambition was the fact that he was accustomed to admit his origin, to demand explanation or satisfaction for every ambiguous smile, and to make merry himself over all the prejudices and vanities of which he was so often the victim.

George strode along, and Willy's last question echoed in his ears. Did he love solitude ? . . . He remembered how he had walked about in Palermo for whole mornings while Grace, following her usual habit, lay in bed till noon. . . . Where was she now . . . ? Since she had said goodbye to him in Naples he had in accordance with their arrangement heard nothing from her. He thought of the deep blue night which had swept over the waters when he had travelled alone to Genoa after that farewell, and of the soft strange fairy-like song of two children who, nestling closely up against each other and wrapped, the pair of them, in one rug, had sat on the deck by the side of their sleeping mother.

With a growing sense of well-being he walked on among the people who passed by him with all the casual nonchalance of a Sunday. Many a glad glance from a woman's eye met his own, and seemed as though it would have liked to console him for strolling about alone and with all the external appearances of mourning on this

beautiful holiday afternoon. And another picture floated
up in his mind.—He saw himself on a hilly sward, after a
hot June day, late in the evening. Darkness all around.
Deep below him a clatter of men, laughter and noise, and
glittering fairy-lamps. Quite near, girls' voices came
out of the darkness. . . . He lit the small pipe which he
usually only smoked in the country ; the flare of the vesta
showed him two pretty young peasant wenches, still almost
children. He chatted to them. They were frightened
because it was so dark ; they nestled up to him. Suddenly
a whizz, rockets in the air, a loud " Ah ! " from down
below. Bengal lights flaring violet and red over the invisible lake beneath. The girls rushed down the hill and
vanished. Then it became dark again and he lay alone
and looked up into the darkness which swam down on him
in all its sultriness. The night before the day on which his
father died had been one such as this. And he thought of
him for the first time to-day.

He had left the Ringstrasse and taken the direction of
the Wieden. Would the Rosners be at home on such a
beautiful day ? At all events the distance was so short
that it was worth trying, and at any rate he fancied going
there rather than to Ehrenbergs'. He was not the least in
love with Else, and it was almost a matter of indifference
to him whether or no she were really engaged to Heinrich
Bermann. He had already known her for a long time.
She had been eleven, he had been fourteen when they had
played tennis with each other on the Riviera. In those
days· she looked like a gipsy girl. Black-blue tresses
tossed round her cheeks and forehead, and she was as
boisterous as a boy. Her brother had already begun to
play the lord, and even to-day George could not help smiling
at the recollection of the fifteen-year old boy appearing
on the promenade one day in a light grey coat with white
black-braided gloves and a monocle in his eye. Frau
Ehrenberg was then thirty-four, and had a dignified

appearance though her figure was too large ; she was still beautiful, had dim eyes, and was usually very tired.

George never forgot the day on which her husband, the millionaire cartridge-manufacturer, had descended on his family and had by the very fact of his appearance made a speedy end of the Ehrenbergian aristocracy. George still remembered in his mind's eye how he had sprung up during the breakfast on the hotel terrace ; a small spare gentleman with a trimmed beard and moustache and Japanese eyes, in badly-creased white flannels, a dark straw hat with a red-and-white striped ribbon on his round head and with dusty black shoes. He always spoke very slowly and in an as it were sarcastic manner even about the most unimportant matters, and whenever he opened his mouth a secret anxiety would always lurk beneath the apparent calm of his wife's face. She tried to revenge herself by making fun of him ; but she could never do anything with his inconsiderate manners. Oskar behaved whenever he had a chance as though he didn't belong to the family at all. A somewhat hesitating contempt would play over his features for that progenitor who was not quite worthy of him, and he would smile meaningly for sympathy at the young baron. Only Else in those days was really nice to her father. She was quite glad to hang on his arm on the promenade and she would often throw her arms round his neck before every one.

George had seen Else again in Florence a year before his mother's death. She was then taking drawing lessons from an old grizzled German, about whom the legend was circulated that he had once been celebrated. He spread the rumour about himself that when he felt his genius on the wane he had discarded his former well-known name and had given up his calling, though what that was he never disclosed. If his own version was to be believed, his downfall was due to a diabolical female who had destroyed his most important picture in a fit of jealousy ; and then ended her life by jumping out of the window. This man who had struck the seventeen-year-old George as a kind of fool and impostor was the object of Else's first infatuation. She was then fourteen years old, and had all the wildness and naïveté of childhood. When she stood in front of the Titian Venus in the Uffizi Gallery her cheeks would flush with curiosity, yearning and admiration, and vague dreams of future experiences would play in her eyes. She often came with her mother to the house which the Wergenthins had hired at Lungarno, and while Frau Ehrenberg tried in her languid blasé way to amuse the ailing baroness, Else would stand at the window with George, start precocious conversations about the art of the Pre-Raphaelites, and smile at her old childish games. Felician too would come in sometimes, slim and handsome, cast his cold grey eyes over the objects and people in the room, murmur a few polite words, sit down by his mother's bedside, and tenderly stroke and kiss her hand. He would usually soon go away again, though not without leaving behind, so far as Else was concerned, a very palpable atmosphere of old-time aristocracy, cold-blooded fascination and elegant contempt of death. She always had the impression that he was going to a gaming-table where hundreds of thousands were at stake, to a duel to the death or to a princess with red hair and a dagger on her dressing-table. George remembered that he had been somewhat jealous both of the erratic drawing-master and of his brother. The master was suddenly dismissed for reasons which were never specified, and soon afterwards Felician left for Vienna with Baron von Wergenthin. George now played to the ladies on the piano more frequently than before, both his own compositions and those of others, and Else would sing from the score easy songs from Schubert and Schumann in her small, rather shrill voice. She visited the galleries and churches with her mother and George ; when spring came there were excursion parties up the Hill Road or to Fiesole, and George and Else exchanged smiling glances which were eloquent of a deeper understanding than actually existed. Their relations went on progressing in this somewhat disingenuous manner, when their acquaintance was renewed and continued in Vienna. Else seemed pleasurably thrilled all over again by the equable friendly manner with which George approached her, notwithstanding the fact that they had not seen each other for some months. She herself, on the other hand, grew outwardly more self-possessed and mentally more unsettled with each succeeding year. She had abandoned her artistic aspirations fairly early, and in the course of time she came to regard herself as destined to the most varied careers.

She often saw herself in the future as a society woman, an organiser of battles of flowers, a patroness of great balls, taking part in aristocratic charity performances ; more frequently she would believe herself called to sit enthroned as a great appreciator in an artistic salon of painters, musicians and poets. She would then dream again of a more adventurous life: a sensational marriage with an American millionaire, the elopement with a violin virtuoso or a Spanish officer, a diabolical ruination of all the men who came near her. Sometimes she would think a quiet life in the country by the side of a worthy landowner the most desirable consummation ; and then she would imagine herself sitting with prematurely grey hair at a simply-laid table in a circle of numerous children while she stroked the wrinkles out of the forehead of her grave husband. But George always felt that her love of comfort, which was deeper than she guessed herself, would save her from any rash step. She would often confide in George without ever being quite honest with him ; for the wish which she cherished most frequently and seriously of all was to become his wife. George was well aware of this, but that was not the only reason why the latest piece of intelligence about her engagement with Heinrich Bermann struck him as somewhat incredible—this Bermann was a gaunt clean-shaven man with gloomy eyes and straight and rather too long hair, who had recently won a reputation as a writer and whose demeanour and appearance reminded George, though he could not tell why, of some fanatical Jewish teacher from the provinces; there was nothing in him which could fascinate Else particularly or even make a pleasurable appeal.

This impression was no doubt dispelled by subsequent conversation. George had left the Ehrenbergs' in company with him one evening last spring, and they had fallen into so thrilling a conversation about musical matters that they had gone on chatting till three o'clock in the morning on a seat in the Ringstrasse.

It is strange, thought George, what a lot of things are running through my mind to-day which I had scarcely thought of at all since they happened. And he felt as though he had on this autumn evening emerged out of the grievous dreary obscurity of so many weeks into the light of day at last.

He was now standing in front of the house in the Paulanergasse where the Rosners lived. He looked up to the second story. A window was open, white tulle curtains pinned together in the centre fluttered in the light breeze.

The Rosners were at home. The housemaid showed George in. Anna was sitting opposite the door, she held a coffee-cup in her hand and her eyes were turned towards the newcomer. On her right her father was reading a paper and smoking a pipe. He was clean-shaven except for a pair of narrow grizzled whiskers on his cheeks. His thin hair of a strange greenish-grey hue was parted at the temples in front and looked like a badly-made wig. His eyes were watery and red-lidded.

The stoutish mother, around whose forehead the memory of fairer years seemed as it were to hover, looked straight

in front of her ; her hands were contemplatively intertwined and rested on the table.

Anna slowly put down her cup, nodded and smiled in
silence. The two old people began to get up when George
came in.

" Please, don't trouble, please don't," said George.

Then there was a noise from the wall at the side of the
room. Josef, the son of the house, got up from the sofa
on which he had been lying. " Charmed to see you, Herr
Baron," he said in a very deep voice, and adjusted the
turned-up collar of his yellow-check rather shabby lounge
jacket.

" And how have you been all this time, Herr Baron ? "
inquired the old man. He remained standing a gaunt and
somewhat bowed figure, and refused to resume his seat
until George had sat down. Josef pushed a chair between
his father and sister, Anna held out her hand to the visitor.

" We haven't seen one another for a long time," she said,
and drank some of her coffee.

" You've been going through a sad time," remarked
Frau Rosner sympathetically.

" Yes," added Herr Rosner. " We were extremely
sorry to read of your great loss—and so far as we knew
your father always enjoyed the best of health."

He spoke very slowly all the time, as if he had still something more to say, stroking his head several times with
his left hand, and nodded while he listened to the answer.

" Yes, it came very unexpectedly," said George gently,
and looked at the faded dark-red carpet at his feet.

" A sudden death then, so to speak," remarked Herr
Rosner and there was a general silence.

George took a cigarette out of his case and offered one to
Josef.

" Much obliged," said Josef as he took the cigarette
and bowed while he clicked his heels together without any
apparent reason ; while he was giving the Baron a light he

2

thought the latter was looking at him, and said apologetically, with an even deeper voice than usual, " Office jacket."

" Office jacket straight from the office," said Anna simply
without looking at her brother.

" The lady fancies she has the ironic gift," answered
Josef merrily, but his manifest restraint indicated that
under other conditions he would have expressed himself
less agreeably.

" Sympathy was universally felt," old Rosner began
again. " I read an obituary in the *Veue Freie Presse* on
your good father by Herr Hoffrat Kerner, if I remember
rightly ; it was highly laudatory. Science too has suffered
a sad loss."

George nodded in embarrassment, and looked at his
hands.

Anna began to speak about her past summer-outing.
" It was awfully pretty in Weissenfeld," she said. " The
forest was just behind our house with good level roads,
wasn't it, papa ? One could walk there for hours and hours
without meeting a soul."

" And did you have a piano out there ? " asked George.
" Oh yes."

" An awful affair," observed Herr Rosner, " a thing fit
to wake up the stones and drive men mad."

" It wasn't so bad," said Anna.

" Good enough for the little Graubinger girl," added
Frau Rosner.

" The little Graubinger girl, you see, is the daughter of
the local shopkeeper," explained Anna : " and I taught
her the elements of pianoforte, a pretty little girl with long
blonde pig-tails."

" Just a favour to the shopkeeper," said Frau Rosner.

" Quite so, but I should like to remind you," supple-
mented Anna, " that apart from that I gave real lessons,
I mean paid-for ones."

" What, also in Weissenfeld ? " asked George.

"Children on a holiday. Anyway, it's a pity, Herr Baron, that you never paid us a visit in the country. I am sure you would have liked it."

George then remembered for the first time that he had promised Anna that he would try to pay her a visit some time in the summer on a cycling tour.

"I am sure the Baron would not have found a place like that really to his liking," began Herr Rosner.

"Why not?" asked George.

"They don't cater there for the requirements of a spoilt Viennese."

"Oh, I'm not spoilt," said George.

"Weren't you at Auhof either?" Anna turned to George.

"Oh no," he answered quickly. "No, I wasn't there," he added less sharply. "I was invited though. . . . Frau Ehrenberg was so kind as to . . . I had various invitations for the summer. But I preferred to stay in Vienna by myself."

"I am really sorry," said Anna, "not to see anything more of Else. You know of course that we went to the same boarding-school. Of course it's a long time ago. I really liked her. A pity that one gets so out of touch as time goes on."

"How is that?" asked George.

"Well, I suppose the reason is that I'm not particularly keen on the whole set."

"Nor am I," said Josef, who was blowing rings into the air. . . . "I haven't been there for years. Putting it quite frankly . . . I've no idea, Baron, of your views on this question . . . I'm not very gone on Israelites."

Herr Rosner looked up at his son. "My dear Josef, the Baron visits the house and it will strike him as rather strange. . . ."

"I?" said George courteously. "I'm not at all on intimate terms with the Ehrenberg family, however much

I enjoy talking to the two ladies." And then he added interrogatively, " But didn't you give singing lessons to Else last year, Fräulein Anna ? "

" Yes. Or rather . . . I just accompanied her. . . ."

" I suppose you'll do so again this year ? "

" I don't know. She hasn't shown any signs of life, so far."

" Perhaps she's giving it all up."

" You think so ? It would be almost better if she did," replied Anna softly, " for as a matter of fact, it was more like squeaking than singing. But anyway," and she threw George a look which, as it were, welcomed him afresh, " the songs you sent me are very nice. Shall I sing them to you ? "

" You've had a look at the things already ? That is nice of you."

Anna had got up. She put both her hands on her temples and stroked her wavy hair gently, as though making it tidy. It was done fairly high, so that her figure seemed even taller than it actually was. A narrow golden watch-chain was twined twice round her bare neck, fell down over her bosom, and vanished in her grey leather belt. With an almost imperceptible nod of her head she asked George to accompany her.

He got up and said, " If you don't mind. . . ."

" Not at all, not at all, of course not," said Herr Rosner. " Very kind of you, Baron, to do a little music with my daughter. Very nice, very nice."

Anna had stepped into the next room. George followed her and left the door open. The white tulle curtains were pinned together in front of the open window and fluttered slightly. George sat down at the cottage-piano and struck a few chords. Meanwhile, Anna knelt down in front of an old black partly gilded whatnot, and got out the music. George modulated the first chords of his song. Anna joined in and sang to George's song the Goethean words,

Deinem Blick mich zu bequemen,
Deinem Munde, deiner Brust,
Deine Stimme zu vernehmen,
War mir erst' und letzte Lust.

She stood behind him and looked over his shoulder
at the music. At times she bent a little forward, and he
then felt the breath of her lips upon his temples. Her voice
was much more beautiful than he remembered its having
ever been before.

They were speaking rather too loudly in the next room.
Without stopping singing Anna shut the door. It had
been Josef who had been unable to control his voice any
longer.

" I'll just pop in to the café for a jiffy," he said.

There was no answer. Herr Rosner drummed gently on
the table and his wife nodded with apparent indifference.

" Goodbye then." Josef turned round again at the door
and said fairly resolutely : " Oh, mamma, if you've got a
minute to spare by any chance——"

" I'm listening," said Frau Rosner. " It's not a secret,
I suppose."

" No. It's only that I've got a running account with
you already."

" Is it necessary to go to the café ? " asked old Rosner
simply, without looking up.

" It's not a question of the café. The fact is . . . you
can take it from me that I'd prefer myself not to have to
borrow from you. But what is a man to do ? "

" A man should work," said old Rosner gently, painfully, and his eyes reddened. His wife threw a sad and
reproachful look at her son.

" Well," said Josef, unbuttoning his office coat, and then
buttoning it up again—" that really is . . . for every single
gulden-note——"

" Pst," said Frau Rosner with a glance towards the door,
which was ajar, and through which, now that Anna had

finished her song, came the muffled sound of George's piano-playing.

Josef answered his mother's glance with a deprecatory wave of his hand. " Papa says I ought to work. As though I hadn't already proved that I can work." He saw two pairs of questioning eyes turned towards him. " Yes of course I proved it, and if it had only depended on me I'd have managed to get along all right. But I haven't got the temperament to put up with things, I'm not the kind to let myself be bullied by any chief if I happen to come in a quarter of an hour late—or anything like that."

" We know all about that," interrupted Herr Rosner wearily. " But after all, as we're already on the subject, you really must start looking round for something."

" Look round . . . good . . ." answered Josef. " But no one will persuade me to go into any business run by a Jew. It would make me the laughing-stock of all my acquaintances . . . of my whole set in fact."

" Your set . . ." said Frau Rosner. " What is your set ? Café cronies ? "

" Well if you don't mind, now that we are on the subject," said Josef—" it's connected with that gulden-note, too. I've got an appointment at the café now with young Jalaudek. I'd have preferred to have told you when the thing had gone quite through . . . but I see now that I'd better show my hand straight away. Well, Jalaudek is the son of Councillor Jalaudek the celebrated paper-merchant. And old Jalaudek is well-known as a very influential personage in the party . . . very intimate with the publisher of the *Christliche Volksbote* : his name is Zell-tinkel. And they're looking out on the *Volksbote* for young men with good manners—Christians of course, for the advertisement business. And so I've got an appointment to-day with Jalaudek at the café, because he promised me his governor would recommend me to Zelltinkel. That would be ripping . . . it would get me out of my mess.

Then it wouldn't be long before I was earning a hundred or a hundred and fifty gulders a month."

" O dear ! " sighed old Rosner.

The bell rang outside.

Rosner looked up.

" That must be young Doctor Stauber," said Frau Rosner and cast an anxious glance at the door, through which the sound of George's piano-playing came in even softer tones than before.

" Well, mamma, what's the matter ? " said Josef.

Frau Rosner took out her purse and with a sigh gave her son a silver gulden.

" Much obliged," said Josef and turned to go.

" Josef," cried Herr Rosner, " it's really rather rude— at the very minute when we have a visitor——"

" Oh thank you, but I mustn't have all the treats."

There was a knock, Doctor Berthold Stauber came in.

" I apologise profusely, Herr Doctor," said Josef, " I'm just going out."

" Not at all," replied Doctor Stauber coldly, and Josef vanished.

Frau Rosner invited the young doctor to sit down. He took a seat on the ottoman and turned towards the quarter from which the piano-playing could be heard.

" Baron Wergenthin, the composer. Anna has just been singing," explained Frau Rosner, somewhat embarrassed. And she started to call her daughter in.

Doctor Berthold gripped her arm lightly but firmly, and said amiably: " No, please don't disturb Fräulein Anna, please don't. I'm not in the least hurry. Besides, this is a farewell visit." The latter words seemed jerked out of his throat ; but Berthold nevertheless smiled courteously, leant back comfortably in his corner and stroked his short beard with his right hand.

Frau Rosner looked at him as if she were positively shocked.

" A farewell visit ? " Herr Rosner asked. " Has the party allowed you to take a holiday, Herr Stauber ? Parliament has only been assembled a short time, as one sees in the papers."

" I have resigned my seat," said Berthold.

" What ? " exclaimed Herr Rosner.

"Yes, resigned," repeated Berthold, and smiled nervously.

The piano-playing had suddenly stopped, the door which had been ajar was now opened. George and Anna appeared.

" Oh, Doctor Berthold," said Anna, and held out her hand to the doctor, who had immediately got up. " Have you been here long ? Perhaps you heard me singing ? "

" No, Fräulein, I'm sorry I was too late for that. I only caught a few notes on the piano."

" Baron Wergenthin," said Anna, as though she were introducing. " But of course you know each other ? "

" Oh yes," answered George, and held out his hand to Berthold.

" The Doctor has come to pay us a farewell visit," said Frau Rosner.

" What ? " exclaimed Anna in astonishment.

" I'm going on a journey, you see," said Berthold, and looked Anna in the face with a serious, impenetrable expression. " I'm giving up my political career . . . or rather," he added jestingly, " I'm interrupting it for a while."

George leant on the window with his arms crossed over his breast and looked sideways at Anna. She had sat down and was looking quietly at Berthold, who was standing up with his hand resting on the back of the sofa, as though he were going to make a speech.

" And where are you going ? " asked Anna.

" Paris. I'm going to work in the Pasteur Institute. I'm going back to my old love, bacteriology. It's a cleaner life than politics."

It had grown darker. The faces became vague, only Berthold's forehead, which was directly opposite the window, was still bathed in light. His brows were twitching. He really has his peculiar kind of beauty, thought George, who was leaning motionless in the window-niche and felt himself bathed in a pleasant sense of peace.

The housemaid brought in the burning lamp and hung it over the table.

" But the papers,"- said Herr Rosner, " have no announcement at all so far of your resigning your seat, Doctor Stauber."

" That would be premature," answered Berthold. " My colleagues and the party know my intention all right, but the thing isn't official yet."

" The news is bound to create a great sensation in the circles affected by it," said Herr Rosner—" particularly after the lively debate the other day in which you showed such spirit and determination. I suppose you've read about it, Baron ? " He turned to George.

" I must confess," answered George, " that I don't follow the parliamentary reports as regularly as I really ought to."

" Ought to," repeated Berthold meditatively. " There's no question of ' ought ' about it really, although the session has not been uninteresting during the last few days—at any rate as a proof of how low a level a public body can sink to."

" The debate was very heated," said Herr Rosner.

" Heated ? . . . Well, yes, what we call heated here in Austria. People were inwardly indifferent and outwardly offensive."

" What was it all about then ? " inquired George.

" It was the debate arising out of the questions on the Golowski case. . . . Therese Golowski."

" Therese Golowski . . ." repeated George. " I seem to know the name."

"Of course you know it," said Anna. "You know Therese herself. She was just leaving the house when you called the last time."

"Oh yes," said George, "one of your friends."

"I wouldn't go so far as to call her a friend ; that seems to imply a certain mental sympathy that doesn't quite exist."

"You certainly don't mean to repudiate Therese," said Doctor Berthold smiling, but dryly.

"Oh no," answered Anna quickly. "I really never thought of doing that. I even admire her ; as a matter of fact I admire all people who are able to risk so much for something that doesn't really concern them at all. And when a young girl does that, a pretty young girl like Therese "—she was addressing herself to George who was listening attentively—"I am all the more impressed. You know of course that Therese is one of the leaders of the Social Democratic Party? "

"And do you know what I took her for ? " said George. "For a budding actress."

"You're quite a judge of character, Herr Baron," said Berthold.

"She really did mean to go on the stage once," corroborated Frau Rosner coldly.

"But just consider, Frau Rosner," said Berthold. "What young girl is there with any imagination, especially if she lives in cramped surroundings into the bargain, who has not at some time or other in her life at any rate coquetted with such an idea."

"Your forgiving her is good," said Anna, smiling.

It struck Berthold too late that this remark of his had probably touched a still sensitive spot in Anna's mind. But he continued with all the greater deliberation. "I assure you, Fräulein Anna, it would be a great pity if Therese were to go on the stage, for there's no getting away from the fact that she can still do her party a tremendous lot of good if she isn't torn away from her career."

" Do you regard that as possible ? " asked Anna.

" Certainly," replied Berthold. " Therese is between two dangers, she will either talk her head off one fine day . . ."

" Or ? " inquired George, who had grown inquisitive.

" Or she'll marry a Baron," finished Berthold curtly.

" I don't quite understand," said George deprecatingly.

" I only said ' Baron ' for a joke, of course. Substitute Prince for Baron and I make my meaning clearer."

" I see . . . I can now get some idea of what you mean, Doctor. . . . But how did Parliament come to bother about her ? "

" Well, it's like this, last year—at the time of the great coal-strike—Therese Golowski made a speech in some Bohemian hole, which contained an expression which was alleged to be offensive to a member of the Imperial family. She was prosecuted and acquitted. One might perhaps draw the conclusion from this that there was no particular substance in the prosecution. Anyway the State Prosecutor gave notice of appeal, there was an order for a new trial, and Therese was sentenced to two months' imprisonment, which she is now serving, and as if that wasn't enough the Judge who had discharged her in the Court of first instance was transferred . . . to somewhere on the Russian frontier, from where no one ever comes back. Well, we put a question over this business, which in my view was extremely tame. The Minister answered somewhat disingenuously amid the cheers of the so-called Constitutional parties. I ventured to reply in possibly somewhat more drastic terms than members are accustomed to use, and as the benches on the other side had no facts with which to answer me they tried to overwhelm me by shouts and abuse. And of course you can imagine what the strongest argument was, which a certain type of Conservatives used against my points."

" Well ? " queried George.

"Hold your jaw, Jew," answered Berthold with tightly compressed lips.

"Oh," said George with embarrassment, and shook his head.

"Be quiet, Jew! Hold your jaw! Jew! Jew! Shut up!" continued Berthold, who seemed somewhat to revel in the recollection.

Anna looked straight in front of her. George thought that this was quite enough. There was a short, painful silence.

"So that was why?" inquired Anna slowly.

"What do you mean?" asked Berthold.

"That's why you're resigning your seat."

Berthold shook his head and smiled. "No, not because of that."

"You are, of course, above such coarse insults, Doctor," said Herr Rosner.

"I won't go quite so far as that," answered Berthold, "but one always has to be prepared for things like that all the same. I'm resigning my seat for a different reason."

"May one ask what it is?" queried George.

Berthold looked at him with an air which was penetrating and yet distrait. He then answered courteously: "Of course you may. I went into the buffet after my speech. I met there, among others, one of the silliest and cheekiest of our democratic popular representatives, who, as he usually does, had made more row than any one else while I was speaking . . . Jalaudek the paper-merchant. Of course I didn't pay any attention to him. He was just putting down his empty glass. When he saw me he smiled, nodded and hailed me as cheerily as though nothing had taken place at all. 'Hallo, Doctor, won't you have a drink with me?'"

"Incredible!" exclaimed George.

"Incredible? . . . No, Austrian. Our indignation is as little genuine as our enthusiasm. The only things genuine with us are our malice and our hate of talent."

" Well, and what did you answer the man ? " asked
Anna.

" What did I answer ? Nothing, of course."

" And you resigned your seat," added Anna with gentle
raillery.

Berthold smiled. But at the same time his eye-brows
twitched, as was his habit when he was painfully or disagreeably affected. It was too late to tell her that as
a matter of fact he had come to ask her for her advice, as
he used to do in the old days. And at any rate he felt
sure of this, he had done wisely in cutting off all retreat
as soon as he entered the room by announcing the resignation of his seat as an already accomplished fact, and his
journey to Paris as directly imminent. For he now knew
for certain that Anna had again escaped him, perhaps for
a long time. He did not believe for a minute that any man
was capable of winning her really and permanently, and
it never entered his head for a minute to be jealous of
that elegant young artist who was standing so quietly by
the window with his crossed arms. It had happened many
times before that Anna had fluttered away for a time, as
though fascinated by the magic of an element which was
strange to her. Why only two years ago, when she was
thinking seriously of going on the stage, and had already
begun to learn her parts, he had given her up for a short
time as completely lost. Subsequently when she had been
compelled to relinquish her artistic projects, owing to the
unreliability of her voice, she seemed as if she wanted to
come back to him again. But he had deliberately refused
to exploit the opportunities of that period. For he wanted
before he made her his wife to have won some triumph,
either in science or in politics, and to have obtained her
genuine admiration. He had been well on the way to it.
In the very seat where she was now sitting as she looked
him straight in the face with those clear but alas ! cold eyes,
she had looked at the proofs of his latest medico-philo-

sophical work which bore the title *Preliminary Observations
on the Physiognomical Diagnosis of Diseases*. And then,
when he finally left science for politics, at the time when he
made speeches at election meetings and equipped himself
for his new career by serious studies in history and political
economy, she had sincerely rejoiced in his energy and his
versatility.

All this was now over. She had grown to eye more and
more severely those faults of his of which he was quite
aware himself, and particularly his tendency to be swept
away by the intoxication of his own words, with the result
that he came to lose more and more of his self-confidence
in his attitude towards her. He was never quite himself
when he spoke to her, or in her presence. He was not
satisfied with himself to-day either. He was conscious,
with an irritation which struck even himself as petty, that
he had not given sufficient force to his encounter with
Jalaudek in the buffet, and that he ought to have made
his detestation of politics ring far more plausibly.

" You are probably quite right, Fräulein Anna," he said,
" if you smile at my resigning my seat on account of that
silly incident. A parliamentary life without its share of
comedy is an absolute impossibility. I should have realised
it, played up to it and taken every opportunity of drinking
with the fellow who had publicly insulted me. It would
have been convenient, Austrian—and possibly even the
most correct course to have taken." He felt himself in
full swing again and continued with animation. " What it
comes to in the end is that there are two methods of doing
anything worth doing in politics. The one is a magnificent
flippancy which looks on the whole of public life as an
amusing game, has no true enthusiasm for anything, and
no true indignation against anything, and which regards
the people whose misery or happiness are ultimately at
stake with consummate indifference. I have not pro-
gressed so far, and I don't know that I should ever have

succeeded in doing so. Quite frankly, I have often wished
I could have. The other method is this : to be ready
every single minute to sacrifice one's whole existence,
one's life, in the truest sense of the word, for what one
believes to be right——"

Berthold suddenly stopped. His father, old Doctor
Stauber, had come in and been heartily welcomed. He
shook hands with George, who had been introduced to him
by Frau Rosner, and looked at him so kindly that George felt
himself immediately drawn towards him. He looked
younger than he was. His long reddish-yellow beard was
only streaked by a few grey hairs, and his smoothly combed
long hair fell in thick locks on to his broad neck. The
strikingly high forehead gave a kind of majesty to the somewhat thick-set figure with its high shoulders. When his
eyes were not making a special point of looking kind or
shrewd they seemed to be resting behind the tired lids
as though to gather the energy for the next look.

" I knew your mother, Herr Baron," he said to George
rather gently.

" My mother, Herr Doctor . . . ? "

" You will scarcely remember it, you were only a little
boy of three or four at the time."

" You attended her ? " asked George.

" I visited her sometimes as deputy for Professor Duchegg,
whose assistant I was. You used to live then in the
Habsburgergasse, in an old house that has been pulled
down long ago. I could describe to you even to-day the
furniture of the room in which I was received by your
father . . . whose premature death I deeply regret. . . . There
was a bronze figure on the secretary, a knight in armour
to be sure with a flag, and a copy of a Vandyck from the
Liechtenstein gallery hung on the wall."

" Yes, quite right," said George, amazed at the doctor's
good memory.

" But I have interrupted your conversation," continued

Doctor Stauber in that droning slightly melancholy and
yet superior tone which was peculiar to him, and sat down
in the corner of the sofa.

" Doctor Berthold has just been telling us, to our great
astonishment," said Herr Rosner, " that he has decided to
resign his seat."

Old Stauber directed a quiet look towards his son,
which the latter answered with equal quietness.   George,
who had watched this play of the eyes, had the impression
that there prevailed between these two a tacit understanding which did not need any words.

" Yes," said Doctor Stauber.   " I wasn't at all surprised.
I've always felt as though Berthold were never really
quite at home in Parliament, and I am really glad that he
has now begun to pine as it were to go back to his real
calling.   Yes, yes, your real calling, Berthold," he repeated,
as though to answer his son's furrowed brow.   " You have
not prejudiced your future by it, in the least.   Nothing
makes life so difficult as our frequent belief in consistency
. . . and our wasting our time in being ashamed of a mistake,
instead of owning up to it and simply starting life again on
a fresh basis."

Berthold explained that he meant to leave in eight days
at the outside.   There would be no point in postponing his
journey beyond that time, it would be possible too that he
might not remain in Paris.   His studies might necessitate
travelling further afield.   Further, he had decided not to
make any farewell visits.   He had, he added by way of
explanation, completely given up all association with
certain bourgeois sets, among whom his father had an
extensive practice.

" Didn't we meet each other once this winter at Ehrenbergs' ? " asked George with a certain amount of satisfaction.

" That's right," answered Berthold.   " We are distantly
related to the Ehrenbergs you know.   The Golowski family
is curiously enough the connecting link between us.   It

would be no good, Herr Baron, if I were to make any attempt to explain it to you in greater detail. I should have to take you on a journey through the registry offices and congregations of Temesvar Tarnopol and similar pleasant localities—and that you mightn't quite fancy."

"Anyway," added old Doctor Stauber in a resigned tone, "the Baron is bound to know that all Jews are related to one another."

George smiled amiably. As a matter of fact it rather jarred on his nerves. There was no necessity at all, in his view, for Doctor Stauber as well officially to communicate to him his membership of the Jewish community. He already knew it and bore him no grudge for it. He bore him no grudge at all for it ; but why do they always begin to talk about it themselves ? Wherever he went, he only met Jews who were ashamed of being Jews, or the type who were proud of it and were frightened of people thinking they were ashamed of it.

" I had a chat with old Frau Golowski yesterday," continued Doctor Stauber.

" Poor woman," said Herr Rosner.

" How is she ? " asked Anna.

" How is she . . . you can imagine . . . her daughter in prison, her son a conscript—he is living in the barracks at the expense of the State . . . just imagine Leo Golowski as a patriot . . . and the old man sits in the café and watches the other people playing chess. He himself can't even run nowadays to the ten kreuzers for the chess money."

" Therese's imprisonment must soon be over anyway," said Berthold.

" It still lasts another twelve, fourteen days," replied his father. . . . " Come, Annerl "—he turned towards the young girl—" it would be réally nice of you if you were to show yourself once more in Rembrandtstrasse ; the old lady has taken an almost pathetic fancy to you. I really

3

can't understand why," he added with a smile, while he looked at Anna almost tenderly.

She looked straight in front of her and made no answer.

The clock on the wall struck seven. George got up as though he had simply been waiting for the signal.

" Going so soon, Herr Baron ? " said Herr Rosner, getting up.

George requested the company not to disturb themselves, and shook hands all round.

" It is strange," said old Stauber, " how your voice reminds one of your poor father."

" Yes, many people have said so," replied George. " I, personally, can't see any trace of it."

" There isn't a man in the world who knows his own voice," remarked old Stauber, and it sounded like the beginning of a popular lecture.

But George took his leave. Anna accompanied him, in spite of his slight remonstrance, into the hall and left the door half open—almost on purpose, so it struck George. " It's a pity we couldn't go on with our music any longer," she said.

" I'm sorry too, Fräulein Anna."

" I liked the song to-day even better than the first time, when I had to accompany myself, only it falls off a bit at the end. . . . I don't know how to express myself."

" Oh, I know what you mean, the end is conventional. I felt so too. I hope soon to be able to bring you something better than that, Fräulein Anna."

" But don't keep me waiting for it too long."

" I certainly won't. Goodbye, Fräulein Anna." They shook hands with each other and both smiled.

" Why didn't you come to Weissenfeld ? " asked Anna lightly.

" I am really sorry, but just consider, Fräulein Anna, I could scarcely get in the mood for society of any kind this year, you can quite appreciate that."

Anna looked at him seriously. "Don't you think,"
she said, "that perhaps one might have been some help
to you in bearing it ? "

"There's a draught, Anna," called out Frau Rosner
from inside.

"I'm coming in a minute," answered Anna with a
touch of impatience. But Frau Rosner had already shut
the door.

"When can I come back ? " asked George.

"Whenever you like. At any rate . . . I really ought
to give you a written time-table, so that you may know
when I'm at home, but that wouldn't be much good either.
I often go for walks or go shopping in town or go to
picture galleries or exhibitions——"

"We might do that together one day," said George.

"Oh, yes," answered Anna, took her purse out of her
pocket and then took out a tiny note-book.

"What have you got there ? " asked George.

Anna smiled and turned over the leaves of a little book.
"Just wait. . . . I meant to go and see the Exhibition
of Miniatures in the Royal Library at eleven on Thursday.
If you too are interested in miniatures, we might meet
there."

"Delighted, I'm sure."

"Right you are then, we can then arrange the next
time for you to accompany my singing."

"Done," said George and shook hands with her. It
struck him that while Anna was chatting with him here
outside, young Doctor Stauber would doubtless be getting
irritated or offended inside, and he was surprised that he
should be more disturbed by this circumstance than
Anna, who struck him as on the whole a perfectly good-
natured person. He freed his hand from hers, said good-
bye and went.

It was quite dark when George got into the streets. He
strolled slowly over the Elizabeth Bridge to the Opera,

past the centre of the town and undisturbed by the hubbub
and traffic around him, listened mentally to the tune of
his song. He thought it strange that Anna's voice which
had so pure and sound a tone in a small room, should have
no future whatsoever before it on the stage and concert
platform, and even stranger that Anna scarcely seemed
to mind this tragic fact. But of course he was not quite
clear in his mind whether Anna's calmness really reflected
her true character.

He had known her more or less casually for some years,
but an evening in the previous spring had been the first
occasion when they had become rather more intimate.
A large party had been got up on that occasion in the
Waldsteingarten. They took their meal in the open air
under the high chestnut-trees, and they all experienced
the pleasure, excitement and fascination of the first warm
May evening of the year. George conjured up in his
mind all the people who had come : Frau Ehrenberg, the
organiser of the party, dressed in an intentionally matronly
style, in a dark loose-fitting foulard dress ; Hofrat Wilt,
wearing as it were the mask of an English statesman with
all the sloppy aristocracy of his nonchalant demeanour, and
his chronic and somewhat cheap superior manner towards
everything and everybody ; Frau Oberberger who looked
like a rococo marquise with her grey powdered hair, her
flashing eyes and her beauty spot on her chin ; Demeter
Stanzides with his white gleaming teeth and that pale
forehead that showed all the weariness of an old race of
heroes ; Oskar Ehrenberg dressed with a smartness that
smacked a great deal of the head clerk in a dressmaking
establishment, a great deal of a young music-hall
comedian and something, too, of a young society man ;
Sissy Wyner who kept switching her dark laughing eyes
from one man to another, as though she had a merry
secret understanding with every single member of the
party ; Willy Eissler who related in his hoarse jovial

voice all kinds of jolly anecdotes of his soldier days and
Jewish stories as well ; Else Ehrenberg in a white English cloth dress with all the delicate melancholy of the
spring flowing around her, while her *grande dame* movements combined with her baby-face and delicate figure
to invest her with an almost pathetic grace ; Felician,
cold and courteous, with haughty eyes which gazed between
the members of the party to the other tables, and from
the other tables beyond into the distance ; Sissy's mother,
young, red-cheeked and a positive chatter-box, who
wanted to talk about everything at the same time and
to listen to everything at the same time ; Edmund Nürnberger with his piercing eyes and his thin mouth curving
into that smile of contempt (which had almost become a
chronic mask) for that whirligig of life, which he thoroughly saw through, though to his own amazement he
frequently discovered that he was playing in the game
himself ; and then finally Heinrich Bermann in a summer
suit that was too loose, with a straw hat that was too
cheap and a tie that was too light, who one moment spoke
louder than the others and at the next moment was more
noticeably silent.

Last of all Anna Rosner had appeared, self-possessed
and without any escort, greeted the party with a slight
nod and composedly sat down between Frau Ehrenberg
and George. " I have asked her for you," said Frau
Ehrenberg softly to George, who prior to this evening had
scarcely given Anna a single thought. These words, which
perhaps only originated in a stray idea of Frau Ehrenberg's,
became true in the course of the evening. From the
moment when the party got up and started on their merry
expedition through the Volksprater George and Anna had
remained together everywhere, in the side-shows and also
on the journey home to town, which for the fun of the
thing was done on foot, and surrounded though they were
by all that buzz of jollity and foolishness they had finished

by starting a perfectly rational conversation. A few days later he called and brought her as he had promised the piano score of " Eugen Onegin " and some of his songs ; on his next visit she sang these songs over to him as well as many of Schubert's, and he was very pleased with her voice. Shortly afterwards they said goodbye to each other for the summer without a single trace of sentimentalism or tenderness. George had regarded Anna's invitation to Weissenfeld as a mere piece of politeness, just in the same way as he had thought his promise to come had been understood ; and the atmosphere of to-day's visit when compared with the innocence of their previous acquaintance was bound to strike George as extremely strange.

At the Stephansplatz George saw that he was being saluted by some one standing on the platform of a horse-omnibus. George, who was somewhat short-sighted, did not immediately recognise the man who was saluting him.

" It's me," said the gentleman on the platform.

" Oh, Herr Bermann, good evening." George shook hands with him. " Which way are you going ? "

" I'm going into the Prater. I'm going to dine down there. Have you anything special on, Baron ? "

" Nothing at all."

" Well, come along with me then."

George swung himself on to the omnibus, which had just begun to move on. They told each other cursorily how they had spent the summer. Heinrich had been in the Salzkammergut and subsequently in Germany, from which he had only come back a few days ago.

" Oh, in Berlin ? " hazarded George.

" No."

" I thought perhaps in connection with a new piece——"

" I haven't written a new piece," interrupted Heinrich somewhat rudely. " I was in the Taunus and on the Rhine in several places."

" What's he got to do on the Rhine ? " thought George, although the topic did not interest him any further. It struck him that Bermann was looking in front of him in a manner that was not only absent-minded but really almost melancholy.

" And how's your work getting on, my dear Baron ? " asked Heinrich with sudden animation, while he drew closer round him the dark grey overcoat which hung over his shoulders.* " Have you finished your quintette ? "

" My quintette ? " repeated George in astonishment. " Have I spoken to you about my quintette, then ? "

" No, not you, but Fräulein Else told me that you were working at a quintette."

" I see, Fräulein Else. No, I haven't got much further with it. I didn't feel quite in the mood, as you can imagine."

" Quite," said Heinrich, and was silent for a while. " And your father was still so young," he added slowly.

George nodded in silence.

" How is your brother ? " asked Heinrich suddenly.

" Quite well, thanks," answered George somewhat coldly.

Heinrich threw his cigarette over the rail and immediately proceeded to light another. Then he said: " You must be surprised at my inquiring after your brother when I have scarcely ever spoken to him. But he interests me. He represents in my view a type which is absolutely perfect of its kind, and I regard him as one of the happiest men going."

" That may well be," answered George hesitatingly. " But how do you come to think so seeing that you scarcely know him ? "

" In the first place his name is Felician Freiherr von Wergenthin-Recco," said Heinrich very seriously, and blew the smoke into the air.

* A special way of wearing a coat affected in Viennese artistic circles.

George looked at him with some astonishment.

"Of course your name is Wergenthin-Recco, too," continued Heinrich, "but only George—and that's not the same by a long way, is it ? Besides, your brother is very handsome. Of course you haven't got at all a bad appearance. But people whose real point is that they're handsome have really a much better time of it than others whose real point is that they're clever. If you are handsome you are handsome for always, while clever people, or at any rate nine-tenths of them, spend their life without showing a single trace of talent. Yes, that's certainly the case. The line of life is clearer so to speak when one is handsome than when one is a genius. Of course all this could be expressed far better."

George was disagreeably affected. What's the matter with him? he thought. Can he perhaps be jealous of Felician . . . on account of Else Ehrenberg?

They got out at the Praterstern. The great stream of the Sunday crowd was flowing towards them. They went towards the Hauptallee, where there was no longer any crush, and strolled slowly on. It had grown cool. George made remarks about the autumnal atmosphere of the evening, the people sitting in the restaurants, the military bands playing in the kiosks.

At first Heinrich answered offhandedly, and subsequently not at all, and finally seemed scarcely to be paying any attention. George thought this rude. He was almost sorry that he had joined Heinrich, all the more so as he made it an almost invariable practice not to respond straight away to casual invitations. The excuse he gave to himself was that it was simply out of absent-mindedness that he had done it on this occasion. Heinrich was walking close to him or even going a few steps in front, as if he were completely oblivious of George's presence. He still held tightly in both hands the overcoat which was swung round him, wore his dark grey felt hat pressed down

over his forehead and looked extremely uncouth. His
appearance suddenly began to jar keenly on George's nerves.
Heinrich Bermann's previous remarks about Felician now
struck him as in bad taste, and as quite devoid of tact,
and it occurred to him at the psychological moment that
practically all he knew of Heinrich's literary productions
had gone against the grain. He had seen two pieces of
his : one where the scene was laid in the lower strata of
society, among artizans or factory workers, and which
finished up with murder and fatal blows ; the other a
kind of satirical society comedy whose first production
had occasioned a scandal and which had soon been
taken out of the repertoire of the theatre. Anyway
George did not then know the author personally, and
had taken no further interest in the whole thing. He
only remembered that Felician had thought the piece
absolutely ridiculous, and that Count Schönstein had
expressed the opinion that if he had anything to do with
it pieces written by Jews should only be allowed to be
performed by the Buda-Pesth Orpheum Company.* But
Doctor von Breitner in particular, a baptised Jew with
a philosophical mind, had given vent to his indignation
that such an adventurer of a young man should have
dared to have put a world on to the stage that was obviously
closed to him, and which it was consequently impossible
for him to know anything about.

While George was remembering all this his irritation at
the rude conduct and stubborn silence of his companion
rose to a genuine sense of enmity, and quite unconsciously
he began to think that all the insults which had been
previously directed against Bermann had been in fact
justified. He now remembered too that Heinrich had
been personally antipathetic to him from the beginning,
and that he had indulged in some ironic remark to Frau
Ehrenberg about her cleverness in having lost no time in

* A company celebrated for its risqué plays.

adding that young celebrity to the tame lions in her drawing-room. Else, of course, had immediately taken Heinrich's part, and explained that he was an interesting man, was in many respects positively charming, and had prophesied to George that sooner or later he would become good friends with him. And as a matter of fact George had preserved, as the result of that nocturnal conversation on the seat in the Ringstrasse in the spring of this year, a certain sympathy for Bermann which had survived down to the present evening.

They had passed the last inns some time ago. The white high road ran by their side out into the night on a straight and lonely track between the trees, and the very distant music only reached them in more or less broken snatches.

" But where are you going to ? " Heinrich exclaimed suddenly, as though he had been dragged there against his will, and stood still.

" I really can't help it," remarked George simply.

" Excuse me," said Heinrich.

" You were so deep in thought," retorted George coolly.

" I wouldn't quite like to say ' deep.' But it often happens that one loses onself in one's thoughts like this."

" I know," said George, somewhat reconciled.

" They were expecting you in August at Auhof," said Heinrich suddenly.

" Expected ? Frau Ehrenberg was certainly kind enough to invite me, but I never accepted. Did you stay there a fairly long time, Herr Bermann ? "

" A fairly long time? No. I was up there a few times, but only for an hour or so."

" I thought you stayed there."

" Not a bit of it. I stayed down at the hotel. I only occasionally went up to Auhof. There was too much noise and bustle there for me. . . . The house was positively packed with visitors. And I can't stand most of the people who go there."

An open fiacre in which a gentleman and lady were sitting passed by.

" Why, that was Oskar Ehrenberg," said Heinrich.

" And the lady ? " queried George, looking towards something bright that gleamed through the darkness.

" Don't know her."

They turned their steps through a dark side-avenue. The conversation stuck again. Finally Heinrich began: " Fräulein Else sang a few of your songs to me at Auhof. I'd heard some of them already too, sung by the Bellini, I think."

" Yes, Bellini sang them last winter at a concert."

" Well, Fräulein Else sang those songs and some others of yours as well."

" Who accompanied her, then ? "

" I myself, as well as I could.   I must tell you, my dear Baron, that as a matter of fact those songs impressed me even more than when I heard them the first time at the concert, in spite of the fact that Fräulein Else has considerably less voice and technique than Fräulein Bellini. Of course one must take into consideration on the other hand that it was a magnificent summer afternoon when Fräulein Else sang your songs.   The window was open, there was a view of the mountains and the deep-blue sky opposite . . . but anyway, you came in for a more than sufficient share of the credit."

" Very flattering," said George, who felt pained by Heinrich's sarcastic tone.

" You know," continued Heinrich, speaking as he frequently did with clenched teeth and unnecessary emphasis, " you know it is not generally my habit to invite people whom I happen to see in the street to join me in an omnibus, and I prefer to tell you at once that I regarded it as—what does one say ?—a sign of fate when I suddenly caught sight of you on the Stephansplatz."

George listened to him in amazement,

"You perhaps don't remember as well as I do," continued Heinrich, "our last conversation on that seat in the Ringstrasse."

George now remembered for the first time that Heinrich had then made a quite casual allusion to the libretto of an opera on which he was busy, and that he had offered himself as the composer of the music with equal casualness and more as a joke than anything else. He answered with deliberate coldness: "Oh yes, I remember."

"Well, that binds you to nothing," answered Heinrich, even more coldly than the other. "All the less so since, to tell you the truth, I've not given my opera libretto a single thought till that beautiful summer afternoon when Fräulein Else sang your song. Anyway, what do you say to our stopping here?"

The restaurant garden which they entered was fairly empty. Heinrich and George sat down in a little arbour next to the green wooden railing and ordered their dinner.

Heinrich leant back, stretched out his legs, looked with probing almost cynical eyes at George, who maintained an obstinate silence, and said suddenly: "I don't think I am making a mistake if I venture to presume that you've not been exactly keen on the things I have done so far."

"Oh," answered George, blushing a little, "what makes you think that?"

"Well, I know my pieces . . . and I know you."

"Me!" queried George, feeling almost insulted.

"Certainly," replied Heinrich in a superior manner. "Besides, I have the same feeling with regard to most men, and I regard this faculty as the only indisputable one I've really got. All my others, I think, are fairly problematical. My so-called art in particular is more or less mediocre, and a good deal too could be said against my character. The only thing which gives me a certain amount of confidence is simply the consciousness of being able to see right into people's souls . . . right deep down, every one,

rogues and honest people, men, women and children,
heathens, Jews and Protestants, yes, even Catholics,
aristocrats and Germans, although I have heard that that
is supposed to be infinitely difficult, not to say impossible,
for people like myself."

George gave a slight start. He knew that Heinrich had
been subjected to the most violent personal attacks by the
clerical and conservative press, particularly with reference
to his last piece. " But what's that got to do with me ? "
thought George. There was another one of them who
had been insulted ! It was really absolutely impossible
to associate with these people on a neutral footing. He
said politely, though coldly, with a semi-conscious recollection of old Herr Rosner's retort to young Dr. Stauber:
" I really thought that people like you were above attacks
of the kind to which you're obviously alluding."

" Really . . . you thought that ? " queried Heinrich, in
that cold almost repulsive manner which was peculiar to
him on many occasions. " Well," he went on more gently,
" that is the case sometimes. But unfortunately not
always. It doesn't need much to wake up that self-
contempt which is always lying dormant within us ; and
once that takes place there isn't a single rogue or a single
scoundrel with whom we don't join forces, and quite sincerely too, in attacking our own selves. Excuse me if I
say ' we.' "

" Oh, I've frequently felt something of the same kind
myself. Of course I have not yet had the opportunity of
being exposed to the public as often as you and in the
same way."

" Well, supposing you did . . . you would never have to
go through quite what I did."

" Why not ? " queried George, slightly hurt.

Heinrich looked him sharply in the face. " You are the
Baron von Wergenthin-Recco."

" So that's your reason ! But you must remember

that there are a whole lot of people going about to-day
who are prejudiced against one for that very reason—and
manage to cast in one's teeth the fact of one's being a baron
whenever they get a chance."

"Yes, yes, but I think you will agree with me that
being ragged for being a baron is a very different matter
than being ragged for being a ' Jew,' although the latter—
you'll forgive me of course—may at times denote the
better aristocracy. Well, you needn't look at me so
pitifully," he added with abrupt rudeness. "I am not
always so sensitive. I have other moods in which
nothing can affect me in any way nor any person either.
Then I feel simply this—what do you all know—what do
you know about me. . . ." He stopped, proudly, with
a scornful look that seemed to pierce through the foliage
of the arbour into the darkness. He then turned his
head, looked round and said simply to George in quite a
new tone : " Just look, we shall soon be the only ones left."

" It is getting quite cold, too," said George.

" I think we might still stroll a bit through the Prater."

" Charmed."

They got up and went. A fine grey cloud hung over
a meadow which they passed.

" The fraud of summer doesn't last after nightfall.
It'll soon all be over," said Heinrich in a tone of unmitigated
melancholy, while he added, as though to console himself :
" Well, one will be able to work."

They came into the Wurstelprater. The sound of music
rang out from the restaurants, and some of the exuberant
gaiety communicated itself to George. He felt suddenly
swung out of the dismalness of an inn garden at autumn
time and a somewhat painful conversation into a new world.
A tout, in front of a merry-go-round, from which a
gigantic hurdy-gurdy sent into the open air the pot-pourri
cut of the " Troubadour " with all the effect of some
fantastic organ, invited people to take a journey to London,

Atzgersdorf and Australia. George remembered again the
excursion in the spring with the Ehrenberg party. It
was on this narrow seat inside the room that Frau Oberberger had sat with Demeter Stanzides, the lion of the
evening, by her side, and had probably told him one of her
incredible stories : that her mother had been the mistress
of a Russian Grand Prince ; that she herself had spent a
night with an admirer in the Hallstadt cemetery, of course
without anything happening ; or that her husband, the
celebrated traveller, had made conquests of seventeen
women in one week in one harem at Smyrna. It was in
this carriage upholstered in red velvet, with Hofrat Wilt
as her *vis-à-vis*, that Else had lounged with lady-like grace,
just as though she were in a carriage on Derby Day, while she
yet managed to show by her manner and demeanour that,
if it came to the point, she herself could be quite as childish
as other persons of happier and less complex temperaments.
Anna Rosner with the reins nonchalantly in her hand,
looking dignified, but with a somewhat sly face, rode a
white Arab ; Sissy rocked about on a black horse that
not only turned round in a circle with the other animals
and carriages, but swung up and down as well. The
boldest eyes imaginable flashed and laughed beneath the
audacious *coiffure* with its gigantic black feather hat, while
her white skirt fluttered and flew over her low-cut patent
leather shoes and open-work stockings. Sissy's appearance
had produced so strange an effect on a couple of strangers
that they called out to her a quite unambiguous invitation.
There had then ensued a short mysterious interview between Willy, who immediately came on the spot, and
the two somewhat embarrassed gentlemen, who first
tried to save their faces by lighting fresh cigarettes with
deliberate nonchalance and then suddenly vanished in the
crowd.

Even the side-show with its " Illusions " and " Illu-
minated Pictures " had special memories for George. It

was here, while Daphne was turning into a tree, that Sissy
had whispered into his ear a gentle " remember " and
thus called to his memory that masked ball at Ehrenberg's
at which she had lifted up her lace veil for a fleeting kiss,
though presumably he had not been the only one.   Then
there was the hut where the whole party had had themselves photographed : the three young girls, Anna, Else
and Sissy in the pose of classical goddesses and the men
at their feet with ecstatic eyes, so that the whole thing
looked like the climax of a transformation scene.   And
while George was thinking of these little episodes there
floated up through his memory the way in which he and
Anna had said goodbye to-day, and it seemed full of the
most pleasant promise.

A striking number of people stood in front of an open
shooting gallery.   Now the drummer was hit in the heart
and beat quick strokes upon his drum, now the glass ball
which was dancing to and fro upon a jet of water broke
with a slight click, now a *vivandière* hastily put her trumpet
to her mouth and blew a menacing blast, now a little railway thundered out of a door which had sprung open,
whizzed over a flying bridge and was swallowed up by
another door.

When the crowd began to thin, George and Heinrich
made their way to the front and recognised that the
good shots were Oskar Ehrenberg and his lady friend.
Oskar was just aiming his gun at an eagle which was
moving up and down near the ceiling with out-
stretched wings, and missed for the first time.   He laid
his weapon down in indignation, gazed round him, saw
the two gentlemen behind him and saluted them.

The young lady with her cheek resting on her gun threw
a fleeting glance at the new arrivals, then aimed again
with great keenness, and pressed the trigger.   The eagle
drooped its hit wings and did not move any more.

" Bravo," shouted Oskar.

The lady laid the weapon before her on the table.
" That's my little lot," she said to the boy who wanted to
load again. " I've won."

" How many shots were there ? " asked Oskar.

" Forty," answered the boy, " that's eighty kreuzers."
Oskar put his hand into his waistcoat pocket, threw a
silver gulden down and received with condescension the
thanks of the loading boy. " Allow me," he then said,
while he placed both his hands on his hips, moved the
top of his body slightly in front and put his left foot forward, " Allow me, Amy, to introduce the gentlemen who
witnessed your triumph, Baron Wergenthin, Herr Von
Bermann . . . Fräulein Amelie Reiter."

The gentlemen lifted their hats, Amelie returned the
greeting by nodding a few times with her head. She wore
a simple foulard dress designed in white, and over it a
light cloak of bright yellow bordered with lace and a
black but extremely lively hat.

" I know Herr Von Bermann already," she said. She
turned towards him. " I saw you at the first night of
your play last winter, when you came on the stage to
bow your acknowledgments. I enjoyed myself very
much. Don't think I am saying this as a mere compli-
ment."

Heinrich thanked her sincerely.

They walked on further between side-shows which were
growing quieter and quieter, past inn gardens which were
gradually becoming empty.

Oskar thrust his right arm through his companion's
left and then turned to George. " Why didn't you come
to Auhof this year ? We were all very sorry."

" Unfortunately I didn't feel much in the mood for
society."

" Of course, I can quite understand," said Oskar with
all proper seriousness. " I was only there myself for a
few weeks. In August I strengthened my tired limbs in the

4

waves of the North Sea; I was in the Isle of Wight, you know."

"That must be very nice," said George. "Who is it that always goes there?"

"You're thinking of the Wyners," replied Oskar. "When they used to live in London they went there regularly, but now they only go there every two or three years."

"But they've kept the Y for Austrian consumption as well," said George with a smile.

Oskar was serious. "Old Herr Wyner," he answered, "honestly earned his right to the Y. He went to England in his thirteenth year, became naturalised there and was made a partner when quite a young man in the great steel manufacturing concern which is still called Black & Wyner."

"At any rate he got his wife from Vienna."

"Yes, and when he died seven or eight years ago she came over here with her two children, but James will never get acclimatised here. . . . Lord Antinous, you know, that's what Frau Oberberger calls him. He is now back at Cambridge again where strangely enough he is studying Greek scholarship. Demeter was a few days in Ventnor, too."

"Stanzides?" added George.

"Do you know Herr Von Stanzides, Herr Baron?" asked Amy.

"Oh yes."

"Then he does really exist?" she exclaimed.

"Yes, but just you listen," said Oskar. "She put a lot of money on him this spring at Freudenau, and won a lot of money, and now she inquires if he really exists."

"What makes you have doubts about Stanzides' existence, Fräulein?" asked George.

"Well, you know, whenever I don't know where he is—Oskar, I mean—it's always a case of 'I've an appointment with Stanzides' or 'I'm riding with Stanzides in the Prater.' Stanzides this and Stanzides that, why it sounds more like an excuse than a name."

"You be quiet now, will you?" said Oskar gently.

"Not only does Stanzides exist," explained George, "but he has the most beautiful black moustache and the most fiery black eyes that are to be found anywhere."

"That's quite possible, but when I saw him he looked more like a jack-in-the-box, yellow jacket, green cap, violet sleeves."

"And she won forty gulden on him," added Oskar facetiously.

"And where are the forty gulden?" sighed Fräulein Amelie. . . . Then she suddenly stood still and exclaimed: "But I've never yet been on it."

"Well, that can be remedied," said Oskar simply.

The Great Wheel was turning slowly and majestically in front of them with its lighted carriages. The young people passed the turnstile, climbed into an empty compartment and swept upwards.

"Do you know, George, whom I got to know this summer?" said Oskar. "The Prince of Guastalla."

"Which one?" asked George.

"The youngest, of course, Karl Friedrich. He was there incognito. He's very thick with Stanzides, an extraordinary man. You take my word for it," he added softly, "if people like us said one hundredth part of the things the prince says, we'd never get out of prison our whole life long."

"Look, Oskar," cried Amy, "at the tables and the people down there. It looks just like a little box, doesn't it? And that mass of lights over there, far off. I'm sure that's going to Prague, don't you think so, Herr Bermann?"

"Possibly," answered Heinrich, knitting his forehead as he stared through the glass wall out into the night.

When they left the compartment and got out into the open air the Sunday hubbub was subsiding.

"Poor little girl," said Oskar Ehrenberg to George, while Amy went on in front with Heinrich, "she has no idea that this is the last time we are going out together in the Prater."

"But why the last time ? " asked George, not feeling particularly interested.

"It's got to be," replied Oskar. "Things like this oughtn't to last longer than a year at the outside. Any way, you might buy your gloves from her after December," he added brightly, though with a certain touch of melancholy. "I am setting her up, you know, in a little business. I more or less owe her that, for I took her away from a fairly safe situation."

"A safe one ? "

"Yes, she was engaged, to a case-maker. Did you know that there were such people ? "

In the meanwhile Amy and Heinrich were standing in front of a narrow moving staircase that went boldly up to a platform and waited for the others. All agreed that they ought not to leave the Prater before going for a ride on the switchback.

They whizzed through the darkness down and up again in the groaning coach under the black tree-tops ; and George managed to discover a grotesque motif in ¾ time in the heavy rhythmic noise.

While he was going down the moving staircase with the others, he knew that the melody should be introduced by an oboe and clarionet and accompanied by a cello and contra bass. It was clearly a *scherzo* probably for a symphony.

"If I were a capitalist," expounded Heinrich with emphasis, "I would have a switchback built four miles long to go over fields and hills, through forests and dancing-halls ; I would also see that there were surprises on the way." Anyway, he thought that the time had come to develop more elaborately the fantastic element in the Wurstelprater. He himself, he informed them, had a rough idea for a merry-go-round that by means of some marvellous machinery was to revolve spiral-fashion above the ground, winding higher and higher till eventually it reached the top of a kind of tower.

Unfortunately he lacked the necessary technical knowledge to explain it in greater detail. As they went on he invented burlesque figures and groups for the shooting galleries, and finally declared that there was a pressing need for a magnificent Punch and Judy show for which original authors should write pieces at once profound and frivolous.

In this way they came to the end of the Prater where Oskar's carriage was waiting. Squashed, but none the less good-tempered, they drove to a wine-restaurant in the town. Oskar ordered champagne in a private room, George sat down by the piano and improvised the theme that had occurred to him on the switchback. Amy lounged back in the corner of the sofa, while Oskar kept whispering things into her ears which made her laugh. Heinrich had grown silent again and twirled his glass slowly between his fingers. Suddenly George stopped playing and let his hands lie on the keys. A feeling of the dreamlike and purposeless character of existence came over him, as it frequently did when he had drunk wine. Ages seemed to have passed since he had come down a badly-lighted staircase in the Paulaner Gasse, and his walk with Heinrich in the dark autumn avenue lay far away in the distant past. On the other hand he suddenly remembered, as vividly as though the whole thing had happened yesterday, a very young and very depraved individual, with whom he had spent many years ago a few weeks of that happy-go-lucky life which Oskar Ehrenberg was now leading with Amy. She had kept him wait ing too long one evening in the street, he had gone away impatiently and had neither heard nor seen anything of her again. How easy life was sometimes. . . .

He heard Amy's soft laugh and turned round. His look encountered that of Oskar, who seemed to be trying to catch his eye over Amy's blonde head. He felt irritated by that look and deliberately avoided it and struck a few chords again in a melancholy ballad-style. He felt a desire to describe all that had happened to him to-day, and looked at the clock over the door. It was past one. He caught Heinrich's eye and they both got up. Oskar pointed to Amy, who had gone to sleep on his shoulder, and intimated by a smile and a shrug of his shoulders that under such circumstances he could not think of going for the present. The two others shook hands with him, whispered good-night and slipped away.

"Do you know what I've done?" said Heinrich. "While you were improvising so extraordinarily finely on that ghastly piano I tried to get the real hang of that libretto that I spoke to you about in the spring."

"Oh, the opera libretto! that *is* interesting. Won't you tell me?"

Heinrich shook his head. "I should like to, but the unfortunate thing is, as you've already seen, that it's really not yet finished—like most of my other so-called plots."

George looked at him interrogatively. "You had a whole lot of things on hand last spring, when we saw each other last."

"Yes, I have made a lot of notes, but to-day I've done nothing more than sentences . . . no words, no, just letters on white paper. It's just as if a dead hand had touched everything. I'm frightened the next time I tackle the thing that it will all fall to pieces like tinder. Yes, I've been going through a bad time, and who knows if there's a better one in store for me?"

George was silent. Then he suddenly remembered the

notice in the papers which he had read somewhere or other about Heinrich's father, the former deputy, Doctor Bermann. He suspected that that might be the reason. " Your father is ill, isn't he ? " he asked.

Heinrich answered without looking at him. " Yes, my father has been in a mental home since June."

George shook his head sympathetically.

Heinrich continued : " Yes, it's an awful business, even though I wasn't on very intimate terms with him during the last months it is indescribably awful, and goes on being so."

" I can quite understand," said George, " not making any headway with one's work under circumstances like that."

" Yes," answered Heinrich hesitatingly. " But it's not that alone. To be quite frank that business plays a comparatively subordinate part in my present mental condition. I don't want to make myself out better than I am. Better . . . ! Should I be better . . . ! " He gave a short laugh and then went on speaking. " Look here, yesterday I still thought that it was the accumulation of every possible misfortune that depressed me so. But to-day I've had an infallible proof that things of no importance at all, positively silly things in fact, affect me more deeply than very real things like my father's illness. Disgusting, isn't it ? "

George looked in front of him. Why do I still go on walking with him, he thought, and why does he take it quite for granted that I should ?

Heinrich went on speaking with clenched teeth and unnecessary vehemence of tone. " I received two letters this afternoon. Two letters, yes . . . one from my mother, who had visited my father yesterday in the home. This letter contained the news that he is bad—very bad ; to come to the point he won't last much longer "—he gave a deep breath—" and as you can imagine that involves all kinds of troubles, responsibilities for my mother and my

sister and for myself.   But just think of it, another letter
came at the same time as that one ; it contained nothing of
importance so to speak—a letter from a person with whom
I have been intimate for two years—and there was a passage
in that letter which struck me as a little suspicious—one
isolated passage . . . otherwise the letter was very affectionate and very nice, like all her other letters . . . and now, just
imagine, the memory of that one suspicious passage, which
another man wouldn't have noticed at all, has been haunting
me and torturing me the whole day.   I've not been thinking
about my father in the lunatic asylum, nor about my mother
and sister who are in despair, but only about that unimportant passage in that silly letter from a really by no
means brilliant female.   It eats up all my strength, it
makes me incapable of feeling like a son, like a human
being . . . isn't it ghastly ? "

George listened coldly.   It struck him as strange that
this taciturn melancholy man should suddenly confide in
so casual an acquaintance as himself, and he could not
help feeling a painful sense of embarrassment when confronted with this unexpected revelation.   He did not
have the impression either that any particular sympathy
for him on Heinrich's part was the real reason for all these
confessions.   He rather felt inclined to put it down to
a want of tact, a certain natural lack of self-control, something which seemed very well described by the expression
" bad breeding," which he had once heard applied to
Heinrich—wasn't it by Hofrat Wilt ?   They went as far
as the Burg gate.   A starless sky lay over the silent town,
there was a slight rustle in the trees of the park, they could
hear somewhere or other the noise of a rolling carriage as
it drove away into the distance.

As Heinrich was silent again, George stood still and said
in as kind a tone as he could: " I must now really say
good-bye, dear Herr Bermann."

" Oh," exclaimed Heinrich, " I now see that you've

come with me quite a long way—and I've been tactless enough to tell you, or rather myself in your presence, a lot of things which can't interest you in the least. . . . Forgive me ! "

" What is there to forgive ? " answered George gently. He felt a little moved by this self-reproach of Heinrich's and held out his hand.

Heinrich took it, said " Good-bye, my dear Baron," and rushed off in a hurry, as though he had suddenly decided that any further word would be bound to be importunate.

George looked after him with a mixture of sympathy and repulsion, and suddenly a free and almost happy mood came over him. He felt young, devoid of care and destined for the most brilliant future. He rejoiced at the winter which was coming, there were all kinds of possibilities : work, amusement, sentiment, while he was absolutely indifferent as to who it was from whom these joys might come. He lingered a moment by the Opera-house. If he went home through the Paulanergasse it would not be appreciably out of his way. He smiled at the memory of the serenades of his earlier years. Not far from here lay the street where he had looked up many a night at a window behind whose curtains Marianne had been accustomed to show herself when her husband had gone to sleep. This woman who was always playing with dangers in whose seriousness she herself did not believe had never really been worthy of George. . . . Another memory more distant than this one was much more gracious. When he was a boy of seventeen in Florence he had walked to and fro many a night before the window of a beautiful girl, the first creature of the other sex who had given her virgin self to him as yet untouched. And he thought of the hour when he had seen his beloved step on the arm of her bridegroom up to the altar, where the priest was to consecrate the marriage, of the look of eternal farewell which she had sent to him from under her white veil. . . .

He had now arrived at his goal. The lamps were still burning at both ends of the short street, so that it was quite dark where he stood opposite the house. The window of Anna's room was open, and the pinned curtains fluttered lightly in the wind, just as in the afternoon. It was quite dark below. A soft tenderness began to stir in George's heart. Of all the beings who had ever refrained from hiding their inclination for him he thought Anna the best and the purest. She was also the first who brought the gift of sympathy for his artistic aspirations. She was certainly more genuine than Marianne, whose tears would roll over her cheeks whatever he happened to play on the piano; she was deeper too than Else Ehrenberg, who no doubt only wanted to confirm herself in the proud consciousness of having been the first to recognise his talent. And if any person was positively cut out to counteract his tendency to dilettantism and nonchalance and to keep him working energetically, profitably and with a conscious object that person was Anna. He had thought only last winter of looking out for a post as a conductor or accompanist at some German Opera; at Ehrenbergs' he had casually spoken of his intentions, which had not been taken very seriously. Frau Ehrenberg, woman of the world that she was, had given him the motherly advice rather to undertake a tour through the United States as a composer and conductor, whereupon Else had cut in, "And an American heiress shouldn't be sniffed at either." As he remembered this conversation he was very pleased with the idea of knocking about the world a bit, he wished to get to know foreign towns and foreign men, to win love and fame somewhere out in the wide world, and finally came to the conclusion that his life was slipping away from him on the whole in far too quiet and monotonous a fashion.

He had long ago left the Paulanergasse, without having taken mentally any farewell of Anna, and was soon home.

As he stepped into the dining-room he saw a light shining from Felician's room.

" Good evening, Felician," he cried out.

The door was opened and Felician came out still fully dressed.

The brothers shook hands with each other.

" Only just got home ? " said Felician. " I thought you had been asleep quite a long time." As he spoke he looked past him, as his manner was, and nodded his head towards the right. " What have you been doing, then ? "

" I've been in the Prater," answered George.

" Alone ? "

" No, I met people. Oskar Ehrenberg with his girl and Bermann the author. We shot and went on the switchback. It was quite jolly. . . . What have you got in your hand ? " he said, interrupting his narrative. " Have you been out for a walk like that ? " he added jestingly.

Felician let the sword which he held in his right hand shine in the light of the lamp. " I've just taken it down from the wall, I begin to-morrow again in earnest. The tournament is in the middle of November, and I want to try what I can do this year against Forestier."

" By Jove ! " cried George.

" A piece of cheek, you think, what ? But it's still a long time before the middle of November. And the strange thing is I've got the feeling as though I had learnt something fresh in the very six weeks of this summer when I didn't have the thing in my hand at all. It's as though my arm had got new ideas in the meanwhile. I can't explain it properly."

" I follow what you mean."

Felician held the sword stretched out in front of him and looked at it affectionately. He then said: " Ralph inquired after you, so did Guido . . . a pity you weren't there."

" You spent the whole day with them ? "

"Oh no, I remained at home after dinner. You must have gone out straight away. I've been studying."

"Studying?"

"Yes, I must really do something serious now. I want to pass my Diplomatic exam. by May at the outside."

"So you've quite made up your mind?"

"Absolutely. There's no point in my remaining on any more in the Stadthalterei. The longer I stay there the clearer it becomes. Anyway, the time won't have been wasted. They don't mind at all if one has spent a year or two in Home Service."

"So you'll probably be leaving Vienna in the autumn."

"Presumably."

"And where will they send you?"

"If one only knew."

George looked in front of him. "So the parting is as near as that?" But why did it affect him so much all of a sudden? . . . Why, he himself had determined to go away, and had quite recently spoken to his brother about his plans for next year. Was he still as sceptical as ever of his seriousness? If only they could have a good frank brotherly heart-to-heart talk as they had had on that evening after their father's funeral. As a matter of fact, it was only when life revealed its gloomy side to them that they felt absolutely in touch. Otherwise there was always this strange constraint between them both. There was obviously no help for it. They just had to talk more or less discreetly to each other like fairly intimate friends. And as though resigned to the situation George went on with his questions. "What did you do in the evening?"

"I had supper with Guido and an interesting young lady."

"Really?"

"He's in silken dalliance again, you know."

"Who is it, then?"

"Conservatoire, Jewess, violin. But she didn't bring it

with her. Not particularly pretty, but clever. She im-
proves him and he respects her; he wants her to be baptised. A humorous affair I can tell you. You would
have had quite a good time."

George turned his eyes towards the sword which Felician
still held in his hand. "Would you like to fence a bit ? "
he asked.

" Why not ? " answered Felician and fetched a second
foil out of his room. Meanwhile George had moved the big
table in the middle up against the wall.

" I haven't had a thing in my hand since May," he
said as he took hold of his sword. They took off their
coats and crossed blades. George cried *touché* the next
second.

" Come on," cried George, and thought himself lucky
that it was his brother whom he had to face as he stood in
an awkward position with the slender flashing weapon in
his hand.

Felician hit him as often as he wanted to without himself being touched a single time. He then lowered his
sword and said : " You're too tired to-day, there's no
point in it. But you should come more often to the club.
I assure you it's a pity, with your talent."

George was pleased by his brotherly praise. He laid his
sword down on the table, took a deep breath and went to
the wide centre window which was open. " What wonderful air," he said. A lonely lamp was shining from the
park, there was absolute silence.

Felician came up to George, and while the latter leant
with both hands on the sill the elder brother remained
upright and swept over street, park and town with one of
his proud quiet glances. They were both silent for a
long time. And they knew they were each thinking of
the same thing : a May night of last spring when they
had gone home together through the park and their father
had greeted them with a silent nod of his head from the

very same window by which they were now standing.
And both felt a little shocked at the thought that they
had enjoyed thè whole day with such full gusto, without
any painful memories of the beloved man who now lay
beneath the ground.

"Well, good-night," said Felician in a softer tone than
usual as he held out his hand to George. He pressed it in
silence and each went into his own room.

George arranged the table lamp, took out some music
paper and began to write. It was not the scherzo which
had occurred to him when he had whizzed through the
night with the others under the black tree-tops a few
hours ago ; and it was not the melancholy folk-ballad of
the restaurant either ; but a quite new *motif* that swam
up slowly and continuously as though from secret depths.
George felt as though he had to allow some mysterious
element to take its course. He wrote down the melody,
which he thought should be sung by an *alto* voice or
played on the viola, and at the same time a strange accompaniment rang in his ears, which he knew would never
vanish from his memory.

It was four o'clock in the morning when he went to bed
with the calmness of a man to whom nothing evil can ever
come in all his life and for whom neither solitude nor
poverty nor death possess any terror.

II

FRAU EHRENBERG sat with her knitting on the green velvet sofa in the raised bow-window. Opposite her Else was reading a book. The white head of the marble Isis gleamed from out the far dark part of the room behind the piano, while a streak of light from the next room played through the open door over the grey carpet. Else looked up from her book through the window to the high tops of the trees in the Schwarzenberg Park which were waving in the autumn wind and said casually: " We might perhaps ring up George Wergenthin, to know if he's coming this evening."

Frau Ehrenberg let her knitting fall on her lap. " I don't know," she said. " You remember what a really charming condolence letter I wrote him and what a pressing invitation I gave him to come to Auhof. He didn't come and the coldness of his answer was quite marked. I wouldn't ring him up."

" One shouldn't treat him like other people," answered Else. " He belongs to the people whom one has occasionally to remind that one is still alive. When he has been reminded he is extremely glad."

Frau Ehrenberg went on with her knitting. " It really won't come to anything," she said quietly.

" It's not meant to come to anything," retorted Else. " I thought you knew that by this time, mamma. We're good friends, nothing more—and even that only at intervals ; or do you really think that I'm in love with him, mamma ? Yes, when I was a little girl I was, in Nice, when we played tennis together, but that is long past."

" Well—and Florence ? "

" In Florence—I was more in love with Felician."

" And now ? " asked Frau Ehrenberg slowly.

" Now . . . you're probably thinking of Heinrich Bermann . . . but you're making a mistake, mother."

" I prefer to be making a mistake. But this summer I really quite had the impression that——"

" I tell you," interrupted Else a little impatiently, " it isn't anything and never was anything. On one solitary occasion, when we went out boating on a sultry afternoon, you saw us from your balcony with your opera-glasses, no doubt—it was only then that it became a little dangerous. And even supposing we had fallen on each other's neck—which as a matter of fact we never did—it wouldn't have meant anything. It was simply a summer flirtation."

" And besides, he's supposed to be involved in a very serious love-affair," said Frau Ehrenberg.

" You mean . . . with that actress, mamma ? "

Frau Ehrenberg looked up. " Did he tell you anything about her ? "

" Tell . . . ? Not in so many words, but when we went for walks together in the park or went out in the evening on the lake, why, he practically spoke of nothing but her— of course without mentioning her name . . . and the better he liked me—men really are such awfully funny people— the more jealous he became about the other woman. . . . But if it were only that ? What young man isn't involved in a serious love affair ? Do you think by any chance, mamma, that George Wergenthin is not ? "

" In a serious one . . . no, that will never happen to him. He's too cold, too superior for that . . . he hasn't got enough temperament."

" That's exactly why," explained Else, airing her knowledge of human nature. " He'll slip into some whirlpool or other and get taken out of his depth without his having noticed it, and some fine day he'll get married . . . out of sheer indolence . . . to some person or other who'll probably be absolutely indifferent to him."

" You must have a definite suspicion," said Frau Ehrenberg.

" I have."

" Marianne ? "

" Marianne ! but that's been over a long time, mamma. And that was never anything particularly serious, either."

" Well, who is it then ? "

" Well whom do you think, mamma ? "

" I have no idea."

" It's Anna," said Else curtly.

" Which Anna ? "

" Anna Rosner, of course."

" But . . ."

" You can say ' but ' as much as you like—it's a fact."

" Else, you don't seriously think that Anna with her reserved character could so far forget herself as to——"

" So far forget herself . . . ? Really, mamma, the number of expressions you keep on using—anyway, I don't think that's quite a case of one's forgetting oneself."

Frau Ehrenberg smiled, not without a certain pride.

The bell rang outside.

" It's he at last," said Else.

" It might quite as well be Demeter Stanzides," observed Frau Ehrenberg.

" Stanzides was to bring the Prince along sometime," said Else casually.

" Do you think that will come off ? " inquired Frau Ehrenberg, letting her knitting fall into her lap.

" Why shouldn't it come off ? " said Else. " They are so intimate."

The door opened. As a matter of fact it was none of the expected visitors who came in, but Edmund Nürnberger. He was dressed, as always, with the greatest care, though not after the latest fashion. His tail coat was a little too short and an emerald pin was stuck in his voluminous satin tie. He bowed as soon as he had got to the door, though his demeanour expressed at the same time a certain irony at his own politeness. " Am I the first ? " he inquired. " No one here yet ? Not a Hofrat—nor a count—nor an author—nor a diabolical female ? "

" Only a woman who never was one, I'm sorry to say," answered Frau Ehrenberg as she shook hands with him.

" And one . . . who will perhaps become one sometime."

" Oh, I am convinced," said Nürnberger, " that if she only takes it seriously, Fräulein Else will succeed in that." He stroked his smooth black somewhat glossy hair slowly with his left hand.

Frau Ehrenberg expressed her regret that their expectation of his coming to Auhof had not been realised. Had he really spent the whole summer in Vienna ?

" Why do you wonder so much, my dear madam ? Whether I am walking up and down among mountain scenery or by the shore of the sea or in my own room, it doesn't really matter much in the end."

" But you must have felt quite lonely," said Frau Ehrenberg.

" You certainly realise solitude more clearly when there's no one in the neighbourhood who shows any desire of talking to you. . . . But let's talk of more interesting and promising men than I am. How are all the numerous friends of your popular family ? "

" Friends ! " repeated Else. " I should like first to know what you mean by the word ? "

" Well, all the people who say something agreeable to you from whatever motive, and whom you believe in when they say it."

The door of the bedroom opened, Herr Ehrenberg appeared and greeted Nürnberger.

" Are you ready packed ? " asked Else.

" Packed and ready," answered Ehrenberg, who had on a grey suit that was far too loose and was biting a fat cigar between his teeth. He turned to Nürnberger to explain. . . . " I'm off to-day, just as I am, to Corfu . . . for the time being; the season is beginning and the Ehrenberg ' at homes ' make me feel sick."

" No one asks you," replied Frau Ehrenberg gently, " to honour them with your presence."

" 'Cute answer, eh," said Ehrenberg, puffing at his cigar. " I don't mind, of course, staying away from your real ' at homes.' But when I'd like to dine quietly at home on a Thursday and there's an attaché sitting in one corner and a hussar in the other, and some one over there is playing his own compositions and some one else on the sofa is being funny, while by the window Frau Oberberger is fixing up an assignation with any one who happens to come along . . . well, it really gets on my nerves. One can stand it once, but not a second time."

" Do you think you'll remain away all the winter ? " asked Nürnberger.

" It's possible. I intend, you know, to go further, to Egypt, to Syria, probably to Palestine as well. Yes, it's perhaps only because one's getting older, perhaps because one reads so much about Zionism and so forth, but I can't help it, I should like to see Jerusalem before I die."

Frau Ehrenberg shrugged her shoulders.

" Those are matters," said Ehrenberg, " which my wife don't understand—and my children even less so. What do you know about it, Else ? no, you don't know anything either. But when one reads what's going on in the world it often makes one inclined to think that there's no other way out for us."

" For us ? " repeated Nürnberger. " I've not observed up to the present that Anti-Semitism has done you any particular harm."

" You mean because I've grown a rich man ? Well if

I were to tell you that I don't give any shakes for money, you would, of course, not believe me, and quite right too. But as sure as you see me here, I swear to you that I would give half my fortune to see the worst of our enemies on the gallows."

" I'm only afraid," remarked Nürnberger, " that you would have the wrong ones hanged."

" There's not much danger," replied Ehrenberg. " Even if you don't catch the man you're after, the man you do catch is bound to be one of them, too, right enough."

" This is not the first time, my dear Herr Ehrenberg, that I observe that your standpoint towards this question is not ideally objective."

Ehrenberg suddenly bit through his cigar and with fingers shaking with rage put it on the ash-tray. " If any one here's to tell me . . . and even . . . excuse me . . . or perhaps you're baptised . . . ? One can really never tell nowadays."

" I'm not baptised," replied Nürnberger quietly. " But on the other hand I am certainly not a Jew either. I've ceased to belong to the congregation for a long time, for the simple reason that I never felt myself to be a Jew."

" If some one were to bash in your top hat in the Ringstrasse because, if you will allow me to say so, you have a somewhat Jewish nose, you'd realise pretty quick that you were insulted because you were a Yiddisher fellow. You take my word for it."

" But, papa, how excited you are getting," said Else, and stroked him on his bald reddish shiny head.

Old Ehrenberg took her hand, stroked it and asked, apparently without any connection with what he had been saying before: " By-the-bye, shall I have the pleasure of seeing my son and heir before I leave ? "

Frau Ehrenberg answered: " Oskar's bound to be home soon."

Ehrenberg turned to Nürnberger. " You will doubtless be glad to know that my son Oskar is an Anti-Semite as well."

Frau Ehrenberg sighed gently. " It's a fixed idea of his," she said to Nürnberger. " He sees Anti-Semites everywhere, even in his own family."

" That is the latest Jewish national disease," said Nürnberger. " I myself have only succeeded up to the present in making the acquaintance of one genuine Anti-Semite. I'm afraid I am bound to admit, dear Herr Ehrenberg, that it was a well-known Zionist leader."

Ehrenberg could only make an eloquent gesture.

Demeter Stanzides and Willy Eissler came in and immediately spread an atmosphere of vivid brilliancy around them. Demeter wore his uniform lightly and magnificently, as though it were a fancy costume rather than a military dress ; Willy stood there in a dinner jacket looking tall and pale and as if he had been keeping late hours, and then immediately gathered up the reins of the conversation, while his pleasantly hoarse voice rasped through the air with amiable imperiousness.

He gave an account of the preparations for an aristo-cratic theatrical performance in which he was adviser, producer and actor, just as he had been last year, and described a meeting of the young lords, where, if his account was to be believed, every one had behaved as though they were in a lunatic asylum, and then went on to treat them to a humorous dialogue between two countesses whose mannerisms he managed to take off in a most delightful way. Ehrenberg was always very amused by Willy Eissler. The vague feeling that this Hungarian Jew managed somehow or other to outwit and make a fool of that whole feudal set, whom personally he hated so much, filled him with respect for the young man.

Else sat at the little table in the corner with Demeter and made him tell her about the *Isle of Wight*. " You were there with your friend ? " she inquired, " weren't you, Prince Karl Friedrich ? "

" My friend the Prince ? . . . that's not quite right, Fräulein Else. The Prince has no friends, nor have I. We're neither of us the type to have friends."

" He must be an interesting man according to all one hears."

" Interesting—I don't know about that. At any rate he's thought over a lot of things which people in his position are not usually accustomed to bother their heads about very much. Perhaps he'd have managed to do all kinds of things too, if he'd been left to himself. Well, who knows, it was perhaps better for him that they kept a tight hold on him, for him and for the country too in the long run. One man alone can do nothing—never in this life. That's why it's best to let matters slide and get out of things, as he did."

Else looked at him somewhat coldly. " You're so philosophical to-day, what is it ? It seems to me that Willy Eissler has spoilt you."

" Willy spoilt me ? "

" Yes, you know you shouldn't associate with such clever people."

" Why not ? "

" You should simply be young, shine, live, and then when there's nothing more to do, do whatever you like . . . but without bothering about yourself and the world."

" You should have told me that before, Fräulein Else ; once a man's started getting clever . . . ."

Else shook her head. " But perhaps in your case it might have been avoided," she said quite seriously. And then they both had to laugh.

The chandelier was lighted up. George Wergenthin and Heinrich Bermann had come in. Invited by a smile George sat down by Else's side.

" I knew that you would come," she said disingenuously

but warmly as she pressed his hand ; she was more glad
than she thought she would have been that he should sit
opposite to her after so long an interval, that she could see
again his proud gracious face and hear again his somewhat
gentle yet warm voice.

Frau Wyner appeared, a little woman with a high
colour, jolly and awkward.   Her daughter Sissy was with
her.   The groups got broken up in the " general post "
of mutual greetings.

" Well, have you composed that song for me yet ? "
Sissy asked George with laughing eyes and laughing lips,
as she played with one of her gloves and moved about like
a snake in her dark-green shimmering dress.

" A song ? " asked George.   He really didn't remember.

" Or waltz or something.   But you promised me to
dedicate something to me."   While she spoke her looks
were wandering round.   They glowed into the eyes of
Willy, passed caressingly by Demeter and addressed a
sphinx-like question to Heinrich Bermann.   It seemed as
though will-o'-the-wisps were dancing through the drawing-
room.

Frau Wyner suddenly came up to her daughter.   She
flushed deeply.   " Sissy is really so silly. . . . What are
you thinking of, Sissy ?   Baron George has had more important things to do this year than to compose things for
you."

" Oh not at all," said George politely.

" You buried your father, that's no trifle."

George looked straight in front of him.

But Frau Wyner went on speaking quite unperturbed.
" And your father wasn't old, was he ?   And such a handsome man. . . . Is it true that he was a chemist ? "

" No," answered George calmly.   " He was President of
the Botanical Society."   Heinrich with one arm on the
shut piano-top was speaking to Else.

" So you've been in Germany ? " she asked.

" Yes," replied Heinrich. " I've been back a fairly long time, four or five weeks."

" And when are you going back again ? "

" I don't know, perhaps never."

" Come, you don't believe that yourself—what are you working at ? " she added quickly.

" All kinds of things," he answered. " I'm going through a rather restless time. I sketch out a lot but I finish nothing. I'm very rarely keen on completing things, obviously I lose all my interest in things too quickly."

" And people too," added Else.

" Possibly. Only unhappily one's emotions remain attached to people after one's reason has long ago decided to have nothing more to do with them. A poet—if you will allow me to use the expression—must go away from every one who no longer presents any riddle to him . . . particularly from any one whom he loves."

" They say," suggested Else, " that it is just those whom we know least that we love."

" That's what Nürnberger makes out, but it's not quite right. If it were really so, my dear Else, then life would probably be much more beautiful than it is. No, we know those whom we love much better than we do other people —but we know them with a feeling of shame, bitterness and with the fear that others may know them as well as we do. Love means this—being afraid that the faults which we have discovered in the person we love may be revealed to others. Love means this—being able to look into the future and curse this very gift. . . . Love means this—knowing some one so that it smashes one."

Else leant on the piano in her childish lady-like way and listened to him curiously. How much she liked him in moments like this ! She would have liked to have stroked his hair again consolingly, as she had done before on the lake when he had been torn by his love for that other woman, but when he suddenly retired into his shell, coldly and drily, and looked as though all his fire had been extinguished she felt that she could never live with him, and she would be bound to run away after a few weeks ... with a Spanish officer or a violin *virtuoso*. " It is a good thing," she said somewhat condescendingly, " that you see something of George Wergenthin. He'll have a sound influence on you. He is quieter than you are. I don't think that he is so gifted as you are, and I am sure that he is not so clever."

" What do you know about his gifts ? " interrupted Heinrich almost rudely.

George came up and asked Else if they couldn't have the pleasure to-night of hearing one of her songs. She didn't want to. Besides she was principally studying opera parts nowadays. That interested her more. As a matter of fact she was far from having a lyrical temperament. George asked her jokingly if she didn't have perhaps the secret intention of going on the stage ?

" With my little bit of a voice ! " said Else.

Nürnberger was standing near them. " That wouldn't be an obstacle," he observed. " Why, I feel quite positive that a modern critic would soon turn up who would boom you as an important singer for the very reason that you have no voice, but who would discover some other gift in you by way of compensation, as, for instance, your gift for characterisation, just as we have to-day certain painters who have no sense of colour but only intellect ; and celebrated authors who never have the vaguest ideas but who succeed in discovering the most unsuitable epithets for every noun they use."

Else noticed that Nürnberger's manner of speaking got on George's nerves. She turned to him. " I should like to show you something," she said, and took a few steps towards the music-case.

George followed her.

" Here is a collection of old Italian folksongs. I should

like you to show me the best. I myself don't know enough
about it."

" I can't understand," said George gently, " how you can
stand any one like that man Nürnberger near you. He
spreads around him an absolute atmosphere of distrust and
malice."

" As I've often told you, George, you're no judge of
character. After all, what do you know about him ? He's
different from what you think he is ; just ask your friend
Heinrich Bermann."

" Oh, I know well enough that he raves about him, too,"
replied George.

" You're speaking about Nürnberger ? " asked Frau
Ehrenberg, who had just joined them.

" George can't stand him," said Else in her casual way.

" Well, you're doing him a great injustice, if that's the
case. Have you ever read anything of his ? "

George shook his head.

" Not even his novel which made so great a sensation
fifteen or sixteen years ago ? That is really a shame.
We've just lent it to Hofrat Wilt. I tell you he was quite
flabbergasted at the way in which the whole of present-
day Austria is anticipated in that book, written all that
time ago."

" Really, is that so ? " said George, without conviction.

" You have no idea," continued Frau Ehrenberg, " of
the applause with which Nürnberger was then hailed ; one
could go so far as to say that all doors sprang open before
him."

" Perhaps he found that enough," observed Else, with
an air of meditative wisdom.

Heinrich was standing by the piano engaged in conversation with Nürnberger, and was making an effort, as
he frequently did, to persuade him to undertake a new
work or to bring out an edition of previous writings.

Nürnberger would not agree. He was filled with positive horror at the thought of seeing his name a prey to publicity again, of plunging again into a literary vortex which seemed to him as repulsive as it was fatuous. He had no desire to enter the competition. What was the point ? Intriguing cliques that no longer made any attempt at concealment were at work everywhere. Did there remain a single man of sound talent and honest aspirations who did not have to face every minute the prospect of being dragged down into the dirt ? Was there a blockhead in the country who could not boast of having been hailed as a genius in some rag or other ? Had celebrity in these days anything at all to do with honour, and was being ignored and forgotten worth even a single shrug of regret ? And who could know after all what verdicts would pass as the correct ones in the future ? Were not the fools really the geniuses and the geniuses really the fools ? It would be ridiculous to allow himself to be tempted to stake his peace of mind and even his self-respect on a game where even the greatest possible win held out no promise of any satisfaction.

" None at all ? " queried Heinrich. " I'll grant you as much as you like about fame, wealth, world-wide influence —but for a man, simply because all these things are of dubious advantage, to relinquish something so absolutely indubitable as the moments of inner consciousness of one's own power——"

" Inner consciousness of power ? Why don't you say straight away the happiness of creating ? "

" It does exist, Nürnberger."

" It may be so; why, I even think I remember that I felt something like that myself now and then, a very long time ago . . . only, as you no doubt know, as the years went by I completely lost the faculty of deceiving myself."

" Perhaps you only think so," replied Heinrich. " Who knows if it is not that very faculty of self-deception which you have developed more strongly than any other as the years went by?"

Nürnberger laughed. "Do you know how I feel when I hear you talk like that? just like a fencing-master feels who gets a thrust in the heart from one of his own pupils."

"And not even one of his best," said Heinrich.

Herr Ehrenberg suddenly appeared in the doorway, to the astonishment of his wife, who had presumed that he would be by now on his way to the station. He led a young lady by the hand. She was dressed simply in black, and had her hair done extraordinarily high after a fashion that was now out of date. Her lips were full and red, the eyes in the pale vivid face had a clear hard gaze.

"Come along," said Ehrenberg with some malice in his small eyes, and led the visitor straight up to Else, who was chatting with Stanzides. "I've brought a visitor for you."

Else held out her hand. "But this is nice." She introduced them—"Herr Demeter Stanzides—Fräulein Therese Golowski."

Therese bowed slightly and let her gaze rest on him for a while with a little embarrassment as though she were scrutinising a beautiful beast, then she turned to Else: "If I had known that you had such a lot of visitors."

"Do you know what she looks like?" said Stanzides softly to George. "Like a Russian student, don't you think?"

George nodded. "That's about it. I know her. She is a school-friend of Fräulein Else's, and now she's playing a leading part among the Socialists. Just think of it! she's just been in prison for *lèse-majesté*, I believe."

"Yes, I think I've read something about it," replied Demeter. "One should really get to know a person of that type more intimately. She's pretty. Her face might be made of ivory."

"And her features show a lot of energy," added George.

" Her brother too is an extraordinary fellow, a pianist and a mathematician, and the father's supposed to be a ruined Jewish skin-dealer."

" It's really a strange race," observed Demeter.

In the meanwhile Frau Ehrenberg had come up to Therese. She considered it correct not to show any surprise. " Sit down, Therese," she said. " And how have you been getting on all this time ? Since you've devoted yourself to political life you don't bother about your old friends any more."

" Yes, I'm afraid my work gives me very little time to pay private visits," replied Therese, thrusting out her chin, in a way that made her face look masculine and almost ugly.

Frau Ehrenberg vacillated as to whether she should or should not make any reference to the term of imprisonment which Therese had just served. It was certainly to be borne in mind there was scarcely another house in Vienna where ladies who had been locked up a short time ago, were allowed to call.

" And how is your brother ? " asked Else.

" He's doing his service this year," answered Therese. " You can imagine pretty well how he's getting on." And she looked ironically at Demeter's hussar uniform.

" I suppose he doesn't get much opportunity there for playing the piano," said Frau Ehrenberg.

" Oh, he's given up all thoughts of being a pianist," replied Therese. " He's all for politics now." And turning with a smile to Demeter she added: " Of course you won't give him away, Herr Oberlieutenant ? "

Stanzides laughed somewhat awkwardly.

" What do you mean by politics ? " asked Herr Ehrenberg. " Does he want to get into the Cabinet ? "

" Not in Austria at any rate," replied Therese. " He is a Zionist, you know."

" What ? " exclaimed Ehrenberg, and his visage beamed.

"That's certainly a subject on which we don't quite agree," added Therese.

"My dear Therese . . . " began Ehrenberg.

"You'll miss your train, my dear," interrupted his wife.

"I'm not going to miss my train, and anyway, another one goes to-morrow. My dear Therese, this is the only thing I want to say—each person should find happiness in his own way. But in this case your brother and not you is the cleverer of you two. Excuse me, I'm perhaps a layman in politics, but I assure you, Therese, exactly the same thing will happen to you Jewish Social Democrats as happened to the Jewish Liberals and German Nationalists."

"How do you mean?" asked Therese haughtily. "In what way will the same thing happen to us?"

"In what way . . . ? I'll tell you soon enough. Who created the Liberal movement in Austria? . . . the Jews. By whom have the Jews been betrayed and deserted? By the Liberals. Who created the National-German movement in Austria? the Jews. By whom were the Jews left in the lurch? . . . what—left in the lurch! . . . Spat upon like dogs! . . . By the National-Germans, and precisely the same thing will happen in the case of Socialism and Communism. As soon as you've drawn the chestnuts out of the fire they'll start driving you away from the table. It always has been so and always will be so."

"We will wait and see," Therese replied quietly.

George and Demeter looked at each other like two friends marooned together on a desert island.

Oskar, who had come in during the middle of his father's speech, compressed his lips and was very embarrassed. But they all felt a kind of deliverance when Ehrenberg suddenly looked at his watch and took his leave.

"We certainly shan't agree to-day," he said to Therese.

Therese smiled. "Scarcely. Hope you will enjoy your

journey and I want once more to . . . to thank you in the name of . . ."

" Hush ! " said Ehrenberg and vanished.

" What are you thanking papa for ? " said Else.

" For a gift of money for which I came to ask him in the most shameless manner. Apart from him there is not a single rich man in the circle of my acquaintances. I am not in a position to speak of the purpose for which it is wanted."

Frau Ehrenberg came up to Bermann and Nürnberger, who were continuing their conversation over the top of the piano, and said softly : " Of course you know that she "— then she looked at Therese—" has just been released from prison."

" I read about it," said Heinrich.

Nürnberger half shut his eyes and cast a glance at the group in the corner where the three girls were talking to Stanzides and Willy Eissler and shook his head.

" What cynicism are you suppressing ? " said Frau Ehrenberg.

" I was just thinking how easily it might have come about for Fräulein Else to have languished two months in prison and for Fräulein Therese to have held receptions in a stylish drawing-room as daughter of the house."

" Easily come about ? "

" Herr Ehrenberg has had good luck, Herr Golowski bad luck. . . . Perhaps that is the only difference."

" Look here, now, Nürnberger," said Heinrich, " you're not going to deny that such a thing as individuality exists in the world. . . . Else and Therese are rather different characters you know."

" I think so too," observed Frau Ehrenberg.

Nürnberger shrugged his shoulders. " They are both young girls, quite gifted, quite pretty . . . everything else is more or less of an accidental appanage, just as it is with most young women—most people, in fact."

Heinrich shook his head energetically. " No, no," he said, " life is really not as simple as all that."

" That doesn't make it simpler, my dear Heinrich."

Frau Ehrenberg turned her eyes towards the door and beamed.

Felician had just come in. With all the sureness of a sleep-walker he walked up to the hostess and kissed her hand. " I have just had the pleasure of meeting Herr Ehrenberg on the steps; he told me he was going off to Corfu. It must be awfully beautiful out there."

" You know Corfu ? "

" Yes, a memory of my childhood." He greeted Nürnberger and Bermann, and they all talked about the South for which Bermann longed and in which Nürnberger did not believe.

George gave his brother a hand-shake which meant a salutation and a goodbye at the same time. As he unobtrusively disappeared through the open door of the dining-room he looked round again, noticed Marianne sitting in the furthest corner of the drawing-room and looking at him ironically through her lorgnette. This woman had always had the mysterious gift of suddenly being present without one realising where she came from. And then a veiled lady came up to him on the steps. " Don't be in such a hurry, you can surely wait another moment," she said. " One really shouldn't spoil women so. . . . I wonder if you'd be in such a hurry, you know, if you were going to keep an appointment with me . . . ? But you prefer to be non-committal. Probably because you're afraid that my husband will shoot you when he comes back from Stockholm. I mean he's probably got as far as Copenhagen to-day. But he places absolute confidence in me. And he's quite right too. For I'm able to swear to you that no one has managed to get any further than a kiss on my hand. . . . No, to tell the full truth, on my neck, here. Of course, you believe, too, that I have had an affair with Stanzides ? No, he wouldn't be at all in my line ! I positively loathe handsome men. I couldn't find anything in your brother Felician either. . . ."

One could form no idea when the veiled lady would leave off speaking, for it was Frau Oberberger. Similar conduct in other women would have betokened a specific overture, but that was not so in her case. In spite of the dubious impression created by her whole manner the world had never been able to fix her so far with a single lover. She lived in a strange, but apparently happy, childless marriage. Her brilliant handsome husband, a geologist by profession, had undertaken scientific expeditions in days gone by, when, so Hofrat Wilt used to assert, he had set more store by the good travelling and facilities and unimpeachable cooking of the districts in question than on their being actually unexplored. But for some years past he had given up travelling in favour of lecturing and ladykilling. When he was at home he lived with his wife in the best *camaraderie*. George had frequently, though never seriously, considered the possibility of a liaison with Frau Oberberger. He was even one of those who had kissed her neck, a fact which she probably did not remember herself. And as she threw back her veil now George again surrendered himself with pleasure to the fascination of this face, which though no longer in its first flush of youth was yet both charming and animated. He wanted to take up the conversation, but she went on speaking. " Do you know you're very pale ? a nice life you must be leading. What kind of a woman is it who is responsible for taking you away from me this time ? "

Hofrat Wilt, with his usual silent step, suddenly stood by them. With a casual air of gallantry and superiority he threw them a " Good-day, beauteous lady, Hullo, Baron," and started to go on.

But Frau Oberberger thought it fitting to inform him

6

first that Baron George was just going to one of his usual orgies—she then followed Hofrat up to the second story at the risk, as she remarked, of his being taken for her ninety-fifth lover if he presented himself at Ehrenberg's at the same time as she did.

It was seven o'clock before George could settle himself in a fly and drive to Mariahilf. He felt quite exhausted by the two hours at Ehrenberg's and he was even more than usually glad at the meeting with Anna which was before him. Since that morning at the miniature exhibition they had seen each other nearly every day ; in parks, picture-galleries, at her house. They usually talked about the little incidents of their life or gossiped about books or music. They did not often talk of the past, but when they did it was without doubts or misgivings. For so far as Anna was concerned the adventures from which George had just come were far from being surrounded with the uncanny atmosphere of mystery ; while George gathered from her own jesting allusions that she herself had already experienced more than one infatuation, though that did not cause him to lose the serenity of his good spirits or even to ask her any further questions.

He had kissed her for the first time eight days ago, in an empty room in the Liechstentein Gallery, and from that moment Anna had employed the familiar 'du,' as though a less intimate appellation would have rung somewhat false. The fly stopped at a street corner. George got out, lit a cigarette and walked up and down opposite the house out of which Anna was due to come.

After a few minutes she came out of the door, he rushed across the street to meet her and kissed her hand ecstatically. Following her habit, for she was in the habit of reading on her journeys, she carried a book with her in a pressed leather cover.

" It is quite cool, Anna," said George, took the book

out of her hand and helped her into the jacket which she
had been carrying over her arm.

" I was a little bit late you see," she said, " and I was
very impatient to see you. Yes," she added with a smile,
"one's temperament will break out now and again. What do
you think of my new dress? " she added as they walked on.

" It suits you very well."

" They thought at my lesson that I looked like a lady-
in-waiting."

" Who thought so ? "

" Frau Bittner herself and her two daughters whom I
am teaching."

" I should rather say, like an Arch-Duchess."

Anna nodded with satisfaction.

" And now tell me, Anna, all that's happened to you
since yesterday."

She began quite seriously: " Twelve o'clock, after I left
you at the door of our house, dinner in the family circle.
Rested a little in the afternoon, and thought about you.
Pupils from four to six-thirty, then read ' Grüner Heinrich,'
and the evening paper. Too lazy to go out again, messed
about at home. Supper. The usual domestic scene."

" Your brother ? " queried George.

She answered with a " Yes " that ruled out all further
questions. " A little music after supper. . . . Even tried
to sing."

" Were you satisfied ? "

" It was quite good enough for me, anyway," she said,
and George thought he detected a slight note of melancholy
in her tone. She quickly went on with her report. " Went
to bed at half-past ten, slept well, got up early at eight . . .
one can't lie in bed any longer in our house . . . dressed till
half-past nine, was about the house till eleven. . . ."

" . . . Messing about," added George.

" Right. Then went on to Weils, gave the boy a lesson,"

" How old is he ? " asked George,

" Thirteen," replied Anna.

" Well, after all that is not so young."

" Quite so," said Anna.   " But you can set your mind at rest when I inform you that he loves his Aunt Adele, a sentimental blonde of thirty-three, and is not thinking for the time being of breaking his troth to her. . . . Well, to continue the record. Got home at one-thirty, had my meal alone, thank Heaven! Father already at the office, mamma in a state of sleep.   Rested again from three to four, thought even more about you, and more seriously too, than yesterday, then went shopping in town, gloves, safety pins and something for mamma, and then drove on the tram, reading all the way to Mariahilf, to the two Bittner kiddies. . . .   So now you know all.   Satisfied ? "

" Except for the boy of thirteen."

" Well, I agree that that might be a bit upsetting. But now we should like to know if you haven't got even more sinister confessions to make to me."

They were in a narrow silent street, which seemed quite strange to George, and Anna took his arm.

" I have just come from Ehrenbergs'," he began.

" Well ? " queried Anna.   " Did they try very much to inveigle you ? "

" No, I can't go so far as that.   Of course they seemed a little hurt that I did not go to Auhof this summer," he added.

" Did dear little Else perform ? " Anna asked.

" No ; of course I don't know what happened after I left."

" It won't be worth the trouble now," said Anna with exuberant mirth.

" You are wrong, Anna.   There are people there for whom it is quite worth while singing."

" Who ? "

" Heinrich Bermann, Willy Eissler, Demeter Stanzides. . . ."

" Oh, Stanzides! " exclaimed Anna. " Now I am really sorry that I wasn't there too."

" It seems to me," said George, "that that is a true word spoken in jest."

" Quite so," replied Anna. " I think Demeter is really desperately handsome."

George was silent for a few seconds and suddenly asked, with more emotion than he usually manifested : " Is it he then . . . ? "

" What ' he ' do you mean ? "

" The one you . . . loved more than me."

She smiled, nestled closer up to him and answered simply, though a little ironically : " Am I really supposed to have been fonder of any one else than of you ? "

" You confessed it to me yourself," replied George.

" But I also confess to you that I should love you in time more than I have loved or ever could love any one else."

" Are you quite sure about that, Anna ? "

" Yes, George, I am quite certain of it."

They had now come again into a more lively street and reluctantly let go of each other's arms.

They remained standing in front of various shops. They discovered a photographer's show-case by a house-door and were very much amused by the laboriously-natural poses in which golden and silver wedding couples, cadets, cooks in their Sunday best and ladies in masked fancy dress were taken.

George asked again in a lighter tone : " So it was Stanzides ? "

" What an idea ! I have never spoken a hundred words to him in my life."

They went on walking.

" Leo Golowski, then ? " asked George.

She shook her head and smiled. " That was calf-love," she replied. " That really doesn't count. I should like

to know the girl of sixteen who wouldn't have fallen
in love in the country with a handsome youth who fights
a duel with a real Count and then goes about for eight
days with his arm in a sling. "

" But he didn't do it on your account, but for his sister's
honour, as it were."

" For Therese's honour ? What makes you think that ? "

" You told me that the young man had spoken to
Therese in the forest while she was studying ' *Emilia
Galotti.* ' "

" Yes, that is quite true. Anyway, she was quite glad
to be spoken to. The only thing Leo objected to was that
the young Count belonged to a club of young men who
really behaved rather cheekily, and I think showed a
touch of Anti-Semitism. So when Therese once went with
her brother for a walk by the lake, and the Count came
up and spoke to Therese as though he had known her for
ages, while he mumbled his name off-handedly, for the
benefit of Leo, Leo made a bow and introduced himself
like this: ' Leo Golowski, Cracow Jew.' I don't know
exactly what happened further; there was an exchange of
words and the duel took place next day in the cavalry
barracks at Klagenfurt."

" So I am quite right," persisted George humorously.
" He did fight for his sister's honour."

" No, I tell you. I was there when he once discussed
the matter with Therese, and said to her: ' So far as I am
concerned you can do whatever amuses you. You can
flirt with any one you like ' . . . ."

" Only it's got to be a Jew, I suppose. . . ." added George.
Anna shook her head. " He's really not like that."

" I know," replied George gently. " We have become
quite good friends lately, your Leo and I.

" Why, only yesterday evening we met at the café
again and he was really quite condescending to me. I
think he really forgives me my lineage. Besides, I haven't

told you that Therese was at Ehrenbergs', too." And he described the appearance of the young girl in the Ehrenberg drawing-room and the impression she had made on Demeter.

Anna smiled with pleasure.

Later on, when they were again walking arm-in-arm in a quieter street, George began again. " But I still don't know who your great passion was."

Anna was silent and looked straight in front of her.

"Come, Anna, you promised me, didn't you ? "

Without looking at him she replied : " If you only had an idea how strange the whole thing seems to me to-day."

"Why strange ? "

" Because the man you're trying to find out was quite an old man."

"Thirty-five," said George jestingly ; " isn't that so ? "

She shook her head seriously. "He was fifty-eight or sixty."

"And you ? " asked George slowly.

"It is two years ago last summer. I was then twenty-one."

George suddenly stood still. " I know now, it was your singing-master. Wasn't it ? "

Anna did not answer.

" So it was he, then ? " said George, without being really surprised, for he was aware that all the celebrated master's pupils fell in love with him in spite of his grey hairs.

" And did you love him most," asked George, " of all the men you had come across ? "

" Strange, isn't it ? but it's a fact all the same."

" Did he know it ? "

" I think so."

They had arrived at an open space with a small garden ... that was only scantily lighted. At the back there towered a church with a reddish glow. As though drawn to a quieter place they wandered on under dark softly-waving branches.

" And what actually was there between you, if it is not a rude question ? "

Anna was silent, and that moment George felt that everything was possible—even that Anna should have been that man's mistress. But underneath the disquiet which he felt at that thought the desire arose gently and unconsciously to hear his fear confirmed. For if Anna had already belonged to some one else before she became his, the adventure could proceed as lightly and irresponsibly as possible.

" I will tell you the whole story," said Anna at last. " It is really not so awful."

" Well ? " asked George, strangely excited.

" Once, after the lesson," Anna began hesitatingly, " he gallantly helped me into my jacket. And then suddenly he drew me to him, took me in his arms and kissed me."

" And you . . . ? "

" I . . . I was quite intoxicated."

" Intoxicated ? . . ."

" Yes, it was something indescribable. He kissed me on the forehead and the hair, and then he took my hand and murmured all sorts of things that I didn't hear properly. . . ."

" And . . ."

" And then . . . then voices came near, he let go my hand and it was all over."

" All over ? "

" Yes, over . . . of course it was all over."

" I certainly don't think it such a matter of course. You saw him again, no doubt."

" Of course, I still went on learning with him."

" And . . . ? "

" I tell you it was over . . . absolutely . . . as though it had never happened."

George was surprised that he should feel reassured. " And he never tried again ? " he asked.

"Never. It would have been so ridiculous, and as he was very clever he knew that quite well himself. It is quite true that up to then I had been very much in love with him, but after this episode he was nothing more to me than my old teacher. In some way he seemed even older than he really was. I don't know if you can really understand what I mean. It was as though he had spent all the remains of his youth in that moment."

"I quite understand," said George. He believed her and loved her more than before. They went into the church. It was almost dark within the large building. There were only some dim candles burning in front of a side altar, and opposite, behind the small statue of a saint, there shone a feeble light. A broad stream of incense flowed between the dome and the flagstones. The verger was walking, jangling his keys softly. Motionless figures appeared vaguely on the seats at the back. George slowly walked forward with Anna and felt like a young husband on his honeymoon going sight-seeing in a church with his young wife. He said so to Anna. She only nodded.

"But it would be very much nicer," whispered George, as they stood nestling close together in front of the chancel, "if we really were together somewhere abroad. . . ."

She looked at him esctatically and yet interrogatively: and he was frightened at his own words. Supposing Anna had taken it as a serious declaration or as a kind of wooing? Was he not obliged to enlighten her that he had not meant it in that way? . . . He remembered the conversation which they had had a short time ago, when they had gone out hanging on to one umbrella on a rainy windy day in the direction of Schönbrunn. He had suggested to her she should drive into the town with him and dine with him in a private room in some restaurant ; she had answered with that iciness in which her whole being was sometimes frozen : "I don't do that kind of thing." He had not pressed her further.

And yet a quarter of an hour later she had said to him, apropos no doubt of a conversation about George's mode of life, but yet with a smile of many possibilities: "You have no initiative, George." And he had suddenly felt at that moment as though depths in her soul were revealing themselves, undreamt-of and dangerous depths, which it would be a good thing to beware of. He could not help now thinking of this again. What was passing within her mind? . . . What did she want and what was she ready for? . . . And what did he desire, what did he feel himself?

Life was so incalculable. Was it not perfectly possible that he should go travelling about the world with her, live with her a period of happiness and finally part from her just as he had parted from many another? . . . Yet when he thought of the end that was inevitably bound to come, whether death brought it or life itself, he felt a gentle grief in his heart. . . . She still remained silent. Did she think again that he was lacking in initiative? . . . Or did she think perhaps "I am really going to succeed, I shall be his wife? . . . ."

He then felt her hand stroke his very gently, with a kind of new tenderness that did him great good.

"George," she said.

"What is it?" he asked.

"If I were religious," she replied, "I should like to pray for something now."

"What for?" said George, feeling almost nervous.

"For you to do something, George—something that really counted. For you to become a genuine artist, a great artist."

He could not help looking at the floor, as though for very shame that her thoughts had travelled on paths that were so much cleaner than his own.

A beggar held open the thick green curtain. George gave the man a coin; they were in the open air. The street lights shone up, the noise of vehicles and closing shutters suddenly grew near. George felt as if a fine veil which the twilight of the church had woven around him and her had now been torn, and in a tone of relief he suggested a little ride. Anna agreed with alacrity. They got into an open fiacre, had the top pulled down over them, drove through the streets, then drove round the Ring, without seeing much of the buildings and gardens, spoke not a word and nestled closer and closer to each other. They were both conscious of each other's impatience and their own, and they knew it was no longer possible to go back.

When they were near Anna's home George said : " What a pity that you have got to go home now."

She shrugged her shoulders and smiled strangely. The depths, thought George again, but without fear and almost gaily. Before the vehicle stopped at the corner they arranged an appointment for the following morning in the Schwarzenberggarten and then got out. Anna rushed home and George slowly strolled towards the town.

He considered whether he should go into the café. He did not really feel keen on it. Bermann would probably stay to supper at the Ehrenbergs' to-day, one could rarely count on Leo Golowski coming: and George was not much attracted by the other young people, most of them Jewish writers, with whom he had recently struck up a casual acquaintance, even though he had thought many of them not at all uninteresting. Speaking broadly, he found their tone to each other now too familiar, now too formal, now too facetious, now too sentimental : not one of them seemed really free and unembarrassed with the others, scarcely indeed with himself.

Heinrich too had declared only the other day that he didn't want to have anything more to do with the whole set, who had become thoroughly antagonistic to him since his successes. George regarded it as perfectly possible that Heinrich, with his characteristic vanity and hypo-

chondria, was scenting enmity and persecution where it
was perhaps merely a case of indifference or antipathy.
He for his part knew that it was not so much friendship
that attracted him to the young author, as the curiosity
to get to know a strange man more intimately. Perhaps
also the interest of looking into a world which up to the
present had been more or less foreign to him. For while
he himself had remained somewhat reserved and had
specially avoided any reference to his own relations with
women, Heinrich had not only told him of his distant
mistress, for whom he asserted he suffered pangs of
jealousy, but also of a blonde and pretty young person
with whom he had recently got into the habit of spending
his evenings—merely to deaden his feelings as he ironically added; he not only told him of his life as a student
and journalist in Vienna, which did not lie so far back,
but also of his childhood and boyhood in that little provincial town in Bohemia where he had come into the world
thirty years ago. The half-affectionate and half-disgusted
tone, with its mixture of attachment and detachment, in
which Heinrich spoke of his family and especially of his
suffering father, who had been an advocate in that little
town and a member of Parliament for a considerable
period, struck George as strange and at times as almost
painful. Why, he seemed to be even a little proud of the
fact that when he was only twenty years old he had
prophesied his blissfully confident parent's fate to the
old man himself, exactly as it had subsequently fulfilled
itself. After a short period of popularity and success the
growth of the Anti-Semitic movement had driven him out
of the German Liberal party, most of his friends had deserted and betrayed him, and a dissipated ' corps ' student,
who described at public meetings the Tsechs and Jews as
the most dangerous enemies of Germanism, propriety
and morality, while at home he thrashed his wife and had
children by his servants, was his successor in the con-

fidence of the electors and in Parliament. Heinrich, who
had always felt a certain amount of irritation at his
father's phrases, honest though they were, about Pan-
Germanism, liberty and progress, had at first gloated
over the spectacle of the old man's downfall. And it
was only when the lawyer who had once been so much
in demand began to lose his practice into the bargain,
and the financial position of the family got worse from
day to day, that the son began to experience a somewhat
belated sympathy. He had given up his legal studies
early enough, and had been compelled to come to the help
of his family with his daily journalistic work. His first
literary successes raised no echo in the melancholy household. There were sinister signs that madness was looming over his father, while now that the latter was falling
into mental darkness his mother, for whom state and
fatherland had ceased to exist, when her husband was
not elected to Parliament, lost her grip of life and of the
world. Heinrich's only sister, once a buxom clever girl,
had developed melancholia after an unhappy passion for
a kind of provincial Don Juan, and with morbid per-
verseness she put the blame for the family misfortune on
the shoulders of her brother, though she had always got
on with him perfectly well in her youth. Heinrich also
told George about other relations whom he remembered
in his early days, and a half-grotesque, half-pathetic series
of strict bigoted old-fashioned Jews and Jewesses swept
by George like shadows from another world. He eventually
realised that Heinrich did not feel himself any homesickness for that small town with its miserable petty
squabbles, or any call to return to the gloomy narrowness
of his almost ruined family, and saw that Heinrich's egoism
was at once his salvation and his deliverance.

It was striking nine from the tower of the Church of
St. Michael when George stood in front of the café. He saw
Rapp the critic sitting by a window not completely

covered by the curtain, with a pile of papers in front of him on the table. He had just taken his glasses off his nose and was polishing them, and the dull eyes brought a look of absolute deadness into a face that was usually so alive with clever malice. Opposite him with gestures that swept over vacancy sat Gleissner the poet in all the brilliancy of his false elegance, with a colossal black cravat in which a red stone scintillated. When George, without hearing their voices, saw the lips of these two men move, while their glances wandered to and fro, he could scarcely understand how they could stand sitting opposite each other for a quarter of an hour in that cloud of hate. It flashed across him at once that this was the atmosphere in which the life of the whole set played its comedy, and through which there darted many a redeeming flash of wit and self-analysis.

What had he in common with these people ? A kind of horror seized on him, he turned away and decided to look up his club once again instead of going into the café, the rooms of which he had not been in for months past. It was only a few steps away. George was soon walking up the broad marble staircase, went into the little dining-room with the light green curtain and was greeted as a long-lost friend by Ralph Skelton, the attaché of the English Embassy, and Doctor von Breitner. They talked about the tournament which was going to take place and about the banquet that was going to be organised in honour of the foreign fencing-masters ; they gossiped about the new operetta at the Wiedner Theatre where Fräulein Lovan as a bayadère had come on to the stage almost naked, and about the duel between the manufacturer Heidenfeld and Lieutenant Novotny, in which the injured husband had fallen. George had a game of billiards with Skelton after the meal and won. He felt in better spirits and resolved henceforth to pay more frequent visits to these airy prettily-furnished rooms frequented by pleasant well-bred young men with whom one could converse lightly and pleasantly.

Felician appeared, told his brother that it had been very amusing at the Ehrenbergs' and that Frau Marianne sent her regards. Breitner, with one of his celebrated huge cigars in his mouth, joined the brothers, and began to speak about the hanging of the portraits of some of those members of the club who had conferred services on it, mentioning particularly the one of young Labinski who had ended all by suicide in the previous year. And George could not help thinking of Grace, of that strange hot-and-cold conversation with her in the cemetery in the melting February snow and of that wonderful night on the moonlit deck of the steamer that had brought them both from Palermo to Naples. He scarcely knew which woman he longed for the most at this particular moment : for Marianne whom he had deserted, for Grace who had vanished, or for the fair young creature with whom he had walked about in a dusky church a few hours ago like a honeymoon couple in a foreign town, and who had wanted to pray to heaven for him to become a great artist. The memory stirred a gentler emotion. Was it not almost as though she set more store by his artistic future than by him himself ? . . . No. . . . Not more. She had only just spoken out what had lain slumbering all the time at the bottom of her soul. It was simply that he forgot as it were only too frequently that he was an artist. But all that must be changed. He had begun and pre-pared so much. Just a little industry and success was assured. And next year he would go out into the world. He would soon get a post as conductor and with a sudden leap he would find himself launched in a profession that brought both money and prestige. He would get to know new people, a different sky would shine above him and white unknown arms stretched towards him mys-teriously as though from distant clouds. And while the young people at his side were weighing very seriously the chances of the champions at the approaching tournament, George went on dreaming in his corner of a future full of work, fame and love.

At the same time Anna was lying in her dark room. She was not asleep and her wide-open eyes were turned towards the ceiling. She had for the first time in her life the infallible feeling that there was a man in the world who could do anything he liked with her. Her mind was firmly made up to take all the happiness or all the sorrow that might lie in front of her, and she had a gentle hope, more beautiful than all her dreams of the past, of a serene and abiding happiness.

III

GEORGE and Heinrich dismounted from their
cycles. The last villas lay behind them and the
broad road with its gradual upward incline led
into the forest. The foliage still hung fairly thickly on the
trees, but every slight puff of wind brought away some leaves
which slowly fluttered down. The shimmer of autumn floated
over the yellow-reddish hills. The road ascended higher past
an imposing restaurant garden approached by a flight of
stone steps. Only a few people sat in the open air, most
of them were in the glass verandah, as though they did
not quite trust themselves to the faltering warmth of this
late October day, through which a dangerous and chilly
draught kept on penetrating.

George thought of the melancholy memory of the winter
evening on which he and Frau Marianne had paid a visit
here, and had had the place to themselves. He had been
bored as he had sat by her side and listened impatiently
to her prattle about yesterday's concert in which Fräulein
Bellini had sung songs ; and when he had been obliged to
get out of the carriage in a suburban street on his way
back on account of Marianne's nervousness, he had taken
a deep breath of deliverance. A similar feeling of release,
of course, almost invariably came over him whenever he
left a mistress, even after some more or less beautiful
hours. Even when he had left Anna on her doorstep a
few days ago, after the first evening of complete happiness,
the first emotion of which he was conscious was the joy
of being alone again. And immediately in its train, even

7

before the feeling of gratitude and the dim realisation of
a genuine affinity with this gentle creature who enveloped
his whole being with such intimate tenderness had
managed to penetrate his soul, there fluttered through it
a wistful dream of voyages over a shimmering sea, of
coasts which approached seductively, of walks along
shores which would vanish again on the next day, of blue
distances, freedom from responsibility and solitude.

The next morning, when the atmosphere of the previous
evening, pregnant as it was with memory and with presage, enveloped him as he woke up, the journey was of
course put off to a later but not so distant though of
course more convenient time. For George knew at this
very hour, though without any touch of horror, that this
adventure was predestined to have an end however sincerely
and picturesquely it had begun. Anna had given herself to him without indicating by a word, a look or gesture
that so far as she was concerned, what was practically a
new chapter in her life was now beginning. And in the
same way George felt quite convinced that the farewell to
her, too, would be devoid of melancholy or of difficulty ;
a pressure of the hand, a smile and a quiet " it was very
beautiful " ; and he felt still easier in his mind when she
came to him at their next meeting with a simple intimate
greeting, quite free from that uneasy tone of nestling
sorrow or accomplished fate which he had heard thrilling
in the voice of many another woman, who had woken up to
such a morning, though not for the first time in her life.

A faintly-defined line of mountains appeared in the
distance and then vanished again as the road mounted
through thick-wooded country up to the heights. Pine-
wood and leaf-bearing wood grew peacefully next to each
other, and the foliage of beeches and birch-trees shimmered
with its autumn tints through the quieter tints of the
firs. Ramblers could be seen, some with knapsack,
alpine-stock and nailed shoes, as though equipped for

serious mountaineering ; now and again cyclists would come whizzing down the road in a feverish rush. Heinrich told his companion of a cycle-tour which he had made along the Rhine at the beginning of September.

"Isn't it strange," said George, "I have knocked about the world a fair bit, but I do not yet know the district where my ancestors' home was."

"Really?" queried Heinrich, "and you feel no emotion when you hear the word Rhine spoken?"

George smiled. "After all it is nearly a hundred years since my great-grandparents left Biebrich."

"Why do you smile, George? It's a much longer time since my ancestors wandered out of Palestine, and yet many otherwise quite rational people insist on my heart throbbing with homesickness for that country."

George shook his head irritably. "Why do you always keep bothering about those people? It will really soon become a positive obsession with you."

"Oh, you think I mean the Anti-Semites? Not a bit of it. I am not touchy any more about them, not usually, at any rate. But you just go and ask our friend Leo what his views are on this question."

"Oh, you mean him, do you? Well, he doesn't take it so literally but more or less symbolically . . . or from the political standpoint," he added uncertainly.

Heinrich nodded. "Both these ideas are very intimately connected in brains of that character." He sank into meditation for a while, thrust his cycle forward with slight impatient spurts and was soon a few paces in front again. He then began to talk again about his September tour. He thought of it again with what was almost emotion. Solitude, change of scene, movement : had he not enjoyed a threefold happiness? "I can scarcely describe to you," he said, "the feeling of inner freedom which thrilled through me. Do you know those moods in which all one's memories near or distant lose, as it were, their oppressive reality? all the people who have meant anything in one's life, whether it be grief, care or tenderness, seem to sweep by more like shadows, or, to put it more precisely, like forms which one has imagined oneself ? And the creations of one's own imagination also come on the scene, of course, and are certainly quite as vivid as the people whom one remembers as having been real ; and then one gets the most extraordinary complications between the figures of reality and of one's imagination. I could describe to you a conversation which took place between my great-uncle who is a rabbi and the Duke Heliodorus, the character you know who is the centre of my opera plot—a conversation which was amusing and profound to a degree which, speaking generally, neither life nor any opera libretto scarcely ever reaches. . . . Yes, such journeys are really wonderful, and so one goes on through towns which one has never seen before, and perhaps will never see again, past absolutely unknown faces which speedily vanish again for all eternity. . . . Then one whizzes again into the street between the rivers and the vineyards. Such moods really cleanse the soul. A pity that they are so rarely vouchsafed to one."

George always felt a certain embarrassment whenever Heinrich became tragic. " Perhaps we might go on a bit," he said, and they jumped on to their machines.

A narrow bumpy byroad between the forest and fields soon led them to a bare unimpressive two-storied house, which they recognised to be an inn by its brown surly signboard. On the green, which was separated from the house by the street, stood a large number of tables, many covered with cloths which had once been white, others with cloths which were embroidered. Ten or twelve young men who were members of a cycling club sat at some pushed-back tables. Several of them had taken off their coats, others with an affectation of smartness wore them with their sleeves hanging down. Designs in magnificent red and green knitting blazed on the sky-blue sweaters with their yellow edges.

A chorus rang out to the sky with more power than purity: "Der Gott der Eisen wachsen liess, der wollte keine Knechte."

Heinrich surveyed the company with a quick glance, half shut his eyes and said to George with clenched teeth and vehement emphasis: "I don't know if these youths are staunch, true and courageous, which they certainly think they are ; but there is no doubt that they smell of wool and perspiration, and so I am all for our sitting down at a reasonable distance from them."

What *does* he want ? thought George. Would he find it more congenial if a party of Polish Jews were to sit here and sing psalms ?

Both pushed their machines to a distant table and sat down. A waiter appeared in black evening dress sprinkled with the relics of grease and vegetables, cleared the table energetically with a dirty napkin, took their orders and went off.

"Isn't it lamentable," said Heinrich, "that in the immediate outskirts of Vienna nearly all the inns should be in such a state of neglect ? It makes one positively depressed."

George thought that this exaggerated regret was out of place. "Oh well, in the country," he said, " you have got to take things as you find them. It is almost part of the whole thing."

Heinrich would not admit the soundness of this point of view. He began to develop a plan for the erection of seven hotels on the borders of the Wienerwald, and was calculating that one would need at the outside three or four millions, when Leo Golowski suddenly appeared. He was in *mufti*, which, as was frequently the case with him, was not without a certain element of bizarreness. He wore to-day, in addition to a light-grey lounge suit, a blue velvet waistcoat and a yellow silk cravat with a smooth steel tie-ring. Both the others greeted him with delight and expressed their astonishment.

Leo sat down by them. " I heard you fixing up your excursion yesterday evening, and when we were discharged from the barracks at nine o'clock to-day, I at once thought how nice it would be to have a chat for an hour or so in the open air with a couple of keen and congenial men. So I went home, threw myself into mufti and started off." He spoke in his usual tone, which always fascinated George with its charm and semi-naïveté, though when he thought of it afterwards it always seemed to possess a certain touch of irony, of insincerity in fact. He had a knack of conducting serious conversations with a cut-and-dried definiteness that really impressed George. He had recently had an opportunity of listening to discussions in the café between Leo and Heinrich on questions dealing with the theory of art, especially the relation between the laws of music and mathematics. Leo thought he was on the track of the fundamental cause of major and minor keys affecting the human soul in such different ways. George took pleasure in following the chain of his acute and lucid analysis, even though he was instinctively on his guard against the audacious attempt to ascribe all the magic and mystery of sound to the rule of laws, which were as inexorable as those in accordance with which the earth and the planets revolved, and must necessarily spring from the same origin as those eternal principles. It was only when Heinrich tried to carry Leo's theories still further, and to apply them for instance to the products of literary style, that George became impatient and immediately felt himself tacit ally of Leo who invariably smiled gently at Heinrich's tangled and fantastic expositions.

The meal was served and the young men ate with appetite ; Heinrich not less than the others, in spite of the fact that he expressed his opinion of the inferiority of the cooking in the most disparaging terms, and was inclined to regard the conduct of the proprietor, not merely as a sign of his personally low mind, but as characteristic of the decay of Austria in many other spheres. The conversation turned on the military position of the country, and Leo gave a satirical description of his comrades and superiors, with which both the others were very much amused. Much merriment, especially, was occasioned by a first-lieutenant who had introduced himself to the volunteer contingent with the ominous words: " I shan't give you anything to laugh about, I am a fiend in human form."

While they were still eating a gentleman came up to the table, clicked his heels together, put his hand to his cycle cap by way of salutation, addressed them with a facetious " All hail," added a friendly " Hallo " for the benefit of Leo, and introduced himself to Heinrich. " My name is Josef Rosner." He then cheerily began the conversation with these words: " I suppose you gentlemen are also on a cycling expedition. . . ." As no one answered him he continued: " One must make the best of the last fine days, the splendid weather won't last much longer."

" Won't you sit down, Herr Rosner ? " asked George politely.

" Much obliged but . . ." He pointed to his party . . . " We have only just started out, we have still got a lot in front of us; going to ride down to Tull and then via Stockerau to Vienna. Excuse me, gentlemen." He took a wooden vesta from the table and lighted his cigarette with dignity.

" What kind of a club are you in then, old chap ? " asked Leo, and George was surprised at the " old chap," till it occurred to him that they had both known each other from boyhood.

" This is the Sechshauser Cycle Club," replied Josef. In spite of the fact that no astonishment was expressed, he added: " Of course you are surprised, gentlemen, at a real Viennese like myself belonging to this suburban club, but it is only because a great friend of mine is the captain there. You see that fat chap there, just slipping into his coat. That is Jalaudek, the son of the town councillor and member of Parliament."

"Jalaudek . . ." repeated Heinrich with obvious loathing in his voice, and said nothing more.

"Oh yes," said Leo, "that's the man, you know, who in a recent debate about the popular education board gave this magnificent definition of science. Didn't you read it ? " He turned to the others.

They did not remember.

"'Science,'" quoted Leo, "'Science is what one Jew copies from another.'"

All laughed. Even Josef, who, however, immediately started explaining : "He is really not that sort at all—I know him quite well—only he is so crude in political life . . . simply because the opposing parties scratch each other's eyes out in our beloved Austria. But in ordinary life he is a very affable gentleman. The boy is much more Radical."

"Is your club Christian Socialist or National German ? " asked Leo courteously.

"Oh, we don't make any distinction. Only of course as things are going nowadays . . ." He stopped with sudden embarrassment.

"Come, come," said Leo encouragingly. " It is perfectly obvious that your club is not tainted by a single Jew. Why, one notices that a mile off."

Josef thought it was best form to laugh. He then said : " Excuse me, no politics in the mountains ! Anyway, as we are on this topic you are labouring under a delusion, gentlemen. For instance, we have a man in the club who is engaged to a Jewish girl. But they are beckoning to me already. Goodbye, gentlemen ; so long, Leo ; goodbye, all." He saluted again and swaggered off.

The others, smiling in spite of themselves, followed him

with their eyes. Then Leo suddenly turned to George
and asked: " And how is his sister getting on with her
singing ? "

" What ? " said George, startled and blushing slightly.

" Therese has been telling me," went on Leo quietly,
" that you and Anna do music together sometimes. Is her
voice all right now ? "

" Yes," replied George, hesitating, " I believe so ; at any
rate I think it is very pleasant, very melodious, especially
in the deeper registers. It is a pity in my view that it is
not big enough for larger rooms."

" Not big enough ? " repeated Leo meditatively.

" How would you describe it ? "

Leo shrugged his shoulders and looked quietly at George.
" It is like this," he said. " I personally like the voice
very much, but even when Anna had the idea of going on
the stage . . . to speak quite frankly, I never thought anything would come of it."

" You probably knew," replied George with deliberate
casualness, " that Fräulein Anna suffers from a peculiar
weakness of the vocal chords."

" Yes, of course I knew that, but if she were cut out
for an artistic career, really had it in her, I mean, she
would certainly have overcome that weakness."

" You think so ? "

" Yes, I do. That is my decided opinion. That's why
I think that expressions like ' peculiar weakness ' or ' her
voice is not big enough ' are more or less euphemisms
for something more fundamental, more psychological.
It's quite clear that her fate line says nothing about her
being an artist, that's a fact. She was, so to speak, predestined from the beginning to end her days in respectable
domesticity."

Heinrich enthusiastically caught up the theory of the
fate line, and led their thoughts in his own erratic way
from the sphere of cleverness to the sphere of sophistry,

and from the sphere of sophistry to the sphere of the nonsensical.

He then suggested that they should bask for half an hour in the meadow in the sun. " It will probably not shine so warm again during this year."

The others agreed.

A hundred yards from the inn George and Leo stretched themselves out on their cloaks. Heinrich sat down on the grass, crossed his arms over his knees, and looked in front of him. At his feet the sward sloped down to the forest. Still deeper down rested the villas of Neuwaldegg, buried in loose foliage. The spire-crosses and dazzling windows of the town shone out from the bluish-grey clouds, and far away, as though lifted up by a moving haze, the plain swept away to a gradual darkness.

Pedestrians were walking over the fields towards the inn. Some gave them a greeting as they passed, and one of them, a slim young man who led a child by the hand, remarked to Heinrich : " This is a really fine day, just like May."

Heinrich felt at first his heart go out as it were involuntarily, as it often did towards casual and unexpected friendliness of this description. But he immediately pulled himself together, for of course he realised that the young man was only intoxicated, as it were, with the mildness of the day and the peace of the landscape ; that at the bottom of his soul he too felt hostile to him, just like all the others who had strolled past him so harmlessly, and he himself found difficulty in understanding why the view of these gently sloping hills and the town merging into twilight should affect him with so sweet a melancholy, in view of the fact that the men who lived there meant so little good by him, and meant him even that little but rarely. The cycling club whizzed along the street which was quite close to them. The jauntily-worn coats fluttered, the badges gleamed and crude laughter rang out over the fields.

" Awful people," said Leo casually without changing his place.

Heinrich motioned down below with a vague movement of his head. " And fellows like that," he said with set teeth, " imagine that they are more at home here than we are."

" Oh, well," answered Leo quietly, " they aren't so far out in that, those fellows there."

Heinrich turned scornfully towards him : " Excuse me, Leo, I forgot for a moment that you yourself wish to count as only here on sufferance."

" I don't wish that for a minute," replied Leo with a smile, " and you need not misunderstand me so perversely. One really can't bear a grudge against these people if they regard themselves as the natives and you and me as the foreigners. After all, it is only the expression of their healthy instinct for an anthropological fact which is confirmed by history. Neither Jewish nor Christian sentimentalism can do anything against that and all the consequences which follow from it." And turning to George he asked him in a tone which was only too courteous : " Don't you think so too ? "

George reddened and cleared his throat, but had no opportunity of answering, for Heinrich, on whose forehead two deep furrows now appeared, immediately began to speak with considerable bitterness.

" My own instinct is at any rate quite as much a rule of conduct for me as the instinct of Herren Jalaudek Junior and Senior, and that instinct tells me infallibly that my home is here, just here, and not in some land which I don't know, the description of which doesn't appeal to me the least bit and which certain people now want to persuade me is my fatherland on the strength of the argument that that was the place from which my ancestors some thousand years ago were scattered into the world. One might further observe on that point that the

ancestors of the Herren Jalaudek and even of our friend
Baron von Wergenthin were quite as little at home here
as mine and yours."

" You mustn't be angry with me," retorted Leo, " but
your standpoint in these matters is really somewhat
limited.   You are always thinking about yourself and
the really quite irrelevant circumstance . . . excuse
my saying irrelevant circumstance, that you are an
author who happens to write in the German language
because he was born in a German country, and happens
to write about Austrian people and Austrian conditions
because he lives in Austria.   But the primary question
is not about you, or about me either, or even about the few
Jewish officials who do not get promoted, the few Jewish
volunteers who do not get made officers, the Jewish lecturers
who either get their Professorship too late or not at all—
those are sheer secondary inconveniences so to speak ;
we have to deal, in considering this question, with quite
another class of men whom you know either imperfectly
or not at all.   We have to deal with destinies to which,
I assure you, my dear Heinrich, that in spite of your
real duty to do so, I am sure you have not yet given
sufficient thorough thought.   I am sure you haven't. . . .
Otherwise you wouldn't be able to discuss all these matters
in the superficial and the . . . egoistic way you are now
doing."

He then told them of his experiences at the Bâle Zionist
Congress in which he had taken part in the previous year,
and where he had obtained a deeper insight into the
character and psychological condition of the Jewish people
than he had ever done before.   With these people, whom
he saw at close quarters for the first time, the yearning for
Palestine, he knew it for a fact, was no artificial pose.   A
genuine feeling was at work within them, a feeling that
had never become extinguished and was now flaming up
afresh under the stress of necessity.   No one could doubt

that who had seen, as he had, the holy scorn shine out in their looks when a speaker exclaimed that they must give up the hope of Palestine for the time being and content themselves with settlements in Africa and the Argentine. Why, he had seen old men, not uneducated men either, no, learned and wise old men, weeping because they must needs fear that that land of their fathers, which they themselves would never be able to tread, even in the event of the realisation of the boldest Zionist plans, would perhaps never be open to their children and their children's children.

George listened with surprise, and was even somewhat moved.

But Heinrich, who had been walking up and down the field during Leo's narrative, exclaimed that he regarded Zionism as the worst affliction that had ever burst upon the Jews, and that Leo's own words had convinced him of it more profoundly than any previous argument or experience.

National feeling and religion, those had always been the words which had embittered him with their wanton, yes malignant, ambiguity. Fatherland. . . . Why, that was nothing more than a fiction, a political idea floating in the air, changeable, intangible. It was only the home, not the fatherland which had any real significance . . . and so the feeling of home was synonymous with the right to a home. And so far as religions were concerned, he liked Christian and Jewish mythology quite as much as Greek and Indian ; but as soon as they began to force their dogmas upon him, he found them all equally intolerable and repulsive. And he felt himself akin with no one, no, not with any one in the whole world : with the weeping Jews in Bâle as little as with the bawling Pan-Germans in the Austrian Parliament ; with Jewish usurers as little as with noble robber-knights ; with a Zionist bar-keeper as little as with a Christian Socialist grocer. And least of all would the consciousness of a persecution which they had all suffered, and of a hatred whose burden fell upon them

all, make him feel linked to men from whom he felt himself
so far distant in temperament. He did not mind recognising Zionism as a moral principle and a social movement,
if it could honestly be regarded in that light, but the idea
of the foundation of a Jewish state on a religious and
national basis struck him as a nonsensical defiance of the
whole spirit of historical evolution. " And you too, at
the bottom of your heart," he explained, standing still in
front of Leo, " you don't think either that this goal will
ever prove attainable; why, you don't even wish it, although
you fancy yourself in your element trying to get there.
What is your home-country, Palestine ? A geographical
idea. What does the faith of your father mean to you ?
A collection of customs which you have now ceased to
observe and some of which seem as ridiculous and in as
bad taste to you, as they do to me."

They went on talking for a long time, now vehemently
and almost offensively, then calmly, and in the honest
endeavour to convince each other. Frequently they were
surprised to find themselves holding the same opinion,
only again to lose touch with each other the next moment
in a new contradiction. George, stretched on his cloak,
listened to them. His mind soon took the side of Leo,
whose words seemed to thrill with an ardent pity for the
unfortunate members of his race, and who would turn
proudly away from people who would not treat him as
their equal. Soon he felt nearer again in spirit to Heinrich,
who treated with anger and scorn the attempt, as wild as
it was short-sighted, to collect from all the corners of the
world the members of a race whose best men had always
merged in the culture of the land of their adoption, or
had at any rate contributed to it, and to send them all
together to a foreign land, a land to which no homesickness called them. And George gradually appreciated how
difficult those same picked men about whom Heinrich
had been speaking, the men who were hatching in their

souls the future of humanity, would find it to come
to a decision. How dazed must be their consciousness
of their existence, their value and their rights, tossed to
and fro as they were between defiance and exhaustion,
between the fear of appearing importunate and their
bitter resentment at the demand that they must needs
yield to an insolent majority, between the inner consciousness of being at home in the country where they lived and
worked, and their indignation at finding themselves per-
secuted and insulted in that very place. He saw for the
first time the designation Jew, which he himself had often
used flippantly, jestingly and contemptuously, in a quite
new and at the same time melancholy light. There dawned
within him some idea of this people's mysterious destiny,
which always expressed itself in every one who sprang from
the race, not less in those who tried to escape from that
origin of theirs, as though it were a disgrace, a pain or a
fairy tale that did not concern them at all, than in those
who obstinately pointed back to it as though to a piece of
destiny, an honour or an historical fact based on an im-
movable foundation.

And as he lost himself in the contemplation of the two
speakers, and looked at their figures, which stood out in
relief against the reddish-violet sky in sharply-drawn,
violently-moving lines, it occurred to him, and not for the
first time, that Heinrich who insisted on being at home
here, resembled both in figure and gesture some fanatical
Jewish preacher, while Leo, who wanted to go back to
Palestine with his people, reminded him in feature and in
bearing of the statue of a Greek youth which he had once
seen in the Vatican or the Naples museum. And he understood again quite well, as his eye followed with pleasure
Leo's lively aristocratic gestures, how Anna could have
experienced a mad fancy for her friend's brother years
ago in that summer by the seaside.

Heinrich and Leo were still standing opposite each other

on the grass, while their conversation became lost in a maze
of words. Their sentences rushed violently against each
other, wrestled convulsively, shot past each other and
vanished into nothingness, and George noticed at some
moment or other that he was only listening to the sound
of the speeches, without being able to follow their
meaning.

A cool breeze came up from the plain, and George got up
from the sward with a slight shiver. The others, who had
almost forgotten his presence, were thus called back again
to actualities, and they decided to leave. Full daylight
still shone over the landscape, but the sun was couched
faint and dark on the long strip of an evening cloud.

" Conversations like this," said Heinrich, as he strapped
his cloak on to his cycle, " always leave me with a sense of
dissatisfaction, which even goes as far as a painful feeling
in the neighbourhood of the stomach. Yes really. They
just lead absolutely nowhere. And after all, what do
political views matter to men who don't make politics
their career or their business ? Do they exert the slightest
influence on the policy and moulding of existence ? You,
Leo, are just like myself ; neither of us will ever do anything
else, can ever do anything else, than just accomplish that
which, in view of our character and our capacities, we are
able to accomplish. You will never migrate to Palestine
all your life long, even if Jewish states were founded and
you were offered a position as prime-minister, or at any
rate official pianist——"

" Oh, you can't know that," interrupted Leo.

" I know it for a certainty," said Heinrich. " That's
why I'll admit, into the bargain, that in spite of my complete
indifference to every single form of religion I would positively
never allow myself to be baptised, even if it were possible—
though that is less the case to-day than ever it was—of
escaping once and for all Anti-Semitic bigotry and villainy
by a dodge like that."

" Hum," said Leo, " but supposing the mediæval stake were to be lighted again."

" In that case," retorted Heinrich, " I hereby solemnly bind myself to take your advice implicitly."

" Oh," objected George, " those times will certainly not come again."

Both the others were unable to help laughing at George being kind enough to reassure them in that way about their future, in the name, as Heinrich observed, of the whole of Christendom.

In the meanwhile they had crossed the field.

George and Heinrich pushed their cycles forward up the bumpy bye-road, while Leo at their side walked on the turf with his cloak fluttering in the wind. They were all silent for quite a time, as though exhausted. At the place where the bad path turned off towards the broad high road, Leo remained stationary and said: " We will have to leave each other here, I am afraid." He shook hands with George and smiled. " You must have been pretty well bored to-day," he said.

George blushed. " I say now, you must take me for a . . ."

Leo held George's hand in a firm grip. " I take you for a very shrewd man and also for a very good sort. Do you believe me ? "

George was silent.

" I should like to know," continued Leo, " whether you believe me, George. I am keen on knowing." His voice assumed a tone of genuine sincerity.

" Why, of course I believe you," replied George, still, however, with a certain amount of impatience.

" I am glad," said Leo, " for I really feel a sympathy between us, George." He looked straight into his eyes, then shook hands once more with him and Heinrich and turned to go.

But George suddenly had the feeling that this young man who with his fluttering cloak and his head slightly

8

bent forward was striding down-hill in the middle of the
broad street was not walking to any " home," but to some
foreign sphere somewhere, where no one could follow him.
He found this feeling all the more incomprehensible since
he had not only spent many hours recently with Leo in
conversation at the café, but had also received all possible
information from Anna about him, his family and his
position in life. He knew that that summer at the seaside,
which now lay six years back, as did Anna's youthful
infatuation, had marked the last summer which the Golowski
family had enjoyed free from trouble, and that the business
of the old man had been completely ruined in the subsequent winter. It had been extraordinary, according to
Anna's account, how all the members of the family had
adapted themselves to the altered conditions, as though
they had been long prepared for this revolution. The
family removed from their comfortable house in the
Rathaus quarter to a dismal street in the neighbourhood
of the Augarten. Herr Golowski undertook all kinds of
commission business while Frau Golowski did needlework
for sale.

Therese gave lessons in French and English and at
first continued to attend the dramatic school. It was a
young violin player belonging to an impoverished noble
Russian family who awakened her interest in political
questions. She soon abandoned her art, for which, as a
matter of fact, she had always shown more inclination
than real talent, and in a short time she was in the full
swing of the Social Democratic movement as a speaker
and agitator. Leo, without agreeing with her views,
enjoyed her fresh and audacious character. He often
attended meetings with her, but as he was not keen on
being impressed by magniloquence, whether it took the
form of promises which were never fulfilled or of threats
which disappeared into thin air, he found it good fun
to point out to her, on the way home, with an irresistible

acuteness, the inconsistencies in her own speeches and those of the members of her party. But he always made a particular point of trying to convince her that she would never have been able to forget so completely her great mission for days and weeks on end, if her pity for the poor and the suffering were really as deep an emotion as she imagined.

Leo's own life, moreover, had no definite object. He attended technical science lectures, gave piano lessons, sometimes went so far as to plan out a musical career, and practised five or six hours a day for weeks on end. But it was still impossible to forecast what he would finally decide on. Inasmuch it was his way to wait almost unconsciously for a miracle to save him from anything disagreeable, he had put off his year of service till he was face to face with the final time-limit, and now in his twenty-fifth year he was serving for the first time.

Their parents allowed Leo and Therese to go their own way, and in spite of their manifold differences of opinion there seemed to be no serious discord in the Golowski family. The mother usually sat at home, sewed, knitted and crocheted, while the father went about his business with increasing apathy, and liked best of all to watch the chess-players in the café, a pleasure which enabled him to forget the ruin of his life. Since the collapse of his business he seemed unable to shake off a certain feeling of embarrassment towards his children, so that he was almost proud when Therese would give him now and again an article which she had written to read, or when Leo was good enough to play a game on Sundays with him on the board he loved so well.

It always seemed to George as though his own sympathy for Leo were fundamentally connected with Anna's long-past fancy for him. He felt, and not for the first time, curiously attracted to a man to whom a soul which now belonged to him, had flown in years gone by.

George and Heinrich had mounted their cycles, and were riding along a narrow road through the thick forest that loomed darker and darker. A little later, as the forest retreated behind them again on both sides, they had the setting sun at their back, while the long shadows of their bodies kept running along in front of their cycles. The slope of the road became more and more pronounced and soon led them between low houses which were overhung with reddish foliage. A very old man sat in a seat in front of the door, a pale child looked out of an open window. Otherwise not a single human being was to be seen.

" Like an enchanted village," said George.

Heinrich nodded. He knew the place. He had been here with his love on a wonderful summer day this year. He thought of it and burning longing throbbed through his heart. And he remembered the last hours that he had spent with her in Vienna in his cool room with the drawn-down blinds, through whose interstices the hot August morning had glittered in : he remembered their last walk through the Sunday quiet of the cool stone streets and through the old empty courtyards—and the complete absence of any idea that all this was for the last time. For it was only the next day that the letter had come, the ghastly letter in which she had written that she had wished to spare him the pain of farewell, and that when he read these words, she would already be quite a long way over the frontier on her journey to the new foreign town.

The road became more animated. Charming villas appeared encircled with cosy little gardens, wooded hills sloped gently upwards behind the houses. They saw once again the expanse of the valley as the waning day rested over meadows and fields. The lamps had been lit in a great empty restaurant garden. A hasty darkness seemed to be stealing down from every quarter simul-

taneously. They were now at the cross-roads. George
and Heinrich got off and lit cigarettes.

" Right or left ? " asked Heinrich.

George looked at his watch. "Six, . . . and I've got
to be in town by eight."

" So I suppose we can't dine together ? " said Heinrich.

" I am afraid not."

"It's a pity. Well, we'll take the short cut then
through Sievering."

They lit their lamps and pushed their cycles through
the forest in a long serpentine. One tree after another in
succession sprang out of the darkness into the radiance
of the globes of light and retreated again into the night.
The wind soughed through the foliage with increased
force and the leaves rustled underneath. Heinrich felt
a quite gentle fear, such as frequently came over him
when it was dark in the open country. He felt, as it
were, disillusioned at the thought of having to spend the
evening alone. He was in a bad temper with George,
and was irritated into the bargain at the latter's reserve
towards himself. He resolved also, and not for the
first time, not to discuss his own personal affairs with
George any more. It was better so. He did not need
to confide in anybody or obtain anybody's sympathy.
He had always felt at his best when he had gone his
own way alone. He had found that out often enough.
Why then reveal his soul to another ? He needed acquaintances to go walks and excursions with, and to discuss
all the manifold problems of life and art in cold shrewd
fashion—he needed women for a fleeting embrace ; but
he needed no friend and no mistress. In that way his
life would pass with greater dignity and serenity. He
revelled in these resolutions, and felt a growing consciousness of toughness and superiority. The darkness of the
forest lost its terror, and he walked through the gently
rustling night as though through a kindred element.

The height was soon reached. The dark sky lay starless over the grey road and the haze-breathing fields that stretched on both sides towards the deceptive distance of the wooded hills. A light was shining from a toll-house quite near them. They mounted their cycles again and rode back as quickly as the darkness permitted. George wished to be soon at the journey's end. It struck him as strangely unreal that he was to see again in an hour and a half that quiet room which no one else knew of besides Anna and himself; that dark room with the oil-prints on the wall, the blue velvet sofa, the cottage piano, on which stood the photographs of unknown people and a bust of Schiller in white plaster; with its high narrow windows, opposite which the old dark grey church towered aloft.

Lamps were burning all the way along. The roads again became more open and they were given a last view of the heights. Then they went at top speed, first between well-kept villas, finally through a populous noisy main road until they got deeper into the town. They got off at the Votive Church.

" Good-bye," said George, " and I hope to see you again in the café to-morrow."

" I don't know . . ." replied Heinrich, and as George looked at him questioningly he added: " It is possible that I shall go away."

" I say, that is a sudden decision."

" Yes, one gets caught sometimes by . . ."

" Lovesickness," filled in George with a smile.

" Or fear," said Heinrich with a short laugh.

" You certainly have no cause for that," said George.

" Do you know for certain ? " asked Heinrich.

" You told us so yourself."

" What ! "

" That you have news every day."

" Yes, that is quite true, every day. I get tender ardent

letters. Every day by the same post. But what does that prove? Why, I write letters which are yet more ardent and even more tender and yet . . ."

" Yes," said George, who understood him. And he hazarded the question : " Why don't you stay with her ? "

Heinrich shrugged his shoulders. " Tell me yourself, George, wouldn't it strike you as slightly humorous for a man to burn his boats on account of a love affair like that and trot about the world with a little actress . . ."

" Personally, I should regret it very much . . . but humorous . . . where does the humour come in ? ''

" No, I have no desire to do it," said Heinrich in a hard voice.

" But if you . . . but if you were to take it very seriously . . . if you asked her point blank . . . mightn't the young lady perhaps give up her career ? "

" Possibly, but I am not going to ask her, I don't want to ask her. No, better pain than responsibility."

" Would it be such a great responsibility ? " asked George. " What I mean is . . . is the girl's talent so pronounced, is she really so keen on her art, that it would be really a sacrifice for her to give the thing up."

" Has she got talent ? " said Heinrich. " Why, I don't know myself. Why, I even think she is the one creature in the world about whose talent I would not trust myself to give an opinion. Every time I have seen her on the stage her voice has rung in my ears like the voice of an unknown person, and as though, too, it came from a greater distance than all the other voices. It is really quite remarkable. . . . But you are bound to have seen her act, George. What's your impression ? Tell me quite frankly."

" Well, quite frankly . . . I don't remember her properly. You'll excuse me, I didn't know then, you see. . . . When you talk of her I always see in my mind's eye a head of reddish-blonde hair that falls a little over the forehead—and very big black roving eyes with a small pale face."

" Yes, roving eyes," repeated Heinrich, bit his lips and was silent for a while. " Good-bye," he said suddenly.

" You'll be sure to write to me ? " asked George.

" Yes, of course. Any way I am bound to be coming back again," he added, and smiled stiffly.

"*Bon voyage*," said George, and shook hands with him with unusual affection. This did Heinrich good. This warm pressure of the hand not only made him suddenly certain that George did not think him ridiculous, but also, strangely enough, that his distant mistress was faithful to him and that he himself was a man who could take more liberties with life than many others.

George looked after him as he hurried off on his cycle. He felt again as he had felt a few hours before, on Leo's departure, that some one was vanishing into an unknown land ; and he realised at this moment that in spite of all the sympathy he felt for both of them he would never attain with either that unrestrained sense of intimacy which had united him last year with Guido Schönstein and previously with poor Labinski.

He reflected whether perhaps the fundamental reason for this was not perhaps the difference of race between him and them, and he asked himself whether leaving out of account the conversation between the two of them, he would of his own initiative have realised so clearly this feeling of aloofness. He doubted it. Did he not as a matter of fact feel himself nearer, yes even more akin, to these two and to many others of their race than to many men who came from the same stock as his own ? Why, did he not feel quite distinctly that deep down somewhere there were many stronger threads of sympathy running between him and those two men, than between him and Guido or perhaps even his own brother ? But if that was so, would he not have been bound to have taken some opportunity

this afternoon to have said as much to those two men ?
to have appealed to them ? " Just trust me, don't shut me
out. Just try to treat me as a friend. . . ." And as he
asked himself why he had not done it, and why he had
scarcely taken any part in their conversation, he realised
with astonishment that during the whole time he had not
been able to shake off a kind of guilty consciousness of
having not been free during his whole life from a certain
hostility towards the foreigners, as Leo called them himself,
a kind of wanton hostility which was certainly not justified
by his own personal experience, and had thus contributed
his own share to that distrust and defiance with which so
many persons, whom he himself might have been glad to
take an opportunity to approach, had shut themselves off
from him. This thought roused an increasing *malaise*
within him which he could not properly analyse, and which
was simply the dull realisation that clean relations could
not flourish even between clean men in an atmosphere of
folly, injustice and disingenuousness.

He rode homewards faster and faster, as though that
would make him escape this feeling of depression. Arrived
home, he changed quickly, so as not to keep Anna waiting
too long. He longed for her as he had never done before.
He felt as though he had come home from a far journey
to the one being who wholly belonged to him.

IV

GEORGE stood by the window. The stone backs of the bearded giants who bore on their powerful arms the battered armorial bearings of a long-past race were arched just beneath him. Straight opposite, out of the darkness of ancient houses the steps crept up to the door of the old grey church which loomed amid the falling flakes of snow as though behind a moving curtain. The light of a street lamp on the square shone palely through the waning daylight. The snowy street beneath, which, though centrally situated, was remote from all bustle, was even quieter than usual on this holiday afternoon, and George felt once more, as indeed he always did when he ascended the broad staircase of the old palace that had been transformed into an apartment house, and stepped into the spacious room with its low-arched ceiling, that he was escaping from his usual world and had entered the other half of his wonderful double life.

He heard a key grating in the door and turned round. Anna came in. George clasped her ecstatically in his arms, and kissed her on the forehead and mouth. Her dark-blue jacket, her broad-rimmed hat, her fur boa were all covered with snow.

"You have been working then," said Anna, as she took off her things and pointed to the table where music paper with writing on it lay close to the green-shaded lamp.

"I have just looked through the quintette, the first movement, there is still a lot to do to it."

"But it will be extraordinarily fine then."

" We'll hope so. Do you come from home, Anna ? "

" No, from Bittner's."

" What, to-day, Sunday ? "

" Yes, the two girls have got a lot behind-hand through the measles, and that has to be made up. I am very pleased too, for money reasons for one thing."

" Making your fortune ! "

" And then one escapes for an hour or two at any rate from the happy home."

" Yes," said George, put Anna's boa over the back of a chair and stroked the fur nervously with his fingers. Anna's remark, in which he could detect a gentle reproach, as it were, a reproach too which he had heard before, gave him an unpleasant feeling. She sat down on the sofa, put her hands on her temples, stroked her dark blonde wavy hair backwards and looked at George with a smile. He stood leaning on the chest of drawers, with both hands in his jacket pocket, and began to tell her of the previous evening, which he had spent with Guido and his violinist. The young lady had, at the Count's wish, been for some weeks taking instruction in the Catholic religion with the confessor of an Arch-duchess ; she, on her side, made Guido read Nietzsche and Ibsen. But according to George's account the only result of this course of study which one could report so far was that the Count had developed the habit of nicknaming his Mistress " the Rattenmamsel," after that wonderful character out of *Little Eyolf*.

Anna had nothing very bright to communicate about her last evening. They had had visitors. " First," Anna told him, " my mother's two cousins, then an office friend of my father's to play tarok. Even Josef was domesticated for once and lay on the sofa from three to five. Then his latest pal, Herr Jalaudek, who paid me quite a lot of atten-tion."

" Really, really."

" He *was* fascinating. I'll just tell you : a violet cravat with yellow spots which puts yours quite into the shade. He paid me the honour too of suggesting that I should help him in a so-called charity-performance at the ' Wild Man,' for the benefit of the Wahringer Church Building Society."

" Of course you accepted ? "

" I excused myself on account of my lack of voice and want of religious feeling."

" So far as the voice is concerned . . ."

She interrupted him. " No, George," she said lightly, " I have given up that hope at last."

He looked at her and tried to read her glance, but it remained clear and free. The organ from the church sounded softly and dully.

" Right," said George, " I have brought you the ticket for to-morrow's ' Carmen.' "

" Thanks very much," she answered, and took the card. " Are you going too, dear ? "

" Yes, I have a box in the third tier, and I have asked Bermann to come. I am taking the music with me, as I did the other day at Lohengrin, and I shall practise conducting again. At the back, of course. You can have no idea what you learn that way. I should like to make a suggestion," he added hesitatingly. " Won't you come and have supper somewhere with me and Bermann after the theatre ? "

She was silent.

He continued : " I should really like it if you got to know him better. With all his faults he is an interesting fellow and . . ."

" I am not a Rattenmamsell," she interrupted sharply, while her face immediately assumed its stiff conventional expression.

George compressed the corners of his mouth. " That doesn't apply to me, my dear child. There are many points

of difference between Guido and me. But as you like."
He walked up and down the room.

She remained sitting on the ottoman. "So you are
going to Ehrenbergs' this evening ? " she asked.

"You know I am. I have already refused twice recently,
and I couldn't very well do so this time."

"You needn't make any excuses, George, I am invited
too."

"Where to ? "

"I am going to Ehrenbergs' too."

"Really ? " he exclaimed involuntarily.

"Why are you so surprised ? " she asked sharply ;
"it is clear that they don't yet know that I am not fit to
be associated with any more."

"My dear Anna, what is the matter with you to-day ?
Why are you so touchy ? Supposing they did know . . .
do you think that would prevent people from inviting you ?
Quite the contrary. I am convinced that you would really
go up in Frau Ehrenberg's respect."

"And the sweet Else, I suppose, would positively envy
me. Don't you think so ? Anyway, she wrote me quite
a nice letter. Here it is. Won't you read it ? " George
ran his eye over it, thought its kindness was somewhat
deliberate, made no further remark and gave it back to
Anna.

"Here is another one too, if it interests you."

"From Doctor Stauber. Indeed ? Would he mind if
he knew that you gave it to me to read ? "

"Why are you so considerate all of a sudden ? " and
as though to punish him she added, " there are probably
a great many things that he would mind."

George read the letter quickly through to himself.
Berthold described in his dry way, with an occasional tinge
of humour, the progress of his work at the Pasteur Institute, his walks, his excursions and the theatres he had
visited, and quite a lot of remarks also of a general character.

But in spite of his eight pages the letter did not contain the slightest allusion to either past or future. George asked casually " How long is he staying in Paris ? "

" As you see he doesn't write a single word about his return."

" Your friend Therese was recently of opinion that his colleagues in the party would like to have him back again."

" Oh, has she been in the café again ? "

" Yes. I spoke to her there two or three days ago. She really amuses me a great deal."

" Really ? "

" She starts off, of course, by always being very superior, even with me. Presumably because I am one of those who rot away their life with art and silly things like that, while there are so many more important things to do in the world. But when she warms up a bit it turns out that she is every bit as interested as we ordinary people in all kinds of silly things."

" She easily gets warmed up," said Anna imperturbably.

George walked up and down and went on speaking. " She was really magnificent the other day at the fencing tournament in the Musikverein rooms. By-the-bye, who was the gentleman who was up there in the gallery with her ? "

Anna shrugged her shoulders. " I did not have the privilege of being at the tournament, and besides, I don't know all Therese's cavaliers."

" I presume," said George, " it was a comrade, in every sense of the term. At any rate he was very glum and was pretty badly dressed. When Therese clapped Felician's victory he positively collapsed with jealousy."

" What did Therese really tell you about Doctor Berthold ? " asked Anna.

" Ho, ho ! " said George jestingly, " the lady still appears to be keenly interested."

Anna did not answer.

"Well," reported George, "I can give you the information that they want to make him stand in the autumn for the Landtag. I can quite understand it too, in view of his brilliant gifts as a speaker."

"What do you know about it? Have you ever heard him speak?"

"Of course I have; don't you remember? At your place."

"There is really no occasion for you to make fun of him."

"I assure you I'd no idea of doing so."

"I noticed at once that he struck you at the time as somewhat funny. He and his father, too. Why, you immediately ran away from them."

"Not at all, Anna. You are doing me a great injustice in making such insinuations."

"They may have their weaknesses, both of them, but at any rate they belong to the people whom one can count on. And that is something."

"Have I disputed that, Anna? Upon my word, I have never heard you talk so illogically. What do you want me to do then? Did you want me by any chance to be jealous about that letter?"

"Jealous? that would be the finishing touch. You with your past."

George shrugged his shoulders. Memories swam up in his mind of similar wrangles in the course of previous relationships, memories of those mysterious sudden discords and estrangements which usually simply meant the beginning of the end. Had he really got as far as all that already with his good sensible Anna? He walked up and down the room moodily and almost depressed. At times he threw a fleeting glance towards his love who sat silent in her corner of the sofa, rubbing her hands lightly as though she were cold. The organ rang out more heavily than before in the silence of the room that had suddenly become so melancholy; the voices of singing men became audible and the window-panes rattled softly. George's glance fell on the little Christmas-tree which stood on the sideboard and whose candles had burnt the evening before last for the benefit of Anna and himself. Half-bored, half-nervous, he took a wooden vesta out of his pocket and began to light the little candles one after another.

Then Anna's voice suddenly rang out to him. "There is no one I should prefer to old Doctor Stauber to confide in about anything serious."

George turned coldly towards her and blew out a burning vesta which he still held in his hand. He knew immediately what Anna meant, and felt surprised that he had never given it another thought since their last meeting. He went up to her and took hold of her hand. Now for the first time she looked up. Her expression was impenetrable, her features immobile. "I say, Anna . . ." He sat down by her side on the ottoman with both her hands in his.

She was silent.

"Why don't you speak ? "

She shrugged her shoulders. "There is nothing new to tell you," she explained simply.

"I see," he said slowly. It passed through his mind that her strange sensitiveness to-day was to be regarded as symptomatic of the condition to which she was alluding, and the uneasiness in his soul increased. "But you can't tell definitely for a good time yet," he said in a somewhat cooler tone than he really meant. "And . . . even supposing . . ." he added with artificial cheerfulness.

"So you would forgive me ? " she asked with a smile.

He pressed her to him and suddenly felt quite transported. A vivid and almost pathetic feeling of love flamed up in him for the soft good creature whom he held in his arms, and who could never occasion him, he felt deeply convinced, any serious suffering. " It really wouldn't be so bad," he said cheerily, " you would just leave Vienna for a time, that's all."

" Well, it certainly wouldn't be as simple as you seem all of a sudden to think it would."

" Why not ? You can soon find an excuse; besides, whom does it concern ? Us two. No one else. But as far as I am concerned. I can get away any day as you know; can stay away too as long as I want to. I have not yet signed any contract for next year," he added with a smile. He then got up to put out the Christmas candles, whose tiny flames had almost burnt down to the end, and went on speaking with increasing liveliness. " It would be positively delightful; just think of it, Anna ! We should go away at the end of February or the beginning of March. South, of course, Italy, or perhaps the sea. We would stay at some quiet place where no one knows us, in a beautiful hotel with enormous grounds. And wouldn't one be able to work there, by Jove ? "

" So that's why ! " she said, as though she suddenly understood him. He laughed, held her more tightly in his arms and she pressed herself against his breast. There was no longer any noise from outside. The last sounds of the organ and the men's voices had died away. The snow curtains swept down in front of the window. . . . George and Anna were happy as they had never been before.

While they were at peace in the darkness he spoke about his musical plans for the near future, and told her, so far as he was able, about Heinrich's opera plot. The room became filled with shimmering shadows. The clatter of a wedding-feast swept through the fantastic hall of an ancient king. A passionate youth stole in and thrust his dagger into the prince. A dark sentence was pronounced more sinister than death itself. A sluggish ship sailed on a darkling flood towards an unknown goal. At the youth's feet there rested a princess, who had

9

once been the betrothed of a duke. An unknown man approached the shining boat with strange tidings ; fools, star-gazers, dancers, courtiers swept past. Anna had listened in silence. When he had finished George was curious to learn what impression the fleeting pictures had made upon her.

" I can't say properly," she replied. " I certainly feel quite puzzled to-day, how you are going to make anything real out of this more or less fantastic stuff."

" Of course you can't realise it yet to-day—particularly after just hearing me describe it. . . . But you do feel, don't you ? the musical atmosphere. I have already noted down a few *motifs*—and I should be really very glad if Bermann would soon get to work seriously."

" If I were you, George . . . may I tell you something ? "

" Of course, fire ahead."

" Well, if I were you, I'd first get the quintette really finished. It can't want much doing to it now."

" Not much, and yet . . . besides, you mustn't forget that I've started all kinds of other things lately. The two pianoforte pieces, then the orchestra *scherzo*—I've already got pretty far with that. But it certainly ought to be made part of a symphony."

Anna made no answer. George noticed that her thoughts were roving, and he asked her where she had run away to this time.

" Not so far," she replied ; " it only just passed through my mind what a lot of things can happen before the opera is really ready."

" Yes," said George slowly, with a slight trace of embarrassment. " If one could just look into the future."

She sighed quite softly and he pressed her nearer to him, almost as though he pitied her. " Don't worry, my darling, don't worry," he said. " I am here all right, and I always shall be here." He thought he felt what

she was thinking; can't he say anything better than
that ? . . . anything stronger ? anything to take away
all my fear—take it away from me for ever ? And he
asked her disingenuously, as though conscious of running
a risk: " What are you thinking of ? " And as she was
obstinately silent he said once more: " Anna, what are
you thinking of ? "

" Something very strange," she answered gently.

" What is it ? "

" That the house is already built, where it will come
into the world—that we have no idea where . . . that is
what I couldn't help thinking of."

" Thinking of that ! " he said, strangely moved. And
pressing her to his heart with a love that flamed up afresh,
" I will never desert you, you two . . ."

When the room was lighted again they were in very
good spirits, plucked the last forgotten sweets from the
branches of the little Christmas-tree and looked forward
to their next meeting among people who were absolutely
indifferent to them, as though it were quite a jolly adventure, laughed and talked exuberant nonsense.

As soon as Anna had gone away George locked his
music manuscript up in a drawer, put out the lamp and
opened the window. The snow was falling lightly and
thinly. An old man was coming up the steps and his
laboured breathing sounded through the still air. Opposite the silent church towered aloft . . . George remained
awhile standing at the window. He felt almost convinced
at this moment that Anna was mistaken in her surmise.
He felt almost reassured as there came into his mind that
remark of Leo Golowski's that Anna was destined to end
her days in respectable middle-class life. Having a child
by a lover really could not be part of her fate line. It
was not part of his fate line either to carry the burden of
serious obligation, to be tied fast from to-day and perhaps
for all time to a person of the other sex ; to become a

father when he was still so young, a father . . . the word
sank into his soul, oppressive, almost sinister.

He went into the Ehrenbergs' drawing-room at eight
o'clock in the evening. He was met by the sound of
waltz music. Old Eissler sat at the piano with his long
grey beard almost drooping on to the keys. George remained at the entrance in order not to disturb him, and
met welcoming glances from every quarter. Old Eissler
was playing his celebrated Viennese dances and songs with
a soft touch and powerful rhythm, and George enjoyed,
as he always did, the sweet crooning melodies.

"Splendid," said Frau Ehrenberg, when the old man
got up.

"Keep your big words for great occasions, Leonie,"
answered Eissler, whose time-honoured privilege it was
to call all women and girls by their Christian names. And
it seemed to do everybody good to hear themselves spoken
to by this handsome old man with his deep ringing voice,
in which there quivered frequently, as it were, a sentimental echo of the vivid days of his youth.

George asked him if all his compositions had appeared in
print.

"Very few, dear Baron. Unfortunately I can scarcely
write a single note."

"It would certainly be an awful pity if these charming melodies were to be absolutely lost."

"Yes, I have often told him that," put in Frau Ehrenberg, "but unfortunately he is one of those men who
have never taken themselves quite seriously."

"No, that is a mistake, Leonie. You know how I began
my artistic career: I wanted to compose a great opera.
Of course I was seventeen years old at the time and
madly in love with a great singer."

Frau Oberberger's voice rang out from the table towards the corner: "I am sure it was a chorus girl."

"You are making a mistake, Katerina," answered

Eissler. " Chorus girls were never my line. It was, as a matter of fact, a platonic love, like most of the great passions of my life."

" Were you so clumsy ? " queried Frau Oberberger.

" I was often that as well," replied Eissler, in his sonorous voice and with dignity. " For as far as I can see I could have had as much luck as a hussar riding-master, but I don't regret having been clumsy."

Frau Ehrenberger nodded appreciatively.

" Then one would not be making a mistake, Herr Eissler," remarked Nürnberger, " if one attributed the chief part in your life to melancholy memories ? "

Frau Ehrenberger nodded again. She was delighted whenever any one was witty in her drawing-room.

" Why did you say," she inquired, " that you could have had as much happiness as a hussar riding-master ? It is not true for a minute that officers have any particular luck with women, even though my sister-in-law once had an affair with a first-lieutenant . . ."

" I don't believe in platonic love," said Sissy, and beamed through the room.

Frau Wyner gave a slight shriek.

" Fräulein Sissy is probably right," said Nürnberger ; " at any rate I am convinced that most women take platonic love either as an insult or an excuse."

" There are young girls here," Frau Ehrenberg reminded him gently.

" One sees that already," said Nürnberger, " from the fact of their joining in the conversation."

" All the same, I would like to take the liberty of adding a little anecdote to the chapter of platonic love," said Heinrich.

" But not a Jewish one," put in Else.

" Of course not. A blonde little girl . . ."

" That proves nothing," interrupted Else.

" Please let him finish his story," remonstrated Frau Ehrenberg.

" Well then, a blonde little girl," began Heinrich again, " once expressed her conviction to me, quite different, you see, from Fräulein Sissy, that platonic love did, as a matter of fact, exist, and do you know what she suggested as a proof of it? giving . . . an experience out of her own life. She had, you know, once spent a whole hour in a room with a lieutenant and . . ."

" That is enough ! " cried Frau Ehrenberg nervously.

" And," finished Heinrich, quite unperturbed and in a reassuring voice, " nothing at all happened in that hour."

" So the blonde girl says," added Else.

The door opened. George saw a strange lady enter in a clear blue square-cut dress, pale, simple and dignified. It was only when she smiled that he realised that the lady was Anna Rosner, and he felt something like pride in her.

When he shook hands with his love he felt Else's look turn towards him.

They went into the next room, where the table was laid with a moderate show of festivity. The son of the house was not there. He was at Neuhaus at his father's factory. But Herr Ehrenberg suddenly turned up at the table when the supper was served. He had just come back from his travels, which as a matter of fact had taken him to Palestine. When he was asked by Hofrat Wilt about his experiences he was at first reluctant to let himself go ; finally it turned out that he had been disappointed in the scenery, annoyed by the fatigue of the journey, and had practically seen nothing of the Jewish settlements which, according to reliable information, were in process of springing up.

" So we have some ground to hope," remarked Nürnberger, " that we may keep you here even in the event of a Jewish state being founded in the imminent future ? "

Ehrenberg answered brusquely : " Did I ever tell you that I intended to emigrate ? I am too old for that."

" Really," said Nürnberger, " I didn't know that you

had only visited the district for the benefit of Fräulein Else and Herr Oskar."

" I am not going to quarrel with you, my dear Nürnberger. Zionism is really too good to serve as small talk at meals."

" We'll take it for granted," said Hofrat Wilt, " that it is too good, but it is certainly too complicated, if only for the reason that everybody understands something different by it."

" Or wants to understand," added Nürnberger, " as is usually the case with most catchwords, not only in politics either—that's why there is so much twaddle talked in the world."

Heinrich explained that of all human creatures the politician represented in his eyes the most enigmatic phenomenon. " I can understand," he said, " pickpockets, acrobats, bank - directors, hotel - proprietors, kings . . . I mean I can manage without any particular trouble to put myself into the souls of all these people. Of course the logical result is that I should only need certain alterations in degree, though no doubt enormous ones, to qualify myself to play in the world the rôle of acrobat, king or bank-director. On the other hand I have an infallible feeling that even if I could raise myself to the nth power I could never become what one calls a politician, a leader of a party, a member, a minister."

Nürnberger smiled at Heinrich's theory of the politician representing a particular type of humanity, inasmuch as it was only one of the superficial and by no means essential attributes of his profession to pose as a special human type, and to hide his greatness or his insignificance, his feats or his idleness behind labels, abstractions and symbols. What the nonentities or charlatans among them represented, why, that was obvious : they were simply business people or swindlers or glib speakers, but the people who really counted, the people who did things—the real geniuses of

course, they at the bottom of their souls were simply
artists. They too tried to create a work, and one, too,
that raised in the sphere of ideas quite as much claim
to immortality and permanent value as any other work
of art. The only difference was that the material in
which they worked was one that was not rigid or re-
latively stable, like tones or words, but that, like living
men, it was in a continual state of flux and movement.

Willy Eissler appeared, apologised to his hostess for
being late, sat down between Sissy and Frau Oberberger
and greeted his father like a friend long lost. It turned
out that though they both lived together they had not
seen each other for several days.

Willy was complimented all round on his success in the
aristocratic amateur performance where he had played the
part of a marquis with the Countess Liebenburg-Rathony
in a French one-act play. Frau Oberberger asked him, in
a voice sufficiently loud for her neighbours to catch it,
where his assignations with the countess took place and
if he received her in the same *pied-à-terre* quarter as his
more middle-class flames. The conversation became more
lively, dialogues were exchanged and became intertwined
all over the room.

But George caught isolated snatches, including part of a
conversation between Anna and Heinrich which dealt with
Therese Golowski. He noticed at the same time that
Anna would occasionally throw a dark inquisitive look
at Demeter Stanzides, who had appeared to-night in evening dress with a gardenia in his buttonhole ; and though
he had no actual consciousness of jealousy he felt strangely
affected. He wondered if at this moment she was really
thinking that she was perhaps bearing a child by him under
her bosom. The idea of " the depths . . ." came to him
again. She suddenly looked over to him with a smile, as
though she were coming home from a journey. He felt
an inner sense of relief and appreciated with a slight

shock how much he loved her. Then he raised his glass
to his lips and drank to her. Else, who up to this time
had been chatting with her other neighbour Demeter,
now turned to George. With her deliberately casual
manner and with a look towards Anna she remarked:
" She does look pretty, so womanly. But that's always
been her line. Do you still do music together ? "

" Frequently," replied George coolly.

" Perhaps I'll ask you to start accompanying me again
at the beginning of the new year. I don't know why we
have not done so before."

George was silent.

" And how are you getting on "—she threw a look at
Heinrich—" with your opera ? "

" Nothing is done so far. Who knows if anything will
come of it ? "

" Of course nothing will come of it."

George smiled. " Why are you so stern with me to-day ? "

" I am very angry with you."

" With me ! Why ? "

" That you always go on giving people occasion to regard
you as a dilettante."

This was a home thrust. George actually felt a slight
sense of malice against Else, then quickly pulled himself
together and answered: " That perhaps is just what I
am. And if one isn't a genius it is much better to be an
honest dilettante than . . . than an artist with a swollen
head."

" Nobody wants you to do great things all at once, but
all the same one really should not let oneself go in the
way you do in both your inner and your outward life."

" I really don't understand you, Else. How can one
contend . . . Do you know that I am going to Germany
in the autumn as a conductor ? "

" Your career will be ruined by your not turning up to
the rehearsals at ten o'clock sharp."

The taunt was still gnawing at George. " And who called me a dilettante, if I may ask ? "

" Who did ? Good gracious, why it has already been in the papers."

" Really," said George feeling reassured, for he now remembered that after the concert in which Fräulein Bellini had sung his songs a critic had described him as an aristocratic dilettante. George's friends had explained at the time that the reason for this malicious critique was that he had omitted to call on the gentleman in question, who was notoriously vain. So that was it once again. There were always extrinsic reasons for people criticising one unfavourably, and Else's touchiness to-day, what was it at bottom but sheer jealousy. . . .

The table was cleared. They went into the drawing-room.

George went up to Anna, who was leaning on the piano, and said gently to her : " You do look beautiful, dear."

She nodded with satisfaction.

He then went on to ask : " Did you have a pleasant talk with Heinrich ? What did you speak about ? Therese, isn't that so ? "

She did not answer, and George noticed with surprise that her eyelids suddenly drooped and that she began to totter. " What is the matter ? " he asked, frightened.

She did not hear him, and would have fallen down if he had not quickly caught hold of her by the wrists. At the same moment Frau Ehrenberg and Else came up to her.

" Did they notice us ? " thought George.

Anna had already opened her eyes again, gave a forced smile and whispered : " Oh, it is nothing. I often stand the heat so badly."

" Come along ! " said Frau Ehrenberg in a motherly tone. " Perhaps you will lie down for a moment."

Anna, who seemed dazed, made no answer and the ladies of the house escorted her into an adjoining room.

George looked round. The guests did not seem to have noticed anything. Coffee was handed round. George took a cup and played nervously with his spoon. "So after all," he thought, "she will not finish up in middle-class life." But at the same time he felt as far away from her psychologically, as though the matter had no personal interest for him.

Frau Oberberger came up to him. "Well, what do you really think about platonic love? You are an expert, you know."

He answered absent-mindedly. She went on talking, as was her way, without bothering whether he was listening or answering. Suddenly Else returned. George inquired how Anna was, with polite sympathy.

"I am certain it is not anything serious," said Else and looked him strangely in the face.

Demeter Stanzides came in and asked her to sing.

"Will you accompany me?" She turned to George.

He bowed and sat down at the piano.

"What shall it be?" asked Else.

"Anything you like," replied Wilt, "but nothing modern." After supper he liked to play the reactionary at any rate in artistic matters.

"Right you are," said Else, and gave George a piece of music.

She sang the *Das Alte Bild* of Hugo Wolf in her small well-trained and somewhat pathetic voice. George played a refined accompaniment, though he felt somewhat *distrait*. In spite of his efforts he could not help feeling a little annoyed about Anna. After all no one seemed to have really noticed the incident except Frau Ehrenberg and Else.

After all, what did it really come to? . . . Supposing they did all know? . . . Whom did it concern? Yes, who bothered about it? Why, they are all listening to Else now, he continued mentally, and appreciating the beauty

of this song. Even Frau Oberberger, though she is not a
bit musical, is forgetting that she is a woman for a few
minutes and her face is quiet and sexless. Even Heinrich
is listening spell-bound and perhaps for the moment is
neither thinking of his work, nor of the fate of the Jews,
nor of his distant mistress. Is perhaps not even giving a
single thought to his present mistress, the little blonde girl,
to please whom he has recently begun to dress smartly.
As a matter of fact he does not look at all bad in evening
dress, and his tie is not a ready-made one, such as he usually
wears, but is carefully tied. . . . Who is standing so close
behind me ? thought George, so that I can feel her
breath over my hair. . . . Perhaps Sissy. . . . If the world
were to be destroyed to-morrow morning it would be
Sissy whom I should choose for to-night. Yes, I am sure
of it. And there goes Anna with Frau Ehrenberg; it seems
I am the only one who notices it, although I have got to
attend simultaneously to both my own playing and Else's
singing. I welcome her with my eyes. Yes, I welcome
you, mother of my child. . . . How strange life is ! . . .

The song was at an end. The company applauded and
asked for more. George played Else's accompaniment to
some other songs by Schumann, by Brahms ; and finally,
by general request, two of his own, which had become
distasteful to him personally, since somebody or other had
suggested that they were reminiscent of Mendelssohn.

While he was accompanying he felt that he was losing
all touch with Else and therefore made a special effort
in his playing to win back again her sense of sympathy.
He played with exaggerated sensibility, he specifically
wooed her and felt that it was in vain. For the first time
in his life he was her unhappy lover.

The applause after George's songs was great.

" That was your best period," said Else gently to him
while she put the music away, " two or three years ago."

The others made kind remarks to him without going

into distinctions about the periods of his artistic development.

Nürnberger declared that he had been most agreeably disillusioned by George's songs. "I will not conceal the fact from you," he remarked, "that going by the views I have frequently heard you express, my dear Baron, I should have imagined them considerably less intelligible."

"Quite charming, really," said Wilt, "all so simple and melodious without bombast or affectation."

"And he is the man," thought George grimly, "who dubbed me a dilettante."

Willy came up to him. "Now you just say, Herr Hofrat, that you can manage to whistle them, and if I know anything about physiognomy the Baron will send two gentlemen to see you in the morning."

"Oh no," said George, pulling himself together and smiling; "fortunately, the songs were written in a period which I have long since got over, so I don't feel wounded by any blame or by any praise."

A servant brought in ices, the groups broke up and Anna stood alone with George by the pianoforte.

He asked her quickly "What does it really mean?"

"I don't know," she replied, and looked at him in astonishment.

"Do you feel quite all right now?"

"Absolutely," she answered.

"And is to-day the first time you have had anything like it?" asked George, somewhat hesitatingly.

She answered: "I had something like it yesterday evening at home. It was a kind of faintness. It lasted some time longer, while we were sitting at supper, but nobody noticed it."

"But why did you tell me nothing about it?"

She shrugged her shoulders lightly.

"I say, Anna dear," he said, and smiled guiltily, "I would like to have a word with you at any rate. Give me

a signal when you want to go away. I will clear out a few
minutes before you, and will wait by the Schwarzenberg-
platz till you come along in a fly. I'll get in and we will
go for a little drive. Does that suit you ? "

She nodded.

He said: "Good-bye, darling," and went into the smoking-
room.

Old Ehrenberg, Nürnberger and Wilt had sat down at
a green card-table to play tarok. Old Eissler and his
son were sitting opposite each other in two enormous green
leather arm-chairs and were utilising the opportunity to
have a good chat with one another after all this time.
George took a cigarette out of a box, lighted it and looked
at the pictures on the wall with particular interest. He
saw Willy's name written in pale red letters down below
in the corner on the green field in a water-colour painted
in the grotesque style, that represented a hurdle race
ridden by gentlemen in red hunting-coats. He turned involuntarily to the young man and said : " I never knew that
one before."

" It is fairly new," remarked Willy lightly.

" Smart picture, eh ? " said old Eissler.

" Oh, something more than that," replied George.

" Yes, I hope to be able to look forward to doing something better than that," said Willy.

" He is going to Africa, lion hunting," explained old
Eissler, " with Prince Wangenheim. Felician is also supposed to be of the party, but he has not yet decided."

" Why not ? " asked Willy.

" He wants to pass his diplomatic examination in the
spring."

" But that could be put off," said Willy ; "lions are dying
out, but unfortunately one can't say the same thing of
professors."

" Book me for a picture, Willy," called out Ehrenberg
from the card-table.

" You play the Mæcenas later on, father Ehrenberg ? " said Willy. " As I've said, I'll take you two on."[1]

" Raise you," replied Ehrenberg, and continued : " If I can order anything for myself, Willy, please paint me a desert landscape showing Prince Wangenheim being gobbled up by the lions . . . but as realistic as possible."

" You are making a mistake about the person, Herr Ehrenberg," said Willy ; " the celebrated Anti-Semite you are referring to is the cousin of my Wangenheim."

" For all I care," replied Ehrenberg, " the lions, too, may be making a mistake. Every Anti-Semite, you know, isn't bound to be celebrated."

" You will ruin the party if you don't look out," admonished Nürnberger.

" You should have bought an estate and settled in Palestine," said Hofrat Wilt.

" God save me from that," replied Ehrenberg.

" Well, since he has done that in everything up to the present," said Nürnberger, and put down his hand.

" It seems to me, Nürnberger, that you are reproaching me again for not goin' about peddlin' ole clo'."

" Then you would certainly have the right to complain of Anti-Semitism," said Nürnberger, " for who feels anything of it in Austria except the peddlars . . . only they, one might almost say."

" And some people with a sense of self-respect," retorted Ehrenberg. " Twenty-seven . . . thirty-one . . . thirty-eight. . . . Well, who's won the game ? "

Willy had gone back into the drawing-room again. George sat smoking on the arm of an easy-chair. He suddenly noticed old Eissler's look directed towards him in a strange benevolent manner and felt himself reminded of something without knowing what.

" I had a few words the other day," said the old gentleman, " with your brother Felician at Schönstein's ; it is

---

[1] A reference to the Faro game.

striking how you resemble your poor father, especially to
one like me, who knew your father as a young man."

It flashed across George at once what old Eissler's look
reminded him of. Old Doctor Stauber's eyes had rested
on him at Rosner's with the same fatherly expression.

" These old Jews ! " he thought sarcastically, but in
a remote corner of his soul he felt somewhat moved. It
came into his mind that his father had often gone for
morning walks in the Prater with Eissler, for whose knowledge of art he had had a great respect. Old Eissler went
on speaking.

" You, George, take after your mother more, I think."

" Many say so. It is very hard to judge, oneself."

" They say your mother had such a beautiful voice."

" Yes, in her early youth. I myself never really heard
her sing. Of course she tried now and again. Two or
three years before her death a doctor in Meran even advised
her to practise singing. The idea was that it should be
a good exercise for her lungs, but unfortunately it wasn't
much of a success."

Old Eissler nodded and looked in front of him. " I
suppose you probably won't be able to remember that
my poor wife was in Meran at the same time as your late
mother ? "

George racked his memory. It had escaped him.

" I once travelled in the same compartment as your
father," said old Eissler, " at night time. We were both
unable to sleep. He told me a great deal about you two—
you and Felician I mean."

" Really. . . ."

" For instance, that when you were a boy you had played
one of your own compositions to some Italian *virtuoso*,
and that he had foretold a great future for you. "

" Great future. . . . Great heavens, but it wasn't a
virtuoso, Herr Eissler. It was a clergyman, from whom, as
a matter of fact, I learned to play the organ."

Eissler continued: "And in the evening, when your mother had gone to bed, you would often improvise for hours on end in the room."

George nodded and sighed quietly. It seemed as though he had had much more talent at that time. "Work!" he thought ardently, "work! . . ."

He looked up again. "Yes," he said humorously, "that is always the trouble, infant prodigies so seldom come to anything."

"I hear you want to be a conductor, Baron."

"Yes," replied George resolutely, "I am going to Germany next autumn. Perhaps as an accompanist first in the municipal theatre of some little town, just as it comes along."

"But you would not have any objection to a Court theatre?"

"Of course not. What makes you say that, Herr Eissler? if it is not a rude question."

"I know quite well," said Eissler with a smile, as he dropped his monocle, "that you have not sought out my help, but I can quite appreciate on the other hand that you would not mind perhaps being able to get on without the intermediaryship of agents and others of that kind. . . . I don't mean because of the commissions."

George remained cold. "When one has once decided to take up a theatrical career one knows at the same time all that one's bargaining for."

"Do you know Count Malnitz by any chance?" inquired Eissler, quite unconcerned by George's air of worldly wisdom.

"Malnitz! Do you mean Count Eberhard Malnitz, who had a suite performed a few years ago?"

"Yes, I mean him."

"I don't know him personally, and as for the suite . . ."

With a wave of the hand Eissler dismissed the composer Malnitz. "He has been manager at Detmold since the beginning of this season," he then said. "That is why I asked you if you knew him. He is a great friend of mine of long standing. He used to live in Vienna. For the last ten or twelve years we have been meeting every year in Carlsbad or Ischl. This year we want to make a little Mediterranean trip at Easter. Will you allow me, my dear Baron, to take an opportunity of mentioning your name to him, and telling him something about your plans to be a conductor ? "

George hesitated to answer, and smiled politely.

" Oh please don't regard my suggestion as officious, my dear Baron. If you don't wish it, of course I will sit tight."

" You misunderstand my silence," replied George amiably, but not without *hauteur* ; " but I really don't know. . . ."

" I think a little Court theatre like that," continued Eissler, " is just the right place for you for the beginning. The fact of your belonging to the nobility won't hurt you at all, not even with my friend Malnitz, however much he likes to play the democrat, or even at times the anarchist . . . with the exception of bombs, of course ; but he is a charming man and really awfully musical. . . . Even though he isn't exactly a composer."

" Well," replied George, somewhat embarrassed, " if you would have the kindness to speak to him. . . . I can't afford to let any chance slip. At any rate, I thank you very much."

" Not at all, I don't guarantee success, it is just a chance, like any other."

Frau Oberberger and Sissy came in, escorted by Demeter.

" What interesting conversation are we interrupting ? " said Frau Oberberger. " The experienced platonic lover and the inexperienced rake ? One should really have been there."

" Don't upset yourself, Katerina," said Eissler, and his voice had again its deep vibrating ring. " One sometimes talks about other things, such as the future of the human race."

Sissy put a cigarette between her lips, allowed George to give her a light and sat down in the corner of the green leather sofa. "You are not bothering about me at all to-day," she began with that English accent of hers which George liked so well. "As though I positively didn't exist. Yes, that's what it is. I am really a more constant nature than you are, am I not?"

"You constant, Sissy?" . . . He pushed an arm-chair quite near to her. They spoke of the past summer and the one that was coming.

"Last year," said Sissy, "you gave me your word you would come wherever I was, and you didn't do it. This year you must keep your word."

"Are you going into the Isle of Wight again?"

"No, I am going into the mountains this time, to the Tyrol or the Salzkammergut. I will let you know soon. Will you come?"

"But you are bound to have a large following any-where."

"I won't trouble about any one except you, George."

"Even supposing Willy Eissler happens to stay in your vicinity?"

"Oh," she said, with a wanton smile and put out her cigarette by pressing it violently upon the glass ash-tray.

They went on talking. It was just like one of those conversations they had had so often during the last few years. It began lightly and flippantly, and eventually finished in a blaze of tender lies which were true for just one moment. George was once again fascinated by Sissy. "I would really prefer to go travelling with you," he whispered quite near her.

She just nodded. Her left arm rested on the broad back of the ottoman. "If one could only do as one wanted," she said, with a look that dreamt of a hundred men.

He bent down over her trembling arm, went on speaking

and became intoxicated with his own words. " Somewhere where nobody knows us, where nobody bothers about any one, that is where I should like to be with you, Sissy, many days and nights."

Sissy shuddered. The word "nights" made her shudder with fear.

Anna appeared in the doorway, signalled to George with a look and then disappeared again. He felt an inward sense of reluctance, and yet he felt that this was just the psychological moment to leave Sissy.

In the doorway of the drawing-room he met Heinrich, who accosted him. " If you are going you might tell me, I should like to speak to you."

"Delighted ! But I must . . . promised to see Fräulein Rosner home, you see. I'll come straight to the café, so till then. . . ."

A few minutes later he was standing on the Schwarzenberg bridge. The sky was full of stars, the streets stretched out wide and silent. George turned up his coat collar, although it was no longer cold, and walked up and down. Will anything come of the Detmold business ? he thought. Oh well, if it is not in Detmold it will be in some town or other. At any rate I mean real business now, and a great deal, a great deal will then lie behind me.

He tried to consider the matter quietly. How will it all turn out ? We are now at the end of December. We must go away in March—at the latest. We shall be taken for a honeymoon couple. I shall go walking with her arm-in-arm in Rome and Posilippo, in Venice. . . . There are women who grow very ugly in that condition . . . but not she, no, not she. . . . There was always a certain touch of the mother in her appearance. . . . She must stay the summer in some quiet neighbourhood where no one knows her . . . in the Thuringian Forest perhaps, or by the Rhine. . . . How strangely she said that to-day. The house in which the child will come into the world is already in existence. Yes. . . . Somewhere in the distance, or perhaps quite near here, that house is standing. . . . And people are living there whom we have never seen. How strange. . . . When will it come into the world ? At the end of the summer, about the beginning of September. By that time, too, I am bound to have gone away. How shall I manage it ? . . . And a year from to-day the little creature will be already four months old. It will grow up . . . become big. There will be a young man there one fine day, my son, or a young girl ; a beautiful little girl of seven, my daughter. . . . I shall be forty-four then . . . When I am sixty-four I can be a grandfather . . . perhaps a director of an opera or two and a celebrated composer in spite of Else's prophecies ; but one has got to work for that, that is quite true. More than I have done so far. Else is right, I let myself go too much, I must be different . . . I shall too. I feel a change taking place within me. Yes, something new is taking place within me also.

A fly came out of the Heugasse, some one bent out of the window. George recognised Anna's face under the white shawl. He was very glad, got in and kissed her hand. They enjoyed their talk, joked a little about the party from which she had just come and found it really ridiculous to spend an evening in so inept a fashion. He held her hands in his and was affected by her presence. He got out in front of her house and rung. He then came to the open door of the carriage and they arranged an appointment for the following day.

" I think we have got a lot to talk about," said Anna.

He simply nodded. The door of the house was open. She got out of the fly, gave George a long look full of emotion and disappeared into the hall.

My love ! thought George, with a feeling of happiness and pride. Life lay before him like something serious and mysterious, full of gifts and full of miracles.

When he went into the café, Heinrich was sitting in a

window niche. Next to him was a pale young beardless man whom George had casually spoken to several times, in a dinner-jacket with a velvet collar but with a shirt-front of doubtful cleanliness.

When George came in the young man looked up with ardent eyes from a paper that he was holding in his restless and not very well-kept hands.

" Am I disturbing you ? " said George.

" Oh, not a bit of it," replied the young man, with a crazy laugh, " the larger the audience the better."

" Herr Winternitz," explained Heinrich, as he shook hands with George, " was just reading me a series of his poems, but we will break off now." Slightly touched by the disappointed expression of the young man George assured him that he would be delighted to hear the poems if he might be permitted to do so.

" It won't last much longer," explained Winternitz gratefully. " It is only a pity that you missed the beginning. I could——"

" What ! Does it all hang together ? " said Heinrich in astonishment.

" What, didn't you notice ? " exclaimed Winternitz, and laughed again crazily.

" I see," said Heinrich. " So it's always the same woman character whom your poems deal with. I thought it was always a different one."

" Of course it is always the same one, but her special characteristic is that she always seems to be a fresh person."

Herr Winternitz read softly but insistently, as though inwardly consumed. It appeared from his series that he had been loved as never a man had been loved before, but also deceived as never a man had been deceived before, a circumstance which was to be attributed to certain metaphysical causes and not at all to any deficiencies in his own personality. He showed himself, however, in his

last poem completely freed of his passion, and declared
that he was now ready to enjoy all the pleasures, which
the world could offer him. This poem had four stanzas ;
the last verse of every stanza began with a " hei," and
it concluded with the exclamation : " Hei, so career I
through the world."

George could not help recognising that the recitation
had to a certain extent impressed him, and when Winternitz
put the book down and looked around him with dilated pupils,
George nodded appreciatively and said : " Very beautiful!"

Winternitz looked expectantly at Heinrich, who was
silent for a few seconds and finally remarked : " It is
fairly interesting on the whole . . . but why do you say
' hei,' if it isn't a rude question ? Positively, no one will
believe it."

" What do you mean ? " exclaimed Winternitz.

" Rather ask your own conscience, if you honestly mean
that ' hei.' I believe all the rest which you read to me, I
mean I believe it in the highest sense of the term, although
not a single word is true. I believe you when you tell
me that you have been seducing a girl of fifteen, that you
have been behaving like a hardened Don Juan, that you
have been corrupting the poor creature in the most dreadful way. That she deceived you with . . . what was it
now ? . . ."

" A clown, of course," exclaimed Winternitz, with a mad
laugh.

" That a clown was the man she deceived you with, that
on account of that creature you had adventures which
grew more and more sinister, that you wanted to kill your
mistress and yourself as well, and that finally you get fed
up with the whole business and go travelling about the
world, or even careering as far as Australia for all I care :
yes, I can believe all that, but that you are the kind of
man to cry out ' hei,' that, my dear Winternitz, is a rank
swindle."

Winternitz defended himself.   He swore that this ' hei '
had come from his most inward being, or at any rate from
a certain element in his most inward being.   When Heinrich
made further objections, he gradually became more and
more reserved, and finally declared that some time or
other he hoped to win his way to that inward freedom
where he would be allowed to cry out " hei."

" That time will never come," replied Heinrich positively.
" You may perhaps get some time to the epic or the
dramatic ' hei,' but the lyrical or subjective ' hei ' will
remain, my dear Winternitz, a closed book to people like
you and me for all eternity."

Winternitz promised to alter the last poem, to make a
point of continuing his development and to work at his
inward purification.

He stood up, a proceeding which caused his starched
shirt front to crack and a stud to break, held out his somewhat clammy hand to Heinrich and George, and went off
to the literary men's table at the back.

George expressed discreet appreciation of the poems which
he had heard.

" I like him the best of the whole set, at any rate personally," said Heinrich.   " He at least has the good sense to
maintain with me a certain mutual reserve in really intimate matters.   Yes, you need not look at me again as
though you were catching me in an attack of megalomania,
but I can assure you, George, I have had nearly enough of
the sort of people " (he swept the further table with a
cursory glance) " who have always got an ' ä soi ' on their
lips."

" What is always on their lips ? "

Heinrich smiled.   " You must know the story of the
Polish Jew who was sitting in a railway compartment with
an unknown man and behaved very conventionally—
until he realised by some remark of the other's that he
was a Jew too, and on the strength of it immediately pro-

ceeded to stretch out his legs on the seat opposite with an ' ä soi ' of relief.''

" Quite good," said George.

" It is more than that," explained Heinrich sternly, " it is deep ; like so many other Jewish stories it gives a bird's-eye view into the tragi-comedy of present-day Judaism. It expresses the eternal truth that no Jew has any real respect for his fellow Jew, never. As little as prisoners in a hostile country have any real respect for each other, particularly when they are hopeless. Envy, hate, yes frequently, admiration, even love ; all that there can be between them, but never respect, for the play of all their emotional life takes place in an atmosphere of familiarity, so to speak, in which respect cannot help being stifled."

" Do you know what I think ? " remarked George. " That you are a more bitter Anti-Semite than most of the Christians I know."

" Do you think so ? " he laughed ; " but not a real one. Only the man who is really angry at the bottom of his heart at the Jews' good qualities and does everything he can to bring about the further development of their bad ones is a real Anti-Semite. But you are right up to a certain point, but I must finish by confessing that I am also an Anti-Aryan. Every race as such is naturally repulsive, only the individual manages at times to reconcile himself to the repulsive elements in his race by reason of his own personal qualities. But I will not deny that I am particularly sensitive to the faults of Jews. Probably the only reason is that I, like all others—we Jews, I mean—have been systematically educated up to this sensitiveness. We have been egged on from our youth to look upon Jewish peculiarities as particularly grotesque or repulsive, though we have not been so with regard to the equally grotesque and repulsive peculiarities of other people. I will not disguise it—if a Jew shows bad form in my presence, or behaves in a ridiculous manner, I have often so painful a sensation that I should like to sink into the earth. It is like a kind of shame that perhaps is akin to the shame of a brother who sees his sister undressing. Perhaps the whole thing is egoism too. One gets embittered at being always made responsible for other people's faults, and always being made to pay the penalty for every crime, for every lapse from good taste, for every indiscretion for which every Jew is responsible throughout the whole world. That of course easily makes one unjust, but those are touches of nervousness and sensitiveness, nothing more. Then one pulls oneself together again. That cannot be called Anti-Semitism. But there are Jews whom I really hate, hate as Jews. Those are the people who act before others, and often before themselves, as though they did not belong to the rest at all. The men who try to offer themselves to their enemies and despisers in the most cowardly and cringing fashion, and think that in that way they can escape from the eternal curse whose burden is upon them, or from what they feel is equivalent to a curse. There are of course always Jews like that who go about with the consciousness of their extreme personal meanness, and consequently, consciously or unconsciously, would like to make their race responsible. Of course that does not help them the least bit. What has ever helped the Jews ? the good ones and the bad ones. I mean, of course," he hastily added, " those who need something in the way of material or moral help." And then he broke off in a deliberately flippant tone: " Yes, my dear George, the situation is somewhat complicated and it is quite natural that every one who is not directly concerned with the question should not be able to understand it properly."

" No, you really should not. . . ."

Heinrich interrupted him quickly. " Yes, I should, my dear George, that is just how it is. You don't understand us, you see. Many perhaps get an inkling, but understand ? no. At any rate we understand you much better than you do us. Although you shake your head ! Do we not deserve to ? We have found it more necessary, you see, to learn to understand you than you did to learn to understand us. This gift of understanding was forced to develop itself in the course of time . . . according to the laws of the struggle for existence if you like. Just consider, if one is going to find one's way about in a foreign country, or, as I said before, in an enemy's country, to be ready for all the dangers and ambushes which lurk there, it is obvious that the primary essential is to get to know one's enemies as well as possible—both their good qualities and their bad."

"So you live among enemies ? Among foreigners ! You would not admit as much to Leo Golowski. I don't agree with him either, not a bit of it. But how strangely inconsistent you are when you——"

Heinrich interrupted him, genuinely pained. " I have already told you the problem is far too complicated to be really solved. To find a subjective solution is almost impossible. A verbal solution even more so. Why, at times one might believe that things are not so bad. Sometimes one really is at home in spite of everything, feels one is as much at home here—yes, even more at home—than any of your so-called natives can ever feel. It is quite clear that the feeling of strangeness is to some extent cured by the consciousness of understanding. Why, it becomes, as it were, steeped in pride, condescension, tenderness ; becomes dissolved—sometimes, of course, in sentimentalism, which is again a bad business."

He sat there with deep furrows in his forehead and looked in front of him.

" Does he really understand me better ? " thought George, " than I do him, or is it simply another piece of megalomania. . . . ? "

Heinrich suddenly started as though emerging from a

dream. He looked at his watch. " Half-past two ! And my train goes at eight to-morrow."

" What, you are going away ? "

" Yes, that is what I wanted to speak to you about so much. I shall have to say goodbye to you for a goodish time, I'm sorry to say. I am going to Prague. I am taking my father away, out of the asylum home to our own house."

" Is he better, then ? "

" No, but he is in that stage when he is not dangerous to those near him. . . . Yes, that came quite quickly too."

" And about when do you think you will be back ? "

Heinrich shook his shoulders. " I can't tell to-day, but however the thing develops, I certainly cannot leave my mother and sisters alone now."

George felt a genuine regret at being deprived of Heinrich's society in the near future. " It's possible that you won't find me in Vienna again when you come back. I shall probably go away this spring, you see." And he almost felt a desire to take Heinrich into his confidence.

" I suppose you are travelling south ? " asked Heinrich.

" Yes, I think so. To enjoy my freedom once again, just for a few months. Serious life begins next autumn, you see. I am looking out for a position in Germany at some theatre or other."

" Really ? "

The waiter came to the table. They paid and went.

They met Rapp and Gleissner together in the doorway. They exchanged a few words of greeting.

" And what have you been doing all this time, Herr Rapp ? " asked George courteously.

Rapp took off his pince-nez. " Oh, my melancholy old job all the time. I am engaged in demonstrating the vanity of vanities."

" You might make a change, Rapp," said Heinrich. " Try your luck for once and praise the splendour of splendours."

" What is the point ? " said Rapp, and put on his glasses.

" That will prove itself in the course of time. But as a rule rotten work only keeps alive during its good fortune and its fame, and when the world at last realises the swindle, it has either been in the grave for a long time or has taken refuge in its presumable immortality."

They were now in the street and all turned up their coat collars, since it had begun again to snow violently.

Gleissner, who had had his first great dramatic success a few weeks ago, quickly told them that the seventh performance of his work, which had taken place to-day, had also been sold out.

Rapp used that as a peg on which to hang malicious observations on the stupidity of the public. Gleissner answered with gibes at the impotence of the critic when confronted with true genius—and so they walked away through the snow with turned-up collar, quite enveloped in the steaming hate of their old friendship.

" That Rapp has no luck," said Heinrich to George. " He'll never forgive Gleissner for not disappointing him."

" Do you consider him so jealous ? "

" I wouldn't go as far as that. Matters are rarely sufficiently simple to be disposed of in a single word. But just think what a fate it is to go about the world in the belief that you carry with you as deep a knowledge of it as Shakespeare had, and to feel at the same time that you aren't able to express as much of it as, for instance, Herr Gleissner, although perhaps one is quite as much good as he is—or even more."

They walked on together for a time in silence. The trees in the Ring were standing motionless with their white branches. It struck three from the tower of the Rathaus. They walked over the empty streets and took the way through the silent park. All around them the continuous fall of snow made everything shine almost brightly.

" By the way, I have not told you the latest news,"

started Heinrich suddenly, looking in front of him and speaking in a dry tone.

"What is it?"

"That I have been receiving anonymous letters for some time."

"Anonymous letters? What are the contents?"

"Oh, you can guess."

"I see." It was clear to George that it could only be something about the actress. Heinrich had returned in greater anguish than ever from the foreign town, where he had seen his mistress act the part of a depraved creature in a new play, with a truth and realism which he found positively intolerable. George knew that he and she had since then been exchanging letters full of tenderness and scorn, full of anger and forgiveness, full of broken anguish and laboured confidence.

"The delightful messages," explained Heinrich, "have been coming along every morning for eight days. Not very pleasant, I can assure you."

"Good gracious, what do they matter to you? You know yourself anonymous letters never contain the truth."

"On the contrary, my dear George, they always do, but letters like that always contain a kind of higher truth, the great truth of possibilities. Men haven't usually got sufficient imagination to create things out of nothing."

"That is a charming way of looking at things. Where should we all get to, then? It makes things a bit too easy for libellers of all kinds."

"Why do you say libellers? I regard it as highly improbable, that there are any libels contained in the anonymous letters which I have been receiving. No doubt exaggerations, embellishments, inaccuracies . . ."

"Lies."

"No, I am sure they are not lies; some, no doubt, but

in a case like this how is one to separate the truth from the lies ? "

" There is a very simple way of dealing with that. You go there."

" Me go there ? "

" Yes, of course that is what you ought to do. When you are on the spot you are bound to get at once to the real truth."

" It would certainly be possible."

They were walking under arcades on the wet stone. Their voices and steps echoed. George began again. " Instead of going on being demoralised with all this annoyance, I should try and convince myself personally as to how matters stood."

" Yes, that would certainly be the soundest thing to do."

" Well, why don't you do it ? "

Heinrich remained stationary and jerked out with clenched teeth : " Tell me, my dear George, have you not really noticed that I am a coward ? "

" Nonsense, one doesn't call that being a coward."

" Call it whatever you like. Words never hit things off exactly. The more precisely they pretend to do so the less they really do. I know what I am. I would not go there for anything in the world. To make a fool of myself once more, no, no, no . . ."

" Well, what will you do ? "

Heinrich shook his shoulders as though the matter really did not concern him.

Somewhat irritated, George went on questioning him. " If you will allow me to make a remark, what does the . . . lady chiefly concerned have to say ? "

" The lady who is chiefly concerned, as you call her, with a wit, which though unconscious is positively in- fernal, does not know for the time being anything about my getting anonymous letters."

" Have you left off corresponding with her ? "

"What an idea! We write daily to each other as we did before. She the most tender and lying letters, I the meanest you can possibly imagine—disingenuous, reserved letters, that torture me to the quick."

"Look here, Heinrich, you are really not a very noble character."

Heinrich laughed out loud. "No, I am not noble. I clearly was not born to be that."

"And when one thinks that after all these are sheer libels——" George for his part had of course no doubt that the anonymous letters contained the truth. In spite of that he was honestly desirous that Heinrich should travel to the actual spot, convince himself, do something definite, box somebody's ears or shoot somebody down. He imagined Felician in a similar position, or Stanzides or Willy Eissler. All of them would have taken it better or in a different way, one for which he certainly could have felt more sympathy. Suddenly the question ran through his brain as to what he would probably do, if Anna were to deceive him. Anna deceive him . . . was that really possible? He thought of her look that evening, that dark questioning look which she had sent over to Demeter Stanzides. No, that did not signify anything, he was sure of it, and the old episodes with Leo and the singing-master, they were harmless, almost childish. But he thought of something that was different and perhaps more significant—a strange question which she had put to him the other day when she had stayed unduly late in his company and had had to hurry off home with an excuse. Was he not afraid, she had asked him, to have it on his conscience that he was making her into a liar? It had rung half like a reproach and half like a warning, and if she herself was so little sure of herself could he trust her implicitly? Did he not love her? He . . . and did he not deceive her in spite of it, or was ready to do so at any moment, which, after all, came to the same thing?

Only an hour ago, in the fly, when he held her in his arms and kissed her, she had of course no idea that he had other thoughts than for her. And yet at a certain moment, with his lips on hers, he had longed for Sissy. Why should it not happen that Anna should deceive him? After all, it might have already happened . . . without his having an idea of it. . . But all these ideas had as it were no substance, they swept through his mind, like fantastic almost amusing possibilities. He was standing with Heinrich in front of the closed door in the Floriani Gassi and shook hands with him.

" Well, God bless you," he said ; " when we see each other again I hope you will be cured of your doubts."

" And would that be much good ? " asked Heinrich. " Can one reassure oneself with certainties in matters of love ? The most one can do is to reassure oneself with bad news, for that lasts, but being certain of something good is at the best an intoxication. . . . Well, goodbye, old chap. I hope we will see each other again in May. Then, whatever happens, I shall come here for a time, and we can talk again about our glorious opera."

" Yes, if I shall be back again in Vienna in May. It may be that I shall not come back before the autumn."

" And then go off again on your new career ? "

" It is quite possible that it will turn out like that," and he looked Heinrich in the face with a kind of childlike defiant smile that seemed to say : " I'm not going to tell you."

Heinrich seemed surprised. " Look here, George, perhaps this is the very last time we are standing together in front of this door. Oh, I am far from thrusting myself into your confidence. This somewhat one-sided relationship will no doubt have to go on on its present lines. Well, it doesn't matter."

George looked straight in front of him.

" I hope things go all right," said Heinrich as the door opened, " and drop me a line now and then."

II

"Certainly," answered George, and suddenly saw Heinrich's eyes resting upon him with an expression of real sympathy which he had never expected. "Certainly . . . and you must write to me, too. At any rate give me news of how things are at home and what you are working at. At all events," he added sincerely, "we must continue to keep in touch with each other."

The porter stood there with dishevelled hair and an angry sleepy expression, in a greenish-brown dressing-gown, with slippers on his bare feet.

Heinrich shook hands with George for the last time. "Goodbye, my dear friend," he said, and then in a gentler voice, as he pointed to the porter: "I cannot keep him waiting any longer. You will find no particular difficulty in reading in his noble physiognomy, which is obviously the genuine native article, the names he is calling me to himself at this particular moment. Adieu."

George could not help laughing. Heinrich disappeared. The door clanged and closed

George did not feel the least bit sleepy and determined to go home on foot. He was in an excited exalted mood. He was envisaging the days which were now bound to come with a peculiar sense of tension. He thought of to-morrow's meeting with Anna, the things they were going to talk over, the journey, the house that already stood somewhere in the world, which his imagination had already roughly pictured like a house out of a box of toys, light-green with a bright red roof and a black chimney. His own form appeared before him like a picture thrown on a white screen by a magic lantern: he saw himself sitting on a balcony in happy solitude, in front of a table strewn with music paper. Branches rocked in front of the railings. A clear sky hung above him, while below at his feet lay the sea, with a dreamy blueness that was quite abnormal.

V

GEORGE gently opened the door of Anna's room.
She still lay asleep in bed and breathed deeply and
peacefully. He went out of the slightly darkened
room, back again into his own and shut the door. Then
he went to the open window and looked out. Clouds bathed
in sunshine were sweeping over the water. The mountains
opposite with their clearly-defined lines were floating in
the brilliancy of the heavens, while the brightest blue was
glittering over the gardens and houses of Lugano.

George was quite delighted to breathe in once more the
air of this June morning, which brought to him the moist
freshness of the lake and the perfume of the plane-trees,
magnolias and roses in the hotel park ; to look out upon
this view, whose spring-like peace had welcomed him like
a fresh happiness every morning for the last three weeks.

He drank his tea quickly, ran down the stairs as quickly
and expectantly as he had once, when a boy, hurried off
to his play, and took his accustomed way along the bank
in the grey fragrance of the early shade. Here he would
think of his own lonely morning walks at Palermo and
Taormina in the previous spring, walks which he had
frequently continued for hours on end, since Grace was
very fond of lying in bed with open eyes until noon.

That period of his life, over which a recent though no
doubt much-desired farewell seemed to squat like a
sinister cloud, usually struck him as more or less bathed in
melancholy. But this time all painful things seemed to
lie in the far distance, and at any rate he had it in his

power to put off the end as long as he wanted, if it did not come from fate itself.

He had left Vienna with Anna at the beginning of March, as it was no longer possible to conceal her condition. In January, in fact, George had decided to speak to her mother. He had more or less prepared himself for it, and was consequently able to make his communication quietly and in well-turned phraseology. The mother listened in silence and her eyes grew large and moist. Anna sat on the sofa with an embarrassed smile and looked at George as he spoke, with a kind of curiosity. They sketched out the plan for the ensuing months. George wanted to stay abroad with Anna until the early summer. Then a house was to be taken in the country in the neighbourhood of Vienna, so that her mother should not be far away in the time of greatest need, and the child could without difficulty be given out to nurse in the neighbourhood of the town. They also thought out an excuse for officious inquisitive people for Anna's departure and absence.

As her voice had made substantial progress of late—which was perfectly true—she had gone off to a celebrated singing mistress in Dresden, to complete her training.

Frau Rosner nodded several times, as though she agreed with everything, but the features of her face became sadder and sadder. It was not so much that she was oppressed by what she had just learnt, as she was by the realisation that she was bound to be so absolutely defenceless, poor middle-class mother that she was, sitting opposite the aristocratic seducer.

George, who noticed this with regret, endeavoured to assume a lighter and more sympathetic tone. He came closer to the good woman, he took her hand and held it for some seconds in his own. Anna had scarcely contributed a word to the whole discussion, but when George got ready to go she got up, and for the first time in front of her mother she offered him her lips to kiss, as though she were now celebrating her betrothal to him.

George went downstairs in better spirits, as though the worst were now really over. Henceforth he spent whole hours at the Rosners' more frequently than before, practising music with Anna, whose voice had now grown noticeably in power and volume. The mother's demeanour to George became more friendly. Why, it often seemed to him as though she had to be on her guard against a growing sympathy for him, and there was one evening in the family circle when George stayed for supper, improvised afterwards to the company from the Meistersingers and Lohengrin with his cigar in his mouth, could not help enjoying the lively applause, particularly from Josef, and was almost shocked to notice as he went home that he had felt quite as comfortable, as though it had been a home he had recently won for himself.

When he was sitting over his black coffee with Felician a few days later the servant brought in a card, the receipt of which made a slight blush mount to his cheek. Felician pretended not to notice his brother's embarrassment, said good-bye and left the room. He met old Rosner in the doorway, inclined his head slightly in answer to his greeting and took no further notice.

George invited Herr Rosner, who came in in his winter coat with his hat and umbrella, to sit down, and offered him a cigar. Old Rosner said: "I have just been smoking," a remark which somehow or other reassured George, and sat down, while George remained leaning on the table.

Then the old man began with his accustomed slowness: "You will probably be able to imagine, Herr Baron, why I have taken the liberty of troubling you. I really wanted to speak to you in the earlier part of the day, but unfortunately I could not get away from the office."

"You would not have found me at home in the morning, Herr Rosner," answered George courteously.

"All the better then that I didn't have my journey for nothing. My wife has told me this morning . . . what has happened. . . ." He looked at the floor.

"Yes," said George, and gnawed at his upper lip. "I myself intended . . . But won't you take off your overcoat? It is very warm in the room."

"No thank you, thank you, it is not at all too warm for me. Well, I was horrified when my wife gave me this information. Indeed I was, Herr Baron. . . . I never would have thought it of Anna . . . never thought it possible . . . it is . . . really dreadful. . . ." He spoke all the time in his usual monotonous voice, though he shook his head more often than usual.

George could not help looking all the time at his head with its thin yellow-grey hair, and felt nothing but a desolate boredom. "Really, Herr Rosner, the thing is not dreadful," he said at last. "If you knew how much I . . . and how sincere my affection for Anna is, you would certainly be very far from thinking the thing dreadful. At any rate, I suppose your wife has told you about our plans for the immediate future . . . or am I making a mistake . . . ? "

"Not at all, Herr Baron, I have been informed of everything this morning. But I must say that I have noticed for some weeks that something was wrong in the house. It often struck me that my wife was very nervous and was often on the point of crying."

"On the point of crying! There is really no occasion for that, Herr Rosner. Anna herself, who is more concerned than any one else, is very well and is in her usual good spirits. . . ."

"Yes, Anna at any rate takes it very well, and that, to speak frankly, is more or less my consolation. But I cannot describe to you, Baron, how hard hit . . . how, I could almost say . . . like a bolt from the blue . . . I could never, no, never have . . . have believed it. . . ." He could not say any more. His voice trembled.

" I am really very concerned," said George, " that you should take the matter like this, in spite of the fact that your wife is bound to have explained everything to you, and that the measures we have taken for the near future presumably meet with your approval. I would prefer not to talk about a time which is further, though I hope not too far off, because phrases of all kinds are more or less distasteful to me, but you may be sure, Herr Rosner, that I certainly shall not forget what I owe to a person like Anna. . . . Yes, what I owe to myself." He gulped.

In all his memory there was no moment in his life in which he had felt less sympathy for himself. And now, as is necessarily the case in all pointless conversations, they repeated themselves several times, until Herr Rosner finally apologised for having troubled him, and took his leave of George, who accompanied him to the stairs.

George felt an unpleasant aftermath in his soul for some days after this visit. The brother would be the finishing touch, he thought irritably, and he could not help imagining a scene of explanation in the course of which the young man would endeavour to play the avenger of the family honour, while George put him in his place with extraordinarily trenchant expressions.

George nevertheless felt a sense of relief after the conversation with Anna's parents had taken place, and the hours which he spent with his beloved alone in the peaceful room opposite the church were full of a peculiar feeling of comfort and safety. It sometimes seemed to them both as though time stood still.

It was all very well for George to bring guide-books, Burckhardt's *Cicerone*, and even maps to their meetings, and to plan out with Anna all kinds of routes ; he did not as a matter of fact seriously think that all this would ever be realised.

So far, however, as the house in which the child was to be born was concerned, they were both impressed with the necessity of its being found and taken before they left Vienna. Anna once saw an advertisement in the paper which she was accustomed to read carefully for that very object, of a lodge near the forest, and not far from a railway station, which could be reached in one and a half hours from Vienna. One morning they both took the train to the place in question and they had a memory of a snow-covered lonely wooden building with antlers over the door, an old drunken keeper, a young blonde girl, a swift sleigh-ride over a snowy winter street, an extraordinarily jolly dinner in an enormous room in the inn, and then home in a badly-lighted over-heated compartment. This was the only time that George tried to find with Anna the house that must be standing somewhere in the world and waiting to be decided upon. Otherwise he usually went alone by train or tramway to look round the summer resorts which were near Vienna. Once, on a spring day that had come straight into the middle of the winter, George was walking through one of the small places situated quite near town, which he was particularly fond of, where village buildings, unassuming villas and elegant country houses lay close upon each other. He had completely forgotten, as often happened, why he had taken the journey, and was thinking with emotion of the fact that Beethoven and Schubert had taken the same walk as he, many years ago, when he unexpectedly ran up against Nürnberger. They greeted each other, praised the fine day, which had enticed them so far out into the open, and expressed regret that they so rarely saw each other since Bermann had left Vienna.

" Is it long since you heard anything of him ? " asked George.

" I have only had a card from him," replied Nürnberger, " since he left. It is much more likely he would correspond regularly with you than with me."

" Why is it more likely ? " inquired George, somewhat irritated by Nürnberger's tone, as indeed he frequently was.

" Well, at any rate you have the advantage over me of being a new acquaintance, and consequently offering more exciting subject-matter for his psychological interest than I can."

George detected in the accustomed flippancy of these words a certain sense of grievance which he more or less understood, for, as a matter of fact, Heinrich had bothered very little about Nürnberger of late, though he had previously seen a great deal of him, it being always his way to draw men to him and then drop them with the greatest lack of consideration, according as their character did or did not fit in with his own mood.

" In spite of that I am not much better off than you," said George. " I haven't had any news of him for some weeks either. His father, too, appears to be in a bad way according to the last letter."

" So I suppose it will soon be all up with the poor old man now."

" Who knows ? According to what Bermann writes me, he can still last for months."

Nürnberger shook his head seriously.

" Yes," said George lightly. " The doctors ought to be allowed in cases like that . . . to shorten the matter."

" You are perhaps right," answered Nürnberger, " but who knows whether our friend Heinrich, however much the sight of his father's incurable malady may put him off his work and perhaps many other things as well—who knows whether he might not all the same refuse the suggestion of finishing off this hopeless matter by a morphia injection ? "

George felt again repulsed by Nürnberger's bitter, ironic tone, and yet when he remembered the hour when he had seen Heinrich more violently upset by a few obscure words in the letter of a mistress than by his father's madness, he could not drive out the impression that Nürnberger's opinion of their friend was correct. " Did you know old Bermann ? " he asked.

" Not personally, but I still remember the time when his name was known in the papers, and I remember, too, many extremely sound and excellent speeches which he made in Parliament. But I am keeping you, my dear Baron. Goodbye. We will see each other no doubt one of these days in the café, or at Ehrenbergs'."

" You are not keeping me at all," replied George with deliberate courtesy. " I am quite at large, and I am availing myself of the opportunity of looking at houses for the summer."

" So you are going in the country, near Vienna this year ? "

" Yes, for a time probably, and apart from that a family I know has asked me if I should chance to run across . . ." He grew a little red, as he always did when he was not adhering strictly to the truth. Nürnberger noticed it and said innocently : " I have just passed by some villas which are to let. Do you see, for instance, that white one with the white terrace ? "

" It looks very nice. We might have a look at it, if you won't find it too dull coming with me. Then we can go back together to town."

The garden which they entered sloped upwards and was very long and narrow. It reminded Nürnberger of one in which he had played as a child. " Perhaps it is the same," he said. " We lived for years and years you know in the country in Grinzing or Heiligenstadt."

This " we " affected George in quite a strange way. He could scarcely realise Nürnberger's ever having been quite young, ever having lived as a son with his father and mother, as a brother with his sisters, and he felt all of a sudden that this man's whole life had something strange and hard about it.

At the top of the garden an open arbour gave a wonderfully fine view of the town, which they enjoyed for some time. They slowly went down, accompanied by the caretaker's wife, who carried a small child wrapped in a grey shawl in her arms. They then looked at the house— low musty rooms with cheap battered carpets on the floor, narrow wooden beds, dull or broken mirrors.

" Everything will be done up again in the spring," explained the caretaker, " then it will look very cheerful." The little child suddenly held out its tiny hand towards George, as if it wanted him to take it up in his arms. George was somewhat moved and smiled awkwardly.

As he rode with Nürnberger into the town on the platform of the tramway and chatted to him he felt that he had never got so close to him on all the many previous occasions when they had been together, as during this hour of clear winter sunshine in the country. When they said goodbye it was quite a matter of course that they should arrange a new excursion on a day in the immediate future. And so it came about that George was several times accompanied by Nürnberger, when he continued his househunting in the neighbourhood of Vienna. On these occasions the fiction was still kept up that George was looking for a house for a family whom he knew, that Nürnberger believed it and that George believed that Nürnberger believed it.

On these excursions Nürnberger frequently came to speak of his youth, to speak about the parents whom he had lost very early, of a sister who had died young and of his elder brother, the only one of his relatives who was still alive. But he, an ageing bachelor like Edmund himself, did not live in Vienna, but in a small town in Lower Austria, where he was a teacher in a public school, where he had been transferred fifteen years ago as an assistant. He could easily have managed afterwards to have got an appointment again in the metropolis, but after a few years of bitterness, and even defiance, he had become so completely acclimatised to the quiet petty life of the place where he was staying that he came to regard a return to

Vienna as more a sacrifice than anything else, and he now lived on, passionately devoted to his profession and particularly to his studies in philology, far from the world, lonely, contented, a kind of philosopher in the little town. When Nürnberger spoke of this distant brother George often felt as though he were hearing him speak about some one who had died, so absolutely out of the question seemed every possibility of a permanent reunion in the future. It was in quite a different tone, almost as though he were speaking of a being who could return once again, that he would talk with a perpetual wistfulness of the sister who had been dead several years. It was on a misty February day, while they were at the railway station waiting for the train to Vienna, and walking up and down with each other on the platform, that Nürnberger told George the story of this sister, who when a child of sixteen had become possessed as it were by a tremendous passion for the theatre, and had run away from home without saying goodbye in a fit of childish romanticism. She had wandered from town to town, from stage to stage, for ten years, playing smaller and smaller parts, since neither her talent nor her beauty appeared to be sufficient for the career which she had chosen, but always with the same enthusiasm, always with the same confidence in her future, in spite of the disillusions which she experienced and the sorrow which she saw. In the holidays she would come to the brothers, who were still living together, sometimes for weeks, sometimes only for days, and tell them about the provincial halls in which she had acted as though they were great theatres ; about her few successes as though they were triumphs which she had won, about the wretched comedians at whose side she worked as though they were great artists, tell them about the petty intrigues that took place around her as though they were powerful tragedies of passion. And instead of gradually realising the miserable world in which she was living a life which was as much to be pitied as that of any one else, she spun every year the essence of her soul into more and more golden dreams. This went on for a long time, until at last she came home, feverish and ill. She lay in bed for months on end with flushed cheeks, raving in her delirium of a fame and happiness which she had never experienced, got up once again in apparent health, and went away once more, only to come back home, this time after a few weeks, in complete collapse with death written on her forehead. Her brother now travelled with her to the South ; to Arco, Meran, to the Italian Lakes, and it was only as she lay stretched out in southern gardens beneath flowering trees, far away from the whirl that had dazed and intoxicated her throughout the years that she realised at last that her life had been simply a racketing about beneath a painted sky and between paper walls— that the whole essence of her existence had been an illusion. But even the little everyday incidents, the apartments and inns of the foreign town, seemed to her memory simply scenes which she had played in as an actress by the footlights, and not scenes which she had really lived, and as she approached nearer and nearer to the grave, there awoke within her an awful yearning for that real life which she had missed, and the more surely she knew that it was lost to her for ever, the clearer became the gaze with which she realised the fullness of the world. And the strangest touch of all was the way in which, in the last weeks of her life, that talent to which she had sacrificed her whole existence without ever really possessing it manifested itself with diabolic uncanniness.

" It seems to me, even to-day," said Nürnberger, " that I have never heard verses so declaimed, never seen whole scenes so acted, even by the greatest actress, as I did by my sister in the hotel room at Cadenabbia, looking out on to the Lake of Como, a few days before she died. Of

course," he added, " it is possible, even probable, that my
memory is deceiving me."

" But why ? " asked George, who was so pleased with
this *finale* that he did not want to have it spoiled. And
he endeavoured to convince Nürnberger, who listened to
him with a smile, that he could not have made a mistake,
and that the world had lost a great actress in that strange
girl who lay buried in Cadenabbia.

George did not find on his excursions with Nürnberger
the house in the country for which he was looking. In
fact it seemed to become more difficult to find every time
he went out. Nürnberger made occasional jokes about
George's exacting requirements. He seemed to be looking for a villa which was to be faced in front by a well-
kept road, while it was to have at the back a garden
door which led into the natural forest. Eventually
George himself did not seriously believe that he would
now succeed in finding the desired house, and relied
on the pressure of necessity after his return from his
travels.

It seemed more essential to get as soon as possible into
touch with a doctor, but George put this off too from one
day to another. But one evening Anna informed him
that she had been suddenly panic-stricken by a new attack
of faintness, had visited Doctor Stauber and explained her
condition to him. He had been very nice, had not expressed any astonishment, had thoroughly reassured
her and only expressed the wish to speak to George before
they went away.

A few days afterwards George went to see the doctor in
accordance with his invitation.

The consultation hours were over. Doctor Stauber received him with the friendliness which he had anticipated,
seemed to treat the whole matter as being as regular and
as much a matter of course as it could possibly be, and
spoke of Anna just as though she had been a young wife,

a method of procedure which affected George in a strange
but not unpleasant way.

When the practical discussion was over the doctor
inquired about the destination of their journey. George
had not yet mapped out any programme, only this much
was decided, that the spring was to be spent in the south,
probably in Italy. Doctor Stauber took the opportunity to
talk about his last stay in Rome, which was ten years back.
He had been in personal touch on this occasion, as he
had been once before, with the director of the excavations
and spoke to George in almost ecstatic terms of the latest
discoveries on the Palatine, about which he had written
monographs as a young man, which he had published in
the antiquarian journals. He then showed George, and
not without pride, his library, which was divided into two
sections, medicine and the history of art, and took out
and offered to lend him a few rare books, one printed in
the year 1834 on the Vatican collections and also a history
of Sicily. George felt highly excited as he realised with
such vividness the rich days that lay in front of him. He
was overcome by a kind of homesickness for places which
he knew well and had missed for a long time. Half-for-
gotten pictures floated up in his memory, the pyramids of
Cestius stood on the horizon in sharp outlines, as they
had appeared to him when he had ridden back as a boy
into the town at evening with the prince of Macedon ; the
dim church, where he had seen his first mistress step up
to the altar as a bride, opened its doors ; a bark under a
dark sky with strange sulphur yellow sails drew near to
the coast. . . . He began to speak about the several
towns and landscapes of the south which he had seen as a
boy and as a youth, explained the longing for those
places which often seized on him like a genuine homesickness, his joy at being able to take in with mature
appreciation all the differing things which he had longed
for, reserved for himself and then forgotten, and many

new things besides, and this time too in the society of a being who was able to appreciate and enjoy everything with him, and whom he held dear.

Doctor Stauber, who was in the act of putting a book back on the shelf, turned round suddenly to George, looked gently at him and said: " I am very glad of that." As George answered his look with some surprise he added: " It was the first tender allusion to your relationship to Annerl that I have noticed in the course of the last hour. I know, I know that you are not the kind of man to take a comparative stranger into your confidence, but if only because I had no reason to expect it, it has really done me good. It came straight from your heart, one could see it ; and I should have been really sorry for Annerl— excuse me, I always call her that—if I had been driven to think that you are not as fond of her as she deserves."

" I really don't know," replied George coolly, " what gave you cause to doubt it, doctor."

" Did I say anything about doubts ? " replied Stauber good-humouredly. " But, after all, it has happened before that a young man who has had all kinds of experiences does not appreciate a sacrifice of this kind sufficiently, for it still is a sacrifice, my dear Baron. We can be as superior to all prejudices as much as we like—but it is not a trifle even to-day for a young girl of good family to make up her mind to do a thing like that, and I won't conceal it from you—of course I did not let Annerl notice anything—it gave even me a slight shock when she came to me the other day and told me all about it."

" Excuse me, Herr Doctor," replied George, irritated but yet polite, " if it gave you a shock that is surely some proof against your being superior to prejudices. . . ."

" You are right," said Stauber with a smile, " but perhaps you will overlook this lapse when you consider that I am somewhat older than you and belong to another age. Even a more or less independent man . . . which I flatter myself I am . . . cannot quite escape from the influence of his age. It is a strange thing, but believe me, even among the young people, who have grown up on Nietzsche and Ibsen, there are quite as many Philistines as there were thirty years ago. They won't own up to it, but it does go against the grain with them, for instance, if some one goes and seduces their sister, or if one of their worthy wives suddenly takes it into her head that she wants to live her own life. . . . Many, of course, are consistent and carry their pose through . . . but that is more a matter of self-control than of their real views, and in the old days, you know, the age to which I belong, when ideas were so immovably hide-bound, when every one for instance was quite sure of things like this : one has to honour one's parents or else one is a knave . . . or . . . one only loves really once in one's life . . . or it's a pleasure to die for one's fatherland. . . . in that time, mind you, when every decent man held up some flag or other, or at any rate had something written on his banner . . . believe me, the so-called modern ideas had more adherents than you suspect. The only thing was that those adherents did not quite know it themselves, they did not trust their own ideas, they thought themselves, as it were, debauchees or even criminals. Shall I tell you something, Herr Baron ? There are really no new ideas at all. People feel with a new intensity—that's what it is. `But do you seriously think that Nietzsche discovered the superman, Ibsen the fraud of life and Anzengruber the truth that the parents who desire love and honour from their children ought to ' come up to the scratch ' themselves ? Not a bit of it. All the ethical ideas have always been there, and one would really be surprised if one knew what absolute blockheads have thought of the so-called great new truths, and have even frequently given them expression long before the geniuses to whom we owe these truths, or rather the courage to regard these truths as true. If I have gone rather too far

12

forgive me. I really only wanted to say . . . and you will believe me, I am sure. . . . I know as well as you, Baron, that there is many a virgin girl who is a thousand times more corrupt than a so-called fallen woman ; and that there is many a young man who passes for respectable who has worse things on his conscience than starting a *liaison* with an innocent girl. And yet . . . it is just the curse of my period . . ." he interpolated with a smile, " I could not help it, the first moment Annerl told me her story certain unpleasant words which in their day had their own fixed meaning began to echo through my old head in their old tones, silly out-of-date words like . . . libertine . . . seduction . . . leaving in the lurch . . . and so on, and that is why I must ask you once more to forgive me, now that I have got to know you somewhat more intimately . . . that is why I felt that shock which a modern man would certainly not own that he experienced. But to talk seriously once again, just consider a minute how your poor father, who did not know Anna, would have taken the matter. He was certainly one of the shrewdest and most unprejudiced men whom one can imagine . . . and all the same you have not the slightest doubt that the matter would not have passed off without his feeling something of a shock as well."

George could not help holding out his hand to the doctor. The unexpectedness of this sudden allusion caused so intense a longing to spring up within him that the only thing he could do to assuage it was to begin to talk of him who had passed away. The doctor was able to tell him of many meetings with the late baron, mostly chance casual encounters in the street, at the sessions of the scientific academy, at concerts. There came another of those moments in which George thought himself strangely guilty in his attitude towards the dead man and registered a mental vow to become worthy of his memory.

" Remember me kindly to Annerl," said the doctor as he said goodbye, " but I would rather you did not tell her anything about the shock. She is a very sensitive creature, that you know well enough, and now it is particularly important to save her any excitement. Remember, my dear Baron, there is only one question before us now—to see that a healthy child comes into the world, everything else. . . . Well, give her my best regards. I hope we shall all see each other again in the summer in the best of health."

George went away with a heightened consciousness of his responsibilities towards the being who had given herself to him and to that other who would wake up to existence in a few months. He thought first of making a will and leaving it behind with a lawyer. But on further consideration he thought it more proper to confide in his brother, who after all stood nearer to him in sentiment than any one else. But with that peculiar embarrassment which was characteristic of the really intimate relationship between the brothers he let day after day go by, until at last Felician's departure on the hunting expedition in Africa was quite imminent.

The night before, on the way home from the club, George informed his brother that he was thinking of taking a long journey in the near future.

" Really! For how long shall you be away ? " asked Felician.

George caught the note of a certain anxiety in these words and felt that it was incumbent on him to add : " It will probably be the last long journey I shall take for some years. I hope to find myself in a permanent position in the autumn."

" So you have quite made up your mind ? "

" Yes, of course."

" I am very glad, George, for different reasons, as you can imagine, that you want at last to do something serious. And besides, it's a very sound thing, that it is not a case of one of us going out into the world while the other remains at home alone. That would really have been rather sad."

George knew quite well that Felician would get a foreign diplomatic post in the following autumn, but he had never realised so clearly that in a few months that brotherly life which had lasted for so many years, that common life in the old house opposite the park, yes, his whole youth so to speak, would be irrevocably over and done with. He saw life lying in front of him, serious, almost menacing. " Have you any idea," he asked, " where they will send you ? "

" There is some chance of Athens."

" Would you like that ? "

" Why not ?   The society ought to be fairly interesting. Bernburg was there for three years and was sorry to leave. And they have transferred him to London, too, and that's certainly not to be sniffed at."

They walked in silence for a while and took their usual way through the park. An atmosphere suggesting the approaching spring was around them, although small white flakes of snow still gleamed on the lawns.

" So you are going to Italy ? " asked Felician.

" Yes."

" As far down South as last spring ? "

" I don't know yet."

Again a short silence.   Suddenly Felician's voice came out of the darkness.   " Have you heard anything of Grace since then ? "

" Of Grace ? " repeated George, somewhat surprised, for it had been a long time since Felician had mentioned that name.   " I have heard nothing more of Grace.   Besides, that is what we arranged.   We took farewell of each other for ever at Genoa.   That is already more than a year ago. . . ."

A gentleman was sitting on a seat quite in the darkness in a fur coat with a top hat and white gloves.   " Ah, Labinski," thought George for a whole minute ;   the next minute he of course remembered that he had shot himself. This was not the first time that he had thought he had seen him. A man had sat in broad daylight in the botanical garden at Palermo under a Japanese ash-tree whom George had taken for a whole second for Labinski; and recently George had thought he had recognised the face of his dead father behind the shut windows of a fiacre.

The houses gleamed behind the leafless branches. One of them was the house in which the brothers lived. The time has come, thought George, for me to mention the matter at last. And to bring matters to a head, he observed lightly: "Besides, I am not going to Italy alone this year."

"Hm! Hm!" said Felician, and looked in front of him.

George felt at the same moment that he had not taken the right tone. He was apprehensive of Felician's thinking something like this: "Oh yes, he has got an adventure again with some shady person or other." And he added seriously: "I say, Felician, I have something serious I should like to talk to you about."

"What! Serious!"

"Yes."

"Well, George," said Felician gently, and looked at him sideways, "what is up, then? You are not thinking of marrying by any chance?"

"Oh no," replied George, and then felt irritated that he had repudiated that possibility with such definiteness. "No, it is not a question of marriage, but of something much more vital."

Felician remained standing for a moment. "You have a child?" he asked seriously.

"No, not yet. That's just it, that is why we are leaving."

"Indeed," said Felician.

They had got out of the park. Involuntarily both looked up to the window of their house, from which only a year ago their father had so often nodded his welcome to them both. Both felt with sorrow that somehow since their father's death they had gradually slipped away from each other—and felt at the same time a slight fear of how much further from each other life could still take them.

" Come into my room," said George when they got upstairs. " That's the most comfortable place."

He sat down on his comfortable chair by his secretary. Felician lounged in the corner on a little green leather ottoman which was near the writing-table and listened quietly.

George told him the name of his mistress, spoke of her with heartfelt sympathy, and asked Felician, in case anything should happen to him, George, in the near future to undertake to look after the mother and her child. He left so much of his fortune as was still available to the child, of course. The mother was to have the usufruct until the child became of age.

When George had finished Felician said with a smile after a short silence : " Oh well, you've got every reason to hope that you will come back as whole and sound from your journey as I will from Africa, and so our conversation has probably only an academic significance."

" I hope so too, of course. But at any rate it reassures me, Felician, that you know all about my secret, and that I can be free from anxiety in every way."

" Yes, of course you can." He shook hands with his brother. Then he got up and walked up and down the room. Finally he said : " You have no thought of legitimising your relationship ? "

" Not for the time being. One can never tell what the future may bring forth."

Felician remained standing. " Well . . ."

" Are you in favour of my marrying ? " exclaimed George with some astonishment.

" Not at all."

" Felician, be frank, please."

" Look here, one should not advise any one in affairs like that. Not even one's own brother."

" But if I ask you, Felician ? It seems to me as though there is something in the business you didn't quite like."

" Well, it is like this, George. . . . You won't misunderstand me. . . . I know of course that you are not thinking of leaving her in the lurch. On the contrary, I am convinced that you will behave all through far more nobly than any ordinary man in your position. But the question is really this, would you have let yourself go into the thing if you had considered the consequences from every point of view ? "

" That of course is very hard to answer," said George.

" I mean just this : Did you intend . . . not to make her your companion for life, but to have a child by her all the same ? "

" Great heavens, who thinks of that ? Of course if one had wanted to be so absolutely on the safe side——"

Felician interrupted him. " Does she know that you are not thinking of marrying her ? "

"Why, you don't think, surely, I promised her marriage?"

",No. But you did not promise to leave her stranded either."

" It would have been equally mean if I had promised, Felician. The whole thing came about as affairs like that always do, developed without any definite plan right up to the present time."

" Yes, that is all right. The only question is whether one is not more or less under an obligation to have definite plans in really vital matters."

" Possibly. . . . But that was never my line, unfortunately."

Felician remained standing in front of George, looked at him affectionately and nodded a few times.

" That is quite true, George. You are not angry with me. . . . But now that we are talking about it. . . . Of course I am not suggesting I have any right to lecture you on your mode of life . . ."

"Go ahead, Felician. . . . I mean if . . . It really does me good." He stroked him lightly on the hand which lay on the back of the ottoman.

"Well, there is not much more to be said. I only mean that in everything you do there is just . . . the same lack of system. Look here, to talk of another important matter, I personally am quite convinced of your talent and many others are, too. But you really work damned little, don't you? And fame doesn't come of itself, even when one . . ."

"Quite so. But I don't work as little as you think, Felician, it is only that work is such a peculiar business with people of my temperament. Frequently when one is out for a walk or even asleep one gets all kinds of ideas. . . . And then in the autumn . . ."

"Yes, yes, we hope so, though I am afraid that you won't be able to live on your salary at the commencement, and it is very questionable how long your little money will hold out with your mode of life. I tell you candidly, when you mentioned a few moments ago the sum which you were able to leave to your child I had quite a shock."

"Be patient, Felician. In three or five years, when I have my opera finished . . ." He spoke in an ironical tone.

"Are you really writing an opera, George?"

"I am beginning one shortly."

"Who is doing the libretto for you?"

"Heinrich Bermann. Of course you scowl again."

"My dear George, I have always been very far from lecturing you in any way about the people you associate with. It is quite natural that you with your intellectual tastes should live in a different set and mix with different people to those I do, people whom I should probably find rather less to my taste. But so long as Herr Bermann's libretto is good you have my blessing . . . and Herr Bermann, of course, too."

" The libretto is not ready yet, only the scenario."

Felician could not help laughing. " So that's how your opera stands! I only hope the theatre is already built at which you are going to get a post as conductor."

" Come, come," said George, somewhat hurt.

" Forgive me," replied Felician, " I have not really any doubts about your future. I should only like you yourself to do a bit more towards it. I really should be so . . . proud, George, if you were to do anything great, and it, I'm sure, only depends on yourself. Willy Eissler, who is a man of genuine musical gifts, told me again only the other day that he thinks more of you than of most of the young composers."

" On the strength of the few songs of mine which he knows? You're a good fellow, Felician, but there is really no need for you to encourage me. I already know what I have got in me, only I must be more industrious, and my going away will do me quite a lot of good. It does one good to get out of one's usual surroundings for a time, like this. And this time it is quite different from last. It is the first time, Felician, that I have had anything to do with a person who is absolutely my equal, who is more . . . whom I can treat as a true friend as well, and the consciousness that I am going to have a child, and by her, too, is, in spite of all the accompanying circumstances, rather pleasant."

" I can quite understand that," said Felician, and contemplated George seriously and affectionately.

The clock on the writing-table struck two.

" What, so late already," cried Felician, " and I have got to pack early to-morrow. Well, we can talk over everything at breakfast to-morrow. Well, good-night, George."

" Good-night, Felician. Thank you," he added with emotion.

" What are you thanking me for, George? You really

are funny ! " They shook hands and then kissed each other, which they had not done for quite a long time, and George resolved to call his child Felician if it was to be a boy, and he rejoiced at the good omen of a name which had so happy a ring.

After his brother's departure George felt as deserted as though he had never had another friend. Living in the great lonely house, where he seemed to be weighed down by a mood like that which had followed the first weeks after his father's death, made him feel depressed.

He regarded the days which still had to elapse before the departure as a transition period, in which it was not worth while starting anything. The hours he spent with his mistress in the room opposite the church became colourless and blank. A psychological change, too, seemed to be now taking place in Anna herself. She was frequently irritable, then taciturn again, almost melancholy, and George was often overcome by so great a sense of *ennui* when he was with her that he felt quite nervous of the next month in which they would be thrown completely into each other's society. Of course the journey in itself promised change enough, but how would it be in the subsequent months which would have to be spent somewhere in the neighbourhood of Vienna ? He must also think about a companion for Anna ; but he was still putting off speaking to her about it, when Anna herself came to him with a piece of news which was calculated to remove that difficulty, and at the same time to raise another one, in the simplest way conceivable. Anna had recently, particularly since she had gradually given up her lessons, become more and more intimate with Therese, and had confided everything to her, and so it soon came about that Therese's mother was also in the secret. This lady was much more congenial to Anna than her own mother, who after a slight glimmer of understanding had held aloof, aggrieved and depressed, from her erring daughter.

Frau Golowski not only declared herself ready to live with Anna in the country, but even promised to discover the little house which George had not been able to find, while the young couple were away. However much this willingness suited George's convenience, he found it none the less somewhat painful to be under an obligation to this old woman, who was a stranger to him, and in moments when he was out of temper it struck him as almost grotesque that it should be Leo's mother and Berthold's father, of all people, who should be fated to play so important a part in so momentous an event in Anna's life.

George paid his farewell visit at Ehrenbergs' on a fine May afternoon three days before he went away.

He had only rarely shown himself there since that Christmas celebration and his conversations with Else had remained on the most innocent of footings. She confessed to him, as though to a friend who could not now misunderstand remarks of that character, that she felt more and more unsettled at home. In particular the atmosphere of the house, as George had frequently noticed before, seemed to be permanently overcast by the bad relations between father and son. When Oskar came in at the door with his nonchalant aristocratic swagger and began to talk in his Viennese aristocratic accent, his father would turn scornfully away, or would be unable to suppress allusions to the fact that he could make an end this very day of all that aristocracy by stopping or lowering his so-called allowance, which as a matter of fact was neither more nor less than pocket-money. If, on his side, his father began to talk Yiddish, as he was most fond of doing in front of company, and with obvious malice, Oskar would bite his lips and make a point of leaving the room. So it was only very rarely during the last few months that father and son stayed in Vienna or in Neuhaus at the same time. They both found each other's presence almost intolerable.

When George came in to Ehrenbergs' the room was almost in darkness. The marble Isis gleamed from behind the pianoforte, and the twilight of the late afternoon was falling in the alcove where mother and daughter sat opposite each other. For the first time the appearance of these two women struck George as somewhat strangely pathetic. A vague feeling floated up in his mind that perhaps this was the last time he would see this picture, and Else's smile shone towards him with such sweet melancholy, that he thought for a whole minute : might I not have found my happiness here, after all ?

He now sat next to Frau Ehrenberg (who was going on quietly knitting) opposite Else, smoked a cigarette and felt quite at home. He explained that, fascinated by the tempting spring weather, he was starting on his projected journey earlier than he had intended, and that he would probably prolong it until the summer.

" And we are going to Auhof as early as the middle of May this time," said Frau Ehrenberg, " and we certainly count upon seeing you down there this year."

" If you are not elsewhere engaged," added Else with a perfectly straight face.

George promised to come in August, at any rate for some days. The conversation then turned on Felician and Willy, who had started with their party a few days ago from Biskra on their hunting expedition in the desert ; on Demeter Stanzides, who announced his immediate intention of resigning from the army and retiring to an estate in Hungary ; and finally on Heinrich Bermann of whom no one had had any news for some weeks.

" Who knows if he will ever come back to Vienna at all ? " said Else.

" Why shouldn't he ? What makes you think that, Fräulein Else ? "

" Upon my word, perhaps he'll marry that actress and trot about the world with her."

George shrugged his shoulders . . . he didn't know personally of any actress with whom Heinrich was mixed up, and he ventured to express a doubt whether Heinrich would ever marry any one, whether she was a Princess or a circus rider.

" It would be rather a pity if Bermann were to," said Frau Ehrenberg, without taking any notice of George's discretion. " I certainly think that young people take these matters either too lightly or too seriously."

Else followed up the idea : " Yes, it is strange, all you men are either cleverer or much sillier in these matters than in any other, although really it is just in such crucial moments of one's life, that one ought as far as possible to be one's ordinary self."

" My dear Else," said George casually, " once one's passions are set going——"

" Yes, when they are set going," emphasised Frau Ehrenberg.

" Passions ! " exclaimed Else. " I believe that like all other great things in the world, they are really something quite rare."

" What do you know, my child ? " said Frau Ehrenberg.

" At any rate I've never so far seen anything of that kind in my immediate environment," explained Else.

" Who knows if you would discover it," remarked George, " even though it did come once in a way quite near you ? Viewed from outside a flirtation and a life's tragedy may sometimes look quite the same."

" That is certainly not true," said Else. " Passion is something that is bound to betray itself."

" How do you manage to know that, Else ? " objected Frau Ehrenberg. " Passions can often conceal themselves deeper than any ordinary trumpery little emotion, for the very reason that there is usually more at stake."

" I think," replied George, " that it is a very personal matter. There are, of course, people who have everything written on their forehead, and others who are impenetrable; being impenetrable is quite as much a talent as anything else."

" It can be trained too, like anything else," said Else.

The conversation stuck for a moment, as is apt to occur when the personal application that lies behind some general observation flashes out only too palpably.

Frau Ehrenberg started a new topic. " Have you been composing anything nice, George ? " she asked.

" A few trifles for the piano. My quintette will soon be ready too."

" The quintette is beginning to grow mythical," said Else discontentedly.

" Else ! " said her mother.

" Well, it really would be a good thing, if he were to be more industrious."

" You are perhaps right about that," replied George.

" I think artists used to work much more in former days than they do now."

" The great ones," qualified George.

" No, all," persisted Else.

" Perhaps it is a good thing that you are going to travel," said Frau Ehrenberg, " for apparently you've too many distractions here."

" He'll let himself be distracted anywhere," asserted Else sternly.   " Even in Iglau, or wherever else he happens to be next year."

" That's why I've never yet thought of your going away," said Frau Ehrenberg and shook her head ; " and your brother will be in Sophia or Athens next year and Stanzides in Hungary . . . it's really a great pity to think of all the nicest men being scattered like this to the four corners of the world."

" If I were a man," said Else, "I would scatter too."

George smiled. " You're dreaming of a journey round the world in a white yacht, Madeira, Ceylon, San Francisco."

" Oh no, I shouldn't like to be without a profession, but I should probably have been an officer in the merchant service."

" Won't you be kind enough "—Frau Ehrenberg turned to George—" to play us one or two of your new things ? "

" Delighted, I'm sure." He got up from the recess and walked towards the window into the darkness of the room. Else got up and turned on the light on top. George opened the piano, sat down and played his ballads.

Else had sat down in an arm-chair and as she sat there, with her arm resting on the side of the chair and her head resting on her arm in the pose of a *grande dame* and with the melancholy expression of a precocious child, George felt again strangely thrilled by her look. He was not feeling very satisfied with his ballad to-day, and was fully conscious that he was endeavouring to help out its effect by putting too much expression into his playing.

Hofrat Wilt stepped softly into the room and made a sign that they were not to disturb themselves. He then remained standing by the door leaning against the wall, tall, superior, good-natured, with his closely-cropped grey hair, until George ended his performance with some emphatic harmonies. They greeted each other. Wilt congratulated George on being a free man and being now able to travel South. " I'm sorry to say I can't do it," he added, " and all the same one has at times a vague notion that even though one were not to visit one's office for a year on end, not the slightest change would take place in Austria." He talked with his usual irony about his profession and his Fatherland. Frau Ehrenberg retorted that there was not a man who was more patriotic, and took his calling more seriously than he himself. He agreed. But he regarded Austria as an infinitely complicated instrument, which only a master could handle properly, and said that the only reason for its sounding badly so often was that every muddler tried his art upon it. " They'll go on knocking it about," he said dismally, "until all the strings break and the frame too."

When George went Else accompanied him into the empty room. She still had a few words to say to him about his ballads. She had particularly liked the middle movement. It had had such an inner glow. Anyway, she hoped he would have a good time on his journey.

He thanked her.

" So," she said suddenly, when he already had his hat in his hand, " it's really a case now of saying a final farewell to certain dreams."

" What dreams ? " he asked in surprise.

" Mine of course, which you are bound to have known about by this time."

George was very astonished. She had never been so specific. He smiled awkwardly and sought for an answer. " Who knows what the future will bring forth ? " he said at last lightly.

She puckered her forehead. " Why aren't you at any rate as straight with me as I am with you ? I know quite well that you are not travelling alone . . . I also know who is going with you . . . what is more I know the whole thing. Good gracious, what haven't I known since we have known each other ? "

And George heard grief and rage quivering below the surface of her words. And he knew that if he ever did make her his wife, she would make him feel that she had had to wait for him too long. He looked in front of him and maintained a silence that seemed at once guilty and defiant.

Then Else smiled brightly, held out her hand and said once again: " *Bon voyage*."

He pressed her hand as though he were bound to make some apology. She took it away from him, turned round and went back into the room. He still waited for a few seconds standing by the door and then hurried into the

street. On the same evening George saw Leo Golowski
again in the café, for the first time for many weeks. He
knew from Anna that Leo had recently had to put up
with a great deal of unpleasantness as a volunteer and
that that " fiend in human form " in particular had perse-
cuted him with malice, with real hatred in fact. It occurred to George to-day that Leo had greatly altered during
the short time in which he had not seen him. He looked
distinctly older.

" I'm very glad to get a chance of seeing you again
before I leave," said George and sat down opposite him at
the café table.

" You are glad," replied Leo, " that you happened to run
across me again, while I positively needed to see you once
again, that is the difference." His voice had even a
tenderer note than usual. He looked George in the face
with a kind, almost fatherly expression.

At this moment George no longer had any doubt that Leo
knew everything. He felt as embarrassed for a few
seconds as though he were responsible to him, was irritated
at his own embarrassment and was grateful to Leo for not
appearing to notice it. This evening they talked about
practically nothing except music. Leo inquired after the
progress of George's work, and it came about during the
course of the conversation that George declared himself
quite willing to play one of his newest compositions to
Leo on the following Sunday afternoon. But when they
took leave of each other, George suddenly had the unpleasant feeling of having passed with comparative success
a theoretical examination, and of being faced to-morrow
with a practical examination. What did this young man,
who was so mature for his years, really want of him ? Was
George to prove to him that his talent entitled him to be
Anna's lover or her child's father ? He waited for Leo's
visit with genuine repugnance. He thought for a minute
of refusing to see him. But when Leo appeared with all

13

that innocent sincerity which he so frequently liked to affect, George's mood soon became less harsh. They drank tea and smoked cigarettes and George showed him his library, the pictures which were hanging in the house, the antiquities and the weapons, and the examination feeling vanished. George sat down at the pianoforte, played a few of his earlier pieces and also his latest ones as well as the ballads, which he rendered much better than he had done yesterday at Ehrenbergs', and then some songs, while Leo followed the melody with his fingers, but with sure musical feeling. Eventually he started to play the quintette from the score. He did not succeed and Leo stationed himself at the window with the music and read it attentively.

" One can't really tell at all so far," he said. " A great deal of it indicates a dilettante with a lot of taste, other parts an artist without proper discipline. It's rather in the songs that one feels . . . but feels what ? . . . talent . . . I don't know. One feels at any rate that you have distinction, real musical distinction."

" Well, that's not so much."

" As a matter of fact it's pretty little, but it doesn't prove anything against you either, since you have worked so little—worked very little and felt little."

" You think . . ." George forced a sarcastic laugh.

" Oh, you've probably lived a great deal but felt . . . you know what I mean, George ? "

" Yes, I can imagine well enough, but you're really making a mistake ; why I rather think that I have a certain tendency to sentimentalism, which I ought to combat."

" Yes, that's just it. Sentimentalism, you know, is something which is the direct antithesis to feeling, something by means of which one reassures oneself about one's lack of feeling, one's essential coldness. Sentimentalism is feeling which one has obtained, so to speak, below cost price. I hate sentimentalism."

" Hm, and yet I think that you yourself are not quite free from it."

" I am a Jew, it's a national disease with us. Our respectable members are working to change it into rage or fury. It's a bad habit with the Germans, a kind of emotional slovenliness so to speak."

" So there is an excuse for you, not for us."

" There is no excuse for diseases either if, fully realising what one is doing, one has missed one's opportunity of protecting oneself against them. But we are beginning to babble in aphorism and are consequently only on the way to half or quarter truths. Let's go back to your quintette. I like the theme of the adagio best."

George nodded. " I heard it once in Palermo."

" What," said Leo, " is it supposed to be a Sicilian melody ? "

" No, it rippled to me out of the waves of the sea when I went for a walk one morning along the shore. Being alone is particularly good for my work, so is change of scene. That's why I promise myself all kinds of things from my trip." He told him about Heinrich Bermann's opera plot, which he found very stimulating. When Heinrich came back again, Leo was to make him seriously start on the libretto.

" Don't you know yet," said Leo, " his father is dead ? "

" Really ? When ? How do you know ? "

" It was in the paper this morning."

They spoke about Heinrich's relationship to the dead man and Leo declared that the world would perhaps get on better if parents would more frequently learn by the experiences of their children instead of asking their children to adapt themselves to their own hoary wisdom. The conversation then turned on the relations between fathers and sons, on true and false kinds of gratefulness, on the dying of people one held dear, on the difference between mourning and grief, on the dangers of memory and the duty of forgetting. George felt that Leo was a very serious thinker, was very solitary and knew how to be so. He felt almost fond of him when the door closed behind him in the late twilight hour and the thought that this man had been Anna's first infatuation did him good.

The remaining days passed more quickly than he anticipated, what with purchases, arrangements and all kinds of preparations. And one evening George and Anna drove after each other to the station in two separate vehicles and jestingly greeted each other in the vestibule with great politeness, as though they had been distant acquaintances who had met by accident.

" My dear Fräulein Rosner, what a fortunate coincidence ! are you also going to Munich by any chance ? "

" Yes, Herr Baron."

" Hullo, that's excellent ! and have you a sleeping-car, my dear Fräulein ? "

" Oh yes, Herr Baron, berth number five."

" How strange now, I have number six."

They then walked up and down on the platform. George was in a very good temper, and he was glad that in her English dress, narrow-brimmed travelling hat and blue veil Anna looked like an interesting foreigner. They went the length of the entire train until they came to the engine, which stood outside the station and was sending violent puffs of light-grey steam up to the dark sky. Outside green and red lamps glowed on the track with a faint light. Nervous whistles came from somewhere out of the distance and a train slowly struggled out of the darkness into the station. A red light waved magically to and fro over the ground, seemed to be miles away, stopped and was suddenly quite near. And outside, shining and losing themselves in the invisible, the lines went their way to near and far, into night and morning, into the morrow, into the inscrutable.

Anna climbed into the compartment. George remained

standing outside for a while and derived amusement from
watching the other travellers, those who were in an excited
rush, those who preserved a dignified calm, and those who
posed as being calm—and all the various types of people
who were seeing their friends off: the depressed, the jolly,
the indifferent.

Anna was leaning out of the window. George chatted
with her, behaved as though he had not the slightest idea
of leaving and then jumped in at the last minute. The
train went away. People were standing on the platform,
incomprehensible people who were remaining behind in
Vienna, and who on their side seemed to find all the others
who were now really leaving Vienna equally incomprehensible. A few pocket-handkerchiefs fluttered. The
station-master stood there impressively and gazed sternly
after the train. A porter in a blue-and-white striped linen
blouse held a yellow bag high up and looked inquisitively
into every window. Strange, thought George casually,
there are people who are going away and yet leave their
yellow bags behind in Vienna. Everything vanished,
handkerchiefs, bags, station-master, station. The brightly-
lighted signal-box, the Gloriette, the twinkling lights of
the town, the little bare gardens along the embankment ;
and the train whizzed on through the night. George turned
away from the window. Anna sat in the corner. She
had taken off her hat and veil. Gentle little tears were
running down her cheeks.

" Come," said George, as he embraced her and kissed her
on the eyes and mouth. " Come, Anna," he repeated
even more tenderly, and kissed her again. " What are you
crying for, dear ? It will be so nice."

" It's easy enough for you," she said, and the tears
streamed on down her smiling face.

They had a beautiful time. They first stopped in
Munich. They walked about in the lofty halls of the
Pinakothek, stood fascinated in front of the old darkening

pictures, wandered into the Glyptothek between marble
gods, kings and heroes ; and when Anna with a sudden
feeling of exhaustion sat down on a settee she felt
George's tender glance lingering over her head. They
drove through the English garden, over broad avenues
beneath the still leafless trees, nestling close to each
other, young and happy, and were glad to think that
people took them for a honeymoon couple. And they
had their seats next to each other at the opera, *Figaro*,
The Meistersingers, and *Tristan*, and they felt as though
a resonant transparent veil were woven around them
alone out of the notes they loved so well, which separated
them from all the rest of the audience. And they
sat, unrecognised by any one at prettily-laid little restaurant tables, ate, drank and talked in the best of spirits.
And through streets that had the wondrous atmosphere
of a foreign land, they wandered home to where the gentle
night waited for them in the room they shared, slept
peacefully cheek by cheek, and when they awoke there
smiled to them from the window a friendly day with
which they could do whatever they liked. They found
peace in each other as they had never done before, and
at last belonged to each other absolutely. Then they
travelled further to meet the call of the spring ; through
long valleys on which the snow shone and melted, then, as
though traversing one last white winter dream, over the
Brenner to Bozen, where they basked in the sunbeams at
noon in the dazzling market-place. On the weather-worn
steps of the vast amphitheatre of Verona, beneath the cool
sky of an Easter evening, George found himself at last in
sight of that world of his heart's desire into which a real
true love was now vouchsafed to accompany him. His
own vanished boyhood greeted him out of the pale reddish
distance together with all the eternal memories, in which
other men and women had their share as well. Why,
even a breath of those bygone days when his mother

had still lived seemed to thrill already through this
air with its familiar and yet foreign atmosphere. He
was glad to see Venice, but it had lost its magic
and was as well known as though he had only left
it yesterday. He was greeted in the Piazza St. Marco
by some casual Viennese acquaintances, and the veiled
lady by his side in the white dress earned many an inquisitive glance. Once only, late at evening, on a gondola
journey through the narrow canals did the looming palaces,
which in the daylight had gradually degenerated into
artificial scenery, appear to him in all the massive splendour of the dark golden glories of their past. Then came
a few days in towns, which he scarcely knew or did not
know at all, in which he had only spent a few hours
as a boy, or had never been in at all. They walked
into a dim church out of a sultry Padua afternoon, and
going slowly from altar to altar contemplated the simple
glorious pictures in which saints accomplished their
miracles and fulfilled their martyrdoms. On a dismal
rainy day a jolty gloomy carriage took them past a brick-
red fort, round which lay greenish-grey water in a broad
moat, through a market-square where negligently dressed
citizens sat in front of the café ; among silent mournful
streets, where grass grew between the cobble-stones, and
they had perforce to believe that this pitifully-dying petty
town bore the resounding name of Ferrara. But they
breathed again in Bologna, where the lively flourishing
town does not simply content itself with a mere pride in
its bygone glories. But it was only when George gazed
at the hills of Fiesole that he felt himself greeted as it
were by a second home. This was the town in which he
had ceased to be a boy, the town in which the stream of
life had begun to course through his veins. At many
places memories floated up in his mind which he kept to
himself ; and when in the cathedral, where the Florentine
girl had given him her final look from beneath her bridal

veil, he only spoke to Anna about that hour in the Altler-
chenfelder Church in that autumn evening, when they had
both begun to talk with some dim presentiment about this
journey, which had now become realised with such inconceivable rapidity. He showed Anna the house in
which he had lived nine years ago. The same shops
in which coral-dealers, watch-makers and lace-dealers
hawked their wares were still underneath. As the second
story was to let George would have had no difficulty
in seeing immediately the room in which his mother
had died. But he hesitated for a long time to set foot
in the house again. It was only on the day before their
departure, as though feeling that he should not put it off
any more, that alone and without any previous word to
Anna, he went into the house, up the stairs and into the
room. The aged porter showed him round and did not
recognise him. The same furniture was still all there.

His mother's bedroom looked exactly the same as it had
done ten years ago, and the same brown wooden bed with
its dark-green silver embroidered velvet coverlet still
stood in the same corner. But none of the emotions which
George had expected stirred within him. A tired memory
which seemed flatter and duller than it had ever been
before, ran through his soul. He stayed a long time in
front of the bed with the deliberate intention of conjuring
up those emotions which he felt it was his duty to feel.
He murmured the word " mother," he tried to imagine
the way in which she had lain here in this bed for many
days and nights. He remembered the hours in which
she had felt better, and he had been able to read aloud
to her or to play to her on the piano in the adjoining
room. He looked at the little round table standing in the
corner over which his father and Felician had spoken in a
soft whisper because his mother had just gone to sleep ;
and finally there arose up in his mind with all the sharp
vividness of a theatrical scene the picture of that dreadful

evening, when his father and brother had gone out, and he
himself had sat at his mother's bedside quite alone with
her hand in his . . . he saw and heard it all over again.
He remembered how she had suddenly felt ill after an
extremely quiet day, how he had hurriedly opened the
windows and the laughter and speeches of strange people
had penetrated into the room with the warm March
air, how she lay there at last with open eyes that were
already blank, while her hair that only a few seconds
ago had streamed in waves over her forehead and temple
lay dry and dishevelled on the pillow, and her left arm hung
down naked over the edge of the bed with still fingers
stretched far apart. This image arose in his mind with
such terrible vividness that he saw again mentally his own
boyish face and heard once again his own long sobbing
. . . but he felt no pain. It was far too long ago—nearly
ten years.

" *E bellissima la vista di questa finestra,*" suddenly said
the porter behind him as he opened the window—and
human voices at once rang into the room from down below
just as they had done on that long-past evening. And
at the same moment he heard his mother's voice in his
ear, just as he had heard it then entreating, dying . . .
" George . . . George " . . . and out of the dark corner in
the place where the pillows had used to lie he saw something pale shine out towards him. He went to the window
and agreed : " *Bellissima vista,*" but in front of the beautiful view there lay as it were a dark veil. " Mother," he
murmured, and once again " Mother " . . . but to his
own amazement he did not mean the woman who had
borne him and had been buried long ago ; the word was
for that other woman, who was not yet a mother but who
was to be in a few months . . . the mother of a child
of which he was the father. And the word suddenly
rang out, as though some melody that had never been
heard or understood before, were now sounding, as though

bells with mystic chiming were swinging in the distant future. And George felt ashamed that he had come here alone, had, as it were, almost stolen here. It was now quite out of the question to tell Anna that he had been here.

The next day they took the train to Rome. And while George felt fresher, more at home, more in the vein for enjoyment, with each succeeding day, Anna began to suffer seriously from a feeling of exhaustion with increasing frequency. She would often remain behind alone in the hotel, while he strolled about the streets, wandered through the Vatican, went to the Forum and the Palatine. She never kept him back, but he nevertheless felt himself bound to cheer her up before he went out, and got into the habit of saying : " Well, you'll keep that for another time, I hope we shall soon be coming here again." Then she would smile in her arch way, as though she did not doubt now that she would one day be his wife ; and he himself could not help owning that he no longer regarded that development as impossible. For it had gradually become almost impossible for him to realise that they were to say goodbye for ever and to go their several ways this autumn. Yet during this period the words with which they spoke about a remote future were always vague. He had fear of it, and she felt that she would be doing well not to arouse that fear, and it was just during these Roman days, when he would often walk about alone in the foreign town for hours on end, that he felt as though he were at times slipping away from Anna in a manner that was not altogether unpleasant.

One evening he had wandered about amid the ruins of the Imperial Palace until the approach of dusk and from the height of the Palatine Hill he had seen the sun set in the Campagna with all the proud delight of the man who is alone. He had then gone driving for a while along the ancient wall of the city to Monte Pincio, and when as

he leant back in the corner of his carriage he swept the
roofs with his look till he saw the cupola of St. Peter's,
he felt with deep emotion that he was now experiencing
the most sublime hour of the whole journey. He did not
get back to the hotel till late, and found Anna standing
by the window pale and in tears, with red spots on her
swollen cheeks. She had been dying of nervousness for
the last two hours, had imagined that he had had an
accident, had been attacked, had been killed. He reassured her, but did not find the words of affection which
she wanted, for he felt in some unworthy way a sense of
being tied and not free. She felt his coldness and gave
him to understand that he did not love her enough; he
answered with an irritation that verged on despair. She
called him callous and selfish. He bit his lip, made no
further answer, and walked up and down the room. Still
unreconciled they went into the dining-room, where they
took their meal in silence, and went to bed without saying
good-night.

The following days were under the shadow of this scene.
It was only on the journey to Naples, when they were alone
in the compartment, that in their joy over the new scenery
to which they were flying they found each other again.
From henceforward he scarcely left her a single minute,
she seemed to him helpless and somewhat pathetic. He
gave up visiting museums since she could not accompany
him. They drove together to Posilippi and walked in
the Villa Nationale. In the excursion through Pompeii
he walked next to her sedan-chair like a patient affectionate
husband, and while the guide was giving his descriptive
account in bad French, George took Anna's hand, kissed it
and endeavoured in enthusiastic words to make her share
in the delight that he himself felt once more in this
mysterious roofless town, which after a burial of two
thousand years had gradually returned street by street,
house by house, to meet the unchanging light of that

azure sky.   And when they stopped at a place where some
labourers were just engaged in extricating with careful
movements of their shovels a broken pillar out of the
ashes he pointed it out to Anna with eyes which shone as
brightly as though he had been storing up this sight for
her for a long time, and as though everything which
had happened before had simply been leading up to the
fulfilment of his purpose of taking her to this particular
place at this particular minute and showing her this
particular wonder.

On a dark blue May night they lay in two chairs covered
with tarpaulins on the deck of the ship that was taking
them to Genoa.   An old Frenchman with clear eyes, who
had sat opposite them at dinner, stood near them for a
while and drew their attention to the stars that hung in
the infinitude like heavy silver drops.   He named some of
them by name, politely and courteously, as though he
felt it incumbent upon him to introduce to each other the
shining wanderers of heaven and the young married couple.
He then said good-night and went down into his cabin.
But George thought of his lonely journey over the same
route and under the same sky in the previous spring after
his farewell from Grace.   He had told Anna about her,
not so much from any emotional necessity, as in order to
free his past from that atmosphere of sinister mystery in
which it often seemed to Anna to disappear, by the conjuring up into life of a specific shape and the designation
of a specific name.   Anna knew of Labinski's death, of
George's conversation with Grace at Labinski's grave, of
George's stay with her in Sicily.   He had even shown her
a picture of Grace ; and yet he thought to himself with
a slight shudder how little Anna herself knew of this
very epoch of his life, which he had described to her with
an almost reckless lack of reserve ; and he felt how
impossible it was to give any other person any idea of a
period which that person had not actually lived through,

and of the contents of so many days and nights every minute of which had been full of vivid life. He realised the comparative insignificance of the little lapses from truth of which he frequently allowed himself to be guilty in his narrative, compared with that ineradicable taint of falseness to which every memory gives birth on its short journey from the lips of one person to the ear of another. And if Anna herself at some later time wanted to describe to some friend, some new lover, as honestly as she possibly could, the time which she spent with George, what after all could that friend really learn ? Not much more than a story such as he had read hundreds of times over in books : a story of a young creature who had loved a young man, had travelled about with him, had felt ecstasy and at times tedium, had felt herself at one with him, and yet had frequently felt lonely. And even if she should make an attempt to give a specific account of every minute . . . there still remained an irrevocable past, and for him who has not lived through it himself the past can never be the truth.

The stars glistened above him. Anna's head had sunk slowly upon his breast and he supported it gently with his hands. Only the slight ripple in the depths betrayed that the ship was sailing onward. But it still went on towards the morning, towards home, towards the future.

The *hour* which had loomed over them so long in silence seemed now about to strike and to begin. George suddenly felt that he no longer had his fate in his own hand. Everything was going its course. And he now felt in his whole body, even to the hairs of his head, that the ship beneath his feet was relentlessly hurrying forward.

They only remained a day in Genoa. Both longed for rest, and George for his work as well. They meant to stay only a few weeks at an Italian lake and to travel home in the middle of June. The house in which Anna was going to live would be bound to be ready by then. Frau Golowski had found out half-a-dozen suitable ones, sent specific

details to Anna and was waiting for her decision, though
she still continued looking for others in case of emergency.
They travelled from Milan to Genoa, but they could not
stand the noisy life of a town any longer and left for
Lugano the very next day.

They had been staying here for a period of four weeks
and every morning George went along the road which took
him, as it did to-day, along the cheerful shore of the lake,
past *Paradiso* to the bend, where there was a view which
every time he longed to see again. Only a few days of
their stay were still before them. In spite of the excellent
state of Anna's health since the beginning of their stay
the time had arrived to return to the vicinity of Vienna,
so as to be able to be ready confidently for all emergencies.
The days in Lugano struck George as the best he had experienced since his departure from Vienna. And he asked
himself during many a beautiful moment, if the time he
was spending here was not perhaps the best time of his
whole life. He had never felt himself so free from desire,
so serene both in anticipation and memory, and he saw with
joy that Anna also was completely happy. Expectant
gentleness shone in her forehead, her eyes gleamed with
arch merriment, as at the time when George had wooed for
their possession. Without anxiety, without impatience
and lifted by the consciousness of her budding motherhood
far above the memory of home prejudices or any question
of future complications, she anticipated with ecstasy the
great hour when she was to give back to the waiting world as
an animate creature, that which her body had drunk in
during a half-conscious moment of ecstasy. George saw
with joy the maturing in her of the comrade that he had
hoped to find in her from the beginning, but who had so
frequently escaped him in the course of the last few months.
In their conversations about his works (all of which she
had carefully gone through), about the theory of the song,
about the more general musical questions, she revealed

to him more knowledge and feeling than he had ever
suspected she had in her. And he himself, though he did
not actually compose much, felt as though he were making
real strides forward. Melodies resounded within him,
harmonies heralded their approach, and he remembered
with deep understanding a remark of Felician's, who had
once said after he had not had a sword in his hand for
months on end, that his arm had had some good ideas
during this period. The future, too, occasioned him no
anxiety. He knew that serious work would begin as soon
as he got back to Vienna, and then his way would lie
before him, clear and unencumbered.

George stood for a long time by the bend in the road
which had been the object of his walk. A short broad
tongue of land, thickly overgrown with low shrubs, stretched
from here straight into the lake, while a narrow gently
sloping path led in a few steps to a wooden seat which
was invisible from the street and on which George was
always accustomed to sit down a little before returning to
the hotel.

" How many more times," he could not help thinking
to-day. " Five or six times perhaps and then back to
Vienna again." And he asked himself what would happen
if they did not go back, if they settled down in some house
somewhere in Italy or Switzerland, and began to build up
with their child a new life in the double peacefulness of
Nature and distance. What would happen ? . . . Nothing.
Scarcely any one would be particularly surprised. And
no one would miss either him or her, miss them with real
grief. These reflections made his mood flippant rather
than melancholy ; the only thought that made him depressed was that he was frequently overcome by a kind of
homesickness, a kind of desire in fact to see certain specific
persons. And even now, while he was drinking in the lake
air, surrendering himself to the blue of this half foreign,
half familiar sky above him and enjoying all the pleasure

of solitude and retirement, his heart would beat when he thought of the woods and hills around Vienna, of the Ringstrasse, the club and his big room with the view of the Stadtpark. And he would have felt anxious if his child had not been going to be born in Vienna. It suddenly occurred to him that another letter from Frau Golowski must have arrived to-day together with many other communications from Vienna, and he therefore decided to take the road round by the post-office before going back to the hotel. For following his habit during the whole trip he had his letters addressed there and not to the hotel, since he felt that this would give him a freer hand in dealing with any outside emergency. He did not, as a matter of fact, get many letters from Vienna. There was usually in spite of their brevity a certain element in Heinrich's letters which, as George quite appreciated, was less due to any particular need of sympathy on the part of the author than to the circumstance that it was an integral part of his literary calling to breathe the breath of life into all the sentences which he wrote. Felician's letters were as cool as though he had completely forgotten that last heartfelt talk in George's room and that brotherly kiss with which they had taken leave of each other. . . . He presumes, no doubt, thought George, that his letters will be read by Anna too, and does not feel himself bound to give this stranger an insight into his private affairs and his private feelings. Nürnberger had sent a few short answers to George's picture-postcards, while in answer to a letter from Rome, in which George had referred to his sincere appreciation of the walks they had had together in the early spring, Nürnberger expressed his regret in ironically apologetic phrases that he had told George on those excursions such a lot about his own family affairs which could not interest him in the slightest. A letter from old Eissler had reached him at Naples, informing him that there was no prospect of a vacancy for the following year at the

Detmold Court Theatre, but that George had been invited through Count Malnitz to be present at the rehearsals and performances as a " visitor by special request," and that this was an opportunity which might perhaps pave the way to something more definite in the future. George had given the proposition his polite consideration, but had little inclination for the time being to stay in the foreign town for any length of time with such vague prospects, and had decided to look out for a permanent appointment as soon as he arrived at Vienna.

Apart from this there was no personal note in any of the letters from home. The remembrances to him which Frau Rosner felt in duty bound to append to her letters to her daughter made no particular appeal, although recently they had been addressed not to the Herr Baron but to George. He felt certain that Anna's parents were simply resigned to what they could not alter, but that they felt it grievously all the same, and had not shown themselves as broad-minded as would have been desirable.

In accordance with his habit George did not go back along the bank. Passing through narrow streets between garden walls, then under arcades and finally over a wide space from which there was another clear view of the lake, he arrived in front of the post-office, whose bright yellow paint reflected the dazzling rays of the sun. A young lady whom George had already seen in the distance walking up and down the pavement, remained standing as he approached. She was dressed in white and carried a white sunshade spread out over a broad straw hat with a red ribbon. When George was quite near she smiled, and he now suddenly saw a well-known face beneath the white spotted tulle veil.

" Is it really you, Fräulein Therese ? " he exclaimed as he took the hand which she held out to him.

" How do you do, Baron ? " she replied innocently, as

14

though this meeting were the most ordinary event imaginable. " How is Anna ? "

" Very well, thanks. Of course you will come and see her ? "

" If I may."

" But tell me now, what are you doing here ? Can it be that you "—and his glance swept her in amazement from top to toe—" are making a political tour ? "

" I can't exactly say.that," she replied, pushing out her chin, without that movement having its usual effect of making her face appear ugly, " it's more of a holdiay jaunt." And her face shone with a genuine smile as she saw George's glance turn towards the door, from which Demeter Stanzides had just come out in a striped black-and-white flannel suit. He lifted his grey felt hat in salutation and shook hands with George.

" Good-morning, Baron. Glad to see you again."

" I am very glad, too, Herr Stanzides."

" No letter for me ? " Therese turned to Demeter.

" No, Therese. Only a few cards for me," and he put them in his pocket.

" How long have you been here ? " inquired George, endeavouring to exhibit as little surprise as possible.

" We arrived yesterday," replied Demeter.

" Straight from Vienna ? " asked George.

" No, from Milan. We have been travelling for eight days. We were first in Venice, that is the orthodox thing to do," added Therese, pulled down her veil and took Demeter's arm.

" You been away much longer ? " said Demeter. " I saw a card from you some weeks back at Ehrenbergs', the house of the Vettii, Pompeii."

" Yes, I've had a wonderful trip."

" Well, we'll have a look round the place a bit," said Therese, " and besides, we don't want to detain the Baron any more. I am sure he wants to go and fetch his letters."

" Oh, there is no hurry about that. Anyway, we'll see each other again."

" Will you give us the pleasure, Baron," said Demeter, " of lunching with us to-day at the Europe ? That's where we put up."

" Thanks very much, but I'm afraid it's impossible. But . . . but perhaps you could manage to dine with . . , with . . . us at the Park Hotel, yes ? At half-past seven if that's all right for you. I'll have it served in the garden, under an awfully fine plane-tree, where we usually take our meals."

" Yes," said Therese, " we accept with thanks. Perhaps I'll come in an hour earlier and have a quiet chat with Anna."

" Good," replied George, " she will be very glad."

" Well, till the evening, Baron," said Demeter, shook hands with him heartily and added: " Please give my kind regards at home."

Therese flashed George an appreciative look, and then went on her way with Demeter towards the bank of the lake.

George looked after them. If I hadn't known her, he thought, Demeter could have introduced her to me straight away as his wife, née Princess X. How strange, those two. . . . He then went into the hall, had his correspondence given to him at the counter and ran cursorily through it. The first thing which caught his eye was a card from Leo Golowski. There was nothing on it except " Dear George, mind you have a good time." Then there was a card from the Waldsteingarten in the Prater, " We have just emptied our glasses to the health of our runaway friend. Guido Schönstein, Ralph Skelton, the Rattenmamsell."

George wanted to read the letters from Felician, Frau Rosner and Heinrich quietly at home with Anna. He was also in a hurry to inform Anna of the news of the

strange couple's arrival. He was not quite free from
anxiety, for Anna's conventional instincts had a knack
of waking up occasionally in a quite unexpected manner.
Anyway, George decided to tell her of his invitation to
Demeter and Therese as though it were an absolute matter
of course and was quite ready, in case she should feel
hurt or irritated or even have doubts about the matter,
to oppose such an attitude firmly and resolutely. He
himself was very glad of the evening which was before
him after the many weeks that he had spent exclusively in
Anna's society. He almost felt a little envious of Demeter,
who was on an irresponsible pleasure-trip like he himself
when he had gone travelling with Grace in the previous
year. Then it occurred to him that he liked Therese
better than ever. In spite of the numerous pretty women
whom he had met in the course of the last month he had
never felt seriously tempted, even though Anna was losing
more and more of her womanly grace. To-day for the
first time he felt a desire for new embraces.

He soon saw Anna's light-blue morning dress shining
through the railings of the balcony. George whistled the
first notes of Beethoven's Fifth Symphony, which was his
usual method of announcing himself, and the pale gentle
face of his beloved immediately appeared over the railings
and her big eyes greeted him with a smile. He held up
the packet of letters, she nodded with pleasure and he
hurried quickly up to her room and on to the balcony.
She was reclining in a cane chair in front of the little
table with the green coverlet, on which some needlework
was lying, as was nearly always the case when George
came home from his morning walk. He kissed her on the
forehead and on the mouth. "Well, whom do you think
I met?" he asked hurriedly.

"Else Ehrenberg," answered Anna, without considering.

"What an idea? How could she get here?"

"Well," said Anna slyly, "she might have travelled off to find you."

"She might, but she didn't. So guess again. I give you three guesses."

"Heinrich Bermann."

"Nowhere near it. Besides there is a letter from him. So guess again."

She reflected. "Demeter Stanzides," she then said.

"What, do you really know something?"

"What should I know? Is he really here?"

"By Jove, you are positively blushing. Ho ho!" He knew of her weakness for Demeter's melancholy cavalier beauty but did not feel the slightest trace of jealousy.

"So it is Stanzides?" she asked.

"Yes, it is Stanzides right enough. But with all the will in the world I can't find anything remarkable about that. It's not remarkable, either. But if you guess whom he is with . . . "

"With Sissy Wyner."

"But . . ."

"Well, I was thinking of marriage. . . . That happens too sometimes."

"No, not with Sissy, and not married, but with your friend Therese, and as unmarried as possible."

"Get along. . . ."

"I tell you, with Therese. They've been travelling for eight days. What have you got to say to that? They have been in Venice and Milan. Had you any idea of it?"

"No."

"Really not?"

"Really not. You know of course that Therese only once wrote me a line, and you read her letter with your well-known interest."

"You're not astonished enough."

"Good gracious, I always knew that she had good taste."

"So has Demeter," exclaimed George with conviction.

"Elective affinities," remarked Anna, elevating her eyebrows, and went on crocheting.

"And so this is the mother of my child," said George, with a merry shake of his head.

She looked at him with a smile. "When is she coming to see me, then?"

"In the afternoon about six, I think. And . . . and Stanzides is coming too . . . a bit later. They are going to dine with us. You don't mind?"

"Mind? I'm very glad," replied Anna simply.

George was agreeably surprised. If Anna in her present condition had met Stanzides in Vienna! . . . he thought. How being away from one's usual environment frees and purifies!

"What news did they tell you?" asked Anna.

"We stood chatting together at the post-office for scarcely three minutes. He sends his regards to you, by the way."

Anna made no answer and it seemed to George as though her thoughts were travelling again on extremely conventional lines.

"Have you been up long?" he asked quickly.

"Yes, I have been sitting here on the balcony for quite a long time. I even went to sleep a bit, the air is so enervating to-day somehow. And I dreamed, too."

"What did you dream about?"

"Of the child," she said.

"Again?"

She nodded. "Just the same as the other day. I was sitting here on the balcony in my dream, and had it in my arms at the breast . . ."

"But what was it, a boy or a girl?"

"I don't know. Just a child. So tiny and so sweet.

And the joy was so . . . No I won't give it up," she said softly with closed eyes.

He stood leaning on the railing and felt the light noon wind stroke his hair. " If you don't want to give it out to nurse," he said, " well you mustn't." And the thought ran through his mind, " Wouldn't it be the most convenient thing to marry her ? . . ." But something or other kept him back from saying so. They were both silent. He had laid the letters in front of him on the table. He now took them up and opened one. " Let's see, first, what your mother writes ? " he said.

Frau Rosner's letter contained the news that all was well at home, that they would all be very glad to see Anna again, and that Josef had got a post on the staff of the *Volksbote* with a salary of fifty gulden a month. Further, an inquiry had come from Frau Bittner as to when Anna was coming back from Dresden, and if it was really certain that she would be back again next autumn, because otherwise they would of course have to look about for a new teacher. . . . Anna stood motionless and expressed no opinion.

Then George read out Heinrich's letter. It ran as follows :

" DEAR GEORGE,

" I am very glad that you will be back so soon, and prefer to tell you so to-day, because once you are there I shall never tell you how very glad I shall be to see you. A few days ago, when I went for a lonely cycle ride along the Danube, I genuinely missed you. What an overwhelming atmosphere of loneliness these banks have ! I remember having once felt like that five or six years ago on a Sunday, when I was in what is technically known as ' jolly company,' and was sitting in the Kloster-neu-burger beer-house in the large garden with its view of the mountains and the fields. How it ascends from the depths

of the waters, loneliness I mean, which certainly is quite
a different thing to what one usually thinks it is. It is
very far from being the opposite of society. Yet it is only
perhaps when one is with other people that one has a
right to feel lonely. Just take this as an aphoristical
humorously untrue special supplement, or treat it as such
and lay it aside. To come back to my ride along the
banks of the Danube—it was on that same rather sultry
evening that I had all kinds of good ideas, and I hope soon
to be able to tell you a lot of startling news about Ägidius,
for that's the name that the murderous melancholy youth
has got at last, about the deep-thinking impenetrable
prince, about the humorous Duke Heliodorus, the name
by which I have the honour of introducing to you the
Princess's betrothed, and especially about the princess
herself, who seems to be a far more remarkable person
than I originally supposed."

"That's to do with the opera plot?" asked Anna,
dropping her work.

"Of course," replied George, and went on reading.

"You must also know, my dear friend, that I have
finished during the last week some verses for the first act,
which so far are not particularly immortal, verses which
until some further development, so long I mean, as they are
without your music, will hop about the world like wingless
angels. The subject-matter appeals to me extraordinarily,
and I myself am curious to know what I am really going
to make of it. I've begun all kinds of other things as well
. . sketched things out . . . thought things over. And
to put it shortly and with a certain amount of cheek I
feel as though a new phase were heralding itself within me.
This sounds of course greater cheek than it really is. For
chimney-sweeps, ice-cream vendors and colour-sergeants
have their phases as well. People of our temperament
always recognise it at once. What I regard as very probable is that I shall soon leave the fantastic element in

which I now feel so much at home, and will either move up or move down into something extremely real. What would you say, for example, if I were to go in for a political comedy ? I feel already that the word 'real' is not quite the right one. For in my view politics is the most fantastic element in which persons can possibly move, the only thing is they don't notice it. . . . This is the point I ought to drive home. This occurred to me the other day when I was present at a political meeting (untrue, I always get these thoughts). Yes—a meeting of working men and women in the Brigittenau in which I found myself next to Mademoiselle Therese Golowski, and at which I was compelled to hear seven speeches about universal suffrage. Each of the speakers—Therese was one of them, too—spoke just as though the solution of that question was the most important thing in the world to him or her personally, and I don't think that any of them had an idea that the whole question was a matter of colossal indifference to them at the real bottom of their hearts. Therese was very indignant of course when I enlightened her on the point, and declared that I had been infected by the poisonous scepticism of Nürnberger, of whom as a matter of fact I'm seeing far too much. She always makes a point of running him down, since he asked her some time ago in the café whether she was going to have her hair done high or in plaits at her next trial for high treason. Anyway, I find it very nice seeing a lot of Nürnberger. When I'm having my bad days, there is no one who receives me with more kindness. Only there are many days whose badness he doesn't suspect or doesn't want to know of. There are various troubles which I feel that he fails to appreciate and which I've given up talking to him about."

" What does he mean ? " interrupted Anna.

" The affair with the actress, clearly," replied George, and went on reading.

" On the other hand he is inclined to make up for that by taking other troubles of mine too seriously. That is probably my fault and not his. He manifested a sympathy towards me for the loss I sustained by my father's death, which I confess made me positively ashamed ; for though it hit me dreadfully hard we had grown so aloof from one another quite a long time before his madness burst upon him, that his death simply signified a further and more ghastly barrier rather than a new experience."

" Well ? " asked Anna, as George stopped.

" I've just got an idea."

" What is it ? "

" Nürnberger's sister lies buried in the Cadenabbia cemetery. I told you about her. I'll run over one of these days."

Anna nodded. " Perhaps I'll go too, if I feel all right. From all I hear of him I find Nürnberger much more sympathetic than that horrible egoist your friend Heinrich."

" You think so ? "

" But really, the way he writes about his father. It is almost intolerable."

" Hang it all ! if people who have grown so estranged as those two——"

" All the same, I haven't really very much in common with my own parents temperamentally either, and yet . . . If I . . . No, no, I prefer not to talk about such things. Won't you go on reading ? "

George read :

" There are more serious things than death, things which are certainly sadder, because these other things lack the finality which takes away the sadness of death, if viewed from the higher standpoint. For instance, there are living ghosts who walk about the streets in the clear daylight with eyes that have died long ago and yet see, ghosts who sit down next to one and talk with a human voice that has a far more distant ring than if it came from a grave. And one might go so far as to say that the essential awfulness of death is revealed to a far greater extent in moments when one has experiences like this, than at those times when one stands near and watches somebody being lowered into the earth . . . however near that somebody was."

George involuntarily dropped the letter and Anna said with emphasis: "Well, you can certainly keep him to yourself—your friend Heinrich."

"Yes," replied George slowly. "He is often a bit affected, and yet . . . hallo, there goes the first bell for lunch. Let's read quickly through to the end."

"But I must now tell you what happened yesterday: the most painful and yet ridiculous affair which I have come across for a long time, and I am sorry to say the persons concerned are our good friends the Ehrenbergs, father and son."

"Oh," cried Anna involuntarily.

George had quickly run through the lines which followed and shook his head.

"What is it ? " inquired Anna.

"It is . . . Just listen," and he went on reading.

"You are no doubt aware of the growing acuteness of the relations between Oskar and the old man in the course of the last year. You also know the real reasons for it, so that I can just inform you of what has taken place without going into the motives for it any further. Well, it's just like this. Yesterday Oskar passes by the Church of St. Michael about twelve o'clock midday and takes off his hat. You know that at the present time piety is about the smartest craze going, and so perhaps it is unnecessary to go into any further explanation, as, for example, that a few young aristocrats happened just to be coming out of

church and that Oskar wanted to behave as a Catholic for
their special benefit. God knows how often he has previously
been guilty of this imposture without being found out,
but as luck would have it, it happens yesterday that old
Ehrenberg comes along the road at the same moment. He
sees Oskar taking off his hat in front of the church door . . .
and attacked by a fit of uncontrollable rage he gives his
offspring a box on the ears then and there. A box on the
ears ! Oskar the lieutenant in the reserve ! Midday in
the centre of the town ! So it is not particularly remarkable
that the story was known all over the town the very same
evening. It is already in some of the papers to-day. The
Jewish ones leave it severely alone, except for a few
scandal-mongering rags, the Anti-Semitic ones of course
go for it hot and strong. The *Christliche Volksbote* is
the best, and insists on both the Ehrenbergs being brought
before a jury for sacrilege or blasphemy. Oskar is said to
have travelled off, no one knows where, for the time being."

"A nice family !" said Anna with conviction.

George could not help laughing against his will. "My
dear girl, Else is really absolutely innocent of the whole
business."

The bell rang for the second time. They went into the
dining-room and took their places at a little table by the
window which was always laid for them alone. Scarcely
more than a dozen visitors were sitting at the long table
in the middle of the room, mostly Englishmen and French-
men, and also a man no longer in the first flush of youth,
who had been there for two days and whom George took
for an Austrian officer in *mufti*. Anyway he bothered
about him as little as he did about the others. George
had put Heinrich's letter in his pocket. It occurred to him
that he had not yet read it through to the end, and he took
it out again over the coffee and perused the remainder.

"What more does he write ?" asked Anna.

" Nothing special," answered George. " About people who probably wouldn't interest you particularly. He seems to have got in again with his café set ; more in fact than he likes and clearly more than he owns up to."

" He'll fit in all right," said Anna flippantly.

George smiled reflectively. " It is a funny set anyway."

" And what is the news with them ? " asked Anna.

George had put the letter down by the cup and now looked a. it. " Little Winternitz. . . . you know . . . the fellow who once recited his poems to me and Heinrich last winter . . . is going to Berlin as reader to a newly-founded theatre. And Gleissner, the man who stared at us once so in the museum . . ."

" Oh yes, that abominable fellow with the eyeglass."

" Well, he declares that he is going to give up writing to devote himself exclusively to sport. . . ."

" To sport ? "

" Yes, quite a sport of his own. He plays with human souls."

" What ? "

" Just listen." He read :

" This buffoon is now asserting that he is simultaneously engaged in the solution of the two following psychological problems, which supplement each other in quite an ingenious way. The first is to bring a young and innocent creature to the lowest depth of depravity, while the second is to make a prostitute into a saint, as he puts it. He promises that he will not rest until the first one finishes up in a brothel, and the second one in a cloister."

" A nice lot," remarked Anna and got up from the table.

" How the sound carries over here," said George and followed her into the grounds.

A dark-blue day, heavy with the sun, was resting on the tops of the trees. They stood for a while by the low balustrade which separated the garden from the street and looked over the lake to the mountains looming behind silver-grey veils that fluttered in the sunlight. They then walked deeper into the grounds, where the shade was cooler and darker, and as they walked arm-in-arm over the softly-crunching gravel along the high brown ivy-grown walls, and looked in at the old houses with their narrow windows, they chatted about the news that had arrived that day, and for the first time a slight anxiety rose up in their minds at the thought that they would so soon have to leave the friendly secrecy of foreign lands for home, where even the ordinary stereotyped day seemed full of hidden dangers. They sat down beneath the plane-tree at the white lacquered table. This place had always been kept free for them, as though it had been reserved. The newly-arrived Austrian gentleman, however, had sat there yesterday afternoon, but driven away by a disapproving glance of Anna's had gone away after a polite salutation.

George hurried up to his room and fetched a few books for Anna and a volume of Goethe's poems and the manuscript of his quintette for himself. They both sat there, read, worked, looked up at times, smiled at each other, exchanged a few words, peered again into their books, looked over the balustrade into the open, and felt peace in their souls and summer in the air. They heard the fountain plashing quite near them behind the bushes, while a few drops fell upon the surface of the water. Frequently the wheels of a carriage would crunch along on the other side of the high wall, at times faint distant whistles would sound from the lake, and less frequently human voices would ring into the garden from the road along the bank. The day, drunken to the full with sunlight, lay heavy on the tree-tops. Later on the noise and the voices increased in volume and number with the gentle wind which was wafted from the lake every afternoon. The beat of the waves on the shore was more audible. The cries of the boatman resounded : on the other side of the wall there rang out the singing of young people. Tiny drops from the fountain were sprinkled around. The breath of approaching evening woke once more human beings, land and water.

Steps were heard on the gravel. Therese, still in white, came quickly through the avenue. George got up, went a few steps to meet her and shook hands. Anna wanted to get up, too, but Therese would not allow it, embraced her, gave her a kiss on the cheek and sat down by her side. "How beautiful it is here!" she exclaimed; "but haven't I come too early?"

"What an idea! I'm really awfully glad," replied Anna.

Therese considered her with a scrutinising smile and took hold of both her hands. "Well, your appearance is reassuring," she said.

"I am very well, as a matter of fact," replied Anna, "and you look as if you were too," she joked good-humouredly.

George's eyes rested on Therese, who was again dressed in white, as she had been in the morning, though now more smartly in English embroidered linen, with a string of light pink corals round her bare throat.

While the two women were discussing the strange coincidence of their meeting George got up to give the orders for dinner. When he returned to the garden the two others were no longer there. He saw Therese on the balcony with her back leaning against the railing, talking with Anna, who was invisible and was presumably in the depths of the room. He felt in good form and walked up and down the avenue, allowed melodies to sing themselves within him, was conscious of his youth and happiness, threw an occasional glance up to the balcony or towards the street, beyond the balustrade, and at last saw Demeter Stanzides arriving. He went to meet him. "Glad to see you," he cried out in welcome from the garden gate. "The ladies are upstairs in the room but will be turning up soon." Would you like to have a look at the grounds in the meanwhile?"

"Delighted."

They went on walking together.

"Do you intend to stay much longer in Lugano?" asked George.

"No, we go to-morrow to Bellaggio, from there to Lake Maggiore, Isola Bella. A really good time never lasts. We have got to be home again in a fortnight."

"Such short leave?"

"Oh, it is not on my account, but Therese has got to go back. I am quite a free man. I have already sent in my papers."

"So you seriously mean to retire to your estate?"

"My estate?"

"Yes, I heard something to that effect at Ehrenbergs'."

"But I haven't got the estate yet, you see. It is simply in the stage of negotiations."

"And where are you going to buy one? if it is not a rude question."

"Where the foxes say good-night to each other. The last place you would think of. On the Hungarian-Croatian frontier, very lonely and remote but very remarkable. I have a certain sympathy for the district. Youthful memories. I spent three years there as a lieutenant. Of course I think I shall grow young again there. Well, who knows?"

"A fine property?"

"Not bad. I saw it again two months ago. I knew it of course in the old days, it then belonged to Count Jaczewicz, finally to a manufacturer. Then his wife died. He now feels lonely down there and wants to get rid of it."

"I don't know," said George, "but I imagine the neighbourhood a little melancholy."

" Melancholy ! Well, it seems to me that at a certain period of one's life every neighbourhood acquires a melancholy appearance." And he looked round the balcony, as though to evolve from his surroundings a new proof of the truth of his words.

" At what period ? "

" Well, when one begins to get old."

George smiled. Demeter struck him as so handsome and as still young in spite of the grey hairs on his temple. " How old are you then, Herr Stanzides? if it isn't a rude question."

" Thirty-seven. I don't say I am old, but I am getting old. Men usually begin to talk about getting old when they have been old for a long time."

They sat down on the seat at the end of the garden, just where it runs into the wall. They had a view of the hotel and of the great terrace on the garden. The upper storeys with their verandahs were hidden from them by the foliage of the trees. George offered Demeter a cigarette and took one himself. And both were silent for a while.

" I heard that you, too, are leaving Vienna," said Demeter.

" Yes, that's very probable . . . if of course I get a job in some opera. Well, even if it isn't this year it is bound to be next."

Demeter sat with legs crossed over each other, gripped one of them tightly by the knee, and nodded. " Yes, yes," he said, and blew the smoke slowly through his lips in driblets. " It is really a fine thing to have a talent. In that case one is bound to feel a bit different sometimes, even about beginning to grow old. That is really the one thing I could envy a man for."

" You have no reason to at all. Anyway, people with talent are not really to be envied. At any rate, only people with genius. And I envy them probably even

15

more than you do. But I think that talents like yours
are something much more definite, something much
sounder so to speak. Of course one doesn't always happen
to be in form. . . . But at any rate, one always achieves
something quite respectable if one can do anything at all,
while people in my line, if they are not in form are no
better than old age pensioners."

Demeter laughed. " Yes, but an artistic talent like
yours lasts longer and develops more and more as the
years go on. Take Beethoven, for instance. The Ninth
Symphony is really the finest thing he did. Don't you
think so. And what about the second part of *Faust*?
. . . While we are bound to go back as the years go on
—we can't help it—even the Beethovens amongst us.
And how early it begins, apart from quite rare exceptions! I was at my prime for instance at twenty-five.
I've never done again what I had in me at twenty-five.
Yes, my dear Baron, those were times."

" Come, I remember seeing you win a race two years
ago against Buzgo, who was the favourite then. . . . Why,
I even betted on him. . . ."

" My dear Baron," interrupted Stanzides, " you take
it from me, I know the reason why I left off improving.
One can feel a thing like that oneself. And that's why
no one knows so well as the sportsman when he's beginning to grow old. And then no further training is any
good. The whole thing then becomes purely artificial.
And if any one tells you that that's not the case, then he's
simply . . . but here come the ladies."

They both got up. Therese and Anna were approaching arm-in-arm, one all in white, the other in a black
dress, which falling to the ground in wide folds completely
hid her figure. The couples met by the fountain.

Demeter kissed Anna's hand. " What a beautiful spot
I have the good fortune to see you again in, my dear
lady."

" It is a pleasant surprise to me, too," replied Anna, " quite apart from the scenery."

" Do you know," said George to Anna, " that these good people are travelling off again to-morrow ? "

" Yes, Therese has told me."

" We want to see as much as possible," explained Demeter, " and so far as my recollection goes the other lakes in upper Italy are even more magnificent than the one here."

" I don't know anything about the others," said Anna. " We haven't done them yet."

" Well, perhaps you will take the opportunity," said Demeter, " and make up a party with us for a little tour : Bellaggio, Pallanza, Isola Bella."

Anna shook her head. " It would be very nice but unfortunately I can't get about enough. Yes, I am incredibly lazy. There are whole days when I never go out of the grounds. But if George fancies running away from me for a day or two, I don't mind at all."

" I have no intention at all of running away from you," said George. He threw a quick glance at Therese, whose eyes were sparkling and laughing.

They all strolled slowly through the garden while it gradually became dusk, and chatted about the places they had recently seen. When they came back to the table under the plane-tree it was laid for dinner and the fairy-lights were burning in the glass holders. The waiter was just bringing the Asti in a bucket. Anna sat down on the seat, which had the trunk of the plane-tree for its back. Therese sat opposite her and George and Demeter on either side.

The meal was served and the wine poured out. George inquired after their Viennese acquaintances. Demeter told them that Willy Eissler had brought back from his trip some brilliant caricatures both of hunters and of beasts. Old Ehrenberg had bought the pictures.

"Do you know about the Oskar affair yet?" said George.

"What affair?"

"Oh, the affair with his father in front of St. Michael's Church." He remembered that he had thought of telling Demeter the story some time back before the ladies had appeared, but that he had thought it right to suppress it. It was the wine, no doubt, which now loosened his tongue against his will. He told them briefly what Heinrich had written him.

"But this is an extremely sad business," said Demeter, very much moved, and all the others immediately felt more serious.

"Why is it a sad business?" asked Therese. "I think it is enough to make one laugh till one cried."

"My dear Therese, you don't consider the consequences it may have for the young man."

"Good gracious, I know well enough. It will make him impossible in a certain set, but that won't do more than make him realise what a silly ass he has been up to the present."

"Well," said George, "if Oskar really is one of those people who can be made to realise anything . . . But I really don't think so."

"Apart from the fact, my dear Therese," added Demeter, "that what you call realising doesn't necessarily mean seeing things in their proper light. All sets of people have their prejudices. Even you are not free from them."

"And what prejudices have we got, I should like to know?" cried Therese, and emptied her glass of wine angrily. "We only want to clear away certain prejudices, particularly the prejudice that there is this privileged caste who regard it as a special honour . . ."

"Excuse, me, Therese dear, but you are not at a meeting now, and I am afraid that the applause at the conclusion of your speech will turn out much fainter than you are accustomed to."

" Look here," Therese turned to Anna, " this is how a cavalry officer argues."

" I beg your pardon," said George, " the whole business has scarcely anything at all to do with prejudices. A box on the ears in the public street, even though it is from one's own father. . . . I don't think one has got to be an officer in the reserve or a student."

" That box on the ears," cried Therese, " gives me a real sense of relief. It represents the well-merited conclusion of a ridiculous and superfluous existence."

" Conclusion! We hope it's not that," said Demeter.

" My letter says," replied George, " that Oskar has travelled off, no one knows where."

" If I am sorry for any one in the business," said Therese, " it is certainly for the old man, who, good-hearted fellow that he is, is probably regretting this very day the unpleasant position in which he has placed his beastly snob of a son."

" Good-hearted!" exclaimed Demeter. " A millionaire! A factory owner! . . . My dear Therese . . . !"

" Yes, it does happen sometimes. He happens to be one of those people who are at one with us at the bottom of their soul. You remember the evening, Demeter, when you had the pleasure of seeing me for the first time. Do you know why I was at Ehrenbergs' then? . . . And do you know the object for which he gave me straight away a thousand gulden . . . ? To . . ." She bit her lips. " I mustn't say, that was the condition."

Suddenly Demeter got up and bowed to somebody who had just passed. It was the Austrian gentleman who had arrived yesterday. He lifted his hat and vanished in the darkness of the garden.

" Do you know that man?" asked George, after a few seconds. " I also seem to know him, but who is it?"

" The Prince of Guastalla," said Demeter.

" Really ! " exclaimed Therese involuntarily, and her eyes pierced into the darkness.

" What are you looking at him for ? " said Demeter. " He is just a man like any one else."

" He is supposed to be banished from Court," said George, " isn't he ? "

" I know nothing about that," replied Demeter, " but he is certainly not a favourite there. He recently published a pamphlet about certain conditions in our army, particularly the life of the officers in the provinces. It went very much against him, although as a matter of fact there is nothing really bad in it."

" He should have applied to me about that," said Therese. " I could have given him a tip or two."

" My dear child," said Demeter deprecatingly, " what you are probably referring to again is simply an exceptional case. You shouldn't jump at once into generalities."

" I am not generalising, but a case like that is sufficient to damn the whole. . . ."

" Don't make a speech, Therese. . . ."

" I am speaking about Leo."   Therese turned to George. " It is really awful what he has been going through this year."

George suddenly remembered that Therese was Leo's sister, as though it were a most remarkable thing which he had completely forgotten. Did he know that she was here and whom she was with ?

Demeter bit his lips somewhat nervously.

" There is an Anti-Semitic First-Lieutenant, you know," said Therese, " who rags him in a particularly mean way because he knows how Leo despises him."

George nodded. He knew all about it.

" My dear child," said Demeter, " I can't make it out, as I have already told you several times. I happen to know First-Lieutenant Sefranek, and I assure you it is possible to get on with him. He is not particularly clever, and it may be quite right to say that he has got no particular liking for the Israelites, but after all one must admit that there are a lot of so-called opprobrious Anti-Semitic expressions which really have no significance at all, and which, so far as my experience goes, are used by Jews quite as much as by Christians. And your worthy brother certainly suffers from a morbid sensitiveness."

" Sensitiveness is never morbid," retorted Therese. " It is only lack of sensitiveness which is a disease, and the most loathsome one I know as a matter of fact. It is notorious that I am as far apart as possible from my brother in my political views. You know that best of all, George. I hate Jewish bankers quite as much as feudal landed proprietors, and orthodox Rabbis quite as much as Catholic priests ; but if a man feels himself superior to me because he belongs to another creed or another race than I do, and being conscious of his greater power makes me feel that superiority, I would . . ♦ Well, I don't know what I would do to a man like that. But anyway I should quite understand Leo if he were to take the next opportunity of going tooth-and-nail for Herr Sefranek."

" My dear child," said Demeter, " if you have the slightest influence with your brother you should try and stop this tooth-and-nail business at any price. In my view by far the best thing to do in a case like that is to go about things in the respectable, I mean the regulation way. It is really not at all true that that never does any good. The superior officers are mostly quiet people, at any rate they are correct and . . ."

" But Leo did that long ago . . . as far back as February. He went to the Major, the Major was very nice to him, and as appears from many indications gave the first-lieutenant a good talking to ; the only thing is it unfortunately wasn't the slightest use. On the contrary, the next chance he had the First-Lieutenant made a special point of starting his beastly tricks again, and he is continuing them with the most refined malice. I assure you, Baron, I am afraid every single day that some misfortune will happen."

Demeter shook his head. " We live in a mad age. I assure you "—he turned to George—" First-Lieutenant Sefranek is no more of an Anti-Semite than you or I. He visits at Jewish houses. I even know that he was extremely intimate for years with a Jewish regimental doctor. It really seems as though everybody were going mad."

" You may be right in that," said Therese.

" Oh, well, Leo is so reasonable," said George. " He is so sensible in spite of all his temperament that I am convinced that he won't let himself be swept away by any foolish impulse. After all he must know that it will all be over in a few months; one can manage to put up with it for that time."

" Do you know, by-the-by, Baron," said Therese, while following the example of the men she took a cigarette out of a box which the waiter had brought, " do you know that Leo was quite charmed with your compositions ? "

" What, charmed ? " said George, while he gave Therese a light. " I really hadn't noticed it at all."

" Well, he liked some things," qualified Therese, " and that's practically the same as somebody else being delighted with them."

" Have you composed anything on your trip ? " asked Demeter courteously.

" Only a few songs."

" I suppose we shall hear them in the autumn ? " said Demeter.

" Good gracious, don't let's talk about the autumn," said Therese. " We may be dead or in prison before then."

" Well, if one really wants to one can manage to avoid the latter alternative," exclaimed Demeter.

Therese shrugged her shoulders. George was sitting near her and believed he could feel the warmth of her body. Lights were shining from the hotel windows and a long reddish strip reached the table at which the two couples were sitting.

" I suggest," said George, " that we make the best of the fine evening and go for another walk along the shore."

" Or take a boat," exclaimed Therese.

They all agreed. George ran up to the room to fetch wraps. When he came down again he found the others standing by the door of the grounds ready to start. He helped Anna into her light-grey cloak, hung his own long overcoat over Therese's shoulders and kept a dark-green rug over his arm. They went slowly through the avenue to the place where the boats were moored. Two boatmen took the party with quick strokes of their oars out of the darkness of the shore into the black shining water. The mountains towered up to the sky, monstrous and gigantic. The stars were not very numerous. Tiny bluish-grey clouds hung in the air. The rowers sat on two cross benches ; in the middle of the boat on narrow seats the two couples sat opposite each other : George and Anna, Demeter and Therese. All were quite silent at first, it was only after some minutes that George broke the silence. He told them the name of the mountain which separated the lake from the South, drew their attention to a village, which though it seemed infinitely far away as it nestled up to the slope of a cliff could nevertheless be reached in a quarter of an hour ; he recognised the white shining house on the height above Lugano as the hotel in which Demeter and Therese were staying and told them about a walk far into the country between sunny vineyards which he had taken the other day.

While he spoke Anna kept hold of his hand underneath the rug. Demeter and Therese sat next to each other staidly and correctly, and not at all like lovers who had only found each other a short time ago. It was only now that George gradually recovered his fancy for Therese, which had almost vanished during her loud violent speechifying.

How long will this Demeter affair last ? he thought. Will it be over when the autumn comes or will it after all last as long or longer than my affair with Anna? Will this row on the dark lake be some time in the future just a memory of something that has completely vanished, just like my row on the Veldeser Lake with that peasant girl, which now comes into my mind again for the first time for years ? . . . Or like my voyage with Grace across the sea ? How strange ! Anna is holding my hand, I am pressing it, and who knows if she isn't feeling at this very minute something similar with regard to Demeter to what I am feeling about Therese ? No, I am sure not. . . . She carries a child under her heart which has already quickened. . . . That's why. . . . Hang it all ! . . . Why, it's my child as well. . . . Our child is now going for a row on the lake of Lugano. . . . Shall I tell it one day that it went for a row round the lake of Lugano before it was born ? How will it all turn out ? We shall be back in Vienna again in a few days. Does Vienna really exist ? It will only slowly begin to come into existence again as we train back. . . . Yes, that's how it is. . . . As soon as I'm home work will start seriously. I shall remain quietly at my home in Vienna and just visit Anna from time to time ; I won't live with her in the country. . . . Or at all events only just before . . . and the autumn. . . . Shall I be in Detmold ? And where will Anna be ? And the child ? . . . With strangers somewhere in the country. How improbable the whole thing seems ! . . . But it was also very improbable a year ago to-day that I and Stanzides should go for a row on the lake of Lugano with Fräulein Anna Rosner and Fräulein Therese Golowski respectively. And now the whole thing couldn't be more of a matter of course. . . . He suddenly heard with abnormal clearness, as though he had just woken up, Demeter's voice quite near him.

" When does our boat leave to-morrow ? "

" Nine o'clock in the morning," replied Therese.

" She maps out the plan of campaign you know," said Demeter. " I don't need to bother about anything."

The moon suddenly shone out over the lake.

It seemed as though it had waited behind the mountains and were now coming out to say goodbye. That infinitely distant village by the mountain-slope suddenly lay quite close in all its whiteness. The boat beached. Therese got up. She was shrouded in the night and looked strikingly tall. George sprang out of the boat and helped her to disembark. He felt her cool fingers, which did not tremble, in his hand, but moved softly as though on purpose, and caught the breath from her lips quite close. Demeter got out after her, then came Anna, tired and awkward. The boatman thanked them for their generous tip and both couples started to walk homewards. The Prince was sitting on a seat in a long dark cloak in the avenue along the bank. He was smoking a cigar, seemed to be looking out on to the nocturnal lake and turned away his head with the obvious intention of avoiding being saluted.

" A man like that could tell a tale," said Therese to George, with whom she had fallen further and further behind, while Demeter and Anna went on in front of them.

" So you are going back to Vienna as soon as all that ? " asked George.

" A fortnight. Do you think that so soon ? At any rate you will be home before us, won't you ? "

" Yes, we shall leave in a few days. We can't put it off any longer. Besides, we shall have to break the journey a few times. Anna doesn't stand travelling well."

" Do you know yet that I found the villa for Anna just before I left ? " said Therese.

" Really, you ? Did you go looking, too ? "

" Yes, I went into the country a few times with my mother. It is a small fairly old house in Salmansdorf with a beautiful garden, which leads straight out to the fields and forest, and the bit of ground in front of the house is quite overgrown. . . . Anna will tell you more about it. I believe it is the last house in the place. Then there comes an inn, but a fair distance away from it."

" I must have overlooked that house on my house-hunting expeditions in the spring."

" Clearly, or you would have taken it. There is a little clay figure standing on a lawn near the garden hedge."

" Can't remember. But do you know, Therese, it is really nice of you to have taken all this trouble for us, as well as your mother. More than nice." He thought of adding " when one takes your strenuous life into consideration," but suppressed it.

" Why are you surprised ? " asked Therese. " I am very fond of Anna."

" Do you know what I once heard some one say about you ? " replied George after a short pause.

" Well, what ? "

" That you would either finish up on the scaffold or as a princess."

" That's a phrase of Doctor Berthold Stauber. He once told it me himself, you know. He is very proud of it, but it is sheer nonsense."

" The betting at present is certainly more on the princess."

" Who says so ? The princess dream will soon be over ! "

" Dream ? "

" Yes, I am just beginning to wake up. It is rather like the morning air streaming into a bedroom."

" And then I suppose the other dream will begin ? "

" What do you mean, the other dream ? "

" This is what I take to be the case with you. When you are in the public eye again, making speeches, sacrific-

ing yourself for some cause or other, then at some
moment or other the whole thing strikes you like a
dream, doesn't it ? And you think real life is somewhere
else."

" There is really something in what you say."

At this moment Demeter and Anna, who were standing
by the garden gate, turned round towards them both
and immediately took the broad avenue towards the
entrance of the hotel. George and Therese also went on
further, unseen outside the railing, into the darkest depths
of the shade.

George suddenly seized hold of his companion's hand.
As though astonished she turned towards him and both
now stood opposite each other, enveloped by the darkness and closer than they could understand. They did
not know how . . . they scarcely meant to, but their lips
rested on each other for a short moment that was more
charged with the doleful joy of deception than with any
other emotion. They then went on, silent, unsatisfied, desirous, and stepped through the garden door.

The two others, who were in front of the hotel, now
turned round and came to meet them.

Therese quickly said to George: "Of course you don't
come with us ? "

George nodded slightly. They were now all standing
in the broad quiet light of the arc-lamps.

" It was really a beautiful evening," said Demeter,
kissing Anna's hand.

" Goodbye then till Vienna," said Therese and embraced Anna.

Demeter turned to George. " I hope we shall see each
other to-morrow morning on the boat."

" Possibly, but I won't promise."

" Goodbye," said Therese and shook hands with George.
She and Demeter then turned round to go away.

" Are you going with them ? " asked Anna, as they

went through the door into the lounge, where men and women were sitting, smoking, drinking, talking.

"What an idea?" replied George. "I never thought of it."

"Herr Baron," suddenly called some one behind him. It was the porter, who held a telegram in his hand.

"What is this?" asked George, somewhat alarmed, opening it quickly. "Oh, how awful!" he exclaimed.

"What is it?" asked Anna.

He read it out while she looked at the piece of paper. "Oskar Ehrenberg tried to commit suicide early this morning in the forest at Neuhaus. Shot himself in the temples, little hope of saving his life, Heinrich."

Anna shook her head. They went up the stairs in silence and into Anna's room. The balcony door was wide open. George stepped into the open air. A heavy perfume of magnolias and roses streamed in out of the darkness. Not a trace of the lake was visible. The mountains towered up as though they had grown out of the abyss. Anna came up to George. He laid his arm on her shoulder and loved her very much. It was as though the serious event of which he had just had tidings, had compelled him to realise the true significance of his own experiences. He knew once more that there was nothing more important for him in the whole world than the well-being of this beloved woman who was standing with him on the balcony and who was to bear him a child.

VI

WHEN George stepped on to the summer heat of the pavement out of the cool central restaurant where he had been accustomed to take his meals for some weeks, and started on his way to Heinrich's apartment, his mind was made up to start his trip into the mountains within the next few days. Anna was quite prepared for it, and appreciating that the monotonous life of the last few weeks was beginning to make him feel bored and mentally restless had even herself advised him to go away for a few days.

They had returned to Vienna six weeks ago on a rainy evening and George had taken Anna straight from the station to the villa, where Anna's mother and Frau Golowski had been waiting for the overdue travellers for the last two hours in a large but fairly empty room, with a dilapidated yellowish carpet under the dismal light of a hanging lamp. The door on to the garden verandah stood open. Outside the pattering rain fell on to the wooden floor and the warm odour of moist leaves and grass swept in. George inspected the resources of the house by the light of a candle which Frau Golowski carried in front of him, while Anna reclined exhausted in the corner of the large sofa covered with fancy calico and was only able to give tired answers to her mother's questions. George had soon taken leave of Anna with mingled emotion and relief, stepped with her mother into the carriage which was waiting outside, and while they rode over the dripping streets into the town he had given the em-

barrassed woman a faithful if forced account of the unimportant events of the last days of their trip. He was
at home an hour after midnight, refrained from waking
up Felician, who was already asleep, and with an undreamt-of joy stretched himself out in his long-lost bed
for his first sleep at home after so many nights.

Since then he had gone out into the country to see
Anna nearly every day. If he did not feel tempted to
make little trips round the summer resorts in the neighbourhood he could easily get to her in an hour on his
cycle. But he more frequently took the horse tram and
would then walk through the little villages till he came
to the low green painted railings behind which stood the
modest country house with its three-cornered wooden
gable in the small slightly sloping garden. Frequently
he would choose a way which ran above the village between garden and fields and would enjoy climbing up
the green slope till he came to a seat on the border of the
forest, from which he could get a clear view of the straggling little place lying in the tiny valley. He saw from
here straight on to the roof beneath which Anna lived,
deliberately allowed his gentle longing for the love who
was so near him to grow gradually more and more
vivid till he hurried down, opened the tiny door and
stepped over the gravel straight through the garden
towards the house. Frequently, in the more sultry hours
of the afternoon, when Anna was still asleep, he would
sit in the covered wooden verandah which ran along the
back of the house in a comfortable easy-chair covered
with embroidered calico, take out of his pocket a book
he had brought with him and read. Then Frau Golowski
in her neat simple dark dress would step out of the dark
inner room and in her gentle somewhat melancholy voice,
with a touch of motherly kindness playing around her
mouth, would report to him about Anna's health, particularly whether she had had a good appetite and if she

had had a proper walk up and down the garden. When
she had finished she always had something to see to in
the kitchen or about the house and disappeared. Then
while George was going on with his reading a fine St.
Bernard dog which belonged to people in the neighbourhood would come out, greet George with serious tearful
eyes, allow him to stroke her short-haired skin and lie
down gratefully at his feet. Later, when a certain stern
whistle which the animal knew well rang out, it would
get up with all the clumsiness of its condition, seem to
apologise by means of a melancholy look for not being
able to stay longer and slink away. Children laughed
and shouted in the garden next door. Now and again
an indiarubber ball came over the wall. A pale nursemaid would then appear at the bottom gate and shyly
request to have the ball thrown back again. Finally,
when it had grown cooler, Anna's face would show itself
at the window that opened on to the verandah, her quiet
blue eyes would greet George, and soon she would come out
herself in a light house-dress. They would then walk up
and down the garden along the faded lilac-bushes and the
blooming currant-bushes, usually on the left side, which
was bounded by the open meadow, and they would take
their rest on the white seat close to the top end of the
garden, underneath the pear-tree. It was only when
supper was served that Frau Golowski would appear again,
shyly take her place at the table and tell them if asked
all the news about her family ; about Therese, who had
now gone on to the staff of a Socialist journal ; about Leo,
who being less occupied by his military duties than before
was enthusiastically pursuing his mathematical studies ;
and about her husband, who while he looked on with
resignation from the corner of a smoky café at the chess
battles of the indefatigable players, always saw new
vistas of regular employment display themselves only to
close again immediately. Frau Rosner only paid an

16

occasional visit and usually went away soon after George's appearance. On one occasion, on a Sunday afternoon, the father had come as well and had a conversation with George about the weather and scenery, just as though they had met by chance at the house of a mutual acquaintance who happened to be ill. It was only to humour her parents that Anna kept herself in complete retirement in the villa. For she herself had grown to lose all consciousness of any false position, feeling just as though she had been George's wedded wife, and when the latter, tired of the monotonous evenings, asked her for permission to bring Heinrich along sometimes she had agreeably surprised him by immediately expressing her agreement.

Heinrich was the only one of George's more intimate friends who still remained in town in these oppressive July days. Felician, who had been as affectionate with his brother since his return home as though the comradeship of their boyhood had been kindled afresh, had just taken his diplomatic examination and was staying with Ralph Skelton on the North Sea. Else Ehrenberg, who had spoken to George once soon after his return by her brother's sick-bed in the sanatorium, had been for a long time at Auhof am See with her mother. Oskar too, whom his unfortunate attempt at suicide had cost his right eye, though it was said to have saved him his lieutenant's commission, had left Vienna with a black shade over his blinded eye. Demeter Stanzides, Willy Eissler, Guido Schönstein, Breitner, all were away, and even Nürnberger, who had declared so solemnly that he did not mean to leave the town this year, had suddenly vanished.

George had visited him before any one else after he came back, to bring him some flowers from his sister's grave in Cadenabbia. He had read Nürnberger's novel on his journey. The scene was laid in a period which was now almost past; the same period, so it seemed to George, as that of which old Doctor Stauber had once spoken to him.

Nürnberger had thrown a grim light over that sickly
world of lies in which adult men passed for mature, old
men for experienced, and people who did not offend
against any written law for righteous ; in which love of
freedom, patriotism and humanitarianism passed *ipso
facto* for virtue, even though they had grown out of the
rotten soil of thoughtlessness or cowardice. He had
chosen for the hero of his book a sterling and energetic
man who, carried away by the hollow phrases of the
period, saw things as they were from the height which he
had reached and seized with horror at the realization of
his own dizzy ascent, precipitated himself into the void
out of which he had come. George was considerably
astonished that a man who had created this strong and
resounding piece of work should subsequently confine
himself to casual cynical comments on the progress of the
age, and it was only a phrase of Heinrich's to the effect that
wrath but not loathing was fated to be fertile that made
him understand why Nürnberger's work had been stopped
for ever. The lonely hour in the Cadenabbia cemetery
on that dark blue late afternoon had made as strange
and deep an impression upon George as though he had
actually known and appreciated the being by whose
grave he stood. It had hurt him that the gold lettering
on the grey stone should have grown faint and that the
beds of turf should have been overgrown with weeds,
and after he had plucked a few yellow-blue pansies for
his friend he had gone away with genuine emotion. He
had cast a glance from the other side of the cemetery
door through the open window of the death-chamber,
and saw a female body on a bier between high burning
candles, covered with a black pall as far as her lips, while
the daylight and candlelight ran into one another over
its small waxen face.

Nürnberger had not been unmoved by this sympathetic attention on the part of George and on that day

they spoke to each other more intimately than they had ever done before.

The house in which Nürnberger lived was in a narrow gloomy street which led out of the centre of the town and mounted in terraces towards the Danube. It was ancient, narrow and high. Nürnberger's apartment was on the fifth and top storey, which was reached by a staircase with numerous turns. In the low though spacious room into which George stepped out of a dark hall stood old but well-preserved furniture, while an odour of camphor and lavender came insistently out of the alcove in the recess in front of which a pale green curtain had been let down. Portraits of Nürnberger's parents in their youth hung on the wall together with brown engravings of landscapes after the Dutch masters. Numerous old photographs in wooden frames stood on the sideboard. Nürnberger fetched a portrait of his dead sister out of a secretary-drawer where it lay beneath some letters that had been yellowed by time. It showed her as a girl of eighteen in a child's costume which seemed to have a kind of historical atmosphere, holding a ball in her hand, and standing in front of a hedge, behind which there towered a background of cliffs. Nürnberger introduced all these unknown faraway and dead persons to his friend to-day by means of their portraits, and spoke of them in a tone which seemed to make the gulf of time between the then and the now both wider and deeper.

George's glance often swept out over the narrow street towards the grey masonry of ancient houses. He saw small cobwebbed panes with all kinds of household utensils behind them. Flower-pots with miserable plants stood on a window-ledge, while fragments of bottles, broken-up barrels, scraps of paper, mouldy vegetables lay in a gutter between two houses, a battered pipe ran down between all this rubbish and disappeared behind a chimney. Other chimneys were visible to right and left, the back of a yellowish stone gable could be seen, towers reared up towards the pale blue heaven and a light grey spire with a broken stone cupola which George knew very well, appeared unexpectedly near. Automatically his eyes tried to find the quarter where he might be able to fix the position of the house in whose entrance the two stone giants bore on their powerful shoulders the armorial bearings of a vanished stock, and in which his child, which was to come into the world in a few weeks, had been begotten.

George gave an account of his trip. He felt the spirit of this hour so deeply that he would have thought himself petty if he had let the matter rest at half-truths. But Nürnberger had known the story, and in its entirety too, long ago, and when George showed a little astonishment at this he smiled mockingly.

" Don't you still remember," he asked, " that morning when we looked over a summer residence in Grinzing ? "

" Of course."

" And don't you remember too that a woman with a little child in her arms took us round the house and garden ? "

" Yes."

" Before we went away the child held out its arms towards you, and you looked at it with a certain amount of emotion in your expression."

" And that's what made you conclude that I. . . ."

" Oh well, you know, you're not the man to go in for thrills over the sight of small children, a bit unwashed, too, into the bargain, if they are not linked on to associations of a personal character."

" One must beware of you," said George jestingly, but not without some sense of uneasiness.

The slight irritation, which he always felt again and again at Nürnberger's superior manner, was far from preventing him from cultivating his society more and more. He frequently fetched him from home to go for walks in the

streets and parks, and he felt a sense of satisfaction, a
sense in fact of personal triumph, when he managed to
draw him from the rarefied regions of bitter wisdom into
the gentler fields of affectionate intercourse. George's
walks with him had become such a pleasant habit that he
felt as though his daily life had been impoverished when
he found one morning that Nürnberger's apartment was
closed. Some days afterwards came a card of apology from
Salzburg, which was also signed by a married couple, a
manufacturer and his wife, good-natured cheery people,
whom George had once got to know slightly through Nürnberger in Graben. According to Heinrich's malicious
description the common friend of this married couple
had been dragged down the stairs, of course after a desperate
resistance, made to sit down in a carriage and been transported to the station more or less like a prisoner. According
to Heinrich, too, Nürnberger had several friends of this
innocent kind who felt the need of getting the celebrated
cynic to let a few drops of his malice trickle into their
palatable cup of life, while Nürnberger on his side liked
to recuperate in their free-and-easy society from the strain
of his acquaintances in literary and psychological circles.

The meeting with Heinrich had meant a disillusionment
to George. After the first words of greeting the author had
as usual only spoken about himself, and that, too, in tones
of the deepest contempt. He had come at last to the
conclusion that he did not really possess any talent but
only intelligence, though that of course to an enormous
degree. The thing about himself that he cursed the most
violently was the lack of harmony in the various phases of
his character, which as he well knew not only occasioned
suffering to himself but to all who came near him. He
was heartless and sentimental, flippant and melancholic,
sensitive and callous, an impossible companion and yet
drawn towards his fellow-beings . . . at any rate at times.
A person with such characteristics could only justify his

existence by producing something immense, and if the
masterpiece which he felt obliged to create did not appear
on the scene very soon he would feel that as a decent
man he would be obliged to shoot himself. But he was not
a decent man. . . . There lay the rub. " Of course you
won't shoot yourself," thought George, " principally because
you haven't got the pluck to do so." Of course he did not
give expression to this thought but on the contrary was
very sympathetic. He talked of the moods to which
after all every artist is liable, and inquired kindly about the
material conditions of Heinrich's life. It soon transpired
that he wasn't in such a bad way by any means. He was
even leading a life which as it appeared to George was freer
from anxiety than it had ever been before. The main-
tenance of his mother and sisters for the ensuing years had
been assured by a small legacy. In spite of all the hostile
influences which were at work against him the fame of his
name was increasing from day to day. The miserable
affair with the actress seemed to be finished once and for
all, and a quite new relationship with a young lady which
was as free and easy as could possibly be desired, was
actually bringing a certain amount of gaiety into his life.
Even his work was making good progress. The first act of
the opera libretto was as good as ready, and he had made
numerous notes for his political comedy. He intended
next year to visit the sittings of Parliament and attend
meetings, and coquetted with the admittedly childish
fantastic plan of posing as a member of the social democratic party, trying to tack himself on to the leaders and
getting himself taken on, if he could get the chance, as an
active member of some organisation or other, simply so as
to get a complete insight into the party machinery. Still,
you know, when he had been talking to any one for five
minutes on end, why he had got him absolutely. He
would find in some casual word, whose significance would
completely escape any one else, a kind of whirlwind which

tore the veil from off the souls of men. His dream was to prove himself a master of imagination in his opera poem and a master of realism in his comedy, and thus show the world that he was equally at home both in heaven and on earth. At a subsequent meeting George got him to read as much of the first act of the opera as he had finished. He found the verses very singable and asked Heinrich to allow him to take the manuscript to Anna. Anna could not bring herself to fancy much what George read out to her; but he asserted, though without any real conviction, that what she felt was just the very longing for these verses to be set to music, and that that must necessarily strike her as a weakness.

When George came into Heinrich's room to-day the latter was sitting at the big table in the middle of the room, which was covered over with papers and letters. Written papers of all kinds lay about on the piano and on the ottoman. Heinrich still had a sheet of faded yellow paper in his hand when he got up and hailed George with the words, " Well, how goes the country ? "

This was the way in which he was accustomed to inquire after Anna's health, a way which George felt afresh every single time to be unduly familiar.

" Quite well, thanks," he replied. " I have just come to ask you if perhaps you would care to come out there with me to-day."

" Oh yes, I should like to very much. The thing is, though, that I am just in the middle of putting various papers in order. I can't come before the evening about seven or so. Will that suit you ? "

" Quite," said George. " But I see I am disturbing you," he added as he pointed to the littered table.

" Not at all," replied Heinrich. " I am only tidying up, as I just told you. They're my father's posthumous papers. Those there are letters to him and here are rough notes more or less like a diary, written for the most part

during his parliamentary period. Tragic, I tell you! How
that man loved his country! And how did they thank him?
You've no idea of the refinement with which they drove
him out of his party. A complicated network of intrigue,
bigotry, brutality. . . . Thoroughly German, to put the
matter in a nutshell."

George felt a sense of antagonism. "And he dares," he
thought, "to hold forth about Anti-Semitism. Is he any
better? any juster? Does he forget that I am a German
myself . . . ?"

Heinrich went on speaking. "But I will give this man
a memorial. . . . He and no other shall be the hero of
my political drama. He is the truly tragi-comic central
figure which I have always been wanting."

George's antagonism became intensified. He felt a
great desire to protect old Bermann against his son. "A
tragi-comic figure," he repeated, almost aggressively.

"Yes," retorted Heinrich unhesitatingly, "a Jew who
loves his country. . . . I mean in the way my father did,
with a real feeling of solidarity, with real enthusiasm for the
dynasty, is without the slightest question a tragi-comic
figure. I mean . . . he belonged to that Liberalising epoch
of the seventies and eighties when even shrewd men were
overcome by the catch-words of the age. A man like
that to-day would certainly appear merely comic. Yes,
even if he had finished up by hanging himself on the first
nail he came across I could not regard his fate as anything
else."

"It is a mania of yours," replied George. "You really
very often give one the impression that you have quite lost
the capacity of seeing anything else in the world except
the Jewish question, you always see it everywhere. If I
were as discourteous as you happen to be at times, I
would . . . you'll forgive me of course, say that you were
suffering from persecution-mania."

"Persecution-mania . . ." replied Heinrich dully, as

he looked at the wall. " I see, so you call it persecution-mania, that. . . . Oh well." And then he continued suddenly with clenched teeth : " I say, George, I want to ask you something on your conscience."

" I'm listening."

He placed himself straight in front of George, and with his eyes pierced his forehead. " Do you think there's a single Christian in the world, even taking the noblest, straightest and truest one you like, one single Christian who has not in some moment or other of spite, temper or rage, made at any rate mentally some contemptuous allusion to the Jewishness of even his best friend, his mistress or his wife, if they were Jews or of Jewish descent ? " And without waiting for George's answer : " There isn't one, I assure you. You can try another test also if you like. Read for instance the letters of any celebrated and otherwise perfectly shrewd and excellent man and observe the passages which contain hostile and ironic expressions about his contemporaries. Ninety-nine times out of a hundred it simply deals with an individual without taking any account of his descent or creed. In the hundredth case, where the miserable victim has the misfortune to be a Jew, the writer will certainly not forget to mention that fact. That's just how the thing is, I can't help it. What you choose to call persecution-mania, my dear George, is in reality simply an extremely intense consciousness that has been kept continuously awake of a condition in which we Jews happen to find ourselves. And as for talking about persecution-mania, why it would be much more logical to talk about a mania for being hidden, a mania for being left alone, a mania for being safe ; which though perhaps a less sensational form of disease is certainly a much more dangerous one for its victims. My father suffered from it, like many others of his generation. He at any rate made such a radical cure that he went mad in the process."

Deep furrows appeared on Heinrich's forehead and he looked again towards the wall, straight past George, who had sat down on the hard black leather ottoman.

" If that's your way of looking at things," replied George," why, you have no other logical alternative but to join Leo Golowski. . . ."

" And migrate to Palestine with him. Is that what you think ? As a matter of symbolical politics or actually— what ?" He laughed. " Have I ever said that I want to get away from here ? That I would prefer to live anywhere else except here ? Above all, have I ever said that I liked living among Jews ? So far as I at any rate am concerned that would be a purely objective solution of an essentially subjective problem."

" I really think so also. And that's why, to tell the truth, I understand less than ever what you want, Heinrich. I had the impression last autumn, when you had your tussle with Golowski on the Sophienalp, that you looked at the matter far more hopefully."

" More hopefully ? " repeated Heinrich in an injured tone.

" Yes. One felt bound to think then that you believed in the possibility of a gradual assimilation."

Heinrich contemptuously contracted the corners of his mouth. " Assimilation. . . . A phrase. . . . Yes, that'll come all right some time or other . . . in a very very long time. It won't come at all in the way many want it to— it won't come either in the way many are afraid it will. . . . Further, it won't be exactly assimilation . . . but perhaps something that beats in the heart of that particular word so to speak. Do you know what it will probably look like in the end ? That we, we Jews I mean, have been a kind of ferment in the brewing of humanity—yes, perhaps that'll come out in anything from one to two thousand years from now. It is a consolation. too. Don't you think so ? " He laughed again.

"Who knows," said George reflectively, "if you won't be regarded as right—in a thousand years? But till then?"

"Why, my dear George, there won't be anything in the way of a solution of the question before then. In our time there won't be any solution, that's absolutely positive. No universal solution at any rate. It will rather be a case of a million different solutions. For it's just a question which for the time being every one has got to settle for himself as best he can. Every one must manage to find an escape for himself out of his vexation or out of his despair or out of his loathing, to some place or other where he can breathe again in freedom. Perhaps there are really people who would like to go as far as Jerusalem to find it . . . I only fear that many of them, once they arrive at their official goal, would then begin to realise that they had made an utter mistake. I don't think for a minute that migrations like that into the open should be gone in for in parties. . . . For the roads there do not run through the country outside but through our own selves. Every one's life simply depends on whether or not he finds his mental way out. To do that of course it is necessary to see as clearly as possible into oneself, to throw the searchlight into one's most hidden crannies, to have the courage to be what one naturally is—not to be led into a mistake. Yes, that should be the daily prayer of every decent man : to make no mistake."

Where is he getting to again now? thought George. He is quite as morbid in his way as his father was. And at the same time one can't say that he has been personally through bad times. And he has asserted on one occasion that he felt there was no one with whom he had anything in common. It is not a bit true. He feels he has something in common with all Jews and he stands nearer to the meanest of them than he does to me. While these thoughts were running through his mind his glance fell on a big envelope lying on the table, and he read the following words written on it in large Roman capitals : " Don't forget. Never forget."

Heinrich noticed George's look and took the envelope up in his hand. Three strong grey seals could be seen on its back. He then threw it down again on the table, drooped his underlip contemptuously and said : " I've tidied up that business as well, you know, to-day. There are days like this when one goes in for a great cleaning-up. Other people would have burnt the stuff. What's the point ? I shall perhaps read it again with pleasure. The anonymous letters I once told you about are in this envelope, you know."

George was silent. Up to the present Heinrich had vouchsafed no information as to the circumstances under which his relations with the actress had come to an end. Only one passage in his letter to Lugano had hinted at the fact that it had not been without a certain deep-felt horror that he had seen his former mistress again. Almost against his own will the following words came out of George's mouth : " You know, of course, the story of Nürnberger's sister who lies buried in Cadenabbia ? "

Heinrich answered in the affirmative. " What makes you think of that ? "

" I visited her grave a few days before I came back." He hesitated. Heinrich was looking fixedly at him with a violently interrogative expression which compelled George to go on speaking. " Just think now, isn't it strange ? since that time those two persons are always associated together in my memory, though I have never seen one of them and have only caught a glimpse of the other one at the theatre—as you know. I mean Nürnberger's dead sister and . . . this actress."

Heinrich grew pale to his very lips. " Are you superstitious ? " he asked scornfully, but it sounded as though he were asking himself.

" Not at all," cried George. " Besides, what has superstition to do with this matter ? "

" I'll only tell you that everything that has any connection at all with mysticism goes radically against the grain with me. Lots of twaddle is passed off in the world for science, but talking about things which one can't know anything about, things whose very essence is that one can never know anything about them, is in my view the most intolerable twaddle of the whole lot."

" Can she have died, this actress ? " thought George.

Suddenly Heinrich took up the envelope again in his hand, and said in that dry tone which he liked to assume at those very moments when he was most deeply harrowed : " Writing out these words here is childish tomfoolery or affectation if you like. I could also have added the words Daudet put before his Sappho : ' To you, my son, when you are twenty years of age. . . .' Too silly, anyway. As though the experiences of one man could be the slightest use to another man. The experiences of one man can often be amusing for another, more often bewildering, but never instructive. . . . And do you know why it is that both those figures are associated in your brain ? I'll tell you why. Simply because in one of my letters I employed the expression ' Ghost ' with reference to my former mistress. So that clears up this mysterious embroglio."

" That's not impossible," replied George. From somewhere or other came the indistinct sound of bad piano-playing. George looked out. The sun lay on the yellow wall opposite. Many windows were open. A boy sat at one of them, his arms resting on the window-ledge, and read. From another two young girls looked down into the garden courtyard. The clattering of utensils was audible. George longed for the open air, for his seat on the border of the forest. Before he turned to go it occurred to him to say : " I wanted to tell you, Heinrich, that Anna too liked your verses very much. Have you written any more ? "

" Not many."

" It would be nice if you brought along to-day all you have done of the libretto and read it to us." He stood by the piano and struck a couple of chords.

" What's that ? " asked Heinrich.

" A theme," replied George " that's just occurred to me for the second act. It is meant to accompany the moment in which the remarkable stranger appears on the ship."

Heinrich shut the window, George sat down and started to go on playing. There was a knock at the door, and Heinrich automatically cried : " Come in."

A young lady came in in a light cloth skirt with a red silk blouse and a white velvet ribbon with a little gold cross round her neck. A Florentine hat trimmed with roses shaded with its broad brim the pale little face from which two big black eyes peered out.

" Good afternoon," said the strange lady in a low voice, which sounded at the same time both defiant and embarrassed. " Excuse me, Herr Bermann, I didn't know that you had visitors," and she looked inquisitively at George, who had at once recognised her.

Heinrich grew paler and puckered his forehead. " I certainly had no idea," he began. He then introduced them and said to the lady : " Won't you sit down ? "

" Thanks," she answered curtly and remained standing. " Perhaps I'll come again later."

" Please don't," cut in George. " I am just on the point of running off."

He watched the look of the actress roving round the room and felt a strange pity for her, such as one frequently feels in dreams for dead people who do not know that they have died. He then saw Heinrich's glance rest on this pale little face with inconceivable hardness. He now remembered very clearly seeing her on the stage, with the reddish-blonde hair that fell over her forehead and her roving eyes. " That's not how persons look," he thought, " who are fated to belong only to *one* man. And to think of Heinrich, who plumes himself so much on his knowledge of character, never having felt that! What did he really want of her ? It was vanity which burnt in his soul, nothing more than vanity."

George walked along the street, which was like a dry oven. The walls of the houses threw back into the air the summer heat which they had absorbed. George took the horse-tram to the hills and woods, and breathed more freely when he was in the country. He walked slowly on between the gardens and villas, then passing the churchyard he took a white road with a gradual incline called Sommerhaidenweg, which he regarded as a good omen, and which was used by practically nobody during this late hour of a sunny afternoon. No shade came from the wooded line of heights on his left, only a gentle purring of breezes which had gone to sleep in the leaves. On the right a green incline sloped downwards towards the long stretch of valley where roofs were gleaming between the boughs and tree-tops. Further down vineyards and tilled fields struggled up behind garden fences towards meadows and quarries, over which shrubbery and bushes hung in the glittering sun. The path along which George was accustomed to wander was just a thin straight line often lost among the fields, and his eye sought the place on the border of the forest where his favourite seat was situated : meadows and wooded heights at the end of the valley with fresh vales and hills. George felt himself strangely wedded to this landscape and the thought that his own career and his own will called him abroad often wove farewell moods around his lonely walks even now.

But at the same time a presentiment of a richer life stirred within him. It was as though many things were

coming to birth in his soul which he had no right to disturb
by anxious reflection ; and there was a murmur of the
melodies of days to come in the lower depths of his soul,
though it was not yet vouchsafed to him to hear them
clearly. He had not been idle, either, in drafting out
clearly the rough plan of his future. He had written a
letter of polite thanks to Detmold, in which he placed himself with reservation at the disposition of the manager for
the coming autumn. He had also looked up old Professor
Viebiger, explained his plans to him and requested him if
the opportunity presented itself to remember his former
pupil. But even though contrary to his expectations
he failed to find a position in the autumn he was determined to leave Vienna, to retire for the time being to a
small town or into the country, and to go on working by
himself amid the quietness. He had not clearly worked
out how his relations to Anna would shape under these
circumstances. He only knew that they must never end.
He thought vaguely that he and Anna would visit each
other and go on journeys together at some convenient time ;
subsequently no doubt she would move to the place where
he lived and worked. But it struck him as useless to go
deeply into these matters before the actual hour arrived,
since his own life had been definitely decided at any rate for
the coming year.

The Sommerhaidenweg ran into the forest, and George
took the broad Villenweg, which crossed the valley at this
point and curved downwards. In a few minutes he found
himself in the street, at the end of which stood the little
villa in which Anna lived. It was close to the forest,
near unpretentious yellow bungalows and only raised
above their level by its attic and balcony with its triangular
wooden gable. He crossed the plot of ground in front
of the house where the little blue clay angel welcomed
him on its square pedestal in the middle of the lawn
between the flower-beds, and went through the narrow

17

passage near which the kitchen lay, and the cool middle room on whose floor the rays of the sun were playing through the dilapidated green Venetian blinds and stepped on to the verandah. He turned towards the left and cast a glance through the open window into Anna's room, which he found empty. He then went into the garden and walking along the lilac and currant-bushes towards the bottom, soon saw Anna some way off, sitting on the white seat under the pear-tree in her loose blue dress. She did not see him coming, but seemed quite plunged in thought. He slowly approached. She still did not look up. He loved her very much at moments like this when she thought she was unobserved and the goodness and peacefulness of her character floated serenely around her clear forehead. The grasshoppers chirruped on the gravel at their feet. Opposite them on the grass the strange St. Bernard dog lay sleeping. It was the animal which first noticed George's arrival as it woke up. It got up and jogged clumsily towards George. Anna now looked up and a happy smile swept over her features. Why am I so seldom here? was the thought which ran through George's mind. Why don't I live out here and work on top on the balcony under the gable, which has a beautiful view on to the Sommerhaidenweg? His forehead had grown damp, for the late afternoon sun was still blazing.

He stood in front of Anna, kissed her on the eyes and mouth and sat down at her side. The animal had slunk after him and stretched itself out at his feet. " How are you, my darling? " he asked, while he put his arm around her neck.

She was very well, as usual, and to-day was a particularly fine day. She had been left quite to herself since the morning, for Frau Golowski had to go to town again to look after her family. It was really not so bad to be so completely alone with oneself. One could sink then into one's dreams undisturbed. They

were of course always the same, but they were so sweet
that one did not get tired of them. She had let herself
dream about her child. How much she loved it to-day,
even before it was born! She would never have considered it possible. Did George understand it too? . . .
And as he nodded absent-mindedly she shook her head.
No, no . . . a man could not understand that, even the
very best and kindest man. Why, she could feel the little
being already moving, could detect the beating of its
tender heart, could feel this new incomprehensible soul
breathe within her, just in the same way as she felt the
flowering and awakening within her of its fresh young
body. And George looked in front of him as though
ashamed that she was facing the near future. It was
true of course that a being would exist, begotten by
himself, like himself and itself destined again to give
life to new beings; it was true that within the blessed
body of that woman, for which he had ceased for a long
time now to feel any desire, there was swelling, according
to the eternal laws, a life that only a year ago had been
undreamt-of, unwished-for, lost in infinity, but which
now was forcing its way up to the light like something
predestined from time immemorial; it was true that he
knew that he was irresistibly drawn into that forged chain
that stretched from primal ancestor to future descendant
and which he grasped as it were with both hands . . .
but he did not feel that this miracle made so potent an
appeal to him as it really ought.

And they spoke to-day more seriously than usual about
what was to happen after the child's birth. Anna, of
course, would keep it with her during the first week, but
then they would have to give it to strangers; but at any
rate it should live quite near, so that Anna could see it
at any time without any difficulty.

" I say, dear," she said quite lightly and suddenly,
" will you often come and visit us ? "

He looked into her arch smiling face, took both her hands and kissed her. " Dearest, what am I to do ? Tell me yourself. You can imagine how hard it will be for me. But what else is there for me to do ? I've got to make a beginning. I've already told you we've given notice to leave the apartment," he added hastily, as though that cut off all retreat. " Felician is probably going to Athens. Yes, it would of course be fine if I could take you with me. But I am afraid that isn't possible. There ought above all to be something more or less certain, I mean one ought—ought at least to be certain that I shall remain in the same place for a longish time."

She had listened with quiet seriousness. She then started to speak about her latest idea. He must not believe, she said, that she was thinking of putting the whole burden of responsibility upon him. She was determined as soon as it was feasible to found a music-school. If he left her alone for a long time the school would be here in Vienna. If he soon came to fetch her it would be wherever she and he had their home. And when she was once in an independent position she meant to take and keep her child whether she was his wife or not. She was very far from being ashamed of it, he knew that quite well. She was rather proud . . . yes, proud of being a mother.

He took her hands in his and stroked them. It would all come right enough, he said, feeling somewhat depressed. He suddenly saw himself sitting at supper between wife and child, beneath the modest light of a hanging lamp in an extremely simple home. And this family scene of his imagination wafted towards him, as it were, an atmosphere of troubled boredom. Come, it was still too early for that, he was still too young. Was it possible, then, that she was to be the last woman whom he was to embrace ? Of course it might come in years, even in months, but not to-day. As for bringing lies and deceit into a well-ordered home, he had a horror of the idea. Yet the thought of rushing away from her to others whom he desired, with the consciousness that he would find Anna again just as he had left her, was at once tempting and reassuring.

The well-known whistle was heard from outside. The dog got up, made George stroke her yellow-spotted back once again and sadly slunk away.

" By Jove," said George, " I had almost forgotten all about it. Heinrich will be here any minute." He told Anna about his visit and did not suppress the fact that he had made the acquaintance of the faithless actress.

" Did she succeed then ? " exclaimed Anna, who did not fancy ladies with roving eyes.

" I don't think that she succeeded at all," replied George. " Heinrich was rather annoyed at her turning up, so far as I could see."

" Well, perhaps he'll bring her along too," said Anna jestingly, " then you will have some one to flirt with again, as you did with the regicide at Lugano."

" Upon my word," said George innocently, and then added casually : " But what's the matter with Therese ? why doesn't she come to see you any more ? Demeter is no longer in Vienna. She would have plenty of time."

" She was here only a few days ago. Why, I told you so. Don't pretend."

" I'd really forgotten it," he answered honestly. " What did she tell you then ? "

" All there was to tell. The Demeter affair is over. Her heart is throbbing once more only for the poor and the miserable—until it is called back." And Anna confided Therese's winter plans to him under the seal of a most rigid silence. Disguised as a poor woman she meant to undertake expeditions through shelters, soup- and tea-kitchens, refuges for the homeless and workmen's dwellings, with a view to shedding a light into the most hidden

corners for the benefit of the so-called golden heart of
Vienna.   She seemed quite ready for it and was perhaps
a little sanguine of discovering some horrors.

George looked in front of him.   He remembered the
stylish lady in the white dress who had stood in the
sunshine in Lugano in front of the post-office, far from
all the cares of the world.   " Strange creature," he
thought.

" Of course she'll make a book out of it," said Anna.
" But mind you don't tell any one, not even your friend
Bermann."

" Shouldn't think of it !   But I say, Anna, hadn't you
better get something ready for this evening ? "

She nodded.   " Come, take me downstairs.   I'll see
what there is and consult Marie too . . . so far as is
possible to do so."

They got up.   The shadows had lengthened.   The children were making a noise in the next garden.   Anna took
her lover's arm and walked slowly with him.   She told
him the newest instances of the fantastic stupidity of
the maid.

The idea of my being a husband, thought George, and
listened reflectively.   When they got to the house he
announced his intention of going to meet Heinrich, left
Anna and went into the street.

At this precise moment a one-horse carriage jogged up.
Heinrich got out and paid the driver.   " Hallo ! "   he
said to George, " have you really waited for me after all ?
It's not so late then ? "

" Not at all.   You're very punctual.   We'll go for a
short walk if it suits you."

" Delighted."

They walked on into the forest past the yellow inn
with the red terraces.

" It is wonderful here," said Heinrich, " and your villa
too looks awfully nice.   Why don't you live out here ? "

" Yes, it's absurd not to," agreed George without further explanation. Then they were silent for a while.

Heinrich was in a light grey summer suit and carried his cloak over his arm, letting it trail a little behind him. " Did you recognise her again ? " he asked suddenly, without looking up.

" Yes," replied George.

" She only came up for one day from her summer engagement. She goes back by train to-night. A surprise attack, so to speak. But it didn't come off." He laughed.

"Why are you so hard ? " asked George, and thought of the big envelope with the grey seals and the silly inscription. " There is really no occasion for you to be so. It is only a fluke that she did not get anonymous letters just like you did, Heinrich. And who knows, if you hadn't left her alone for God knows what reasons . . ."

Heinrich shook his head and looked at George almost as though he pitied him. " Do you mean by any chance that it is my intention to punish her or avenge myself ? Or do you think I'm one of those mugs who don't know what to make of the world because something has happened to them which they know has already happened to thousands before them and will happen to thousands after them ? Do you think I despise the ' faithless woman ' or that I hate her ? Not a bit of it. Of course I don't mean to say that I don't at times assume the pose of hatred and contempt, only of course to produce better results upon her. But as a matter of fact I understand all that has happened far too well for me to . . ." He shrugged his shoulders.

" Well, if you do understand it ? . . ."

" But, my dear friend, understanding a thing is no earthly good at all. Understanding is a game like anything else. A very ' classy ' game and a very expensive one. One can spend one's whole soul over it and finish up a poor devil. But understanding hasn't got the least thing in the world to do with our feelings, almost as little as it has to do with our actions. It doesn't protect us from suffering, from revulsion, from ruin. It leads absolutely nowhere. It's a kind of *cul-de-sac.* Understanding always signifies the end."

As they walked slowly and silently up a side path with a moderate incline, each one engrossed in his own thoughts, they emerged out of the woods into open meadowland, which gave a clear view of the valley. They looked out over the town and then further on towards the haze-breathing plain through which the river ran shining ; they looked towards the far line of the mountains, over which a thin haze was spreading.   Then in the peace of the evening sun they walked on further towards George's favourite seat on the border of the forest. The sun was not visible. George watched the track of the Sommer-haidenweg on the other side of the valley run along the wooded hills ; it looked pale and cooled. He then looked down and knew that in the garden at his feet there was a pear-tree, beneath which he had sat a few hours before with some one who was very dear to him, and who carried his child under her bosom, and he felt moved. He felt a slight contempt for the women who were perhaps waiting for him somewhere, but that did not extinguish his desire for them. Summer visitors were walking about down below on the path between the garden and the meadows. A young girl looked up and whispered something to nother.

" You are certainly a popular personality in the place here," remarked Heinrich, contracting the corners of his mouth ironically.

" Not that I know of."

" Those pretty girls looked at you with great interest. People always find an inexhaustible source of excitement in other people not being married. Those holiday-makers down there are bound to look upon you as a kind of Don Juan and . . . your friend as a seduced maiden who has gone wrong, don't you think so ? "

" I don't know," said George, anxious to cut short the conversation.

"And I wonder what I represented," continued Heinrich unperturbed, " to the theatrical people in the little town. Clearly the deceived lover. Consequently an absolutely ridiculous character. And she ? Well, one can imagine. Things are awfully simple for lookers-on. But when one gets to close quarters everything looks utterly different. But the question is whether the complexion it has in the distance isn't the right one ? Whether one does not persuade oneself into believing a lot of rot, if one's got a part to play in the comedy oneself? "

He might quite as well have stayed at home, thought George. But as he could not send him home, and with the object at any rate of changing the conversation, he asked him quickly: " Do you hear anything from the Ehrenbergs ? "

" I had a rather sad letter from Fräulein Else a few days ago," replied Heinrich.

" You correspond with her ? "

" No, I don't correspond with her. At any rate I have not yet answered her."

" She is taking the Oskar business much more to heart than she will own," said George. " I spoke to her once in the nursing-home. We remained standing quite a time outside in the passage in front of the white varnished door behind which poor Oskar was lying. At that time they were afraid of the other eye as well. It's really a tragic affair."

" Tragi-comic," corrected Heinrich with hardness.

" You see the tragi-comic in everything. I'll tell you why, too. Because you're more or less callous. But in this case the comic element takes a back seat."

" You make a mistake," replied Heinrich. " Old Ehren-berg's box on the ear was a piece of crudeness, Oskar's suicide a piece of stupidity, his making such a bad shot at himself a piece of bungling. These elements certainly can't produce anything really tragic. It is a rather disgusting business, that's all."

George shook his head angrily. He had felt genuine sympathy for Oskar since his misfortune. He was also sorry for old Ehrenberg, who had been staying in Neuhaus since then, was only living for his work and refused to see any one. They had both paid their penalty, which was heavier than they had deserved. Couldn't Heinrich see that and feel it just as he did ? They really got on one's nerves at times, these people, with their exaggerated Jewish smartness and their relentless psychology—these Bermanns and Nürnbergers. Their principal object in life was to be surprised by nothing whatsoever. What they lacked was kindness. It was only when they grew older that a certain gentleness came over them. George thought of old Doctor Stauber, of Frau Golowski, of old Eissler, but so long as they were young . . . they always kept on the *qui vive*. Their one ideal was not to be scored off ! A disagreeable lot. He felt more and more that he missed Felician and Skelton, who as a matter of fact were really quite clever enough. He even missed Guido Schönstein.

" But in spite of all her melancholy," said Heinrich after a time, " Fräulein Else seems to be having a pretty good time of it. They are having people down again at Auhof. The Wyners were there the other day, Sissy and James. James got his doctor's degree the other day at Cambridge. Classy, eh ? "

The word Sissy darted through George's heart like a flashing dagger. He realised it all of a sudden. He would be with her in a few days. His desire surged up so strongly that he himself scarcely understood it.

The dusk came down. George and Heinrich got up, went down the fields and entered the garden. They saw Anna come down the centre path accompanied by a gentleman.

" Old Doctor Stauber," said George. " You know him, I suppose ? "

They exchanged greetings.

" I am very glad," said Anna to Heinrich, " that you should come and see us at last."

" Us ! " repeated George to himself, with a sense of surprise which he immediately repudiated. He went in front with Doctor Stauber. Heinrich and Anna slowly followed.

" Are you satisfied with Anna ? " George asked the doctor.

" Things couldn't be going on better," replied Stauber, " only she must continue to take exercise regularly and properly."

It struck George, who had not seen the doctor before since his return, that he had not yet given him back the books which he had borrowed and he made his apologies.

" There's time enough for that," replied Stauber. " I am only too glad if they came in handy." And he asked what impressions he had brought home from Rome.

George told him of his wanderings through the old imperial palaces, of his drives through the Campagna in the evening light, of a sultry hour in Hadrian's garden just before a storm. Doctor Stauber begged him to stop, otherwise he might be induced to leave all his patients here in the lurch so as to run away at once to the city he loved so much. Then George made polite inquiries after Doctor Berthold. Was there any foundation for the rumour that he would be engaged again in active political life in the approaching winter ?

Doctor Stauber shrugged his shoulders. " He comes back in September, that's the only thing certain so far. He has been very industrious at Pasteur's and he wants to

elaborate at the pathological institute here a great piece
of serum research work which he began in Paris. If he
takes my advice he'll stick to it, for in my humble
opinion what he is now doing is much more important for
humanity than the most glorious revolution. Of course
talents vary, and I've certainly nothing to say against
revolutions now and again. But speaking between ourselves, my son's talent is far more on the scientific side.
It's rather his temperament which drives him in the other
direction . . . perhaps only his temper. Well, we shall
see. But how about your plans for the autumn ? " he
added suddenly, as he looked at George with his good-
natured fatherly expression. " Where are you going to
swing your bâton ? "

" I only wish I knew myself," replied George.

Doctor Stauber was walking by his side, his lids half closed
and his cigar in his mouth, and while George told him
about his efforts and his prospects with self-important
emphasis he thought he felt that Doctor Stauber simply
regarded everything he said as nothing more than an
attempted justification of his putting off his marriage
with Anna. A slight irritation against her arose within
him ; she seemed to be standing behind them and perhaps
was enjoying quietly that he was, as it were, being cross-
examined by Doctor Stauber.

He deliberately assumed a lighter and lighter tone, as
though his own personal plans for the future had nothing
at all to do with Anna, and finished up by saying merrily:
" Why, who knows where I shall be this time next year ?
I may finish up in America."

" You might do worse," replied Doctor Stauber quietly.
" I have a cousin who is a violinist in Boston, a man named
Schwarz, who earns there at least six times as much as he
gets here at the opera."

George did not like being compared with violinists of the
name of Schwarz and asserted with an emphasis which he

himself thought rather exaggerated that it was not at all a question of money-making, at any rate at the beginning. Suddenly, he did not know where the thought came from, the idea ran through his mind : " Supposing Anna dies. . . . Supposing the child were her death. . . ." He felt deeply shocked, as though he had committed a crime by the very thought, and he saw in his imagination Anna lying there with the shroud drawn over her chin and he saw the candlelight and daylight streaming over her wax-pale face. He turned round almost anxiously, as though to assure himself that she was there and alive. The features of her face were blurred in the darkness and this frightened him. He remained standing with the doctor till Anna arrived with Heinrich. He was happy to have her so near him. " You must be quite tired now, dear," he said to her in his tenderest tone.

" I've certainly honestly performed my day's work," she replied. " Besides," and she pointed to the verandah, where the lamp with the green paper shade was standing on the laid table, " supper will soon be ready. It would be so nice, Doctor, if you could stay; won't you ? "

" I'm afraid it's impossible, my dear child. I ought to have been back in town ages ago. Remember me kindly to Frau Golowski. See you again soon. Good-bye, Herr Bermann. Come," he added, " is one going to get another chance soon of seeing or reading one of your fine pieces of work ? "

Heinrich shrugged his shoulders, vouchsafed a social smile and was silent. Why, he thought, are even the best-bred men usually tactless when they meet people like myself ? Do I ask him about his affairs ?

The doctor went on to express in a few words his sympathy with Heinrich over old Bermann's death. He remembered the dead man's celebrated speech in opposition to the introduction of Tschech as the judicial language in certain Bohemian districts. At that time the Jewish provincial advocate had come within an ace of being Minister of Justice. Yes, times had changed.

Heinrich started to listen. After all this could be made use of in the political comedy.

Doctor Stauber took his leave. George accompanied him to the carriage which was waiting outside, and availed himself of the opportunity to ask the doctor some medical questions. The latter was able to reassure him in every respect.

" It's only a pity," he continued, " that circumstances do not allow Anna to nurse the child herself."

George stood still meditatively. It could not hurt her, could it ? . . . At any rate, only the child ? Or her as well ? . . . He asked the doctor.

" Why talk about it, my dear Baron, if it's not practicable ? That's all right, don't you worry," he added, with one foot already in the carriage. " One needn't be nervous about the child of people like you two."

George looked him straight in the eye and said : " I will at any rate take care that he lives the first years of his life in healthy air."

" That's very nice," said Doctor Stauber gently. " But speaking generally there is no healthier air in the world for children than their parents' home."

He shook hands with George and the carriage rolled away.

George remained standing for a moment and felt a lively irritation against the doctor. He vowed mentally that he would never allow the conversation with him to take a turn that would as it were entitle him to give unsolicited advice or make veiled reproaches. What did the old man know ? What did he really understand about the whole thing ? George's antagonism became more and more violent. When I choose to, he said to himself, I will marry her. Can't she have the child with her anyway ? Hasn't she said herself that she will be proud of having a child ? I am not going to repudiate it either, and I will do everything in my power. And later on sometime. . . . But I should be doing an injustice to myself, to her, to the child if I were to make up my mind to-day to do something which at any rate is still premature.

He had slowly walked past the short side of the house into the garden. He saw Anna and Heinrich sitting on the verandah. Marie was just coming out of the house, very red in the face, and putting a warm dish on the table, from which the steam mounted up. How quiet Anna sits there, thought George, and remained standing in the darkness. How serene, how free from care, as though she could trust me implicitly, as though there were no such things as death, poverty, treacherous desertion, as though I loved her as much as she deserves. And again he felt alarmed. Do I love her less ? Is she not right in trusting me ? When I sit over there on my seat on the edge of the forest so much tenderness often wells up in me that I can scarcely stand it. Why do I feel so little of that now ? He was standing only a few paces away and watched her first carve and then stare into the darkness out of which he was to come, while her eyes began to shine as he stepped suddenly into the light. My one true love, he thought.

When he sat down by the others Anna said to him: " You've had a very long consultation with the doctor."

" It wasn't a consultation. We were chatting. He also told me about his son who is coming back soon."

Heinrich inquired after Berthold. The young man interested him and he hoped very much to make his acquaintance next winter. His speech last year on the Therese Golowski case, together with his open letter to his constituents, in which he had explained the reasons for his resignation, yes, they had been really first-class per-formances. . . . Yes, and more than that—documents of the period.

A light almost proud smile flew over Anna's face.

She looked down to her place and then quickly up to George. George also was smiling. Not a trace of jealousy stirred within him. Did Berthold have any idea . . . ? Of course. Did he suffer ? . . . Probably. Could he forgive Anna ? To think of having to forgive at all ! What nonsense.

A dish of mushrooms was served. On its appearance Heinrich could not refrain from asking if it were at all poisonous.

George laughed.

" You needn't make fun of me," said Heinrich. " If I wanted to kill myself I wouldn't choose either poisoned mushrooms or decayed sausage, but a nobler and swifter poison. At times one is sick of life, but one is never sick of health, even in one's last quarter of an hour. And besides, nervousness is a perfectly legitimate, though usually shamefully repudiated, daughter of reason. What does nervousness really mean ? considering all the possibilities that may result from an action, the bad and good ones equally. And what is courage ? I mean, of course, real courage, which is manifested far more rarely than one thinks. For the courage which is affected or the result of obedience or simply a matter of suggestion doesn't count. True courage is often really nothing else than the expression of an as it were metaphysical conviction of one's own superfluity."

" Oh, you Jew ! " thought George, though without malice, and then said to himself, " Perhaps he isn't so far out after all."

They found the beer so good, although Anna did not drink any, that they sent Marie to the inn for a second jugful. Their mood became genial. George described his trip again. The days at Lugano in the broiling sun, the journey over the snowy Brenner, the wandering through the roofless city, which after a night of two thousand years had surged up again to the light ; he conjured up again the minute in which they had been present, he and Anna, when workmen were carefully and laboriously excavating a pillar out of the ashes. Heinrich had not yet seen Italy. He meant to go there next spring. He explained that he was frequently torn by a desire for, if not exactly Italy, at any rate foreign lands, distance, the world. When he heard people talking about travels he often got heart palpitation like a child the evening before its birthday. He doubted whether he was destined to end his life in his home. It might be, perhaps, that after wandering about for years on end he would come back and find in a little house in the country the peace of his later manhood. Who knew—life was so full of coincidences—if he were not destined to finish his life in this very house in which he was now a guest and felt better than he had for a long time?

Anna thanked him with an air which indicated that she was not merely the hostess of the country house but of the whole world itself with its evening calm.

A soft light began to shine out of the darkness of the garden. A warm moist odour came from the grass and flowers. The long fields which ran down to the railing swept into view in the moonlight and the white seat under the pear-tree shimmered as though very far away. Anna complimented Heinrich on the verses in the opera libretto which George had read to her the other day.

" Quite right," remarked George, smoking a cigar with his legs comfortably crossed, " have you brought us anything fresh ? "

Heinrich shook his head. " No, nothing."

" What a pity ! " said Anna, and suggested that Heinrich should tell them the plot consecutively and in detail. She had been wanting to know about it for a long time. She was unable to get any clear idea of it from George's account.

They looked at each other. There came up in their

18

minds that sweet dark hour when they had lain in peace
with breast close to breast in a dark room in front of
whose windows, behind its floating curtain of snow, a
grey church had loomed, and into which the notes of an
organ had boomed heavily. Yes, they now knew where
the house stood in which the child was to come into the
world. Perhaps another house, too, thought George, stands
somewhere or other in which the child that has not yet
been born will end its life. Death! As a man—or as
an old man, or . . . . Oh, what an idea, away with it . . .
away with it!

Heinrich declared his readiness to fulfil Anna's wish,
and stood up. "I shall perhaps find it useful myself,"
he said apologetically.

"But mind you don't suddenly switch off into your
political tragi-comedy," remarked George. And then,
turning to Anna: "He's writing a piece, you know, with
a National German corps student for its hero who poisons
himself with mushrooms through despair of emancipation
of the Jews."

Heinrich nodded dissent. "One glass of beer less and
you'd never have made that epigram."

"Jealousy!" replied George. He felt extraordinarily
pleased with life, particularly now that he had firmly made
up his mind to leave the day after to-morrow. He sat
quite close to Anna, held her hand in his and seemed to
hear the melody of future days singing in the deepest
recesses of his soul.

Heinrich had suddenly gone into the garden outside the
verandah, reached over the railing, took his cloak from
the chair and threw it romantically around him. "I'm
going to begin," he said. "Act I."

"First, an overture in D. minor," interrupted George.
He whistled an impressive melody, then a few notes and
finished with an " and so on."

"The curtain rises," said Heinrich. "Feast in the

King's garden. Night. The princess is to be married to
the Duke Heliodorus next day. I call him Heliodorus
for the time being, he will probably have another name
though. The king adores his daughter and can't stand
Heliodorus, who is a kind of popinjay with the tastes of a
mad Cæsar. The king has really given the feast to annoy
Heliodorus, and not only are all the nobles in the land
invited but the youth of all classes, in so far as they
have won a right to be invited by their beauty. And on
this evening the princess is to dance with any one who
pleases her. And there is some one in particular, his
name is Ägidius, with whom she seems quite infatuated.
And no one is more pleased about it than the king.
Jealousy on the part of Heliodorus. Increased pleasure
on the part of the king. Scene between Heliodorus and
the king. Scorn. Enmity. Then something highly unexpected takes place. Ägidius draws his dagger against
the king. He wants to murder him. The motives for
this attempted murder of course would have to be very
carefully worked in if you had not been kind enough,
my dear George, to set the thing to music! So it will be
enough to hint that the youth hates tyrants, is a member
of a secret society, is perhaps a fool or a hero off his own
bat. I don't know yet, you see. The attempted murder
fails. Ägidius is arrested. The king wishes to be left alone
with him. Duet. The youth is proud, self-possessed,
great. The king superior, cruel, inscrutable. That's
about my idea of him. He had already sent many men
to their death and already seen many die, but his own
inner consciousness is so awfully vivid and intense that
all other men seem to him to be living in a state of mere
semi-consciousness, so that their death has practically
no other significance except the step from twilight into
gloom. A death like that strikes him as too gentle or
too banal for a case like this. He wishes to plunge this
youth from a daylight such as no mortal has yet enjoyed

into the most dreadful darkness. Yes, that's how his mind works. How much he says or sings about this I don't yet know of course. Ägidius is taken away just like a prisoner condemned, so everybody thinks, to immediate death, and on the very same ship, too, as that on which Heliodorus was to have started on his journey with the princess in the evening. The curtain falls. The second act takes place on the deck. The ship under weigh. Chorus. Isolated figures come up. Their significance is only revealed later. Dawn. Ägidius is led up from the hold below. To his death, as he is bound, of course, to think. But it turns out otherwise. His fetters are loosed. All bow down to him. He is hailed as a prince. The sun rises. Ägidius has an opportunity of noticing that he is in the very best society—beautiful women, nobles. A sage, a singer, a fool, are intended for important parts. But who should come out of the chorus of women but the princess herself ; she belongs absolutely to Ägidius, like everything else on the ship."

" What a splendid father and king ! " said George.

" No price is too dear for him to pay ! " explained Heinrich, " for a really ingenious idea. That's his line. There follows a splendid duet between Ägidius and the princess. Then they sit down to the meal. After the meal dancing. High spirits. Ägidius naturally thinks he has been saved. He is not inordinately surprised, because his hatred for the king was always to a great extent inspired by admiration. The twilight begins to loom. Suddenly a stranger is at Ägidius' side. Perhaps he has been there for a long time, one among the many, un-noticed, mute. He has a word to say to Ägidius. The feasting and dancing proceed meanwhile. Ägidius and the stranger. ' All this is yours,' says the stranger. ' You can rule according to your humour. You can take pos-session and kill just as you wish. But to-morrow . . . or in two or seven years or in one year or in ten, or still later, this ship will approach an island on whose shore a marble hall towers aloft upon a cliff. And there death waits for you—death. Your murderer is with you on the ship. But only the one whose mission it is to be your murderer knows it. Nobody else knows who he is. Nay, nobody else on this ship has any inkling that you are consecrated to death. Remember that. For when you let any one notice that you yourself know your fate you are doomed to death that very hour.'"

Heinrich spoke these words with exaggerated pathos, as though to conceal his embarrassment. He went on more simply. "The stranger vanishes. Perhaps I shall have him disembarked on the mainland by two silent attendants who have accompanied him. Ägidius remains among the hundreds of men and women of which one or the other is his murderer. Which one? The sage or the fool? The star-gazer yonder? One of those yonder, ruminating in the darkness? Those men stealing up the steps yonder? One of the dancers? The princess herself? She comes up to him again, is very tender, nay, passionate. Hypocrite? Murderess? His love? Does she know? At any rate she is his. All this is to be his to-day. Night on the sea. Terror. Delight. The ship goes slowly on towards that shore that lies hours or years away in the distance of the far-off mist. The princess is nestling at his feet. Ägidius stares into the night and watches." Heinrich stopped as though personally affected.

Melodies rang in George's ear. He heard the music for the scene when the stranger disappears escorted by the mutes, and then gradually the noise of the feast comes to the front of the stage. He did not feel it within him as a mere melody, but he already felt it with all its fulness of instruments. Were there not flutes sounding and oboes and clarionets? Was not the 'cello singing and the violin? Was not a faint beat of a drum droning out of a corner of the orchestra? Involuntarily he held up his right arm, as though he had his conductor's bâton in his hand.

"And the third act ? " asked Anna, as Heinrich remained silent.

"The third act," repeated Heinrich, and there was a touch of depression in his voice. "The scene of the third act, of course, will be laid in that hall on the cliff—don't you think so ? It must, I think, begin with a dialogue between the king and the stranger. Or with a chorus ? There are no choruses on uninhabited islands. Anyway, the king is there and the ship is in sight. But look here, why should the island be uninhabited ? " He stopped.

"Well ? " asked George impatiently.

Heinrich laid both his arms on the railing of the verandah. "I'll tell you something. This isn't an opera at all . . ."

"What do you mean ? "

"There are very good reasons for my not getting as far as this part of it. It is a tragedy clearly. I just haven't got the courage to write it. Do you know what would have to be described ? The inner change in Ägidius would have to be described. That is clearly both the difficulty and the beauty of the subject-matter. In other words it is a thing which I daren't do. The opera idea is simply a way of getting out of it, and I don't know if I ought to take on anything like that." He was silent.

"But at any rate," said Anna, " you must tell us the end of the opera as you have got it in your mind. I must really admit that I'm quite excited."

Heinrich shrugged his shoulders and answered in a tired voice: "Well, the ship hoves to. Ägidius lands. He is to be hurled into the sea."

"By whom ? " asked Anna.

"I've no idea at all," replied Heinrich unhappily. "From this point my mind is an absolute blank."

"I thought it would be the princess," said Anna, and waving her hand through the air executed a death signal.

Heinrich smiled gently. " I thought of that, of course, also, but . . . He broke off and suddenly looked up to the night sky in a state of nervous tension.

" It was to finish with a kind of pardon, so far as your original draft went," remarked George irritably. " But that, of course, is only good enough for an opera. But now, as your Ägidius is the hero of a tragedy, of course he will have to be really hurled into the sea."

Heinrich raised his forefinger mysteriously and his features became animated again. " I think something is just dawning upon me. But don't let's talk about it for the time being, if you don't mind. It's perhaps really been a sound thing that I told you the beginning."

" But if you think that I am going to do *entr'acte* music for you," said George, without particular emphasis, " you are under a delusion."

Heinrich smiled, guiltily, indifferently and yet quite good-humouredly. Anna felt with concern that the whole business had fizzled out. George was uncertain whether he ought to be irritated at his hopes being disappointed or be glad at being relieved of a kind of obligation. But Heinrich felt as though the creations of his own mind were deserting him in shadowy confusion, mockingly, without farewell and without promising to come again.

He found himself alone and deserted in a melancholy garden, in the society of quite a nice man whom he knew very well, and a young lady who meant nothing at all to him. He could not help thinking all of a sudden of a person who was travelling at this very hour in a badly-lighted compartment in despair and with eyes red with crying, towards dark mountains, worrying whether she would get there in time to-morrow for her rehearsal. He now felt again that since that had come to an end he was going downhill, for he had nothing left, he had no one left. The suffering of that wretched person, the victim of his own agonizing hatred, was the only thing in the world.

And who knew ? She might be smiling at another the very next day, with those tearful eyes of hers, with her grief and longing still in her soul and a new *joie de vivre* already in her blood.

Frau Golowski appeared on the verandah. She was flurried and somewhat late, and still carried her umbrella and had her hat on. Therese sent her remembrances from town and wanted to arrange to come and see Anna again the next day or so.

George, who was leaning up against a wooden pillar of the verandah, turned to Frau Golowski with that studious politeness which he always ostentatiously assumed when talking to her. " Won't you ask Fräulein Therese in both our names if she wouldn't care to stay out here for a day or two ? The top room is quite at her service. I'm on the point of going into the mountains for a short time, you know," he added, as though he regularly slept in the little room at all other times.

Frau Golowski expressed her thanks. She would tell Therese. George looked at his watch and saw that it was time to start for home. He and Heinrich then said good-bye. Anna accompanied both of them as far as the garden door, remained standing a little while and watched them till they got on to the height where the Sommerhaidenweg began.

The little village at the bottom of the valley flowed past them in the moonlight. The hills loomed pale like thin walls. The forest breathed darkness. In the distance thousands of lights glittered out f the night mist of the summer town. Heinrich and George walked by each other in silence and a sense of estrangement arose between them. George remembered that walk in the Prater in the previous autumn, when their first almost confidential talk had brought them near to each other. How many talks had they not had since ? But had they not all, as it were, gone into thin air ? And to-day, too, George was

unable to walk through the night with Heinrich without
exchanging a word, as he used to do many a time with
Guido or with Labinski without feeling any loss of real
sympathy. The silence became a strain. He began to
talk of old Stauber, as that was the first subject to occur
to him, and praised his reliability and versatility. Heinrich
was not very taken with him and thought him somewhat
intoxicated with the sense of his own kindness, wisdom
and excellence. That was another kind of Jew which he
could not stand—the self-complacent kind. The conversation then turned on young Stauber, whose vacillation
between politics and science had something extremely
attractive about it for Heinrich. From that they turned
into a conversation about the composition of parliament,
about the squabbles between the Germans and the Tschechs
and the attacks of the Clericals on the Minister of Education.
They talked with that strained assiduousness with which
one is accustomed to talk about things which are absolutely
indifferent to one in one's heart of hearts. Finally they
discussed the question whether the Minister ought to
remain in office or not after the dubious figure he had cut
over the civil marriage question, and had the vaguest ideas
after they had finished as to which of them had been in
favour of his resignation and which of them against it.
They walked along the churchyard. Crosses and gravestones towered over the walls and floated in the moonlight. The path inclined downwards to the main road.
They both hurried so as to catch the last tram, and standing on the platform in the sultry scented night air drove
towards the town. George explained that he thought of
doing the first part of his tour on his cycle. Obeying a
sudden impulse, he asked Heinrich if he wouldn't like to
join him. Heinrich agreed and after a few minutes manifested great keenness. They got out at the Schottentor,
found out a neighbouring café and after an exhaustive consultation managed, with the help of special maps which

they found in encyclopædias, to decide on every possible
route. When they left each other their plan was not
indeed quite definite, but they already knew that they
would leave Vienna early, the day after the next, and
would mount their cycles at Lambach.

George stood quite a long time by the open window of
his bedroom. He felt intensely awake. He thought of
Anna, from whom he was to part to-morrow for a few
days, and visualised her as sleeping at this hour out
there in the country in the pale twilight between the
moonlight and the morning. But he felt dully as though
this image had nothing at all to do with his own fate, but
with the fate of some unknown man, who himself knew
nothing about it. And he was absolutely unable to realise
that within that slumbering being there slept another
being in still deeper mystery, and that this other being was
to be his own child. Now that the sober mood of the early
dawn stole almost painfully through his senses the whole
episode seemed more remote and improbable than it had
ever been before. A clearer and clearer light showed
above the roofs of the town, but it would be a long time
before the town woke up. The air was perfectly motionless. No breeze came from the trees in the park opposite,
no perfume from the withered flower-beds. And George
stood by the window; unhappy and without compre-
hension.

VII

GEORGE slowly climbed up from the hold on narrow carpeted steps between long oblique mirrors and wrapped in a long dark green rug which trailed behind him, wandered up and down on the empty deck beneath the starry sky. Motionless as ever, Labinski stood in the stern and turned the wheel, while his gaze was directed towards the open sea. "What a career!" thought George. "First a dead man, then a minister, then a little boy with a muff and now a steersman! If he knew that I were on this ship he would certainly hail me." "Look out!" cried behind George the two blue girls, whom he had met on the sea-shore, but he rushed on, wrapped himself in his rug and listened to the flapping of white gulls over his head. Immediately afterwards he was in the saloon, down below, sitting at the table, which was so long that the people at the end were quite small. A gentleman near him, who looked like the elder Grillpazer, remarked irritably: "This boat's always late. We ought to have been in Boston a long time ago." George then felt very nervous; for if he could not show the three music scores in the green cover when he disembarked, he would certainly be arrested for high treason. That was why the prince who had been rushing all over the deck with the wheel all day long often cast such strange sideglances at him. And to intensify his suspicions still more he was compelled to sit at table in his shirtsleeves while all the other gentlemen wore generals' uniforms, as they always did on boats, and all the ladies wore red velvet

dresses. "We shall soon be in America," said a raucous
steward who was serving asparagus. "Only one more
station."

"The others can sit there quietly," thought George.
"They have nothing to do, but I must swim to the
theatre straight away." The coast appeared opposite him
in the great mirror; nothing but houses without roofs,
whose tiers of terraces towered higher and higher, and the
orchestra was waiting impatiently up above in a quiet
kiosk with a broken stone cupola. The bell on the deck
pealed and George tumbled down the steps into the park
with his green rug and two pocket handkerchiefs. But
they had shipped the wrong one across; it was the
Stadtpark, as a matter of fact; Felician was sitting on
a seat, an old lady in a cloak close to him put her fingers
on her lips, whistled very loudly and Felician said, with
an unusually deep voice: "Kemmelbach—Ybs." "No,"
thought George, "Felician never uses a word like that . . ."
rubbed his eyes and woke up.

The train was just starting again. Two red lamps were
shining in front of the closed window of the compartment.
The night ran past, silent and black. George drew his
travelling rug closer round him and stared at the green
shaded lamp in the ceiling. "What a good thing that I'm
alone in the compartment," he thought. "I have been
sound asleep for at least four or five hours. What a strange
confused dream that was!" The white gulls first came
back into his memory. Did they have any significance?
Then he thought of the old woman in the cloak, who of
course was no other than Frau Oberberger. The lady
would not feel particularly flattered. But really, hadn't
she looked quite like an old lady, when he had seen her a
few days ago by the side of her beaming husband in the
box of the little red-and-white theatre of the watering-
place? And Labinski, too, had appeared to him in his
dream as a steersman, strangely enough. And the girls

in blue dresses, also, who had looked out of the hotel garden into the piano room through the window as soon as they heard him playing. But what was the really ghostly element in that dream?

Not the girls in blue, not even Labinski, and not the Prince of Guastalla, who had rushed like mad to the wheel over the deck. No, it was his own figure which had appeared to him so ghostly as it had slunk along by his side multiplied a hundred times over in the long oblique mirrors on both sides. He began to feel cold. The cool night air penetrated into the compartment through the ventilator in the ceiling. The deep black darkness outside gradually changed into a heavy grey and there suddenly rang in George's ears in a sad whisper the words he had heard only a few hours ago in a woman's low voice: How soon will it take you to forget me? . . . He did not wish to hear those words. He wished they had already become true, and in desperation he plunged back into the memory of his dream. It was quite clear that the steamer on which he had gone to America on his concert tour really meant the ship on which Ägidius had sailed towards his sinister fate. And the kiosk with the orchestra was the hall where Ägidius had waited for death. The starry sky which spread over the sea had been really wonderful. The air had been bluer and the stars more silvery than he had ever seen them in waking life, even on the night when he had sailed with Grace from Palermo to Naples. Suddenly the voice of the woman he loved rang through the darkness again, whispering and mournful: "How long will it take you to forget me?" . . . And he now visualised her as he had seen her a few hours ago, pale and naked, with her dark hair streaming over the pillows. He did not want to think of it, conjured up other images from the depths of his memory and deliberately chased them past him. He saw himself going round a cemetery in the thawing February snow with Grace; he saw him-

self riding with Marianne over a white country road towards the wintry forest. He saw himself walking with
his father over the Ringstrasse in the late evening; and
finally a merry-go-round whirled past him. Sissy with
her laughing lips and eyes was rocking about on a brown
wooden horse. Else, graceful and ladylike, was sitting
in a little red carriage, and Anna rode an Arab with the
reins nonchalantly in her hand. Anna! How young and
graceful she looked! Was that really the same being
whom he was to see again in a few hours? and had he
really only been away from her for ten days? And was
he ever to see again all that he had left ten days ago?
The little angel in blue clay between the flower-beds, the
verandah with the wooden gable, the silent garden with
the currant- and the lilac-bushes? It all seemed absolutely inconceivable. She will wait for me on the white
seat under the pear-tree, he thought, and I will kiss her
hands as though nothing had happened.

"How are you, George dear?" she will ask me. "Have
you been true to me?" No . . . . That's not her way
of asking, but she will feel without asking at all or my
answering that I have not come back the same as I went
away. If she only does feel it! If I am only saved from
having to lie! But haven't I done so already? And he
thought of the letters which he had written from the lake,
letters full of tenderness and yearning, which had really
been nothing but lies. And he thought of how he had
waited at night with a beating heart, his ear glued to the
door, till all was quiet in the inn; of how he had then
stolen over the passage to that other woman who lay
there pale and naked, with her dark eyes wide open,
enveloped in the perfume and bluish shimmer of her
hair. And he thought of how he and she one night, half
drunken with desire and audacity, had stepped out on to
the verandah, beneath which the water plashed so seductively. If any one had been out on the lake in the deep

darkness of this hour he would have seen their white bodies shining through the night. George thrilled at the memory. We were out of our senses, he thought; how easily it might have happened that I should be lying to-day with a bullet through my heart six feet under the ground. Of course there's still a chance of it. They all know. Else knew first, though she scarcely ever came down from Auhof into the village. James Wyner, who saw me with the other woman one evening standing on the landing-stage is bound to have told her. Will Else marry him ? I can understand her liking him so much. He is handsome, that chiselled face, those cold grey eyes which look shrewd and straight into the world, a young Englishman. Who knows if he wouldn't have turned into a kind of Oskar Ehrenberg in Vienna ? And George remembered what Else had told him about her brother. He had struck George as so self-possessed, almost mature in fact, on his sick-bed in the nursing-home. And now he was said to be leading a wild life in Ostend, to be gambling and gadding about with the most evil associates, as though he wanted to go thoroughly to the dogs. Did Heinrich still find the matter so tragi-comic ? Frau Ehrenberg had grown quite white with grief. And Else had cried her eyes out in front of George one morning in the grounds; but had she only been crying about Oskar ?

The grey in front of the compartment window slowly cleared. George watched the telegraph wires outside sweeping and shifting across each other with swift movements and he thought of how, yesterday afternoon, his own lying words to Anna had travelled across one of these wires : "Shall be with you early to-morrow morning. Fondest love, your own George." . . . He had hurried back straight from the post-office to an ardent and desperate final hour with the other woman, and he could not realise that even at this very minute, when he had already been

away from her for a whole eternity, she should still be
lying asleep and dreaming in that same room with the
fast-closed windows. And she will be home this evening
with her husband and children. Home—just as he would
be. He knew that it was so and he could not understand
it. For the first time in his life he had been near doing
something which people would probably have had to call
madness. Only one word from her . . . and he would
have gone out with her into the world, have left everything
behind, friends, mistress and his unborn child. And was
he not still ready to do so? If she called him would he
not go? And if he did do so would he not be right?
Was he not far more cut out for adventures of that kind
than for the quiet life full of responsibilities which he had
chosen for himself? Was it not rather his real line to career
boldly and unhesitatingly about the world than to be
stuck somewhere or other with his wife and child, with all
the bothers about bread-and-butter, his career and at
the best a little fame? In the days from which he had
just come he had felt that he was living, perhaps for the
first time. Each moment had been so rich and so full,
and not only those spent in her arms. He had suddenly
grown young again. The country had flowered with a
greater splendour, the arc of the sky had grown wider, the
air which he drank had exhaled a finer spice and strength,
and melodies had rippled within him as never before.
Had he ever composed anything better than that wordless
song to be sung on the water with its sprightly rocking
melody? And that fantasy had risen strangely by the
shore of the lake one hour out of depths of his which he
had never dreamt of, after he had seen the wondrous
woman for the first time. Well, Herr Hofrat Wilt would
no longer have occasion to regard him as a dilettante.
But why did he think of him of all people? Did the others
know what kind of a man he was any better? Didn't it
often seem to him as though even Heinrich, who had

once wanted to write an opera libretto for him, had failed to judge him any more accurately ? And he heard again the words which the author had spoken to him that morning when they had cycled from Lambach to Gmunden through the dew-wet forest. "You need not do creative work in order to realise yourself . . . you do not need work . . . only the atmosphere of your art. . . ." He suddenly remembered an evening in the keeper's lodge on the Alamsee when a huntsman of seventy-three had sung some jolly songs and Heinrich had wondered at any one of that age being still so jolly, since one would be bound to feel oneself so near one's death. Then they had gone to bed in an enormous room which echoed all their words, philosophised about life and death for a long time, and suddenly fallen asleep.

George was still motionless as he lay stretched out in his rug and considered whether he should tell Heinrich anything about his meeting with his actress. How pale she had grown when she had suddenly seen him. She had listened, with roving eyes, to his account of the cycle tour with Heinrich and then begun to tell him straight away about her mother and her little brother who could draw so wonderfully finely. And the other members of the company had kept staring all the time from the stage door, particularly a man with a green tyrol hat, in which a chamois' beard was stuck. And George had seen her play the same evening in a French farce, and asked himself if the pretty young person who acted and pranced about so wildly down on the stage of the little holiday theatre could really be so desperate as Heinrich imagined. Not only he but James and Sissy as well had liked her very much. What a jolly evening it had been ! And the supper after the theatre with James, Sissy, old mother Wyner and Willy Eissler ! And next day the ride in the four-in-hand of old Baron Löwenstein, who drove himself. In less than an hour they had reached the lake. A boat

19

was rowing near the bank in the early sunshine. And the woman he loved sat on the rowing-seat with a green silk shawl over her shoulders. But how was it that Sissy also had divined the relationship between him and her? And then the merry dinner at the Ehrenbergs' up at Auhof! George sat between Else and Sissy, and Willy told one funny story after the other. And then on the afternoon, George and Sissy had found each other without any rendezvous in the dark green sultriness of the park amid the warm scent of the moss and the pines, while all the others were resting. It had been a wonderful hour, which had floated through this day as lightly as a dream, without vows of troth and without fear of fulfilment. How I like thinking every single minute of it all over again, savouring it to the full, that golden day! I see both of us, Sissy and myself, going down over the fields to the tennis-court, hand in hand. I think I played better than I ever did in my life. . . . And I see Sissy again lounging in a cane chair, with a cigarette between her lips and old Baron Löwenstein at her side, while her looks flamed towards Willy. What had become of me at that moment, so far as she was concerned? And the evening! How we swam out in the twilight into the lake, while the warm water caressed me so deliciously. What a delight that was! And then the night . . . the night. . . .

The train stopped again. It was already quite light outside. George lay still, as before. He heard the name of the station called out; the voices of waiters, conductors and travellers; heard steps on the platform, station-signals of all kinds, and he knew that in an hour he would be in Vienna. . . . Supposing Anna had received information about him, just as Heinrich had about his mistress the previous winter? He could not imagine that a thing like that could make Anna lose control of herself, even if she believed in it. Perhaps she would cry, but certainly only to herself, quite quietly. He resolved firmly not to

let her notice anything. Was not that his plain duty?
What was the important thing now? Only this, that
Anna should spend the last weeks quietly and without
excitement, and that a healthy child should come into the
world. That was all that mattered. How long had it
been since he had heard Doctor Stauber say those words?
The child . . . ! How near the hour was, the child. . . .
He thought again ; but he could think of nothing except
the mere word. He then endeavoured to imagine a tiny
living being. But as though to mock him figures of
small children kept appearing, who looked as though they
had stepped out of a picture-book, drawn grotesquely and
in crude colours. Where will it spend its first years? he
thought. With peasants in the country, in a house with
a little garden. But one day we will fetch it and take
it home with us. It might, too, turn out differently. One
gets a letter like this : Your Excellency, I have the honour
to inform you that the child is seriously ill. . . . Or . . .
What is the point of thinking about things like that?
Even though we kept it with us it might fall ill and die.

Anyway, it must be given to people who are highly
responsible. I'll see about it myself . . . .He felt as
though he were confronted with new duties which he had
never properly considered and which he had not yet
grown able to cope with. The whole business was beginning, as it were, over again. He came out of a world
in which he had not bothered about all these things,
where other laws had prevailed than those to which he
must now submit.

And had it not been as though the other people, too,
had felt that he was not really one of them, as though
they had been steeped in a kind of respect, as though they
had been seized by a feeling of veneration for the power
and holiness of a great passion, whose sway they witnessed in their own neighbourhood? He remembered an
evening on which the hotel visitors had disappeared from

the piano-room one after another, as though they had been conscious of their duty to leave him alone with her. He had sat down at the piano and begun to improvise. She had remained in her dark corner in a big arm-chair. First of all he had seen her smile, then the dark shining of her eyes, then only the lines of her figure, then nothing more at all. But he had been conscious the whole time " She is there ! " Lights flashed out on the other bank opposite. The two girls in the blue dresses had peered in through the window and had quickly disappeared again. Then he stopped playing and remained sitting by the pianoforte in silence. Then she had come slowly out of the corner like a shadow and had put her hand upon his head. How ineffably beautiful that had been ! And it all came into his mind again. How they had rested in the boat in the middle of the lake, with shipped oars, while his head was in her lap ! And they had walked through the forest paths on the opposite bank until they came to the seat under the oak. It had been there that he had told her everything—everything as though to a friend. And she had understood him, as never another woman had understood him before. Was it not she whom he had always been seeking ? she who was at once mistress and comrade, with a serious outlook upon everything in the world, and yet made for every madness and for every bliss ? And the farewell yesterday. . . . The dark brilliance of her eyes, the blue-black stream of her loosened hair, the perfume of her white naked body. . . . Was it really possible that this was over for ever ? that all this was never, never to come again ?

George crumpled the rug between his fingers in his helpless longing and shut his eyes. He no longer saw the softly moving lines of the wooded hills, which swept by in the morning light, and as though for one last happiness he dreamed himself back again into the dark ecstasies of that farewell hour. Yet against his will he was overcome by fatigue after the jar and racket of the night in the train, and he was swept away out of the images which he had himself called up, in a route of wild dreams which it was not vouchsafed him to control. He walked over the Sommerhaidenweg in a strange twilight that filled him with a deep sadness. Was it morning ? Was it evening ? Or just a dull day ? Or was it the mysterious light of some star over the world that had not yet shone for any one except him ? He suddenly stood upon a great open meadow where Heinrich Bermann ran up and down and asked him : Are you also looking for the lady's castle ? I have been expecting you for a long time. They went up a spiral staircase, Heinrich in front, so that George could only see a tail of the overcoat which trailed behind. Above, on an enormous terrace which gave a view of the town and the lake, the whole party was assembled. Leo had started his dissertation on minor harmonies, stopped when George appeared, came down from his desk and himself escorted him to a vacant chair which was in the first row and next to Anna. Anna smiled ecstatically when George appeared. She looked young and brilliant in a splendid *décolletée* evening dress. Just behind her sat a little boy with fair hair, in a sailor suit with a broad white collar, and Anna said " That's he." George made her a sign to be silent, for it was supposed to be a secret. In the meanwhile Leo played the *C sharp minor* Nocturne by Chopin in order to prove his theory, and behind him old Bösendorfer leaned against the wall in his yellow overcoat, tall, gaunt and good-natured. They all left the concert-room in a great crush. Then George put Anna's opera cloak round her shoulders and looked sternly at the people round him. He then sat in the carriage with her, kissed her, experienced a great delight in doing so and thought : " If it could only be like this always." Suddenly they stopped in front of the house in Mariahilf. There were already many pupils waiting upstairs by the window and beckoning. Anna got

out, said good-bye to George with an arch expression and
vanished behind the door, which slammed behind her.

" Excuse me, sir. Ten minutes more," some one said.
George turned round. The conductor stood in the doorway
and repeated : " We shall be in Vienna in ten minutes."

" Thank you," said George and got up, with a more or
less confused head. He opened the window and was glad
it was fine weather outside in the world. The fresh morning
air quite cheered him up. Yellow walls, signal-boxes, little
gardens, telegraph poles, streets, flew past him, and finally
the train stood in the station. A few minutes later George
was driving in an open fiacre to his apartment, saw workmen, shop girls and clerks going to their daily callings ;
heard the rattle of rolling shutters and in spite of all the
anxiety which awaited him, in spite of all the desire which
drew him elsewhere, he experienced the deep joy of once
more being at home.

When he went into his room he felt quite hidden. The
old secretary, covered with green baize, the malachite
letter-weight, the glass ash-tray with its burnt-in cavalier,
the slim lamp with the broad green thick glass shade, the
portrait of his father and mother in the narrow mahogany
frames, the round little marble table in the corner with its
silver case for cigars, the Prince of the Electorate, after
Vandyck on the wall, the high bookcase with its olive-
coloured curtains ; they all gave him a hearty greeting.
And how it did one good to have that good home look over
the tree tops in the park, towards the spires and roofs.
An almost undreamt-of happiness streamed towards him
from everything which he found again here, and he felt
sore at heart that he would have to leave it all in a few
weeks. And how long would it last until one had a home,
a real home ? He would have liked to have stopped for a
few hours in his beloved room but he had no time. He
had to be in the country before noon.

He had thrown off his clothes and let the warm water

swirl round him deliciously in his white bath. To avoid going to sleep in his bath he chose a means he had often employed before. He rehearsed in his mind note by note a fugue of Bach's. He thought of a pianoforte that would have to be diligently practised and music scores which would have to be read. Wouldn't it really be more sensible to devote another year to study ? Not to enter into negotiations straight away or to take a post, which he would turn out to be unable to fill ? Rather to stay here and work. Stay here ? But where ? Notice had been given. It occurred to him for a moment to take the apartment in the old house opposite the grey church, where he had spent such beautiful hours with Anna, and it was as though he were remembering a long-past episode, an adventure of his youth, gay and yet a little mysterious, that had been over long ago. . . .

He went back into his room, refreshed and wearing a brand-new suit, the first light one which he had put on since his father's death. A letter lay on the secretary which had just arrived by the first post, from Anna. He read it. It was only a few words : " You are here again, my love—I welcome you. I do long to see you. Don't keep me waiting too long. Your Anna. . . ."

George got up. He did not himself know what it was in the short letter that touched him so strangely. Anna's letters had always retained, in spite of all their tenderness, a certain precise, almost conventional element, and he had frequently jokingly called them " proclamations." This was couched in a tone that reminded him of the passionate girl of by-gone days, of that love of his whom he had almost forgotten, and a strangely unexpected anxiety seized on his heart. He rushed downstairs, took the nearest fiacre and drove to the country. He soon felt agreeably distracted by the sight of the people in the streets who meant nothing to him at all ; and later, when he was near the wood, he felt soothed by the charm of the blue summer day.

Suddenly, sooner than George had anticipated, the vehicle stopped in front of the country house. Involuntarily George first looked up to the balcony under the gable. A little table was standing there with a white cover and a little basket on it. Oh yes, Therese had been staying here for a few days. He now remembered for the first time. Therese . . . ! Where was it now ? He got out, paid the carriage and went into the front garden where the blue angel stood on its unpretentious pedestal amid the faded flower-beds. He stepped into the house. Marie was just laying the table in the large centre room. " Madam's over there in the garden," she said.

The verandah door was open. The planks of its floor creaked underneath George's feet. The garden with its perfume and its sultriness received him. It was the old garden. During all the days in which George had been far away it had lain there silently, just as it was lying at this minute ; in the dawn, in the sunshine, in the twilight, in the darkness of night ; always the same. . . . The gravel path cut straight through the field to the heights. There were children's voices on the other side of the bushes from which red berries were hanging. And over there on the white seat, with her elbow on its arm, very pale, in her flowing blue morning dress, yes, that was Anna. Yes, really she. She had seen him now. She tried to get up. He saw it, and saw at the same time that she found it difficult. But why ? Was she spell-bound by excitement ? Or was the hour of trial so near ? He signed to her with his hand that she was to remain seated, and she really did sit down again, and only just stretched out her arms lightly towards him. Her eyes were shining with bliss. George walked very quickly, with his grey felt hat in his hand, and now he was at her side.

" At last," she said, and it was a voice which came from as far back as those words in her letter of this morning. He took her hands, shook them in a strange clumsy way, felt a lump in his throat, but was still unable to articulate anything and just nodded and smiled. And suddenly he knelt before her on the grass, with her hands in his and his head in her lap. He felt her lightly taking her hands away, and putting them on his head ; and then he heard himself crying quite softly. And he felt as though he were in a sweet vague dream, a little boy again and lying at his mother's feet, and this moment were already a mere memory, painful and far away, even while he was living it.

VIII

FRAU GOLOWSKI came out of the house. George could see her from the top end of the garden as she stepped on to the verandah. He hurried excitedly towards her, but as soon as she saw him in the distance she shook her head.

" Not yet ? " asked George.

" The Professor thinks," replied Frau Golowski, " some time before dark."

" Some time before dark," said George and looked at his watch. And now it was only three.

She held out her hand sympathetically and George looked into her kind eyes, which were somewhat tired by her nocturnal vigils. The white transparent curtain in front of Anna's window had just been slightly drawn back. Old Doctor Stauber appeared by the window, threw George a friendly reassuring glance, disappeared again and the curtains were drawn. Frau Rosner was sitting in the large centre room by the round table. George could only see from the verandah the outlines of her figure ; her face was quite in the shade. Then a whimpering and then a loud groan forced their way from the room in which Anna lay. George stared up at the window, stood still for a while, then turned round and walked for the hundredth time to-day up the path to the top of the garden. It is clear that she is already too weak to shriek, he thought ; and his heart pained him. She had lain in labour for two whole days and two whole nights. The third day was now approaching its end,—and now it was still to last until evening came. On the evening of the first day Doctor Stauber had called in the Professor, who had been there twice yesterday and had remained in the house since noon to-day. While Anna had gone to sleep for a few minutes, and the nurse was watching by her bed, he had walked up and down in the garden with George and had endeavoured to explain to him all the peculiar features of the case. For the time being there was no ground for anxiety. They could hear the child's heart beating quite clearly. The Professor was a still fairly young man with a long blonde beard, and his words trickled gently and kindly like drops of some anodyne drug. He spoke to the sick woman like a child, stroked her over the hair and forehead, caressed her hands and gave her pet names. George had learned from the nurse that this young doctor exhibited the same devotion and same patience at every sick-bed. What a profession ! thought George, who had once, during these three bad days, fled to Vienna for a few hours, which enabled a man to have a sound dreamless sleep for six good hours up there in the attic this very night while Anna was writhing in pain.

He walked along by the faded lilac-bushes, tore off leaves, crunched them in his hand and threw them on the ground. A lady in a black-and-white striped morning dress was walking in the next garden on the other side of the low bushes. She looked at George seriously and almost sympathetically. Quite so ! thought George. Of course she heard Anna's screams the day before yesterday, yesterday and to-day. The whole place in fact knew of what was happening there ; even the young girls in the *outré* Gothic villa, who had once taken him for the interesting seducer ; and there was real humour in the fact that a strange gentleman with a reddish pointed beard, who lived two houses away, should have suddenly greeted him yesterday in the village with respectful understanding.

Remarkable, thought George, how one can make oneself

popular with people. But Frau Rosner let it be seen that even though she did not regard George as mainly responsible for the seriousness of the position she certainly regarded him as somewhat callous. He did not bear any grudge for this against the poor good woman. She could not of course have any idea how much he loved Anna. It was not long since he had known it himself. She had not addressed any question to him on that morning of his arrival when George had lifted his head off her lap after a long silent fit of weeping, but he had read in the painful surprise of her eyes that she guessed the truth, and he thought he understood why she did not question him. She must realise how completely she possessed him again, how henceforth he belonged to her more than he had ever done before, and when he told her in the subsequent hours and days of the time which he had spent far away from her, and that now fateful name resounded casually but yet insistently out of the catalogue of the women whom he had met, she smiled, no doubt, in her slightly mocking way, but scarcely differently than when he spoke of Else or Sissy, or the little girls in their blue dresses who had peeped into the music-room when he was playing.

He had been living in the villa for two weeks, had been feeling well and in good form for serious work. He spread out every morning on the little table, where Therese's needlework had lain a short time ago, scores, works on musical theory, musical writing-paper, and occupied himself with solving problems in harmony and counterpoint. He often lay down in the meadow by the edge of the forest and read some favourite book or other, let melodies ring within him, indulged in day-dreams and was quite happy, with the rustling of the trees and the brilliance of the sun. In the afternoon, when Anna was resting, he would read aloud or talk to her. They often talked with affectionate anticipation about the little creature that was soon to come into the world, but never about their own future, whether distant or immediate. But when he sat by her bed, or walked up and down the garden with her arm-in-arm, or sat by her side on the white seat under the pear-tree, where the shining stillness of the late summer day rested above them, he knew they were tied fast to each other for all time, and that even the temporary separation with which they were faced could have no power to affect them in view of the certain feeling that they were all in all to each other.

It was only since the pains had come upon her that she seemed removed from him to a sphere where he could not follow her. Yesterday he had sat by her bed for hours and had held her hand in his. She had been patient, as always, had anxiously inquired if he were quite comfortable in the house, had begged him to work and go for walks as he had done before, since after all he could not help her, and had assured him that since she was suffering she loved him even more. And yet she was not the same, George felt, as she had been during these days. Particularly when she screamed out—as she had this morning in her worst pains—her soul was so far away from him that he felt frightened.

He was near the house again. No noise came from Anna's room, in front of the window of which the curtains moved slightly. Old Doctor Stauber was standing on the verandah. George hastened towards him with a dry throat. "What is it?" he asked hastily.

Doctor Stauber put his hand on his shoulder. "Going on nicely."

A groan came from within, grew louder, grew into a wild frenzied scream. George passed his hand over his damp forehead and said to the doctor with a bitter smile: "Is that what you mean by going on nicely?"

Stauber shrugged his shoulders. "It is written, 'With pain shalt thou . . .'"

George felt a certain sense of resentment. He had

never believed in the God of the childishly pious, who
was supposed to reveal himself as the fulfiller of the wishes
of wretched men and women, as the avenger and forgiver
of miserable human sins.   The Nameless One which he
felt in the infinite beyond his senses, and transcending all
understanding, could only regard prayer and blasphemy
as poor words out of a human mouth.   Not even when
his mother had died, after the senseless martyrdom of her
suffering, not even when his father had died, passing away
painlessly so far as he could understand, had he presumed
to indulge in the belief that his own personal misfortunes
in the world's progress signified more than the falling of
a leaf.   He had not bowed down in cowardly humility
to any inscrutable solution of the riddle, nor had he
foolishly murmured against an ungracious power of whose
decrees he was the personal victim.

To-day he felt for the first time as though somewhere
or other in the clouds an incomprehensible game was being
played in which his own fortunes were the stakes.   The
scream within had died away and only groans were
audible.

" And the beating of the heart ? " asked George.

Doctor Stauber looked at him.   " It could still be heard
clearly ten minutes ago."

George fought against a dreadful thought which had been
hounded up out of the depths of his soul.   He was healthy,
she was healthy, two strong young people. . . . Could
anything like that be really possible ?

Doctor Stauber put his hand on his shoulder again.
" Go for a walk," he said.   " We'll call you as soon as
it's time."   And he turned away.

George remained standing on the verandah for another
minute.   He saw Frau Rosner sitting huddled up in solitary brooding on the sofa near the wall in the large room
that was beginning to grow dim in the shade of the late
afternoon.   He went away, walked round the house

and went up the wooden stairs into his attic. He threw
himself on the bed and shut his eyes. After a few minutes
he got up, walked up and down in the room, but gave up
doing so as the floor creaked. He went on to the balcony. The score of *Tristan* lay open on the table. George
looked at the music. It was the prelude to the third act.
The music rang in his ears. The sea waves were beating
heavily on a cliff shore, and out of the mournful distance
rang the sad melody of an English horn. He looked
over the pages far away into the silver-white brilliance of
the daylight. There was sunshine everywhere—on the
roofs, paths, gardens, hills and forests. The sky was
spread out in its azure vastness and the smell of the har-
vest floated up from the depths. How were things with
me a year ago ? thought George. I was in Vienna, quite
alone. I had not an idea. I had sent her a song . . .
' *Deinem Blick mich zu bequemen* ' . . . but I scarcely
gave her a thought . . . and now she lies down there
dying. . . . He gave a violent start. He had meant to
say mentally . . . " She is lying in labour," and the words
"lies dying" had as it were stolen their way on to his lips.
But why was he so frightened ? How childish ! As
though there existed presentiments like that ! And if
there really were danger, and the doctors had to decide,
then of course they would have to save the mother. Why,
Doctor Stauber had only explained that to him a few
days ago. What, after all, is a child that hasn't yet
lived ? Nothing. He had begotten it at some moment
or other without having wished it, without having even
thought of the possibility that he might have become a
father. How did he know either that in that dark hour
of ecstasy, behind closed blinds a few weeks ago he had
not . . . also become a father without having wished it,
without having even thought of the possibility ; and perhaps it might have happened without his ever knowing !

He heard voices and looked down ; the Professor's

coachman had caught hold of the arm of the housemaid, who was only slightly resisting. Perhaps the foundations are being laid here too of a new human life, thought George, and turned away in disgust. Then he went back into his room, carefully filled his cigarette-case out of the box that stood on the table, and it suddenly seemed to him that his excitement was baseless and even childish, and it occurred to him: " My mother, too, once lay like that before I came into the world, just as Anna is doing now. I wonder if my father walked about as nervously as I am doing? I wonder if he would be here now if he were still alive? I wonder if I would have told him at all? I wonder if all this would have happened if he had lived? He thought of the beautiful serene summer days by the Veldeser Lake. His comfortable room in his father's villa swept up in his memory and in some vague way, almost dreamwise, the bare attic with the creaking floor in which he now found himself seemed to typify his whole present existence in contrast to that former life which had been so free from care and responsibility. He remembered a serious talk about the future which he had had a few days ago with Felician. Immediately after this thought there came into his mind the conversation which he had had with a woman in the country, who had introduced herself with the offer to take charge of the child. She and her husband possessed a small property near the railway, only an hour away from Vienna, and her only daughter had died in the previous year. She had promised that the little one should be well looked after, as well, in fact, as though it were not a stranger's at all, and as George thought of this he suddenly felt as though his heart were standing still. It will be there before dark. . . . The child. . . . His child, but a strange woman was waiting somewhere to take it away with her. He was so tired after the excitement of the last few days that his knees hurt him. He remembered having previously felt similar physical sensations, the evening after his "leaving-examination" and the time when he had learnt of Labinski's suicide. How different, how joyful, how full of hope had been his mood three days ago, just before the pains began! He now felt nothing except an unparalleled dejection, while he found the musty smell of the attic more and more unpleasant. He lit a cigarette and stepped on to the balcony again. The warm silent air did him good. The sunshine still lay on the Sommerhaidenweg and a gilded cross shone over the walls from the direction of the churchyard.

He heard a noise beneath him. Steps? Yes, steps and voices too. He left the balcony and the room and rushed down over the creaking wooden staircase. A door opened, steps were hurrying over the floor. The next moment he was on the bottom step opposite Frau Golowski. His heart stood still. He opened his mouth without asking.

"Yes," she nodded, "a boy."

He gripped both her hands and felt, while he was beaming all over, a stream of happiness was running through his soul with a potency and intense warmth that he had never anticipated. He suddenly noticed that Frau Golowski's eyes were not shining as brightly as they certainly ought to have. The stream of happiness within him ebbed back. Something choked his throat. "Well?" he said. Then he added, almost menacingly: "Does it live?"

"It just breathed once. . . . The Professor hopes . . ."

George pushed the woman on one side, reached the great centre room in three strides and stood still as though spell-bound. The Professor, in a long white linen apron, held a small creature in his arms and rocked it hurriedly to and fro. George stood still. The Professor nodded to him and went on undisturbed with what he was doing. He was examining the little creature in his arms with

20

scrutinising eyes, he put it on the table, over which a white linen cloth had been spread, made the child's limbs execute violent exercises, rubbed its breast and face, then lifted it high up several times in succession, and George always saw how the child's head drooped heavily on to its breast. Then the doctor put it on to the linen cloth, listened with his ear on its bosom, got up, put one hand on its little body and motioned gently with the other to George to approach.

Involuntarily holding his breath George came quite near him. He looked first at the doctor and then at the little creature which lay on the white linen. It had its eyes quite open, strangely big blue eyes, like those of Anna. The face looked quite different from what George had expected, not wrinkled and ugly like that of an old dwarf, no ; it was really a human face, a silent beautiful child-face, and George knew that these features were the image of his own.

The Professor said gently: " I've not heard its heart beat for the last hour."

George nodded. Then he asked hoarsely: " How is she ? "

" Quite well, but you mustn't go in yet, Herr Baron."

" No," replied George and shook his head. He stared at the immobile little body with its bluish shimmer and knew that he was standing in front of the corpse of his own child. Nevertheless he looked at the doctor again and asked: " Can nothing more be done ? "

He shrugged his shoulders.

George breathed deeply and pointed to the closed bedroom door. " Does she know yet——" He asked the doctor.

" Not yet. Let's be thankful for the time being that it is over. She has gone through a lot, poor girl. I only regret that it should turn out to have been for nothing."

" You expected it, Herr Professor ? "

" I feared it since this morning."

" And why . . . why ? "

The doctor answered softly and gently: " A very exceptional case, as I told you before."

" You told me . . . ? "

" Yes, I tried to explain to you that this possibility . . . it was strangled, you see, by the umbilical cord. Scarcely one or two per cent. of births end like that." He was silent.

George gazed at the child. Quite right, the Professor had prepared him in advance only he had not taken it seriously. Frau Rosner was standing by him with helpless eyes. George held out his hand to her and they looked at each other like persons whom the sore stress of circumstances has made companions in misfortune. Then Frau Rosner sank down on a chair by the wall.

The Professor said to George: " I will now go and just have a look at the mother."

" Mother ! " repeated George, and gazed at him.

The doctor looked away.

" You will tell her ? " asked George.

" No, not at once. Anyway, she will be ready for it. She asked several times in the course of the day if it was still alive. It will not have so dreadful an effect upon her as you fear, Herr Baron . . . at any rate during the first hours, the first days. You mustn't forget what she has gone through."

He pressed George's limply-hanging hand and went.

George stood there motionless. He was gazing continually at the little creature, and it seemed to him a picture of undreamt-of beauty. He touched its cheeks, shoulders, arms, hands, fingers. How mysteriously complete it all was ! And there it lay, having died without having lived, destined to go from one darkness into another, through a senseless nothingness. There it lay, the sweet tiny body which was ready for life and yet was unable to

move. There they shone, those big blue eyes, as though
with desire to drink in the light of heaven, and completely
blind before they had seen a ray. And there was the small
round mouth which was open as though with thirst, but yet
could never drink at a mother's breast. There it gazed,
that white child-face with its perfect human features,
which was never to receive or feel the kiss of a mother,
the kiss of a father. How he loved this child! How he
loved it, now that it was too late! A choking despair
rose within his throat. He could not cry. He looked
around him. No one was in the room and it was quite still
next door. He had no desire to go into that other room,
nor had he any fear. He only felt that it would have
been rather senseless. His eye returned to the dead child,
and suddenly the poignant question thrilled through him
whether it was really bound to be true. Could not every
one make a mistake, a physician as much as a layman?
He held his open palm before the child's open lips and it
was as though something cool was breathed towards him.
And then he held both hands over the child's breast and
again it seemed as though a light puff were playing over
the tiny body. But it felt just the same as in the other
place: no breath of life had blown towards him. He
now bent down again and his lips touched the child's cool
forehead. Something strange, something he scarcely felt
tingled through his body to the very tips of his toes. He
knew it now; he had lost the game up there in the clouds,
his child was dead. Then he slowly lifted his head and
turned away. The sight of the garden tempted him into
the open. He stepped on to the verandah and saw Doctor
Stauber and Frau Rosner sitting on the seat that was
propped against the wall—both silent. They looked at
him. He turned away as though he did not know them
and went into the garden. The shadow of the house fell
obliquely over the lawn, there was still sunlight higher up
but it was dull and as though without the strength to

illumine the air. Why did he want to think of that light
which was sun and yet did not shine, that blue in the
heights which was heaven and yet did not bless him?
What was the point of the silence of this garden, which
should console and comfort him, and yet received him
to-day as though it were some strange inhospitable place?
It gradually occurred to him that just such a twilight
had enveloped him in a dream a short time ago with a
dreariness of which he had previously had no idea, and
had filled his soul with incomprehensible melancholy.
What now? he said to himself aloud. He did not seek
for any answer, and only knew that something unforeseen
and unalterable had happened that must change the face
of the world for him for all time. He thought of the day
when his father had died. A wild grief had overwhelmed
him then; yet he had been able to cry and the world
had not suddenly become dark and void. His father had
really lived, had once been young, had worked, loved,
had children, experienced joys and sorrows. And the
mother who had borne him had not suffered in vain. And
even if he himself should have to die to-day, however early
it might be, he had nevertheless a life behind him, a life
full of light and music, happiness and suffering, hope and
anxiety, steeped in all the fulness of the world. And even
if Anna had passed away to-day, in the hour when she
gave life to a new being, she would as it were have fulfilled
her lot and her end would have had its terrible but none the
less deep significance. But what had happened to his child
was senseless, was revolting—a piece of irony from somewhere or other, whither one could send no question and no
answer. What was the point of it all? What had been
the significance of these past months with all their dreams,
their troubles and their hopes? For he knew, all in a
flash, that the expectation of the wonderful hour in which
his child was to be born had always lain in the depths of
his soul every single day, even those which were most

matter-of-fact, those which were most vacant, or those which were most wanton. And he felt ashamed, impoverished, miserable.

He stood by the garden fence at the top end and looked towards the edge of the forest, towards his seat on which he had rested so often, and he felt as though forest and field and seat had previously been his possessions, and that he must now surrender them too, like so much else. In a corner of the garden stood a dark grey neglected summer-house with three little window-apertures and a narrow opening for a door. He had always disliked it, and had only gone in once for a few moments. To-day he felt drawn inside. He sat down on the cracked seat and suddenly felt hidden and soothed, as though all that had happened were less true or could in some inconceivable way be undone. Yet this hallucination soon vanished, he left the inhospitable room and stepped into the open.

I must now go back into the house again, he thought with a sense of exhaustion, and could not quite realise that the dead body of his child must be resting in the dark room, which he could see from here stretching behind the verandah like an unfathomable darkness. He walked slowly down the garden. Anna's mother was standing with a gentleman on the verandah. George recognised old Rosner. He stood there in his overcoat, he had laid his hat in front of him on the table. He passed a pocket handkerchief over his forehead and his red-lidded eyes twitched. He went towards George and pressed his hand. "What a pity that it turned out differently," he said, "than we had all hoped and expected!"

George nodded. He then remembered that the old gentleman's heart had not been quite right during the past week and inquired after his health.

"It is kind of you to ask, Herr Baron. I am a little better, only I find going uphill rather troublesome."

George noticed that the glass door that led to the centre

room was closed. " Excuse me," he said to old Rosner, strode straight to the door, opened it and quickly closed it behind him. Frau Golowski and Doctor Stauber were standing near the table and speaking to each other. He walked up to them and they suddenly stopped talking.

" Well ? " he inquired.

Doctor Stauber said : " We have been speaking about the . . . formalities. Frau Golowski will be kind enough to see to all that."

" Thank you," replied George and held out his hand to Frau Golowski.

" All that," he thought. A coffin, a funeral, a notification to the local registry ; a son born of Anna Rosner, spinster, died on the same day. Nothing about the father of course. Yes, his part was finished. Only to-day ? Had it not been finished the very second when quite by chance he became a father ?

He looked at the table. The cloth was spread over the tiny corpse. Oh, how quick ! he thought bitterly. Am I never to see it again ? I suppose I may be allowed to, once. He drew the cloth a little away from the body and held it high up. He saw a pale child-face which was quite familiar to him, only since then some one had closed the eyes. The old grandfather's clock in the corner ticked. Six o'clock. Scarcely an hour had passed since his child had been born and died : the fact was already as indisputably certain as though it could never have been otherwise.

He felt a light touch on the shoulder.

" She took it quietly," said Doctor Stauber, standing behind him.

George dropped the cloth over the child's face and turned his head towards the side. " She already knows, then . . . ? "

Doctor Stauber nodded. Frau Golowski had turned away.

"Who told her ? " asked George.

" It wasn't necessary to tell her," replied Doctor Stauber, " was it ? "   He turned to Frau Golowski.

The latter explained :   " When I went in to her she just looked at me, and then I saw at once that she already knew."

" And what did she say ? "

" Nothing—nothing at all.   She turned her eyes towards the window and was quite still.   She asked where you had gone, Herr Baron, and what you were doing."

George breathed deeply.   The door of Anna's room opened.   The Professor came out in a black coat.   " She is quite quiet," he said to George.   " You can go in to her."

" Did she speak to you about it ? " asked George.

The Professor shook his head.   Then he said : " I am afraid I must go into town now ; you'll excuse me, won't you ?   I hope things will go on all right.   I shall be here early to-morrow any way.   Good-bye, dear Herr Baron." He pressed his hand sympathetically.   " You'll drive in with me, Doctor Stauber, won't you ? "

" Yes," said Doctor Stauber, " I only want to say good-bye to Anna."   He went.

George turned to the Professor.   " May I ask you something ? "

" Please do."

" I should very much like to know, Herr Professor, whether this is simply imagination.   It seems to me, you know "—and he again lifted up the cloth from the tiny corpse—" as though this child did not look like a new-born one, more beautiful, so to speak.   I feel as though the faces of new-born children were bound to be more wrinkled, more like old men.   I can't tell you whether I have ever seen one or whether I've only read about it."

" You are quite right," replied the Professor.   " It is just in cases of this kind, and also of course when things turn out more fortunately, that the features of the children

are not distorted, are frequently, in fact, quite beautiful."
He contemplated the little face with professional sympathy,
nodded a few times: "Pity, pity" . . . let the cloth fall
down again, and George knew that he had seen his child's
face for the last time. What name would it have had?
Felician. . . . Good-bye, little Felician!

Doctor Stauber came out of the next room and gently
closed the door. "Anna is expecting you," he said to
George. The latter gave him his hand, shook hands with
the Professor again, nodded to Frau Golowski and went
into the next room.

The nurse got up from Anna's side and disappeared out
of the room. Opposite the door hung a mirror in which
George saw an elegant young gentleman who was pale
and was smiling. Anna lay in her bed, which stood clear
in the middle of the room, with big clear eyes, which looked
straight at George.

"What kind of a figure do I cut?" he thought. He
pushed the chair close to her bed with some ceremonious-
ness, sat down, grasped her hand, put it to his forehead
and then kissed her fingers long and almost ardently.

Anna was the first to speak. "You were in the garden?" she asked.

"Yes, I was in the garden."

"I saw you come down from the top some time ago."

"You had better not talk, Anna. Don't you feel it a
strain?"

"These few words! Oh no. But you can tell me
something. . . ."

He was holding her hand in his all the time and looking
at her fingers. Then he said: "Do you know that there
is a little summer-house at the top end of the garden?
Yes, of course you know. . . . I only mean, we'd never
properly realised it."

"I was in there a few times during the first week," said
Anna. "I don't like it."

"No, indeed!"

"Have you done any work this morning?" she then asked.

"What an idea, Anna!"

She shook her head quite gently. "And recently you have been getting on so well with it."

He smiled.

She remained serious. "You were in town yesterday?" she asked.

"You know I was."

"Did you find any letters? I mean important ones."

"You should really not talk so much, Anna. I'll tell you everything right enough. Well then, I found no letters of any importance. There was nothing from Detmold either. Anyway, I'll go and see Professor Viebiger one of these days. But we can talk about these things another time, don't you think? And so far as work goes . . . I've been having another look at *Tristan* this morning. I even know it down to the smallest detail. I could trust myself to conduct it to-day, if it came to the point."

She was silent and looked at him.

He remembered the evening when he had sat by her side at the Munich opera, as though enveloped in a transparent veil of the notes he loved so well. But he said nothing about it.

It grew dark. Anna's features began to grow dim. "Are you going to town to-day?" she asked.

He had not thought of doing so. But he now felt as though a kind of relief were beckoning to him. Yes, he would go in. What, after all, could he do out here? But he did not answer at once.

Anna began again: "I think you would perhaps like to speak to your brother."

"Yes, I should like to very much. I suppose you are going to sleep soon?"

"I hope so."

" How tired you must be," he said as he stroked her arm.

" No, it is rather different. I feel so awake . . . I can't tell you how awake I feel. . . . It seems as though I had never been so awake in my whole life. And I know at the same time that I'm going to sleep more deeply than I ever have . . . as soon as I've once closed my eyes."

" Yes, of course you will. But may I stay a bit longer with you ? I'd really like to go on sitting here till you've fallen asleep."

" No, George, if you are here I can't go to sleep. But just stay a bit longer. It's so nice."

He held her hand all the time and looked out on to the garden, which was now lying in the twilight.

" You weren't very much up at Auhof this year ? " said Anna indifferently, as though simply making conversation.

" Oh yes, nearly every day. Didn't I tell you ?—I think Else will marry James Wyner and go with him to England."

He knew that she was not thinking of Else but of some one quite different. And he asked himself : Does she perhaps mean . . . that that is the reason ?

A warm puff blew in from outside. Children's voices rang in. George looked out. He saw the white seat gleaming under the pear-tree and thought of how Anna had waited for him there in her flowing dress, beneath the fruit-laden branches, girdled by the gentle miracle of her motherhood. And he asked himself: " Was it fated then that it must end like this ? Or was it after all so fated at the moment when we embraced each other for the first time ? " The Professor's remark that one to two per cent. of all births ended like that came into his mind. So it was a fact that since people had started being born one or two in every hundred must perish in this senseless fashion at the very moment when they were brought into the light !

And so many must die in their first years, and so many in the
flower of their youth, and so many as men.   And again a
fated number put an end to their own lives, like Labinski.
And so many were doomed to fail in their attempt, as in
Oskar Ehrenberg's case. Why search for reasons ? Some
law is at work, incomprehensible and inexorable, which
we men cannot struggle against. Who is entitled to complain ? why should I be the victim ? If it doesn't happen
to one, it will happen to another . . . whether innocent or
guilty like he was. One to two per cent. get hit, that is
heavenly justice. The children who were laughing in the
garden opposite, they were allowed to live. Allowed ?
No, they *must* live, even as his own child had had to die,
after the first breath it drew, doomed to travel from one
darkness into another, through a senseless nothingness.

It was twilight outside and it was almost night in the
room. Anna lay still and motionless. Her hand did not
move in George's, but when George got up he saw that
her eyes were open. He bent down, hesitated a moment,
then put his arm round her neck and kissed her on her
lips, which were hot and dry and did not answer his touch.
Then he went. In the next room the hanging lamp was
alight over the table on which the dead child had lain
some while back. The green tablecloth was now spread
out as though nothing had happened. The door of Frau
Golowski's room was open. The light of a candle shone
in, and George knew that his child was sleeping in there,
its first and last sleep.

Frau Golowski and Frau Rosner sat next to each other
on the sofa by the wall, dumb, and as though huddled
together. George went up to them. " Has Herr Rosner
gone already ? " He turned to Frau Rosner.

" Yes, he rode into the town with the doctors," she
answered, and looked at him questioningly.

" She is quiet." George answered her look. " I think she
will sleep soundly."

" Won't you take something ? " asked Frau Golowski.
" You haven't since one o'clock had . . ."

" No thanks, I'm going into town now. I want to speak
to my brother. I am also expecting important letters.
I'll be here again early to-morrow." He took his leave,
went up to his attic, fetched the *Tristan* score from the
balcony into the room, took his stick and overcoat, lit a
cigarette and left the house. As soon as he was in the
street he felt freer. An awful upheaval lay behind him.
It had ended unhappily, but at any rate it had ended.
And Anna was bound to be all right. Of course with
mothers as well there was the fated percentage. But it
was clear that the possibility of an unfortunate issue
was according to the law of probabilities necessarily much
less than if the child had remained alive.

He walked through the straggling village with swift
strides, tried not to think of anything and looked with
forced attention at every single house by which he passed.
They were all mean, most of them positively dreary and
squalid. Behind them little gardens sloped up to vineyards, cultivated fields and meadows in the evening mist.
In an almost empty inn garden a few musicians were
sitting by a long table, playing a melancholy waltz on
violins, guitars and a concertina. Later on he passed
more presentable houses, and he looked in through open
windows into decently lighted rooms in which there were
tables laid for dinner. He eventually took his seat in a
cheerful inn garden, as far away as possible from the other
not very numerous customers. He took his meal and soon
felt a salutary fatigue come over him. On the tram he almost
dozed off in his corner. It was only when the conveyance was driving through more lively streets that he
thoroughly woke up and remembered what had happened,
with an agonising but arid precision. He got out and
walked home through the moist sultriness of the Stadtpark. Felician was not at home. He found a telegram

lying on his secretary. It was from Detmold and ran as follows : "We request you kindly to inform us if you can possibly come to us within the next three days. This offer is to be considered for the time being as binding on neither party ; travelling expenses paid in any event.——Faithfully, Manager of the Hoftheater." Next to it lay the red form for the answer.

George was in a state of nervous tension. What should he answer now ? The telegram clearly indicated that there was a vacancy for the post of conductor. Should he ask for a postponement ? After eight days it would be quite easy to go there for an interview and then come back at once. He found thinking about it a strain. At any rate the matter could wait till to-morrow, and if that was too late then there would be no essential change in the position after all. He would always be welcomed as a special visitor, he knew that already. It was perhaps better not to bind himself . . . to go on working at his training somewhere, without yet taking obligations or responsibilities upon himself, and then to be ready and equipped for the following year. But what paltry considerations these were, when compared with the terrible event of his life which had occurred to-day ! He took up the malachite paper-weight and put it on the telegram. What now . . . ? he asked himself. Go to the club and rout out Felician ? Yet that was not quite the place to tell him about the matter. It would really be best to stay at home and wait for him. It was in fact a little tempting to undress at once and lie down. But he certainly would not be able to sleep. So he came to think of tidying up his papers a little once again. He opened the drawer in his secretary, sorted bills and letters and made notes in his note-book. The noise of the street came in through the open windows as though from a distance. He thought of how he had read the letters of his dead parents in the same place in the previous summer after his father's death, and how the

same noise of the town and the same perfume **from**
the park had streamed in to him just like to-day. **The**
year that had elapsed since then seemed in his **tired**
mind to extend into eternities, then contracted again **into**
a short span of time, and something kept whispering in **his**
soul: What for . . . what for? His child was dead. It
would be buried in the churchyard by the Sommerhaidenweg. It would rest there in consecrated ground, from the
toilsome journey which it was fated to take from one darkness into another through a senseless nothingness. It would
lie under a little cross, as though it had lived and suffered
a whole human life. . . . As though it had lived! It had
really lived from the moment when its heart had already
begun to beat in its mother's body. No, even earlier. . . . It
had belonged to the realm of the living from the very moment when its mother's body had received it. And George
thought of how many children of men and women were fated
to perish even earlier than his own child, how many, wished
and unwished, were fated to die in the first days of their
life without their own mothers even having an idea. And
while he dozed with shut eyes, half asleep and half awake,
in front of his secretary, he saw nothing but shining crosses
standing up on tiny mounds, as though it were a toy
cemetery and a reddish yellow toy sun were shining over
it. But suddenly the image represented the Cadenabbia
cemetery. George was sitting like a little boy on the
stone wall which surrounded it, and suddenly turned his
gaze down towards the lake. And then there rode in a
very long narrow boat, beneath dull yellow sails, with a
green shawl on her shoulders, a woman, sitting motionless
on the rowing bench, a woman whose face he tried to
recognise with vague and almost painful efforts.

The bell rang. George got up. What was it? Oh, **of**
course, there was no one there to open. The servant **had**
been discharged since the first day of the month, and **the**
porter's wife, who now looked after the brothers, was **not**

in the apartment at this hour.   George went into the hall
and opened the door.   Heinrich Bermann was standing in
the hall.

" I saw a light in your room from down below," he said.
" It was a good idea my first going past your house.   I was
going, as a matter of fact, to drive out to your place in the
country."

Is his manner really so excited ? thought George, or do
I only think it is ?   He asked him to come in and sit down.

" Thanks, thanks, I prefer to walk up and down.   No,
don't light the high lamp.   The table lamp's quite enough.
. . . Anyway—how are you getting on out there ? "

" A child was born this morning," replied George quietly.
" But unfortunately it was dead."

" Still-born ? "

" I don't know if one can say that," replied George with
a bitter smile ; " for it is supposed to have drawn one
breath according to the doctor.   The pains lasted for three
days on end.   It was ghastly.   Now it's all over."

" Dead !   I'm very sorry—I really am."   He held out
his hand to George.

" It was a boy," said George, " and strangely enough,
very beautiful.   Quite different from what new-born children usually look like."   He then told him, too, how he
had stayed quite a time in an inhospitable summer-house
which he had never gone into before, and the strange way
in which the lighting of the country had suddenly altered.
" It was a light," said George, " that places in one's
dreams sometimes have.   Quite indefinite . . . like twilight . . . but rather mournful."   While he said this, he
knew that he would have described the whole matter
quite differently to Felician.

Heinrich sat in the corner of the ottoman and let the
other speak.   He then began : " It is strange.   All this
affects me very much, of course, and yet . . . it calms me
at the same time."

" Calms you ? "

" Yes. As though certain things which I unhappily
had to fear had suddenly grown less probable."

" What kind of things ? "

Without listening to him Heinrich went on speaking
with set teeth. " Or is it only because I am in the
presence of another man's grief ? Or is it because I am
somewhere else, in a strange flat ? That would be quite
possible. Haven't you noticed that even one's own death
strikes one as something highly improbable, when one is
travelling for instance ; frequently in fact when one is
out for a walk. Man is subject to incomprehensible illusions like that."

Heinrich turned round after a few seconds, as though
he had regained his self-control, but remained standing by
the window with both hands resting on the sill behind
him, and said laconically in a hard voice : " There's
the possibility, you see, of the girl whose acquaintance
you casually made the other day at my place having
committed suicide. Please don't look so startled. As you
know, many of her letters hinted that she would do it."

" Well ? " said George.

Heinrich lifted his hand deprecatingly. " I never took
it seriously at all. But I got a letter this morning which,
I don't quite know how to express it, had an uncanny
ring of truth about it. As a matter of fact there is nothing in it which she hasn't already written to me ten or
twenty times over; but the tone . . . the tone . . . To
come to the point, I am as good as convinced that it has
happened this time. Perhaps at this very minute ! " He
stopped and stared in front of him.

" No, Heinrich." George stepped up to him and put
his hand on his shoulder. " No ! " he added, more firmly,
" I don't believe it at all. I spoke to her a few weeks
ago. You know about that. And then she certainly did
not give me the impression . . . I also saw her playing

21

comedy . . . If you had seen her acting in that impudent farce, you wouldn't believe it either, Heinrich. She only wants to revenge herself on you for your cruelty. Unconsciously, perhaps. Probably she has convinced herself on many occasions that she cannot go on living, but the fact that she has stuck it out till to-day . . . Of course, if she had done it at once . . ."

Heinrich shook his head impatiently. " Just listen, George. I telegraphed to the Summer Theatre. I inquired if she were still there, suggesting that it was a question of a new part for her, rehearsal of a new piece of mine, or something like that. I have been waiting at home . . . till now . . . but there is no answer. If I don't get one, or not a satisfactory one, I'll certainly go there."

" Yes, but why didn't you simply ask if she . . ."

" If she has killed herself ? One doesn't want to make oneself ridiculous, George. I might have asked for news on that point every other day or so, of course. . . . It would certainly have had a kind of grotesque humour right enough."

" Look here now—you don't believe it yourself ? "

" I'll go home now to see if there's a telegram there. Good-bye, George. Forgive me. I couldn't stand it any more at home, you see. . . . I am really sorry to have bothered you with my own affairs at a time like this. Once more, I ask you to forgive me."

" You had no idea . . . And even if you had known . . . In my case, it's quite—a finished chapter, so to speak. In my case, there is unfortunately nothing more to do."

He looked excitedly out of the window, over the tops of the trees, towards the red spires and roofs which towered up out of the faint red light of the evening town. Then he said : " I'll come with you, Heinrich. I can't start anything at home. I mean . . . If you don't mind my society."

" Mind ! . . . My dear George ! . . . " He pressed his hand.

They went. At first they walked along the park in silence. George remembered his walk with Heinrich through the Prater Allee last autumn, and immediately after that he remembered the May evening when Anna Rosner had appeared in the Waldsteingarten later than the others, and Frau Ehrenberg had whispered to him, " I have asked her specially for you." Yes, for him. If it had not been for that evening Anna would never have become his mistress, and none of all the events which lay heavy on him to-day would ever have happened. Was there some law at work in this ? Of course ! So many children had to come into the world every year, and a certain number of those out of wedlock, and good Frau Ehrenberg had imagined that inviting Fräulein Anna Rosner for Baron Von Wergenthin had been a matter of her own personal fancy.

" Is Anna quite out of danger ? " asked Heinrich.

" I hope so," replied George. Then he spoke about the pain which she had suffered, her patience, and her goodness. He felt the need of describing her as a perfect angel, as though he could thereby atone a little for the wrong he had done her.

Heinrich nodded. " She really seems to be one of the few women who are made to be mothers. It isn't true, you know, that there are many of that kind. Having children—that's what they're all there for; but being mothers ! And to think of her, of all people, having to suffer like that ! I really never had an idea that anything like that could happen."

George shrugged his shoulders. Then he said : " I had been expecting to see you out there again. I think you even made some promise to that effect when you dined with us and Therese a week ago."

" Oh yes. Didn't we squabble dreadfully, Therese

and I? It got even more violent on the way home.
Really quite funny. We walked, you know, right into
the town. The people who met us are absolutely bound
to have taken us for a couple of lovers, we quarrelled so
dreadfully."

" And who won in the end ? "

" Won? Does it ever happen that any one wins?
One only argues to convince oneself, never to convince the
other person. Just imagine Therese eventually realising
that a rational person can never become a member of any
party! Or if I had been driven to confess that my independence of party betokened a lack of philosophy of
life, as she contended! Why, we could both have shut
up shop straight away. But what do you think of all
this talk about a philosophy of life? As though a philosophy of life were anything else than the will and the
capacity to see life as it really is. I mean, to envisage it
without being led astray by any preconceived idea, without having the impulse to deduce a new law straight away
from our particular experience, or to fit our experience
into some existing law. But people mean nothing more
by the expression ' philosophy of life ' than a higher kind of
devotion to a pet theory, devotion to a pet theory within
the sphere of the infinite, so to speak. Or they go on talking
about a gloomy or cheerful philosophy according to the
colours in which their individual temperament and the
accidents of their personal life happen to paint the world
for them. People in the full possession of their senses have a
philosophy of life and narrow-minded people haven't. That's
how the matter stands. As a matter of fact, one doesn't
need to be a metaphysician to have a philosophy of life.
. . . Perhaps in fact one shouldn't be one at all. At any
rate, metaphysics have nothing at all to do with the
philosophy of life. Each of the philosophers really knew
in his heart of hearts that he simply represented a kind of
poet. Kant believed in the Thing In Itself, and Schopen-

hauer in the World as Will and Representation, just
like Shakespeare believed in Hamlet, and Beethoven
in the Ninth Symphony. They knew that another work
of art had come into the world, but they never imagined
for a single minute that they had discovered a final
' truth.' Every philosophical system, if it has any rhythm
or depth, represents another possession for the world.
But why should it alter a man's relationship to the world
if he himself has all his wits and senses about him ? "
He went on speaking with increasing excitement and
fell, as it seemed to George, into a feverish maze. George
then remembered that Heinrich had once invented a
merry-go-round that turned in spirals higher and higher
above the earth, to end finally in the top of a tower.

They chose a way through suburban streets, with few
people and only moderate lighting. George felt as though
he were walking about in a strange town. Suddenly a
house appeared that was strangely familiar to him, and
he now noticed for the first time that they were passing
the house of the Rosner family. There were lights in the
dining-room. Probably the old man was sitting there
alone, or in the company of his son. Is it possible, thought
George, that in a few weeks Anna will be sitting there
again at the same table as her mother and father and
brother as though nothing had happened ? That she
will sleep again night after night behind that window with
its closed blinds and leave that house day after day to
give her wretched lessons . . . That she will take up
that miserable life again as though nothing at all had
changed ? No. She should not go back to her family.
It would be quite senseless. She must come to him, live
with him, the man she belonged to. The Detmold telegram ! He had almost forgotten it, but he must talk it
over with her. It showed hope and prospects. Living
was cheap in a little town like that. Besides, George's
own fortune was a long way from being eaten up.

One would be justified in chancing it. Besides, this post simply represented the beginning. Perhaps he would get another one soon in a larger town. In a single night one might be a success without expecting it—that was always the way—and one would have a name, not only as a conductor, but also as a composer, and it need only be two or three years before they could have the child with them. . . . The child . . . how the thought raged through his brain ! . . . To think of one being able to forget a thing like that even for a minute.

Heinrich went on speaking all the time. It was quite obvious that he wanted to stupefy himself. He continued to annihilate philosophers. He had just degraded them from poets to jugglers. Every system, yes, every philosophic system and every moral system was nothing but a juggle of words, a flight from the animated fulness of phenomena into the marionette fixity of categories. But that was the very thing which mankind desired. Hence all the philosophies, all the religions, all the moral laws. They were all taking part in that identical flight.

A few, a very few, were given the awful inner faculty of being ready to feel every experience as new and individual—were given the strength to endure standing in a new world as it were, every single minute. And the truth was this : only the man who conquered the cowardly impulse of imprisoning all experiences in words was shown life—that manifold unity, that wondrous thing, in its own true shape.

George had the feeling that Heinrich, with all his talk, was simply trying to succeed in shaking off any sense of responsibility towards a higher law by refusing to recognise any. And with a kind of growing antagonism to Heinrich's silly and extraordinary behaviour he felt that the scheme of the world that had threatened some hours ago to fall to pieces was gradually beginning to put itself together again within his own soul. He had only recently rebelled against the senselessness of the fate which had struck him, and yet he already began to feel vaguely that even what had appeared to him as a grievous misfortune had not been precipitated upon his head out of the void, but that it had come to him along a way which, though darker, was quite as preordained as that which approached him along a far more visible road and which he was accustomed to call necessity.

They were in front of the house in which Heinrich lived. The concierge stood at the door and informed them that he had put a telegram in Heinrich's room a short time ago.

"Oh," said Heinrich indifferently, and slowly went up the stairs. George followed. Heinrich lit a candle in the hall. The telegram lay on the little table. Heinrich opened it, held it near to the flickering light, read it himself and then turned to George. "She's expected for the rehearsal to-morrow, and has not yet turned up." He took the light in his hand and followed by George went into the next room, put the light on the secretary, and walked up and down. George heard through the open window the strumming of a piano resounding over the dark courtyard.

"Is there nothing else in the telegram ? " he asked.

"No. But it's obvious that not only has she been absent from the rehearsal, but that she wasn't to be found in her lodgings either. Otherwise, they would certainly have telegraphed that she was ill, or given some explanation or other. Yes, my dear George," he breathed deeply, " it has happened this time."

"Why ? There is no proof of it. Scarcely anything to go on."

Heinrich cut short the other's remarks with a curt gesture. He then looked at his watch and said : " There are no more trains to-day. . . . Yes. . . . What should one do first ? " He stopped, remained standing, and suddenly

said: " I'll go to her mother's. Yes. That's the best. . . .
Perhaps—perhaps . . ."

They left the apartment. They took a conveyance at
the next corner.

" Did the mother know anything ? " asked George.

" Damn it all," said Heinrich, " about as much as mothers
usually know. It is incredible the small amount of thought
people give to what is taking place under their very noses,
if they are not compelled to do so by some actual occasion.
And most people have no idea how much they really know
at the bottom of their hearts without owning up to it.
The good woman is bound of course to be somewhat
surprised at my springing up so suddenly. . . . I haven't
seen her for a long time."

" What will you say to her ? "

" Yes, what will I say to her ? " repeated Heinrich, and
bit at his cigar. " I say, I've got a splendid idea. You'll
come with me, George. I'll introduce you as a manager,
eh ? You are travelling through, have got to catch a
special train for St. Petersburg at eleven o'clock this very
day. You've heard somewhere or other that the young
lady is staying in Vienna, and I as an old friend of the
family have been kind enough to introduce you."

" Do you feel in the mood for comedies like that ? "
asked George.

" Please forgive me, George, it's really not at all necessary. I'll just ask the old woman if she has any news. . . .
What do you say ? . . . How sultry it is to-night ! "

They drove over the Ring, through the echoing Burghof,
through the streets of the town. George felt in a strange
state of tension. Supposing the actress were now really
sitting quietly at home with her mother ? He felt that
it would mean a kind of disillusionment for him. And
then he felt ashamed of that emotion. Do I look upon the
whole thing as simply a distraction ? he thought. What
happens to other people . . . is rarely more than that,

Nürnberger would say . . . A strange way of distracting oneself in order to forget the death of one's child. . . . But what is one to do? . . . I can't alter things. I shall be going away in a few days, thank heaven.

The vehicle stopped in front of a house in the neighbourhood of the Praterstein. A train was growling over the viaduct opposite; underneath the avenues of the Prater ran into the darkness. Heinrich dismissed the conveyance. "Thank you very much," he said to George. "Good-bye."

"I'll wait for you here."

"Will you really? Well, I should be awfully grateful if you would."

He disappeared through the door. George walked up and down.

In spite of the lateness of the hour it was still fairly lively in the street. The strains of a military band in the Prater carried to the place where he was. A man and a woman went past him; the man carried in his arms a sleeping child, which had slung its hands round its father's neck. George thought of the garden in Grinzinger, of the unwashed little thing which had stretched out its tiny hands to him from its mother's arms. Had he been really touched then, as Nürnberger had asserted? No, it was certainly not emotion. Something else perhaps. The vague consciousness of standing with both hands linked in that riveted chain which stretches from ancestors to descendants, of participating in the universal human destiny. Now, he stood suddenly released again, alone . . . as though spurned by a miracle whose call he had heard without sufficient veneration. It struck ten o'clock from a neighbouring church tower. Only five hours, thought George, and how far away it all seemed! Now he was at liberty to knock about the world as he had done before. . . . Was he really at liberty?

Heinrich came out of the doorway. The door closed behind him. "Nothing," he said. "The mother has no

idea. I asked her for the address, as though I had something important to communicate to her. I had just come
from the Prater, and it had occurred to me . . . and so on.
A nice old woman. The brother sits at a table and copies
on a drawing-board out of an illustrated paper a mediæval
castle with innumerable turrets."

"Be candid, for once in a way," said George. "If you
could save her by doing so, wouldn't you forgive her
now ? "

"My dear George, don't you see yet that it is not a
question of whether I want to forgive her or not ? Just
remember this, I could just have stopped loving her,
which can frequently happen without one's being deceived
at all. Imagine this—a woman who loves you pursuing
you, a woman whose contact for some reason or other
makes you shudder swearing to you that she'll kill
herself if you reject her. Would it be your duty to give
in ? Could you reproach yourself the slightest bit if she
really went to her death, through the so-called pangs of
despised love ? Would you regard yourself as her murderer ? It is sheer nonsense, isn't it ? But if you think
that it's what other people call conscience which is now
torturing me, you are making a mistake. It is simply
anxiety about what has happened to a person who was
once very dear to me, and is I suppose still very dear to
me. The uncertainty . . ." He suddenly stared fixedly in
one direction.

"What is the matter with you ? " asked George.

"Don't you see ? A telegraph messenger is coming towards the door of the house." Before the man had time to
ring Heinrich was at his side, and said a few words which
George could not understand.

The messenger seemed to be making objections. Heinrich was answering and George, who had come nearer,
could hear him.

"I have been waiting for you here in front of the door

because the doctor gave me stringent orders to do so. This telegram contains . . . perhaps . . . bad news . . . and it might be the death of my mother. If you don't believe me, you just ring and I'll go into the house with you." But he already had the telegram in his hands, opened it hurriedly and started to read it by the light of the street lamp. His face remained absolutely immobile. Then he folded the telegram together again, handed it to the messenger, pressed a few silver coins into his hand. " You must now take it in yourself."

The messenger was surprised, but the tip put him in a better temper.

Heinrich rang and turned away. " Come ! " he said to George. They went silently down the street. After a few minutes Heinrich said : " It has happened."

George felt more violently shocked than he had anticipated. " Is it possible . . . ? " he exclaimed.

" Yes," said Heinrich. " She drowned herself in the lake— where you spent a few days this summer," he added in a tone which seemed to imply that George too was some- how partly responsible for what had happened.

" What's in the telegram ? " inquired George.

" It's from the manager. It contains the news that she has had a fatal accident while out boating. Requests her mother to give further directions."

He spoke in a cool hard voice, as though he were reading an announcement out of a paper.

" That poor woman ! I say, Heinrich, oughtn't you to . . ."

" What ! . . . Go to her ? What should I be doing there ? "

" Who is there, except you, who can at a time like this stand by her . . . ought to, in fact ? "

" Who except me ? " He remained standing. " You think that because it happened more or less on my account ? I tell you positively that I feel absolutely innocent. The boat out of which she let herself drop, and the waves which

received her could not feel more innocent than I do.   I
just want to settle that point. . . . But that I should go in
and see the mother . . . Yes, you are quite right about it."
And he turned again in the direction of the house.

" I will remain with you if you like," said George.

" What an idea, George !   Just go quietly home.   What
more am I to ask you to do ?   And remember me to Anna,
and tell her how sorry I am. . . . Well, you know that. . . .
Ah, here we are.   You don't mind my keeping you a few
seconds more before I . . ."   He stood silently there.   He
then began again, and his features became distorted.   " I'll
tell you something, George.   It's like this.   It's a great
happiness that at certain times one doesn't know what has
really happened to one.   If one immediately realised the
awfulness of moments like this, you know, to the extent
one realises them afterwards in one's memory, or realises
them before in anticipation—one would go mad.   Even
you, George—yes, even you.   And many do really go mad.
Those are probably the people who are granted the gift of
realising straight away . . . My mistress has drowned herself,
do you see ?   That's all one can say.   Has the same kind
of thing really happened to any one else before ?   Oh no.
Of course you think that you have read or heard of something similar.   It is not true.   To-day is the first time—
the first time since the world's been in existence—that
anything like this has ever happened."

The door opened and closed again.   George was alone in
the street.   His head was dazed, his heart oppressed.   He
went a few steps, then took a fly and drove home.   He saw
the dead woman in front of him, just as she had stood in
front of the stage door on that bright summer day in her
red blouse and short white skirt, with the roving eyes
beneath the reddish hair.   He would have sworn at the
time that she had a *liaison* with the comedy actor who
looked like Guido.   Perhaps that really was the case.
That might be *one* kind of love and what she felt for Hein-

rich another.   Really there were far too few words.   You
go to your death for one man, you go to bed with another—
perhaps the very night before you drown yourself for the
first.   And what, after all, does a suicide really mean ?
Only perhaps that at some moment or other one has failed
to appreciate death.   How many tried again if they had
failed once ?   The conversation with Grace came into his
mind, that hot-and-cold conversation by Labinski's grave
on the sunny February day in the thawing snow.

She had confessed to him then that she had not felt
any fear or horror when she had found Labinski shot in
front of the door of her flat.   And when her little sister
had died many years ago she had watched the whole night
by the death-bed without feeling even a trace of what other
people called horror.   But, so she told George, she had
learned to feel in men's embraces something that might
be rather like that feeling.   At first the thing had puzzled
her acutely, subsequently she thought she could understand it, but according to what the doctors said she was
doomed to barrenness, and that must be the reason why
it came about that the moment of supreme delight, which
was rendered as it were pointless by this fate, plunged
her in terror and apprehension.   This had struck George
at the time as a piece of affectation.   To-day he felt a
breath of truth in it for the first time.   She had been a
strange creature.   Would he ever meet again a person of
a similar type ?   Why not ?   Quite soon, as a matter of
fact.   A new epoch in his life was now beginning and the
next adventure was perhaps waiting for him somewhere or
other.   Adventure . . . ?   Had he a right still to think
about such things ? . . . Were not, from to-day onwards,
his responsibilities more serious than they had ever been ?
Did he not love Anna more than he had ever done before ?
The child was dead, but the next one would live . . . Heinrich
had spoken the truth : Anna was simply cut out to be a
mother.   A mother. . . . But he thought with a shiver :

Was she cut out at the same time to be the mother of *my* children ? The fly stopped. George got out and went up the two storeys to his apartment. Felician was not yet home. Who knows when he will come ? thought George. I can't wait for him, I'm too tired. He undressed quickly, sank into bed, and a deep sleep enveloped him.

When he woke up his eyes tried to find through the window a white line between field and forest, the Sommerhaidenweg which he had been accustomed to look at for some days. But he only saw the bluish empty sky which a tower was piercing, and suddenly realised that he was at home, and all that he had lived through yesterday came into his mind. Yet he felt fresh and alert in mind and body, and it seemed to him as though apart from the calamity which had befallen him there was a piece of good fortune which he had to remember. Oh yes, the Detmold telegram. . . . Was it really so lucky ? He had not thought so yesterday evening.

There was a knock at his door. Felician came into the room with his hat and stick in his hand. " I didn't know that you slept at home last night," he said. " Glad to see you. Well, what's the news out there ? "

George rested his arm on the pillow and looked up towards his brother. " It's over," he said ; " a boy, but dead," and he looked straight in front of him.

" Not really," said Felician with emotion, came up to him and instinctively put his hand upon his brother's head. He then put hat and stick on one side and sat down on the bed by him, and George could not help thinking of the morning hours of the years of his childhood, when he had often seen his father sitting like that on the edge of the bed when he woke up. He explained to Felician how it had all happened, laying especial stress on Anna's patience and gentleness ; but he felt with a certain sense of misgiving that he had to force himself a bit **to** keep the tone of seriousness and depression which was appropriate to his news. Felician listened sympathetically, then got up and walked up and down the room. Then George got up, began to dress and told his brother of the remarkable developments of the rest of the evening. He spoke about his walks and drives with Heinrich Bermann and of the strange way in which they had learned at last of the actress's suicide.

" Oh, that's the one," said Felician. " It's already in the papers, you know."

" Well, what happened ? " asked George curiously.

" She rowed out into the lake and slipped into the water out of the boat. . . . Well, you can read it. . . . I suppose you're now going straight out into the country again ? " he added.

" Of course," replied George, " but I have still got something to tell you, Felician, something which may interest you." And he told his brother about the Detmold telegram.

Felician seemed surprised. " This is getting serious," he exclaimed.

" Yes, it's getting serious," replied George.

" You have not yet answered ? "

" No, how could I ? "

" And what do you mean to do ? "

" Frankly, I don't know. You understand I can't go straight away, particularly under circumstances like this."

Felician looked reflective. " A little delay probably wouldn't hurt," he said then.

" I agree. I must first find out how they're getting on out there. Of course I should also like to talk it over with Anna."

" Where have you put the telegram ? Can I read it ? "

" It's lying on the secretary," said George, who was at the moment engaged in tying up his shoes.

Felician went into the next room, took the telegram in

his hand and read it. " It is much more urgent," he observed, " than I thought."

" It seems to me, Felician, that it still strikes you as strange that I am shortly going to have a real profession."

Felician stood at his brother's side again and stroked his hair. " It is perhaps rather providential that the telegram should have come yesterday."

" Providential ! How so ? "

" I mean that after such a sad business the prospect of practical occupation ought to do you twice as much good. . . . But I am afraid I must leave you now. I've still got quite a lot to do. Farewell visits among other things."

" When are you going then, Felician ? "

" A week to-day. I say, George, I suppose you are probably coming back from the country to-day ? "

" Certainly, if everything is all right out there."

" Perhaps we might see each other again in the evening."

" I should like to very much, Felician."

" Well then, if it suits you I'll be at home at seven. We might go and have supper together—but alone, not at the club."

" Yes, with pleasure."

" And you might do me a favour," began Felician again after a short silence. " Remember me out there very very kindly . . . tell her that I sympathise most sincerely."

" Thank you, Felician. I will tell her."

" Really, George, I can't tell you how much it touched me," continued Felician with warmth. " I only hope that she'll soon get over it. . . . And you, too."

George nodded. " Do you know," he said gently, " what it was going to be called ? "

Felician looked at his brother's eyes very seriously, then he pressed his hand. " Next time," he said with a kindly smile. He shook hands with his brother again and went.

George looked after him, torn by varying emotions. Yet he's not altogether sorry, he thought, that it should have turned out like that.

He got ready quickly and decided to cycle into the country again to-day. It was only when he had got past most of the traffic that he really became conscious of himself. The sky had grown a little dull and a cool wind blew from the hills towards George, like an autumn greeting. He did not want to meet any one in the little village where yesterday's events were bound to be already known, and took the upper road between the meadows and the garden to the approach from the back. The nearer the moment came when he was to see Anna again, the heavier his heart grew. At the railing he dismounted from his cycle and hesitated a little. The garden was empty. At the bottom lay the house sunk in silence. George breathed deeply and painfully. How different it might have been! he thought, walked down and heard the gravel crunch beneath his feet. He went on to the verandah, leaned his cycle against the railing and looked into the room through the open window. Anna lay there with open eyes. " Good morning," he cried, as cheerfully as he could.

Frau Golowski, who was sitting by Anna's bed, got up and said at once : " We've had a good sleep, a good sound sleep."

" That's right," said George, and vaulted over the railing into the room.

" You're very enterprising to-day," said Anna with her arch smile, which reminded George of long-past times. Frau Golowski informed him that the Professor had been early in the morning, had expressed himself completely satisfied and taken Frau Rosner with him in his carriage into the town. She then went away with a kindly glance.

George bent down over Anna, kissed her with real feeling on the eyes and mouth, pushed the chair nearer, sat down and said: " My brother—sends you his sincere wishes."

Her lips quivered imperceptibly. " Thank you," she replied gently, and then remarked: " So you came out on your cycle ? "

" Yes," he replied. " One has to keep a look-out you know on the way, and there are times when it's rather a sound thing one has to do so." He then told her how last evening had finished up. He related the whole thing as an exciting story, and it was only in the orthodox way at the end that Anna was allowed to find out how Heinrich's mistress had ended her life. He expected to see her moved, but she kept a strangely hard expression about her mouth. " It's really dreadful," said George. " Don't you think so ? "

" Yes," replied Anna shortly, and George felt that her kindness completely failed her here. He saw the loathing flowing out of her soul, not tepidly, as though from one person to another, but strong and deep like a stream of hate from world to world.

He dropped the subject and began again. " Now for something important, my child." He was smiling but his heart beat a little.

" Well ? " she asked tensely.

He took the Detmold telegram out of his breast pocket and read it to her. " What do you think of that ? " he asked with affected pride.

" And what did you answer ? "

" Nothing so far," he replied casually, as though he had never thought of taking the matter seriously. " Of course I wanted first to talk it over with you."

" Well, what do you think ? " she asked imperturbably.

" I . . . shall refuse of course. I'll wire that I . . . at any rate, can't come yet awhile." And he seriously ex-

plained to her that nothing would be lost by a postponement, that he would at any rate be welcomed as a special
visitor, and that this pressing request was only due to an
accident that one had no right to expect.

She let him go on speaking for a while, then she said:
" There you go being casual again. I think you should
have made a special point of answering at once and . . ."

" Well, and . . ."

" Perhaps have even taken the train there straight away
this morning,"

" Instead of coming out to see you—eh ? " he jested.

She remained serious. " Why not ? " she said, and
noticing him jerk his head up in surprise, " I'm getting on
very well, thank heaven, George. And even if I were
a bit worse you couldn't do any good, so . . ."

" Yes, my child," he interrupted, " it seems to me you
don't appreciate what it really means ! Going there, of
course, is a fairly simple matter—but—staying there !
Staying there at least till Easter ! The season lasts till
then."

" Well, George, I think it quite right that you haven't
gone away without first saying goodbye to me. But
look here, you've got to go anyway, haven't you ? Even
though we didn't actually speak about it during the last
weeks we were both quite well aware of it. For whether
you go away in a month's time or the day after to-morrow
—or to-day . . ."

George now began to argue seriously. It was not at all
the same thing whether he went away in a month's time
or to-day. One could manage to get used to certain
thoughts in the course of a month, and besides, talk over
everything properly—with regard to the future.

" What is there so much to talk over ? " she replied in
a tired voice. " Why, in a month's time you'll be . . .
You'll have as little chance of taking me with you as you
have to-day. I even think that there won't be any point

in our talking seriously about anything until after your return. A great deal will be bound to be cleared up by then. . . . At any rate, with regard to your prospects . . ." She looked out of the window into the garden.

George showed mild indignation at her matter-of-fact coolness, which never deserted her, even at a moment like that. " Yes, indeed," he said, " when one considers— what it means for you to stay here, and me . . ."

She looked at him. " I know what it means," she said.

Instinctively he avoided her look, took her hands and kissed them. He felt inwardly harrowed. When he looked up again he saw her eyes resting on him quite maternally, and she spoke to him like a mother. She explained to him that it was *just* because of the future— and there swept around that word a gentle suggestion of actual hope—that he should not miss an opportunity like that. In two or three weeks he could come back from Detmold to Vienna for a few days, for the people there would certainly appreciate that he must put his affairs over here in order. But above all it was necessary to give them a proof of his seriousness. And if he set any store by her advice there was only one thing to do : take the train that very evening. He need have no anxiety about her. She felt that she was quite out of danger. She felt that quite unmistakably. Of course he would hear from her every day, twice a day if he liked, morning and evening.

He did not yield at once, coming back again to the point that the unexpectedness of this separation would occasion a relapse. She answered that she would much prefer a quick separation like this to the prospect of another four weeks spent in anxiety, emotion and the fear of losing him. And the essential point remained that it was not a question of more than half the year, so they had half the year for themselves, and if everything went all right there would not be many periods of separation for the—the future.

He now began again: "And what will you do in this half-year, while I'm away? It is really . . ."

She interrupted him. "For the time being it will go on just as it has been going on for years; but I have been thinking this morning about a lot of things."

"The school for singing?"

"That, too. Although of course that is neither so easy nor so simple. And besides," she added, with her arch expression, "it would be a pity if one had to shut it up again too soon. But we'll talk about all that later on. You go now and telegraph."

"Yes, but what!" he exclaimed in such desperation that she could not help laughing.

Then she said: "Quite simple, 'Shall have the honour to present myself at your office to-morrow noon. Yours very obediently or faithfully . . . or very proudly. . . .'"

He looked at her. Then he kissed her hand and said: "You're certainly the cleverer of us two."

His tone seemed to hint "the cooler too." But a gentle, tender and somewhat mocking look from her turned away the *innuendo*.

"Well, I'll be back again in ten minutes." He left her with a cheerful face, went into the next room and shut the door. Opposite, in that other room, it now occurred to him again forcibly—his dead child lay in its coffin. . . . For the necessary steps, to use Doctor Stauber's expression of yesterday, were bound to have been already taken. He felt a paroxysm of grievous yearning.

Frau Golowski came out of the hall. She came up to him and spoke with admiration of Anna's resignation and calmness.

George listened somewhat absent-mindedly. His looks kept always glancing through the doorway and at last he said gently: "I should like to see it once more."

She looked at him, at first slightly shocked and then sympathetically.

" Nailed down already ? " he asked anxiously.

" Sent away already," replied Frau Golowski slowly.

" Sent away ! "   His face became convulsed with such
agony that the old woman laid her hands on his arm as
though to calm him.

" I went to notify it quite early," she said, " and then
the other matter took place very quickly.   They took it
away an hour ago to the mortuary."

" To the mortuary . . ." George shuddered. He was
silent for a long time as though unnerved from having
just learned a terrible and completely unexpected piece of
news.   When he recovered himself again he still felt Frau
Golowski's friendly hand upon his arm and saw her kind
eyes with their tired lines resting on his face.   " So it's
all finished," he said, with an indignant look upwards, as
though his last hope had been maliciously stolen from him.
He then shook hands with Frau Golowski.   " And you've
undertaken all this, dear lady. . . . I really don't know . . .
how I can ever . . ."

A gesture from the old woman deprecated any further
thanks.

George left the house, threw a contemptuous glance at
the little blue angel, which seemed to look anxiously down
at the faded flower-beds, and went into the street.   On his
way to the post-office he worried over the wording of the
telegram that was to announce his arrival at the place of
his new profession and his new prospects.

IX

OLD Doctor Stauber and his son sat over their coffee. The old man held a paper in his hand and seemed to be trying to find something. "The hearing of the case," he said, "is not yet fixed."

"Really!" replied Berthold, "Leo Golowski thinks that it will take place in the middle of November, that is to say in about three weeks. Therese, you know, visited her brother a few days ago in prison. They say he is perfectly calm and in quite good spirits."

"Well, who knows? perhaps he will be acquitted," said the old man.

"That's highly improbable, father. He ought to be glad, on the other hand, that he isn't being prosecuted for ordinary murder. An attempt was certainly made to get him prosecuted for it."

"You certainly can't call it a serious attempt, Berthold. You see the Treasury didn't bother about the silly libel to which you are referring."

"But if they had regarded it as a libel," retorted Berthold sharply, "they would have been under an obligation to prosecute the libellers. Beside, it is common knowledge that we are living in a state where no Jew is safe from being convicted to death for ritual murder; so why should the authorities shrink from taking official cognisance of the theory that Jews when they fight duels with pistols with Christians manage—perhaps for religious reasons—to ensure for themselves a criminal advantage? That the Court didn't lack the good-will to take another opportunity of doing a service to the party in power is best seen by the fact that he still remains under arrest pending the trial, in spite of the fact that the high bail was tendered."

"I don't believe the story about the bail," said the old doctor. "Where's Leo Golowski to get fifty thousand gulden from?"

"It wasn't fifty thousand, father, but a hundred thousand, and so far Leo Golowski knows nothing about it. I can tell you in confidence, father, that Salomon Ehrenberg put up the money."

"Indeed! Well, I'll tell you something in confidence too, Berthold."

"Well?"

"It's possible that it won't go to trial at all. Golowski's advocate has presented a petition to quash the proceedings."

Berthold burst out laughing. "On those grounds! And do you think, father, that that can have the slightest prospect of success? Yes, if Leo had fallen and the First-Lieutenant had survived . . . then perhaps."

The old man shook his head impatiently. "You must always make opposition speeches, my boy, at any price."

"Forgive me, father," said Berthold, twitching his brows. "Every one hasn't got the enviable gift of being able to ignore certain tendencies in public life when they don't concern him personally."

"Is that what I am in the habit of doing, then?" retorted the old man vehemently, and the half-shut eyes beneath the high forehead opened almost bitterly. "But it is you, Berthold, much more than I, who refuse to look where you don't want to see. I think you're beginning to brood over your ideas. You're getting morbid. I had hoped that a stay in another city, in another country, would cure you of certain petty narrow ideas, but they have grown worse instead. I notice it. I can neither understand nor approve any one starting fighting like Leo Golowski did. But to go on standing with your clenched fist in your pocket, so to speak—what's the point of it ? Pull yourself together, man. Character and industry always pull through in the end. What's the worst that can happen to you ? That you get your professorship a few years later than any one else. I don't think it is so great a misfortune. They won't be able to ignore your work if it is worth anything. . . ."

" It is not only a question of myself," objected Berthold.

" But it is mostly a matter of second-class interests of that kind. And to come back to our previous topic, it is really very questionable whether if it had been the First-Lieutenant who had shot down Leo Golowski an Ehrenberg, or Ehrenmann* for that matter, would have turned up with a hundred thousand gulden for him. Yes, to be sure, and now you are quite at liberty to take me for an Anti-Semite too, if it amuses you, although I am driving straight into the Rembrandtstrasse to see old Golowski. Well, good-bye, try and come to reason at last." He held out his hand to his son. The latter took it without changing countenance. The old man turned to go. At the door he said : " I suppose we shall see each other this evening at the Medical Society ? "

Berthold shook his head. " No, father, I am spending this evening in a less edifying place—the ' Silberne Wein-traube,' where there is a meeting of the Social Political Union."

" Which you can't miss ? "

" Impossible."

" Well, I wish you would tell me straight out, Are you going to stand for the Landtag ? "

" I . . . am going to stand."

" Indeed ! You think you're capable now of being able to face the . . . unpleasantness which you ran away from last year ? "

* A pun on the word *Ehre* which means honour.

Berthold looked through the window at the autumn rain. "You know, father," he replied, twitching his brows, "that I wasn't in the right frame of mind then. I now feel strong and armed, in spite of your previous remarks, which have really touched the actual point. And above all I know precisely what I want."

The old man shrugged his shoulders. "I can't understand how any one can give up a definite work . . . and you will certainly have to give it up, for a man can't serve two masters . . . to think of dropping something definite to . . . to make speeches to people whose profession, so to speak, it is to have preconceived opinions—to fight for opinions which are usually not even believed in by the man who puts you forward to represent them."

Berthold shook his head. "I assure you, father, I'm not tempted this time by any oratorical or dialectical ambition. This time I have discovered the sphere in which I hope it will be possible for me to do quite as definite work as in the laboratory. I intend, you know, if I do any good at all, to bother about nothing else except questions of public health. Perhaps I can count on your blessing, father, for this kind of political activity."

"On mine . . . yes. But how about your own ?"

"What do you mean ?"

"The blessing to which one might give the name of the inner call."

"You doubt even that," replied Berthold, really hurt.

The servant came in and gave the old doctor a visiting card. He read it. "Tell him I'll be glad to see him in a minute."

The servant went away.

Berthold went on speaking in a state of some excitement. "I feel justified in saying that my training, my knowledge . . ."

His father interrupted him as he played with the card. "I don't doubt your knowledge or your energy or your industry, but it seems to me that to be able to do any particular good in the sphere of public health you need as well as those excellent qualities another one too, which in my view you only have to a very small extent : kindness, my dear Berthold, love of mankind."

Berthold shook his head vehemently. " I regard the love of humanity which you mean, father, as absolutely superfluous and rather injurious. Pity—and what else can loving people whom one doesn't personally know really be ?—necessarily leads to sentimentalism, to weakness. And when one wants to help whole groups of men then, above all, you must be able to be hard at times, hard to individuals—yes, be ready in fact to sacrifice them if the common good demands it. You only need to consider, father, that the most honest and consistent social hygiene would have the direct result of annihilating diseased people, or at any rate excluding them from all enjoyment of life, and I don't deny that I have all kinds of ideas tending in that way which may seem cruel at the first glance. But the future, I think, belongs to ideas. You needn't be afraid, father, that I shall begin straight away to preach the murder of the unhealthy and the superfluous. But theoretically that's certainly what my programme leads to. Do you know, by the way, whom I had a very interesting conversation with the other day on this very subject ? "

" What subject do you mean ? "

" To put it precisely, a conversation on the right to kill. With Heinrich Bermann the author, the son of the late Deputy."

" But where did you get the opportunity of seeing him then ? "

" The other day at a meeting. Therese Golowski brought him along. You know him, too, don't you, father ? "

" Yes," replied the old man, " I've known him for quite

a long time." And he added : " I met him again this year in the summer at Anna Rosner's."

Berthold's eyebrows again twitched violently. Then he said sarcastically: " I thought it was something like that. Bermann mentioned, you know, that he had seen you some time ago, but he wouldn't remember exactly where. I concluded that it must have been a case of—discretion. I see. So the Herr Baron thought he would introduce his friends into her house."

" My dear Berthold, your tone seems to suggest that you have not got over a certain matter as completely as you previously hinted."

Berthold shrugged his shoulders. " I have never denied that I have an antipathy for Baron Wergenthin. That is why the whole business was so painful to me from the very beginning."

" Is that why ? "

" Yes."

" And yet I think, Berthold, that you would regard the matter differently if you were to meet Anna Rosner again some time or other as a widow—even assuming that her late husband was even more antipathetic to you than Baron von Wergenthin."

" That's possible. One can certainly presume that she has been loved—or at any rate respected, not just taken and—chucked away as soon as the spree was over. I'd have found that rather . . . Well, I won't put it any more definitely."

The old man shook his head as he looked at his son. " It really seems as though all the advanced views of you young people break down as soon as your passions and vanities come into question."

" So far as certain questions of cleanness or cleanliness are concerned I do not know that I am guilty of any so-called advanced views, father, and I don't think that you would be particularly delighted either if I felt any desire to be the successor of a more or less dead Baron Wergenthin."

" Certainly not, Berthold. For her sake, especially, for you would torture her to death."

" Don't be uneasy," replied Berthold, " Anna's in no peril from my quarter. It's all over."

" That's a good reason. But, happily, there's an even better one. Baron Wergenthin's neither dead nor has he cleared out. . . ."

" It doesn't matter, you know, about the actual word."

" He has, as you know, a position as a conductor in Germany . . ."

" What a piece of luck ! He has really been very fortunate over the whole thing. Not even having to provide for a child."

" You have two faults, Berthold. In the first place you are really an unkind man, and in the second place you never let one finish. I was just on the point of saying that it doesn't seem to be anything like all over between Anna and Baron Wergenthin. Only the day before yesterday she gave me his kind regards."

Berthold shrugged his shoulders as though the matter were finished so far as he was concerned. " How's old Rosner ? " he asked.

" He'll pull through all right this time," replied the old man. " Anyway, I hope that you've retained a sufficient sense of detachment to realise that his attacks are not due to his grief about the prodigal daughter, but to a sclerosis of the arteries that is unfortunately fairly far advanced."

" Is Anna giving lessons again ? " asked Berthold after some hesitation.

" Yes," replied the old man, " but perhaps not much longer." And he showed his son the visiting card which he was still holding in his hand.

Berthold contracted the corners of his mouth. " Do

you think," he asked ironically, " he has come here to celebrate his wedding, father ? "

" I shall soon find that out," replied the old man. " At any rate I'm very glad to see him again—for I assure you he's one of the most charming young men I've ever met."

" Extraordinary ! " said Berthold. " A quite unique winner of hearts. Even Therese raves about him. And Heinrich Bermann the other day, it was almost funny . . . Oh well, a slim handsome blonde young man, a baron, a German, a Christian—what Jew could withstand the magic ? . . . Goodbye, father."

" Berthold ! "

" Well, what ? "   He bit his lips.

" Pull yourself together !   Remember what you are."

" I . . . remember."

" No, you don't.   Otherwise you couldn't forget so often who the others are."

Berthold lifted his head interrogatively.

" You should really go to Rosner's some time. It is not worthy of you to let Anna see your disapproval in so —childish a fashion.   Goodbye . . . hope you'll have a good time in the ' Silberne Weintraube." He shook hands with his son and then went into his consulting-room. He opened the door of the waiting-room and with a friendly nod of the head invited George von Wergenthin, who was turning over the leaves of an album, to come in.

" I must first apologise to you, Herr Doctor," said George, after he had sat down. " My departure was so sudden. . . . Unfortunately I had no opportunity of saying goodbye to you, of thanking you personally for your great . . ."

Doctor Stauber deprecated his thanks. " I am very glad to see you again," he said, " I suppose you are here in Vienna on leave ? "

" Of course," replied George.   " I've only got three

days' leave ; they need me there so urgently, you see," he added with a modest smile.

Doctor Stauber sat opposite him in the chair behind his secretary and contemplated him kindly. " You feel very satisfied with your new position, so Anna says."

" Oh yes ; of course there are all kinds of difficulties when one plunges into a new kind of life like I did. But taking it all round everything has turned out much easier than I expected."

" So I hear. And that you have already had a very good introduction at Court."

George smiled. " Anna of course imagines that episode to be more magnificent than it really was. I played once at the Hereditary Prince's and a lady member of the theatre sang two songs of mine there ; that's all. But what is much more important is that I have a chance of being appointed conductor this very season."

" I thought you were already."

" No, Herr Doctor, not yet officially. I have already conducted a few times as deputy, *Freischütz* and *Undine*, but for the time being I am only accompanist."

In response to further questions from the doctor he told him some more about his activities at the Detmold Opera. He then got up and said goodbye.

" Perhaps I can give you a lift part of the way in my carriage," said the doctor. " I am driving to the Rembrandtstrasse to the Golowskis'."

" Thanks very much, Herr Doctor, but that's not on my way. Anyway, I intend to visit Frau Golowski in the course of to-morrow. She's not ill, is she ? "

" No. Of course the excitement of the last weeks is bound to have had some effect upon her."

George mentioned that he had written a few words to her and also to Leo immediately after the duel. " When one thinks that it might have turned out differently . . ." he added.

Doctor Stauber looked in front of him. " Having children," he said, " is a happiness which one pays for by instalments."

At the door George began somewhat hesitatingly: " I also wanted . . . to inquire of you, Herr Doctor, about the real state of Herr Rosner's health. . . . I must say I found him looking better than I had expected from Anna's letters."

" I hope that he will get all right again," replied Stauber. " But of course one must remember that he's an old man. He's even old for his years."

" But it's not a case of anything serious ? "

" Old age is a serious business in itself," replied Doctor Stauber, " especially as his whole antecedent life, his youth and manhood, were not particularly cheerful."

George, whose eyes had been roving round the room, suddenly exclaimed: " I've just thought of it, Herr Doctor. I've never sent you back the books you were good enough to lend me in the spring. And now I'm afraid all our things are at the depository, silver, furniture, pictures and the books as well. So I must ask you, Herr Doctor, to have patience till the spring."

" If you have no worse troubles than that, my dear Baron . . ."

They went slowly down the stairs and Doctor Stauber inquired after Felician.

" He's in Athens," replied George, " I've heard from him twice, not yet in any great detail. . . . How strange it is, Herr Doctor, coming back as a stranger to a town where one was at home a short time ago, and staying at an hotel as a gentleman from Detmold ! . . ."

Doctor Stauber got into his carriage. George asked him to give his very best regards to Frau Golowski.

" I'll tell her. And I wish you all further success, my dear Baron. Goodbye."

It was five by the Stephanskirche clock. George was

faced with an empty hour. He decided to stroll slowly into the suburb in the thin tepid autumn rain. He had scarcely slept at all in the train and he had been at the Rosners' two hours after his arrival. Anna herself had opened the door to him, greeted him with an affectionate kiss, and quickly taken him into the room, where her parents welcomed him with more politeness than sincerity. The mother, who preserved her usual embarrassed and slightly injured tone, did not say much. The father, sitting in the corner of the ottoman, with a blue-coloured rug over his knees, felt it incumbent on him to inquire about the social and musical conditions of the little capital from which George had come. Then he had remained alone awhile with Anna. They first exchanged question and answer with undue quickness, and subsequently endearments, which were both flat and awkward, and they both seemed disappointed that they did not feel the happiness of seeing each other again with anything like the intensity which their love had given them to expect. Very soon a pupil of Anna's put in an appearance. George took his leave and hurriedly arranged an appointment for the evening with his mistress. He would fetch her from Bittner's and then take her to the opera to see the performance of *Tristan.*

He had then taken his midday meal by the big window of a restaurant in the Ringstrasse, made purchases and given orders at his tradesmen's, looked up Heinrich, whom he did not find at home, and finally, obeying a sudden idea, decided to pay his " return-thanks" visit to Doctor Stauber. He now walked on slowly through the streets which he knew so well and which already seemed to have an atmosphere of strangeness ; and he thought of the town from which he came and in which he was feeling at home far more quickly than he had expected. Count Malnitz had received him with great kindness from the very first moment. He had the plan of reforming the opera in

23

accordance with modern ideas and wanted to win George
to him, so the latter thought, as a collaborator and friend
in his far-reaching projects. For the first conductor,
excellent musician no doubt though he might be, was
nowadays more of a court official than an artist. He had
been appointed when he was five-and-twenty and had
now been stationed in the little town for thirty years, a
paterfamilias with six children, respected, contented and
without ambition. Soon after his arrival George heard
songs sung at a concert which a long time ago had spread
the fame of the young conductor throughout almost the
whole world. George was unable to understand the impression produced by these quite out-of-date pieces, but
none the less warmly complimented the composer with a
kindly sympathy for the ageing man in whose eyes there
seemed to shine the distant glamour of a richer and more
promising past. George frequently asked himself if the old
conductor still thought of the fact that he had once been
taken for a man who was destined to go far, and whether
he, like so many other of the inhabitants, regarded the
little town as a hub from which the rays of influence and
of fame fell far around. George had only found in a few
any desire for a larger and more complex sphere of activity ;
it often seemed to him as though they rather treated him
with a kind of good-natured pity because he came from a
great town, and in particular from Vienna. Whenever
the name of that town was mentioned in front of
people George noticed in their smug and somewhat
sarcastic manner that almost as regularly as harmonies
accompany the bass, certain other words would be immediately switched into the conversation, even though
they were not specifically mentioned : waltzes . . . café . . .
süsses Mädel* . . . grilled chicken. . . fiacre. . . parliamentary
scandal. George was often irritated by this and made

* Literally " sweet girl." The phrase was invented by Schnitzler
himself.

up his mind to do all he could to improve his countrymen's reputation in Detmold. He had been asked to come because the third conductor, a quite young man, had suddenly died, and so George, on the very first day, had to sit at the piano in the little rehearsal-room and perform singing accompaniments. It went off excellently. He rejoiced in his gifts, which were stronger and surer than he had himself hoped, and it seemed to him, so far as he could recollect, that Anna had slightly underestimated his talent. Apart from this he threw himself more seriously into his compositions than he had ever done before. He worked at an overture which had originated out of the *motifs* of Bermann's opera. He had begun a violin sonata, and the mythical quintette, as Else had called it once, was nearly finished. It was going to be performed this very winter in one of the Court *soirées*, which were under the direction of the deputy-conductor of the Detmold orchestra, a talented young man, the only person in fact in his new home with whom George had so far become at all intimate, and with whom he was accustomed to take his meals at the " Elephant."

George still inhabited a fine room in this inn, with a view on to the big square planted with lindens, and from day to day put off taking an apartment. He was quite uncertain whether he would be still in Detmold next year and he also had the feeling that it would be bound to wound Anna, if he were to do anything which looked like settling down as a bachelor for any length of time. Yet he had said no word in his letters to her about any of the prospects of the future, just as she, on her side, left off addressing to him doubting or impatient questions. They practically only communicated to each other actual facts. She wrote of her gradual return into her old groove of life, and he of all the new surroundings among which he must first settle down. Although there was practically nothing which he had to keep from her, he made a special point of slurring over many things that might easily lead to a misunderstanding. How was one to express in words the strange atmosphere which permeated in the morning the rehearsals in the half-dark body of the theatre, when the odour of cosmetics, perfumes, dresses, gas, old wood and fresh paint came down from the stage to the stalls, when figures which one did not at first recognise hopped to and fro between the rows of seats in ordinary or stage dress, when some breath which was heavy and scented blew gently against one's neck? And how was one to describe a glance which flashed down from the eyes of a young singer while one looked up to her from the keys . . . ? Or when one saw this young singer home through the Theaterplatz and the Königsstrasse in the broad light of noon and used the opportunity not merely to talk about the part of Micaela, which one had just been studying with her, but also about all kinds of other, though no doubt fairly innocent, things? Could one recount this to one's mistress in Vienna without her reading something suspicious between the lines? And even if one had laid stress on the fact that Micaela was engaged to a young doctor in Berlin who adored her as much as she did him it would scarcely have improved matters, for that would really have looked as though one felt obliged to answer and reassure.

How strange, thought George, that it is just this very evening that she is singing the Micaela which I practised with her, and that I am going here along this same road out to Mariahilf which I used to take a year ago so frequently and so gladly. He thought of a specific evening when he had fetched Anna from out there, walked about with her in the quiet streets, looked at funny photographs in a doorway and finally walked with her on the cool stone flags of an ancient church, in a soft but how ominous conversation about an unknown future. . . . And now all had turned out quite differently to what he had hoped—quite differently. . . . Why did it strike him like that ? . . . What had he anticipated then at that time ? . . . Had not the year that had just passed been wonderfully rich and beautiful with its happiness and its grief ? And did he not love Anna to-day better and more deeply than ever ? And had he not frequently yearned for her in that fresh town as hotly as though for a woman who had never yet belonged to him ? To-day's early meeting with its flat and awkward endearments in the sinister atmosphere of a grey hour really ought not to lead him astray. . . .

He was at the appointed place. When he looked up to the lighted windows, behind which Anna was giving her lesson, a slight emotion came over him, and when she came out of the door the next minute, in a simple English dress and a grey felt hat on her rich dark blonde hair, holding a book in her hand, just as she had appeared a year ago, an unexpected feeling of happiness suddenly streamed over him. She did not see him at once, for he was standing in the shadow of a house. She opened her umbrella and went as far as the corner where she had been in the habit of waiting for him the previous year. He gazed at her for a while and was glad that she looked so fine and distinguished. Then he followed her quickly, and caught her up in a few strides. She informed him at once that she could not go to the opera with him. Her father had been taken ill this afternoon.

George was very disappointed. "Won't you at any rate come with me for the first act ? "

She shook her head. " No, I am not very keen on that sort of thing. It is much better for you to give the seat to some friend. Go and fetch Nürnberger or Bermann."

" No," he replied, " if you can't come with me I'd rather go alone. I should have enjoyed it so much. I am not very keen on the performance personally. I'd prefer to stay with you . . . so far as I am concerned, even at your people's ; but I must go. I have—to make a report."

Anna backed him up. " Of course you must go," and she

added: " I wouldn't advise you, too, to spend an evening with us. It's really not particularly jolly."

He had taken the umbrella out of her hand and held it over her, while she held his arm. " I say, Anna," he said, " I should like to make a suggestion ! " He was surprised that he should be looking for a way of leading up to it, and began hesitatingly: " My few days in Vienna are, of course, more or less unsettled and cut up—and now there's this depressed atmosphere at your people's as well. . . . We are not really managing to see anything of each other: don't you agree ? "

She nodded without looking at him.

" So wouldn't you like to come part of the way with me, Anna, when I go back again ? "

She looked at him sideways in her arch way and did not answer.

He went on speaking. " I can, you see, quite well manage to get an extra day's leave if I wire to the theatre. It would really be awfully nice if we had a few hours all to ourselves."

She consented with sincerity but not enthusiasm and made her decision depend on the state of her father's health. She then asked him how he had spent the day.

He told her in detail, and also added his programme for to-morrow. " So we two will see each other in the evening," he said. " I'll come to your place if that's convenient, and then we'll arrange further details."

" Yes," said Anna, and looked in front of her down the damp brown-grey street.

He tried again to persuade her to come to the opera with him, but it was futile. He then inquired about her singing lessons and followed that up by speaking about his own activity, as though he had to convince her that after all he was not having a much better time than she was. And he referred to his letters, in which he had written about everything in full detail.

" So far as that's concerned . . . " she said suddenly in quite a hard voice . . . And when, hurt by her tone, he could not help throwing back his head, she proceeded : " What is there really in letters, however detailed they are ? "

He knew what she was thinking about—he felt a certain heaviness at heart. Was there not in the very inexorableness of this silence all that she refused to voice aloud ?—question, reproach and rage. He had already felt this morning and now felt again that a certain sense of positive enmity to himself was rising within her, against which she herself seemed to be struggling in vain. Was this morning the first time . . . ? Had it not dated far longer back ? Perhaps it had been always there, from the very first moment when they had belonged to each other, and even in the moments of their supreme happiness ? Had not this hostile feeling been present when she pressed her bosom against his behind dark curtains to the music of the organ, when she waited for him in the room at the hotel in Rome, with eyes red with tears, while he had been watching with delight from Monte Pincio the sun setting in the Campagna, and had realised that he was finding this hour of solitary enjoyment the most wonderful in the whole journey ? Had it not been present when he ran down the gravel path on a hot morning, dropped down at her feet and cried in her lap as though it had been the lap of a mother ? And when he had sat by her bedside and looked out into the garden at eventime, while the dead child she had borne an hour ago lay silent on the white linen cloth, had it not been there again, drearier than ever, so that it would have been almost unbearable, if they had not long ago managed to put up with it, in the way one manages to endure so much of the unsatisfactoriness and so much of the sorrow that comes up out of the depths of human intercourse ? And now how painfully did he feel this sense of hostility as he walked arm-in-arm with her, holding the umbrella carefully over her, down the damp streets ? It was there again—

menacing and familiar.   The words which she had spoken
were still ringing in his ears : "What is there really in letters,
however detailed they are ? " . . . But even more solemnly
there rang in his ears the unspoken words : What does the
most ardent kiss in which body and soul seem to fuse really
come to ?   What does the fact that we travelled together
for months through strange lands really come to ?   What
does the fact that I had a child by you come to ?   What
does the fact that you cried out in my lap your remorse
for your deception ?   What does it all come to, when
you still go and leave me quite alone ? . . . Why, I was alone
at the very moment when my body drank in the germ of
life which I carried within me for nine months, which was
intended to live amongst strangers, though our own child,
and which did not wish to remain on earth !

But while all this sank heavily into his soul he agreed
in a light tone that she was really quite right and that
letters—even though they were actually twenty pages long
—could not contain much in particular ; and while a
harrowing pity for her sprang up in him he gently expressed
the hope that there would be a time in which they would
neither of them any longer be thrown back upon mere letters.
And then he found words of greater tenderness, told her of
those lonely walks of his in the outskirts of the strange town
when he thought of her ; told her of the hours in that
meaningless hotel room, with its view of the linden-planted
square, and of his yearning for her, which was always
present whether he sat alone at his work or accompanied
singers at the pianoforte or chatted with new acquaintances.   But when he stood with her in front of the house
door, with her hand in his, and looked up into her eyes as
he murmured a bright goodbye, he was shocked to see in
them the flickering out of a jaded sense of disillusionment
that had almost ceased to be painful.   And he knew that
all the words which he had spoken to her had meant nothing
to her, had meant less than nothing, since the one word,

the word she scarcely hoped for any more, and yet longed
for all the time, had not come.

A quarter of an hour later George was sitting in his
stall at the opera. He was first a little depressed and limp,
but the pleasure of enjoyment soon began to course through
his veins. And when Brangäne threw the king's cloak over
her mistress's shoulders, Kurwenal announced the king's
approach and the ship's crew on the deck hailed the land
amid all the glory of the resplendent heavens, George had
long ago forgotten a bad night in the train, some boring commissions, an extremely forced conversation with an old
Jewish doctor and a walk on the wet pavement which
mirrored the light of the lamps by the side of a young lady
who looked decent, distinguished and somewhat depressed.
And when the curtain fell for the first time and the light
streamed through the enormous room, upholstered in red
and gold, he did not feel any unpleasant sense of being
brought back to sober life, but he rather felt as though he
were plunging his head out of one dream into another ;
while a reality which was full of all kinds of wretched
complications flew impotently past somewhere outside.
The atmosphere of this house, so it seemed to him, had
never made him so intensely happy as it did to-day. He
had never felt so palpably that all the audience, so long as
they were here, were protected in some mystic way against
all the pain and all the dirt of life. He stood up in his
corner seat, which was in front by the middle gangway,
saw many a pleased glance turn towards him and felt
conscious of looking handsome, elegant and even somewhat
unusual. And besides that he was—and this filled him
with satisfaction—a man who had a profession, a position,
a man who sat in this very theatre with a responsible commission to perform, as a kind of envoy from a German
court theatre. He looked round with his opera-glass.
From the back of the stalls Gleissner greeted him with a
somewhat too familiar nod of his head and seemed im-

mediately afterwards to be expatiating on George's personal characteristics to the young lady who sat next to him. Who could she be ? Was it the harlot which the author, with his hobby for experimenting on souls, wanted to make into a saint, or was it the saint whom he wanted to make into a harlot ? Hard to say, thought George. They'd both look about the same, halfway.

George felt the lens of an opera-glass burning on the top of his head. He looked up. It was Else, who was looking down to him from a box in the first tier. Frau Ehrenberg sat near her and between them there bowed over the front of the box a tall young man who was no other than James Wyner. George bowed and two minutes later stepped into the box, to find himself greeted with friendliness but not a trace of surprise. Else, in a low-cut black velvet dress, with a small pearl necklet round her throat and a somewhat strange though interesting coiffure, held out her hand to him. " And how did you manage to get here ? On leave ? Sacked ? Run away ? "

George explained, briefly and good-humouredly.

" It was very nice of you," said Frau Ehrenberg, " to have sent us a line from Detmold."

" He really shouldn't have done that, either," remarked Else. " It was quite calculated to make one think that he had gone off to America with some one or other."

James was standing in the middle of the box, tall and gaunt, with his chiselled face and his dark smooth hair parted at the side. " Well, George, how do you like Detmold ? "

Else was looking at him with dropped eyelashes. She seemed delighted with his way of still always speaking German as though he had to translate it to himself out of English. Anyway, she employed the occasion to make a joke and said : " How George likes it in Detmold ! I am afraid your question is indiscreet, James." Then she turned to George. " We are engaged, you know."

" We haven't yet sent out any cards, you know," added Frau Ehrenberg.

George offered his congratulations.

"Lunch with us to-morrow," said Frau Ehrenberg. "You will only meet a few people. I'm sure they'll all be very glad to see you again—Sissy, Frau Oberberger, Willy Eissler."

George excused himself. He could not bind himself to any specific time, but if he possibly could he would very much like to look in during the course of the afternoon.

"Quite so," said Else in a low voice, without looking at him, while her arm, in its long white glove, lay carelessly on the ledge of the box. "You are probably spending the middle of the day in the family circle."

George pretended not to hear and praised to-night's performance. James declared that he liked *Tristan* better than all the other operas by Wagner, including the *Meistersingers*.

Else simply remarked: "It's awfully fine, but as a matter of fact I'm all against love-philtres and things in that line."

George explained that the love-philtre was to be regarded as a symbol, whereupon Else declared that she had a distaste for symbols as well. The first signal for the second act was given. George took his leave and rushed downstairs with only just enough time to take his place before the curtain rose. He remembered again the semi-official capacity in which he was sitting in the theatre to-night, and determined not to surrender himself unreservedly to his impressions. He soon managed to discover that it was possible to produce the love-scene quite differently from the way in which it was being done to-night. Nor did he think it right that Melot, by whose hand Tristan was doomed to die, should be represented by a second-rate singer, as was nearly always the case. After the fall of the curtain on the second act he got up with a kind of increased self-consciousness, stood up in his seat and looked frequently up to the box in the first tier, from which Frau Ehrenberg nodded to him benevolently, while Else spoke to James, who was standing still behind her with crossed arms. It struck George that he would see James's sister again to-morrow. Did she still often think of that wonderful hour in the park in the afternoon, amid the dark green sultriness of the park, in the warm perfume of the moss and the pines ? How far away that was ! He then remembered a fleeting kiss in the nocturnal shadow of the garden wall at Lugano. How far away that was too ! He thought of the evening under the plane-tree, and the conversation about Leo came again into his mind. A remarkable fellow that Leo, really. How consistently he had stuck to his plan ! For he must have formed it a long time ago. And obviously Leo had only waited for the day when he could doff his uniform to put it into execution. George had received no answer to the letter which he had immediately written him after hearing about the duel. He resolved to visit Leo in prison if it were possible.

A man in the first row greeted him. It was Ralph Skelton. George arranged by pantomimic signs to meet him at the end of the performance.

The lights were extinguished, the prelude to the third act began. George heard the tired sea-waves surging against the desolate beach and the grievous sighs of a mortally wounded hero were wafted through the blue thin air. Where had he heard this last ? Hadn't it been in Munich . . . ? No, it couldn't be so far back. And he suddenly remembered the hour when the sheets of the *Tristan* music had been spread open before him on a balcony beneath a wooden gable. A sunny path opposite ran to the churchyard between field and forest, while a cross had flashed with its golden light ; down in the house a woman he loved had groaned in agony and he had felt sick at heart. And yet this memory, too, had its own melancholy sweetness, like all else that had completely passed. The balcony, the little blue angel between the flowers, the white seat under the pear-tree, where was it all now ? He would see the house again once more, once more before he left Vienna.

The curtain rose. The shawm rang out yearningly beneath the pale expanse of an unsympathetic heaven. The wounded hero slumbered in the shade of the linden branches, and by his head watched Kurwenal the faithful. The shawm was silent, the herdsman bent questioningly over the wall and Kurwenal made answer. By Jove, that was a voice of unusual timbre ! If we only had a baritone like that, thought George. And many other things, too, which we need ! If he were only given the requisite power he felt himself able, in the course of time, to turn the modest theatre at which he worked into a first-class stage. He dreamed of model performances to which people would stream from far and wide. He no longer sat there as an envoy, but as a man to whom it was perhaps vouchsafed to be himself a leader in not too distant days. Further and higher coursed his hopes. Perhaps just a few years—and his own original harmonies would be ringing through a spacious hall of a musical festival, and the audience would be listening as thrilled as the one to-day, while somewhere outside a hollow reality would be flowing impotently past. Impotently ? That was the question. Did he know whether it was given him to compel human beings by his art as it had been given to the master to whom they were listening to-day—to triumph over the difficulty, wretchedness and awfulness of everyday life? Impatience and doubt tried to rise out of his soul ; but his will and common-sense quickly banished them and he now felt again the pure happiness he always experienced when he heard beautiful music, without thinking of the fact that he often wished himself to do creative work and obtain recognition for doing it.

In moments like this the only relation to his beloved

art of which he was conscious was that he was able to understand it with deeper appreciation than any other human being. And he felt that Heinrich had spoken the truth when they had ridden together through a forest damp with the morning dew : it was not creative work— it was simply the atmosphere of his art which was necessary to his existence. He was not one of the damned, like Heinrich, who always felt driven to catch hold of things, to mould them, to preserve them, and who found his world fall to pieces whenever it tried to escape from his creative hand.

Isolde in Brangäne's arms had dropped dead over Tristan's body, the last notes were dying away, the curtain fell. George cast a glance up to the box in the first tier. Else stood by the ledge with her look turned towards him, while James put her dark-red cloak over her shoulders, and it was only now, that after a nod of the head as quick as though she had meant no one to notice it, she turned towards the exit. Remarkable, thought George from a distance : there is a certain . . . melancholy romantic something about the way she carries herself, about many of her movements. It is then that she reminds me most of the gipsy girl of Nice, or the strange young person with whom I stood in front of the Titian Venus in Florence. . . . Did she ever love me ? No. And she doesn't love her James either. Who is it then ? . . . Perhaps . . . it was really that mad drawing-master in Florence. Or no one at all. Or Heinrich, of all people ? . . .

He met Skelton in the *foyer*. " Back again ? " queried the latter.

" Only for a few days," replied George.

It transpired that Skelton had not really known what George was doing and had thought that he was on a kind of musical tour through the German towns for the purposes of study. He was now more or less surprised to hear that George was here on leave and had been practically com-

missioned by the manager to inspect the new production of
Tristan. " Will this suit you ? " said Skelton. " I've got
an appointment with Breitner; at the ' *Imperial,*' the
white room."

" Excellent," replied George. " I'm staying there."

Doctor von Breitner was already smoking one of his
celebrated big cigars when the two men appeared at his
table. " What a surprise ! " he exclaimed, when George
greeted him. He had heard that George was engaged as
conductor in Düsseldorf.

" Detmold," said George, and he thought : " The people
here don't bother about me particularly. . . . But what
does it matter ? "

Skelton described the *Tristan* performance and George
mentioned that he had spoken to the Ehrenbergs.

" Do you know that Oskar Ehrenberg is on his way to
India or Ceylon ? " asked Doctor von Breitner.

" Really ! "

" And whom do you think with ? "

" Some woman, I suppose ? "

" Oh, of course. I've even heard they've got five or
seven women with them."

" Who ?—' they.' "

" Oskar Ehrenberg . . . and . . . have a guess . . . Well,
the Prince of Guastalla ! "

" Impossible ! "

" Funny, eh ? They became very thick this year at
Ostend or at Spa. . . . *Cherchez* . . . et cetera. It seems
that just as there are women, you know, for whom people
fight duels there's also another class across whom, as it
were, you shake hands. Now they've left Europe together.
Perhaps they'll found a kingdom on some island or other
and Oskar Ehrenberg will be prime minister."

Willy Eissler appeared. His complexion was sallow,
his voice hoarse and he looked as if he had been keeping
late hours. " Hullo, Baron ! Forgive me not being

thunderstruck but I have already heard that you are here. Some one or other saw you in the Kärtnerstrasse."

George requested Willy to remember Count Malnitz to his father. He himself, he was sorry to say, had no time on this occasion to look up the old gentleman, to whom, as he observed with a pretty mock-modesty, he owed his position in Detmold.

" So far as your future is concerned, Baron," said Willy, " I never had any anxiety about it, particularly since I heard Bellini sing your songs last year—or was it further back ? But it is quite a good idea of yours, deciding to leave Vienna. You'd have been bound to have been taken for a dilettante here for a cool twenty or thirty years. That's always the way in Vienna. I know it. When people know that a man comes of a good family, has a taste too for pretty ties, good cigarettes and various other amenities of life, they don't believe that he has real artistic capacity. You wouldn't be taken seriously here without proof from outside. . . . So hurry up and furnish us with a brilliant one, Baron."

" I'll make an effort to," said George.

" By the way, have you heard the latest, gentlemen ? " began Willy again. " Leo Golowski, the one-year-volunteer who shot First-Lieutenant Sefrenek, is free."

" Let out on bail ? " asked George.

" No, he's quite free. His advocate addressed a petition to the Emperor to quash the proceedings, and it turned out successful to-day."

" Incredible ! " exclaimed Breitner.

" Why are you so surprised, Breitner ? " said Willy. " It is possible, you know, for something sensible to happen in Austria once in a blue moon."

" A duel is never sensible," said Skelton, " and therefore a pardon for a duel can't be sensible either."

" A duel, my dear Skelton, is either something very much worse or something very much better than sensible," replied Willy. " It is either a ghastly folly or a relentless necessity, either a crime or an act of deliverance. It is not sensible and doesn't need to be so. In exceptional cases, one can't make any headway at all with common-sense, and I am sure you too will concede, Skelton, that in a case like the one of which we have just been speaking a duel was inevitable."

" Absolutely," said Breitner.

" I can imagine a polity," observed Skelton, " in which differences of that kind were settled by a court."

" Differences of that kind settled by a court ! Oh, I say ! . . . Do you really think, Skelton, that in a case where there is no question of right or of possession at issue, but where men confront each other with a stupendous hate, do you really think that a proper settlement could be arrived at by means of a fine or imprisonment ? The fact, gentlemen, that refusal to fight a duel in such cases is regarded as a piece of cowardice by all people who possess temperament, honour and honesty has a fairly deep significance. In the case of Jews at any rate," he added. " So far as the Catholics are concerned it is well known that it is only their orthodoxy which keeps them from fighting."

" That's certainly the case," said Breitner simply.

George wanted to know details of the affair between Leo Golowski and the First-Lieutenant.

" Quite so," said Willy. " Of course you've only just arrived. Well, the First-Lieutenant gave him a fine ragging for the whole year, and as a matter of fact——"

" I know the prelude," interrupted George. " Part of it from first-hand information."

" Really ! Well, the prelude, to stick to that ex-pression, was over on the first of October. I mean Leo Golowski had finished his year of service. And on the second he placed himself in front of the barracks early in the morning and quietly waited till the First-Lieutenant came out of the door. As soon as he did he stepped up to

24

him ; the First-Lieutenant reached for his sword, but Leo
Golowski grabs hold of his hand, doesn't let it go, puts his
other fist in front of his forehead. There is a story, too,
that Leo is supposed to have flung the following words at
the First-Lieutenant. . . . I don't know if it's true."

" What words ? " asked George curiously.

" ' You were worth more than I was yesterday, Herr
First-Lieutenant ; now we are on an equality for the time
being—but one of us will be worth more than the other
again by this time to-morrow.' "

" Somewhat Talmudic," remarked Breitner.

" You,of course, must be the best judge of that, Breitner,"
replied Willy, and went on with his story.   " Well, the duel
took place next morning in the fields by the Danube—
three exchanges of ball at twenty paces without advancing.
If that proved abortive the sword till one or other was *hors
de combat*. . . . The first shots missed on both sides, and
after the second . . . after the second, I say, Golowski
was really worth more than the First-Lieutenant, for the
latter was worth nothing, less than nothing—a dead man."

" Poor devil," said Breitner.

Willy shrugged his shoulders.   " He just happened to
have caught a tartar.   I'm sorry, too, but one must admit
that Austria would be a different place in many respects
if all Jews would behave like Leo Golowski in similar cases.
Unfortunately . . ."

Skelton smiled.   " You know, Willy, I don't like any one
to say anything against the Jews when I am there.   I like
them, and I should be sorry if people wanted to solve
the Jewish question by a series of duels, for when it was
all over there wouldn't be a single male specimen left of
that excellent race."

At the end of the conversation Skelton had to admit
that the duel could not be abolished in Austria for the
present.   But he reserved the right of putting the question
whether that fact was really an argument in favour of the

duel, and not rather an argument against Austria, since many other countries—he refrained from mentioning any out of a sense of modesty—had discarded the duel for centuries. And did he go too far if he ventured to designate Austria—the country, too, in which he had felt really at home for the last six years—as the country of social shams? In that country more than anywhere else there existed wild disputes without a touch of hate and a kind of tender love without the need of fidelity. Quite humorous personal likings existed or came into existence between political opponents; party colleagues, on the other hand, reviled, libelled and betrayed each other. You would only find a few people who would vouchsafe specific views on men and things, and anyway even these few would be only too ready to make reservations and admit exceptions. The political conflict there gave one quite the impression as though the apparently most bitter enemies, while exchanging their most virulent abuse, winked to each other: "It's not meant so seriously."

"What do you think, Skelton?" asked Willy. "Would you wink, too, if the bullets were flying on both sides?"

"You certainly would, Willy, unless death were staring you in the face. But that circumstance, I think, doesn't affect one's mood but only one's demeanour."

They went on sitting together for a long time and continued gossiping. George heard all kinds of news. He learned among other things that Demeter Stanzides had concluded the purchase of the estate on the Hungarian-Croatian frontier, and that the Rattenmamsell was looking forward to a happy event. Willy Eissler was much excited at the result of this crossing of the races, and amused himself in the meanwhile by inventing names for the expected child, such as Israel Pius or Rebecca Portiuncula.

Subsequently the whole party betook itself to the neighbouring café. George played a game of billiards with Breitner and then went up to his room. He made out in bed a time-table for the next day and finally sank into a deliciously deep sleep.

The paper he had ordered the day before was brought in with the tea in the morning, together with a telegram. The manager requested him to report on a singer. To George's delight it was the one he had heard yesterday in Kurwenal. He was also allowed to stay three days beyond his specified leave, " in order to put his affairs in order at his convenience," since an alteration of the programme happened to allow it. Excellent, really, thought George. It struck him that he had completely forgotten his original intention of wiring for a prolongation of his leave. I have got even more time for Anna now than I thought, he reflected. We might perhaps go into the mountains. The autumn days are fine and mild, and at this time one would be pretty well alone and undisturbed anywhere. But supposing there is an accident again— an—accident—again ! . . . Those were the very words in which the thought had flown through his mind. He bit his lips. Was that how he had suddenly come to regard the matter ? An accident. . . . Where was the time when he had thought of himself almost with pride as a link in an endless chain which went from the first ancestors to the last descendants ? And for a few moments he seemed to himself like a failure in the sphere of love, somewhat dubious and pitiable.

He ran his eye over the paper. The proceedings against Leo Golowski had been quashed by an Imperial pardon. He had been discharged from prison last evening. George was very glad and decided to visit Leo this very day. He then sent a telegram to the Count, and made out a report with due formality and detail on yesterday's performance. When he got out into the street it was nearly eleven. The air had the cool clearness of autumn. George felt thoroughly rested, refreshed and in a good temper. The day lay before him rich with hopes and promised all kinds of excitement. Only something troubled him without his immediately knowing what it was. . . . Oh yes, the visit in the Paulanergasse, the depressing rooms, the ailing father, the aggrieved mother. I'll simply fetch Anna, he thought, take her for a walk and then go and have supper somewhere with her. He passed a flower shop, bought some wonderful dark-red roses and had them sent to Anna with a card on which he wrote: " A thousand wishes. Goodbye till the evening." When he had done this he felt easier in his mind. He then went through the streets in the centre of the town to the old house in which Nürnberger lived. He climbed up the five storeys. A slatternly old servant with a dark cloth over her head opened the door and ushered him into her master's room. Nürnberger was standing by the window with his head slightly bent, in the brown high-cut lounge-suit which he liked to wear at home. He was not alone. Heinrich, of all people, got up from the old arm-chair in front of the secretary with a manuscript in his hand. George was heartily welcomed.

" Has your being in Vienna anything to do with the crisis in the management of the opera ? " asked Nürnberger. He refused to allow this observation to be simply passed over as a joke. " Look here," he said, " if little boys who a short time ago were only in a position to give formal proof of their connection with German literature on the strength of the regularity of their visits to a literary café, are invited to take appointments as readers on the Berlin stage, well, in an age like this I see no occasion for astonishment if Baron Wergenthin is fetched in triumph to the Vienna opera after his no doubt strenuous six weeks' career as the conductor of a German Court theatre."

George paid a tribute to truth by explaining that he had only obtained a short leave to put his Vienna affairs in order, and did not forget to mention that he had seen the new production of *Tristan* yesterday as a kind of agent for his manager, but he smiled ironically at himself all the time. Then he gave a short and fairly humorous description of his experiences up to the present in the little capital. He even touched jestingly on the Court concerts as though he were far from taking his position, his present successes, the theatre, or indeed life in general with any particular seriousness.

Conversation then turned on Leo Golowski's release from prison. Nürnberger rejoiced at this unhoped-for issue, but yet firmly refused to be surprised at it, for the most highly improbable things always happened in life, and particularly in Austria, as they all knew very well. But when George mentioned the rumour of Oskar Ehrenberg's yachting trip with the Prince as a new proof of the soundness of Nürnberger's theory, he was at first inclined nevertheless to be slightly sceptical. Yet he finished by admitting its possibility, since his imagination, as he had known for a long time, was invariably surpassed by reality.

Heinrich looked at the time. It was time for him to say goodbye.

" Haven't I disturbed you, gentlemen ? " asked George. " I think you were reading something, Heinrich, when I came in ? "

" I had already finished," replied Heinrich.

" You'll read me the last act to-morrow, Heinrich ? " said Nürnberger.

" I have no intention of doing so," replied Heinrich with a laugh. " If the first two acts are as great a frost in the theatre as they were with you, my dear Nürnberger, it will be positively impossible to play the thing through to the end. We'll assume, Nürnberger, that you rush indignantly out of the stalls into the open air. I'll let you off the cat-calls and the rotten eggs."

" Hang it all ! " exclaimed George.

" You're exaggerating again, Heinrich," said Nürnberger. " I only ventured to make a few objections," he said, turning to George, " that's all. But he's an author, you know."

" It all depends on what you mean by 'objection,'" said Heinrich. " After all, it is only an objection to the life of a fellow human being if you cut his head open with a hatchet ; only it's a fairly effective one." He pointed to his manuscript and turned to George. " You know what that is ? My political tragi-comedy. No wreaths, by request."

Nürnberger laughed. " I assure you, Heinrich, you could still make something really splendid out of your subject. You can even keep the whole scenario and a number of the characters. All you need to do is to make up your mind to be less fair when you revise your draft."

" But surely his fairness is a fine thing," said George.

Nürnberger shook his head. " One may be anywhere else, only not in the drama," and turning to Heinrich again : " In a piece like that, which deals with a question of the day, or indeed several questions, as you really intended, you'll never do any good with a purely objective treatment. The theatre public demands that the subjects tackled by the author should be definitely settled, or that at any rate some illusion of that kind should be created. For of course there never is any real solution, and an apparent solution can only be made by a man who has the courage or the simplicity or the temperament to take sides. You'll soon appreciate the fact, my dear Heinrich, that fairness is no good in the drama."

" Do you know, Nürnberger," said Heinrich, " one perhaps might do some good even with fairness. I think I simply haven't got the right kind. As a matter of fact, you know, I've no desire at all to be fair. I imagine it must be so wonderfully nice to be unfair. I think it would be the most healthy gymnastic exercise for one's soul that one could possibly practise. It must do one such a lot of good to be able really to hate the man whose views you are combating. It saves one, I'm sure, a great deal of inner strength which you can expend far better yourself in the actual fight. Yes, if one still preserves fairness of heart. . . . But my fairness is here," and he pointed to his forehead. " I do not stand above parties either, but I belong to them all in a kind of way, or am against them all. I have not got the divine but the dialectical fairness. And that's why "—he held his manuscript high up—" it has resulted in such a boring and fruitless lot of twaddle."

" Woe to the man," said Nürnberger, " who is rash enough to write anything like that about you."

" Well, you see," replied Heinrich with a smile, " if some one else were to say it, one couldn't suppress the slight suspicion that he might be right. But now I must really go. Good-bye, George. I'm very sorry that you missed me yesterday. When are you leaving again ? "

" To-morrow."

" Anyway, I shall see you before you leave. I'm home to-day the whole afternoon and evening. You will find a man who has resolutely turned away from the questions of the day and devoted himself again to the eternal problems, death and love. . . . Do you believe in death, by-the-bye, Nürnberger ? I am not asking you about love."

" That somewhat cheap joke from a man in your position," said Nürnberger, " makes me suspect that in spite of your very dignified demeanour my criticism has. . . ."

" No, Nürnberger, I swear to you that I am not wounded. I have rather a comfortable sensation of the whole thing being finished with."

" Finished with, why so ? It is still quite possible that I've made a mistake, and that this very piece, which I didn't think quite a success, will have a success on the stage which will make you into a millionaire. I should be deeply grieved if on account of my criticism, which may be very far from being authoritative . . ."

" Quite so, quite so, Nürnberger. We must all of us

always admit the possibility that we may be mistaken. And the next time I'll write another piece, and one with the following title too: '*Nobody's going to take me in,*' and you shall be the hero of it, Nürnberger."

Nürnberger smiled. " . . . I ? That means you'll take a man whom you imagine you know, that you'll try to describe those sides of his character which suit your game —that you'll suppress others which are no use to you, and the result . . ."

" The result," interrupted Heinrich, " will be a portrait taken by a mad photographer with a spoilt camera during an earthquake and an eclipse of the sun. Is that right, or is there anything missing ? "

" The psychology ought to be exhaustive," said Nürnberger.

Heinrich took his leave in boisterous spirits and went away with his rolled-up manuscript. When he had gone George remarked: " His good temper strikes me as a bit of a pose, you know."

" Do you think so ? I have always found him in remarkably good form lately."

" In really good form ? Do you seriously think so ? After what he has gone through ? "

" Why not ? Men who are so almost exclusively self-centred as he is get over emotional troubles with surprising quickness. Characters of that type, and as a matter of fact other kinds of men as well, feel the slightest physical discomfort far more acutely than any kind of sentimental pain, even the faithlessness and death of the persons they happen to love. It comes no doubt from the fact that every emotional pain flatters our vanity somehow or other, and that you can't say the same thing about an attack of typhoid or a catarrh in the stomach. Then there is this additional point about artistic people, for while catarrh of the stomach provides positively no copy at all (at any rate that used to be reasonably certain a short time ago) you can get anything you jolly well like out of your emotional pains, from lyric poems down to works on philosophy."

" Emotional pains are of very different kinds, of course," replied George. " And being deceived or deserted by a mistress . . . or even her dying a natural death . . . is still rather a different thing to her killing herself on our account."

" Do you know for a certainty," replied Nürnberger, " that Heinrich's mistress really killed herself on his account ? "

" Didn't Heinrich tell you, then ? . . ."

" Of course, but that doesn't prove much. Even the shrewdest amongst us are always fools about the things which concern ourselves."

Such remarks as these on the part of Nürnberger produced a strangely disconcerting effect on George. They belonged to the class of which Nürnberger was rather fond, and which, as Heinrich had once observed, quite destroyed all the point of all human intercourse, and in fact of all human relations.

Nürnberger went on speaking. " We only know two facts. One is that our friend once had a *liaison* with a girl and the other that the girl in question threw herself into the water. We both of us know practically nothing about all the intervening facts, and Heinrich probably doesn't know anything more about them either. None of us can know why she killed herself, and perhaps the poor girl herself didn't know either."

George looked through the window and saw roofs, chimneys and weather-beaten pipes, while fairly near was the light-grey tower with the broken stone cupola. The sky opposite was pale and empty. It suddenly occurred to George that Nürnberger had not yet made any inquiry about Anna. What was he probably thinking ? Thinking no doubt that George had deserted her, and that she had already consoled herself with another lover. Why did I come to Vienna ? he thought desultorily, as though his

journey had had no other purpose than to listen to Nürnberger giving him what had now turned out to be a sufficiently pessimistic analysis of life. It struck twelve. George
took his leave. Nürnberger accompanied him as far as
the door and thanked him for his visit. He inquired
earnestly about what George was doing in his new home,
about his work and his new acquaintances, as though
their previous conversation on the subject had not really
counted, and now learned for the first time of the accident
which was responsible for George's sudden appointment
in the little town.

" Yes, that's just what I always say," he then remarked.
" It is not we who make our fate, but some circumstance
outside us usually sees to that—some circumstance which
we were not in a position to influence in any way, which
we never have a chance of bringing into the sphere of our
calculations. After all, do you deserve any credit . . . ? I
feel justified in putting this question, much as I respect your
talent. Nor does old Eissler, whose interest in your affairs
you once told me about, deserve any credit either for your
being wired to from Detmold and finding your true sphere
of work there so quickly. No. An innocent man, some
one you don't know, had to die a sudden death to enable you
to find that particular place vacant. And what a lot of
other things which you were equally unable to influence,
and which you were quite unable to foresee, had to come
on the scene to enable you to leave Vienna with a light
heart—to enable you, in fact, to leave it at all."

George felt hurt. " What do you mean by a light
heart ? " he asked.

" I mean a lighter heart than you would have had under
other circumstances. If the little creature had remained
alive who knows whether you . . ."

" You can take it from me that I would have gone away,
even then. And Anna would have taken it quite as much
as a matter of course as she does now. Don't you believe

me ? Why, perhaps I'd have gone with an even lighter heart if that matter had turned out otherwise. Why, it was Anna who persuaded me to accept. I was quite undecided. You have no idea what a good sensible creature Anna is."

" Oh, I don't doubt it at all. According to all you have told me about her from time to time, she certainly seems to have behaved with more dignity in her position than young ladies of her social status are usually accustomed to exhibit on such occasions."

" My dear Herr Nürnberger, the position really wasn't as dreadful as all that."

" Come, don't say that. For however much things may have been made easier by your courtesy and consideration, take it from me that the young lady is bound to have felt frequently during the last months the irregularity of her position. I am sure there isn't a single member of the feminine sex, however daring and advanced may be her views, who doesn't prefer in a case like that to have a ring on her finger. And it's all in favour, too, of your friend's sensible and dignified behaviour that she never allowed you to notice it, and that she took the bitter disillusionment at the end of these nine months, which were certainly not entirely a bed of roses, with calmness and self-possession."

" Disillusionment is rather a mild word. Pain would perhaps be more correct."

" I dare say it was both. But in this case, as in most others, the burning wound of pain heals more quickly than the throbbing piercing wound of disillusionment."

" I don't quite understand."

" Well, my dear George, you don't doubt, do you, that if the little creature had remained alive you two would have married very quickly ; why, you'd even be married this very day."

" And you think that now, just because we have no child . . . Yes, you seem to be of the opinion that . . . that . . .

it's all over between us. But you are quite wrong, quite wrong, my dear friend."

"My dear George," replied Nürnberger, "both of us would prefer not to speak about the future. Neither you nor I know the place where a strand of our fate is being spun at this very moment. You didn't have the slightest inkling, either, when that conductor was attacked by a stroke, and if I now wish you luck in your future career I don't know whose death I have not conjured down by that very wish."

They took leave of each other on the landing. Nürnberger cried after George from the stairs : " Let me hear from you now and then."

George turned round once more. "And mind you do the same." He only saw Nürnberger's gesture of resigned remonstrance, smiled involuntarily, hurried down the stairs and took a conveyance at the nearest corner.

He pondered over Nürnberger and Bermann on his way to the Golowskis'. What a strange relationship it was between them. A scene which he thought he had seen some time or other in a dream came into George's mind. The two sat opposite each other, each held a mirror in front of the other. The other saw himself in it with the mirror in his hand, and in that mirror the other again with his mirror in his hand, and so on to infinity ; but did either of them really know the other, did either of them really know himself ? George's mind became dizzy. He then thought of Anna. Was Nürnberger right again ? Was it really all over ? Could it really ever end ? Ever ? . . . Life is long ! But were even the ensuing months dangerous ? No. That was not to be taken seriously, however it might turn out. Perhaps Micaela . . . And in Easter he would be in Vienna again. Then there came the summer, they would be together, and then ? Yes, what then ? Engagement ? Herr Rosner and Frau Rosner's son-in-law, Joseph's brother-in-law ! Oh well, what did

he care about the family ?   It was Anna after all who
was going to be his wife, that good gentle sensible creature.

The fly stopped in front of an ugly fairly new house,
painted yellow, in a wide monotonous street.   George
told the driver to wait and went into the doorway.   The
house looked quite dilapidated from inside.   Mortar had
crumbled away from the walls in many places and the steps
were dirty.   There was a smell of bad fat coming out of
some of the kitchen windows.   Two fat Jewesses were
talking on the landing of the first storey in a jargon which
George found positively intolerable.   One of them said
to a boy whom she held by the hand : " Moritz, let the
gentleman pass."

Why does she say that ? thought George, there's plenty
of room ; she obviously wants to get into conversation with
me.   As though I could do her any harm or any good !   An
expression of Heinrich's in a long-past conversation came
into his mind : " An enemy's country."

A servant-girl showed him into a room which he immediately recognised as Leo's.   Books and papers on the
writing-table, the piano open, a Gladstone bag, which was
still not completely unpacked, open on the sofa.   The door
opened the next minute.   Leo came in, embraced his
visitor and kissed him so quickly on both cheeks that the
man who was welcomed with such heartiness had no time
to be embarrassed.

" This is nice of you," said Leo, and shook both his
hands.

" You can't imagine how glad I was . . ." began George.

" I believe you. . . . But please come in with me.   We are
having dinner, you know, but it's nearly over."

He took him into the next room.   The family was
gathered round the table.

" I don't think you know my father yet," observed Leo,
and introduced them to each other.

Old Golowski got up, put away the serviette which he

had tied round his neck and held out his hand to George. The latter was surprised that the old man should look so completely different from what he had expected. He was not patriarchal, grey-bearded and venerable, but with his clean-shaven face and broad cunning features looked more like an ageing provincial comedian than anything else.

" I am very glad to make your acquaintance, Herr Baron," he said, while one could read in his crafty eyes . . . " I know everything."

Therese hastily asked George the conventional questions : when he had come, how long he was staying, how he was ; he answered patiently and courteously, and she looked him in the face with animation and curiosity.

Then he asked Leo about his plans for the near future.

" I must first practise the piano industriously, so as not to make a fool of myself before my pupils. People were very nice to me, of course. I had books, as many as I wanted, but they certainly didn't put a piano at my disposition." He turned to Therese. " You should certainly flog that point to death in one of your next speeches. This bad treatment of prisoners awaiting trial must be abolished."

" It was no laughing matter for him this time yesterday," said old Golowski.

" If you think by any chance," said Therese, " that the good luck which happened to come your way will alter my views you are making a violent mistake. On the contrary." And turning to George she continued: " Theoretically, you know, I am absolutely against their having let him out. If you'd simply knocked the fellow down dead, as you would have been quite entitled to do, without this abominable farce of a duel you'd never have been let out, but would have served your five to ten years for a certainty. But since you went in for this ghastly life-and-death gamble which is favoured by the State, because you cringed down to the military point of view you've been pardoned. Am I not right ? " She turned again to George.

The latter only nodded and thought of the poor young man whom Leo had shot, who as a matter of fact had had nothing else against the Jews except that he disliked them just as much as most people did after all—and whose real fault had only been that he had tried it on the wrong man.

Leo stroked his sister's hair and said to her : " Look here, if you say publicly in your next speech what you've just said to-day within these four walls you'll really impress me."

" Yes, and you'll impress me," replied Therese, " if you take a ticket to Jerusalem to-morrow with old Ehrenberg."

They got up from the table. Leo invited George to come into his room with him.

" Shall I be disturbing you ? " asked Therese. " I too would like to see something of him, you know."

They all three sat in Leo's room and chatted. Leo seemed to be enjoying his regained freedom without either scruples or remorse. George felt strangely affected by this. Therese sat on the sofa in a dark well-fitting dress. To-day was the first occasion on which she resembled the young lady who had drunk Asti under a plane-tree in Lugano, when she was the mistress of a cavalry officer, and who had subsequently kissed some one else. She asked George to play the piano. She had never yet heard him. He sat down, played something from *Tristan* and then improvised with happy inspiration. Leo expressed his appreciation.

" What a pity that he is not staying," said Therese, as she leaned against the wall and crossed her hands over her high coiffure.

" I am coming back at Easter," replied George, and looked at her.

" But only to disappear again," said Therese.

" That may be," replied George, and the thought that

his home was no longer here, that he had no home at all anywhere, and would not have for a long time, suddenly overwhelmed him.

" How would it be," said Leo, " if we went on a tour together in the summer ?—you, Bermann and I ? I promise you that you won't be bored by theoretical conversation like you were once last autumn . . . do you still remember ? "

" Oh well," said Therese, stretching herself, " nothing will come of it anyway. Deeds, gentlemen ! "

" And what comes of deeds ? " asked Leo. " Putting them at the highest, they simply save individual situations for the time being."

" Yes, deeds which you do for yourself," said Therese. " But I only call a real deed what one is capable of doing for others, without any feeling of revenge, without any personal vanity, and if possible anonymously."

At last George had to go. What a lot of things he still had to see to.

" I'll come part of the way with you," said Therese to him.

Leo embraced him again, and said : " It really was nice of you."

Therese disappeared to fetch her hat and jacket. George went into the next room. Old Frau Golowski seemed to have been waiting for him ; with a strangely anxious face she came up to him and put an envelope in his hand.

" What is that ? "

" The account, Herr Baron. I didn't want to give it to Anna. . . . It might perhaps have upset her too much."

" Oh yes. . . ." He put the envelope in his pocket and thought that it felt strangely different to any other. . . .

Therese appeared with a little Spanish hat, ready to go out. "Here I am. Goodbye, mamma. Shan't be home for dinner."

She went down the stairs with George and threw him sideways a glance of pleasure.

" Where can I take you ? " asked George.

" Just take me along with you. I'll get out somewhere."

25

They got in, the vehicle went on. She put to him all kinds of questions which he had already answered in the apartment, as though she took it for granted that he was now bound to be more candid with her than before the others. She did not learn anything except that he felt comfortable in his new surroundings and that his work gave him satisfaction. Had his appearance been a great surprise for Anna? No, not at all. He had of course given her notice of it. And was it really true that he meant to come back again at Easter? It was his definite intention. . . .

She seemed surprised. "Do you know that I had almost imagined . . ."

"What?"

"That we would never see you again!"

He was somewhat moved and made no answer. The thought then ran through his mind: Would it not have been more sensible . . . ? He was sitting quite close to Therese and felt the warmth of her body, as he had done before in Lugano. In what dream of hers might she now be living—in the dark jumbled dream of making humanity happy, or the light gay dream of a new romantic adventure? She kept looking insistently out of the window. He took her hand, without resistance, and put it to his lips.

She suddenly turned round to him and said innocently: "Yes, stop now. I'd better get out here."

He let go her hand and looked at Therese.

"Yes, my dear George. What wouldn't one fall into," she said, "if one didn't"—she gave an ironic smile— "have to sacrifice oneself for humanity? Do you know what I often think? . . . Perhaps all this is only a flight from myself."

"Why . . . Why do you take to flight?"

"Goodbye, George."

The vehicle stopped. Therese got out, a young man stood still and stared at her, she disappeared in the crowd.

I don't think she'll finish up on the scaffold, thought George. He drove to his hotel, had his midday meal, lit a cigarette, changed his clothes and went to Ehrenbergs'.

James, Sissy, Willy Eissler and Frau Oberberger were with the ladies of the house in the dining-room taking black coffee. George sat down between Else and Sissy, drank a glass of Benedictine and answered with patience and good humour all the questions which his new activities had provoked. They soon went into the drawing-room, and he now sat for a time in the raised alcove with Frau Oberberger, who looked young again to-day and was particularly anxious to hear more intimate details about George's personal experiences in Detmold. She refused to believe him when he denied having started intrigues with all the singers in the place. Of course she simply regarded theatrical life as nothing but a pretext and opportunity for romantic adventures. Anyway, she always made a point of thinking she detected the most monstrous goings-on in the *coulisses* behind the curtain, in the dressing-rooms and in the manager's office. When George had no option but to disillusion her, by his report of the simple, respectable, almost philistine life of the members of the opera, and by the description of his own hardworking life, she visibly began to go to pieces, and soon he found himself sitting opposite an aged woman, in whom he recognised the same person as had appeared to him last summer, first in the box of a little white-and-red theatre and later in a now almost forgotten dream. He then went and stood with Sissy near the marble Isis, and each sought to find in the eyes of the other during their harmless chatter a memory of an ardent hour beneath the deep shade of a dark green park in the afternoon. But to-day that memory seemed to them both to be plunged in unfathomable depths.

Then he went and sat next to Else at the little table on which books and photographs were lying. She first addressed to him some conventional questions like all the rest. But suddenly she asked quite unexpectedly and somewhat gently: "How is your child?"

"My child. . . ." He hesitated. "Tell me, Else, why do you ask me . . . ? Is it simply curiosity?"

"You are making a mistake, George," she replied calmly and seriously. "You usually make mistakes about me, as a matter of fact. You take me for quite superficial, or God knows what. Well, there's no point in talking about it any more. Anyway, my asking after the child is not quite so incomprehensible. I should very much like to see it sometime."

"You would like to see it?" He was moved.

"Yes, I even had another idea. . . . But one which you will probably think quite mad."

"Let's hear it, Else."

"I was thinking, you know, we might take it with us."

"Who, we?"

"James and I."

"To England?"

"Who's told you we're going to England? We are staying here. We've already taken a place in 'Cottage' * outside. No one need know that it is your child."

"What a romantic thought!"

"Good gracious, why romantic? Anna can't keep it with her, and you certainly can't. Where could you put it during the rehearsals? In the prompter's box, I suppose?"

George smiled. "You are very kind, Else."

"I'm not kind at all. I only think why should an innocent little creature pay the penalty or suffer for . . . Oh well, I mean it can't help it. . . . After all . . . is it a boy?"

"It was a boy." He paused, then he said gently: "It's dead, you know." And he looked in front of him.

"What! Oh, I see . . . you want to protect yourself against my officiousness."

* A fashionable district in Vienna.

" No, Else, how can you ? . . . No, Else, in matters like that one doesn't lie."

" It's true, then ?   But how did it . . . ? "

" It was still-born."

She looked at the ground. " No ?   How awful ! "   She shook her head. " How awful ! . . . And now she's lost everything quite suddenly."

George gave a slight start and was unable to answer. How every one seemed to take it for granted that the Anna affair was finished. And Else did not pity him at all. She had no idea of how the death of the child had shocked him.   How could she have an idea either ?   What did she know of the hour when the garden had lost its colour for him and the heavens their light, because his own beautiful child lay dead within the house ?

Frau Ehrenberg joined them. She declared that she was particularly satisfied with George.   Anyway, she had never doubted that he would show what he was made of as soon as he once got started in a profession. She was firmly convinced, too, that they would have him here in Vienna as a conductor in three to five years.   George pooh-poohed the idea.   For the time being he had not thought of coming back to Vienna. He felt that people worked more and with greater seriousness outside in Germany.   Here one always ran the danger of losing oneself.

Frau Ehrenberg agreed, and took the opportunity to complain about Heinrich Bermann, who had lapsed into silence as an author and now never showed himself anywhere.

George defended him and felt himself obliged to state positively that Heinrich was more industrious than he had ever been.   But Frau Ehrenberg had other examples of the corrupting influence of the Vienna air, particularly Nürnberger, who now seemed to have cut himself completely off from the world.   As for what had happened to Oskar . . . could that have happened in any other town except Vienna ? Did George know, by-the-by, that Oskar was travelling

with the Prince of Guastalla ? Her tone did not indicate
that she regarded that as anything special, but George
noticed that she was a little proud of it, and entertained the
opinion somewhere at the back of her mind that Oskar had
turned out all right after all.

While George was speaking to Frau Ehrenberg he noticed that Else, who had retired with James into the recess,
was directing glances towards him—glances full of melancholy and of knowledge, which almost frightened him. He
soon took his leave, had a feeling that Else's handshake
was inconceivably cold, while those of the others were
amiably indifferent, and went.

" How funny it all is," he thought in the vehicle which
drove him to Heinrich's. People knew everything before he
did. They had known of his *liaison* with Anna before it
had begun, and now they knew that it was over before he
did himself. He had half a mind to show them all that
they were making a mistake. Of course, in so vital an
affair as that one should be very careful not to decide on
one's course of action out of considerations of pique. It
was a good thing that a few months were now before him in
which he could pull himself together and have time for
mature reflection. It would be good for Anna, too,
particularly good for her, perhaps. Yesterday's walk with
her in the rain over the brown wet streets came into his
mind again, and struck him as ineffably sad. Alas, for
the hours in the arched room into which the strains of the
organ opposite had vibrated through the floating curtain
of snow—where were they ? Yes, where had these hours
gone to ? And so many other wonderful hours as well !
He saw himself and Anna again in his mind's eye, as a young
couple on their honeymoon, walking through streets which
had the wonderful atmosphere of a strange land ; common-
place hotel rooms, where he had only stayed with her for
a few days, suddenly presented themselves before him,
consecrated as it were by the perfume of memory. . . .

Then his love appeared to him, sitting on a white seat, beneath the heavy branches, with her high forehead girdled with the deceptive presentiment of gentle motherhood. And finally she stood there with a sheet of music in her hand while the white curtain fluttered gently in the wind. And when he realised that it was the same room in which she was now waiting for him, and that not more than a year had gone by since that evening hour in the late summer when she had sung his own songs for the first time to his own accompaniment, he breathed heavily and almost anxiously in his corner.

When he was in Heinrich's room a few minutes afterwards he asked him not to look upon this as a visit. He only wanted to shake hands with him. He would fetch him for a walk to-morrow morning if that suited him. . . . Yes—the idea occurred to him while he was speaking—for a kind of farewell walk in the Salmansdorf Forest.

Heinrich agreed, but asked him to stay just a few minutes. George asked him jestingly if he had already recovered from his failure of this morning.

Heinrich pointed to the secretary, on which were lying loose sheets covered with large nervous writing. " Do you know what that is ? I have taken up *Ägidius* again, and just before you came I thought of an ending which was more or less feasible. I'll tell you more about it to-morrow if it will interest you."

" By all means. I am quite excited about it. It's a good thing, too, that you have settled down to a definite piece of work again."

" Yes, my dear George, I don't like being quite alone, and must create some society for myself as quickly as possible, people I choose myself . . . otherwise, any one who wants to come along, and one is not keen on being at home to every chance ghost."

George told him that he had called on Leo and found him in far better spirits than he had ever expected.

Heinrich leaned against the secretary with both his hands buried in his trouser pockets and his head slightly bent ; the shaded lamp made uncertain shadows on his face. "Why didn't you expect to find him in good spirits ? If it had been us . . . if it had been me, at any rate, I should probably have felt exactly the same."

George was sitting on the arm of a black leather arm-chair with crossed legs and his hat and stick in his hand. "Perhaps you are right," he said, "but I must confess all the same that when I saw his cheerful face I found it very strange to realise that he had a human life on his conscience."

"You mean," said Heinrich, beginning to walk up and down the room, "that it is one of those cases where the relationship of cause and effect is so illuminating that you are justified in saying quietly ' he has killed ' without its looking like a mere juggle of words. . . . But speaking generally, George, don't you think that we regard these matters a little superficially ? We must see the flash of a dagger or hear the whistle of a bullet in order to realise that a murder has been committed. As though any man who let any one else die would be in most cases different from a murderer in anything else except having managed the business more comfortably and being more of a coward. . . ."

"Are you really reproaching yourself, Heinrich ? If you had really believed that it was bound to turn out like thàt . . . I am sure you would not have . . . let her die."

"Perhaps . . . I don't know. But I can tell you one thing, George : if she were still alive—I mean if I had forgiven her, to use the expression you are so fond of using now and then—I should regard myself as guiltier than I do to-day. Yes, yes, that's how it is. I will confess to you, George, there was a night . . . there were a few nights, when I was practically crushed by grief, by despair, by . . . Other people would have taken it for remorse, but it was nothing of the kind. For amid all my grief, all my despair,

I knew quite well that this death meant a kind of re-
demption, a kind of reconciliation, a kind of cleanness. If I
had been weak or less vain . . . as you no doubt regard it . . .
if she had been my mistress again, something far worse
than that death would have happened for her as well . . .
loathing and anguish, rage and hate, would have crawled
around our bed . . . our memories would have rotted bit
by bit—why, our love would have decomposed whilst its
body was still alive. It had no right to be. It would have
been a crime to have protracted the life of this love affair
which was sick unto death, just as it is a crime—and what
is more, will be regarded so in the future—to protract the
life of a man who is doomed to a painful death. Any
sensible doctor will tell you as much. And that is why I'm
very far from reproaching myself. I don't want to justify
myself before you or before any one else in the world, but
that is just how it is. I *can't* feel guilty. I often feel very
bad, but that hasn't the least thing in the world to do with
any consciousness of guilt."

"You went there just afterwards ? " asked George.

"Yes, I went there. I even stood by when they lowered
the coffin into the ground. Yes, I trained there with the
mother." He stood by the window, quite in the darkness,
and shook himself. "No, I shall never forget it. Besides,
it is only a lie to say that people come together in a common
sorrow. People never come together if they're not natural
affinities. They feel even further away from each other
in times of trouble. That journey ! When I remember it !
I read nearly the whole time, too. I found it positively
intolerable to talk to the silly old creature. There is no
one one hates more than some one who is quite indifferent to
you and requires your sympathy. We stood together by
her grave, too, the mother and I—I, the mother, and a
few actors from the little theatre. . . . And afterwards I
sat in the inn with her alone, after the funeral—a *tête-à-
tête* wake. A desperate business, I can tell you. Do you

know, by-the-by, where she lies buried ? By your lake, George. Yes. I have often found myself driven to think of you. You know of course where the churchyard is ? Scarcely a hundred yards from Auhof. There's a delightful view on to our lake, George ; of course, only if one happens to be alive."

George felt a slight horror. He got up. " I am afraid I must leave you, Heinrich. I am expected. You'll excuse me ? "

Heinrich came up to him out of the darkness of the window. " Thank you very much for your visit. Well, to-morrow, isn't it ? I suppose you are going to Anna now ? Please give her my best wishes. I hear she is very well. Therese told me."

" Yes, she looks splendid. She has completely recovered."

" I'm very glad. Well, till to-morrow then. I'm extremely glad that I shall be able to see you again before you leave. You must still have all kinds of things to tell me. I've done nothing again but talk about myself."

George smiled. As though he hadn't grown used to this with Heinrich. " Good-bye," he said, and went.

Much of what Heinrich had said echoed in George's mind when he sat again in his fiacre. " We must see the flash of a dagger in order to realise that a murder has been committed." George felt that there was a kind of subterranean connection, but yet one which he had guessed for a long time, between the meaning of these words and a certain dull sense of discomfort which he had frequently felt in his own soul. He thought of a past hour when he had felt as though a gamble over his unborn child was going on in the clouds, and it suddenly struck him as strange that Anna had not yet spoken a word to him about the child's death, that she had even avoided in her letters any reference, not only to the final misfortune, but also to the whole period when she had carried the child under her bosom.

The conveyance approached its destination. Why is my heart beating ? thought George. Joy ? . . . Bad conscience ? . . . Why to-day all of a sudden ? She can't have any grievance against me. . . . What nonsense! I am run down and excited at the same time, that's what it is. I shouldn't have come here at all. Why have I seen all these people again ? Wasn't I a thousand times better off in the little town where I had started a new life, in spite of all my longings ? . . . I ought to have met Anna somewhere else. Perhaps she will come away with me. . . . Then everything will still come right in the end. But is anything wrong ? . . . Are our relations really in a bad way ? And is it a crime to prolong them ? . . . That may be a convenient excuse on certain occasions.

When he went into Rosners' the mother, who was sitting alone at the table, looked up from her book and shut it with a snap. The light of a lamp that was swinging gently to and fro flowed from overhead on to the table, distributing itself equally in all directions. Josef got up from a corner of the sofa. Anna, who had just come out of her room, stroked her high wavy hair with both hands, welcomed George with a light nod of the head and gave him at this moment the impression of being rather an apparition than real flesh and blood. George shook hands with every one and inquired after Herr Rosner's health.

" He is not exactly bad," said Frau Rosner, " but he finds it difficult to stand up."

Josef apologised at being found sleeping on the sofa. He had to use the Sunday in order to rest himself. He was occupying a position on his paper which often kept him there till three o'clock in the morning.

" He is working very hard now," said his mother corroboratively.

" Yes," said Josef modestly, " when a fellow gets real scope, so to speak. . . ." He went on to observe that the *Christliche Volksbote* was enjoying a larger and larger circulation, particularly in Germany. He then addressed some questions to George about his new home, and showed a keen interest in the population, the condition of the roads, the popularity of cycling and the surrounding neighbourhood.

Frau Rosner, on her side, made polite inquiries about the composition of the repertoire. George supplied the information and a conversation was soon in progress, in which Anna also played a substantial part, and George found himself suddenly paying a visit to a middle-class and conventional family where the daughter of the house happened to be musical. The conversation finally finished up in George feeling himself bound to express a wish to hear the young lady sing once more—and he had as it were to pull himself together to realise that the woman whose voice he had asked to hear was really his own Anna.

Josef made his excuses; he was called away by an appointment with club friends in the café. "Do you still remember, Herr Baron . . . the classy party on the Sophienalp ? "

" Of course," replied George, smiling, and he quoted: " Der Gott, der Eisen wachsen liess. . . ."

" Der wollte keine Knechte," added Josef. " But we have left off singing that now for a long time. It is too like the ' Watch on the Rhine,' and we don't want to have it cast in our teeth any more that we have a sneaking fancy for the other side of the frontier. We had great fights about it on the committee. One gentleman even sent in his resignation. He's a solicitor, you know, in the office of Doctor Fuchs, the National German Deputy. Yes, it's all politics, you know." He winked. They must not think, of course, that now that he himself had an insight into the machinery of public life he still took the swindle seriously. With the scarcely surprising remark that he could tell a tale or two if he wanted, he took his leave. Frau Rosner thought it time to go and look after her husband.

George sat alone with Anna, opposite her by the round table, over which the hanging lamp shed its light.

"Thank you for the beautiful roses," said Anna. "I have them inside in my room." She got up, and George followed her. He had quite forgotten that he had sent her any flowers. They were standing in a high glass in front of the mirror. They were dark red and their reflection was opaque and colourless. The piano was open, some music stood ready and two candles were burning at the side. Apart from that all the light in the room was what came from the adjoining apartment through the wide opening left by the door.

"You've been playing, Anna?" He came nearer. "The Countess's Aria? Been singing, too?"

"Yes—tried to."

"All right?"

"It is beginning to . . . I think so. Well, we'll see. But first tell me what you have been doing all to-day."

"In a minute. We haven't welcomed each other at all so far." He embraced and kissed her.

"It is a long time since——" she said, smiling past him.

"Well?" he asked keenly, "are you coming with me?"

Anna hesitated. "But what do you really think of doing, George?"

"Quite simple. We can go away to-morrow afternoon. You can choose the place. Reichenau, Semmering, Brühl, anywhere you like. . . . And I'll bring you back in the morning the day after to-morrow." Something or other kept him back from mentioning the telegram which gave him three whole days to do what he liked with.

Anna looked in front of her. "It would be very nice," she said tonelessly, "but it really won't be possible, George."

"On account of your father?"

She nodded.

"But he is surely better, isn't he?"

"No, he is not at all well. He is so weak. They

wouldn't of course reproach me directly in any way. But I . . . I can't leave mother alone now, for that kind of excursion."

He shrugged his shoulders, feeling slightly wounded at the designation which she had chosen.

" Come, be frank," she added in a jesting manner. " Are you really so keen on it ? "

He shook his head, almost as if in pain, but he felt that this gesture also was lacking in sincerity. " I don't understand you, Anna," he said, more weakly than he really meant. " To think that a few weeks of being away from each other, to think of . . . well, I don't know what to call it. . . . It is as though we had got absolutely out of touch. It's really me, Anna, it's really me. . . ." he repeated in a vehement but tired voice. He got up from the chair in front of the piano. He took her hands and put them to his lips, feeling nervous and somewhat moved.

" What was *Tristan* like ? " she inquired.

He gave her a conscientious account of the performance and did not leave out his visit to the Ehrenbergs' box. He spoke of all the people whom he had seen and conveyed to her Heinrich Bermann's wishes. He then drew her on to his knee and kissed her. When he removed his face from hers he saw tears running over her cheeks. He pretended to be surprised, " What's the matter, child ? . . . But why, why . . . ? "

She got up and went to the window with her face turned away from him.

He stood up too, feeling somewhat impatient, walked up and down the room once or twice, then went up to her, pressed her close to him, and then immediately began again in great haste : " Anna, just think it over and see if you really can't come with me ! It would all be so different from what it is here. We could really talk things over thoroughly. We have got such important matters to discuss. I need your advice as well, about the plans I am to make for next year. I've written to you about it, haven't I ? It is very probable, you see, that I shall be asked to sign a three years' contract in the next few days."

"What am I to advise you ?" she said. "After all, you know best whether it suits you there or not."

He began to tell her about the kind and talented manager who clearly wished to have him for a collaborator ; about the old and sympathetic conductor who had once been so famous ; about a very diminutive stage-hand who was called Alexander the Great ; about a young lady with whom he had studied the Micaela, and who was engaged to a Berlin doctor ; and about a tenor, who had already been working at the theatre for twenty-seven years and hated Wagner violently. He then began to talk about his own personal prospects, artistic and financial. There was no doubt that he could soon attain an excellent and assured position at the little Court Theatre. On the other hand one had to bear in mind that it was dangerous to bind oneself for too long ; a career like that of the old conductor would not be to his taste. Of course . . . temperaments varied. He for his part believed himself safe from a fate like that.

Anna looked at him all the time, and finally said in a half jesting, half meditative tone, as though she were speaking to a child: "Yes, isn't he trying hard ?"

The thrust went home. "In what way am I trying hard ?"

"Look here, George, you don't owe me explanations of any kind."

"Explanations ? But you are really . . . Really, I'm not giving you any explanations, Anna. I'm simply describing to you how I live and what kind of people I have to deal with . . . because I flatter myself that these things interest you, in the same way that I told you where I had been yesterday and to-day."

She was silent, and George felt again that she did not believe him, that she was justified in not believing him—

even though now and again the truth happened to come from his lips. All kinds of words were on the tip of his tongue, words of wounded pride, of rage, of gentle persuasion—each seemed to him equally worthless and empty. He made no reply, sat down at the piano and gently struck some notes and chords. He now felt again as though he loved her very much and was simply unable to tell it her, and as though this hour of meeting would have been quite different if they had celebrated it elsewhere. Not in this room, not in this town ; in a place, for preference, which they neither of them knew, in a new strange environment, yes, then perhaps everything would have been again just as it had been once before. Then they would have been able to have rushed into each other's arms—as once before, with real yearning, and found delight—and peace. The idea occurred to him : " If I were to say to her now 'Anna ! Three days and three nights belong to us ! ' If I were to beg her . . . with the right words . . . Entreat her at her feet. . . . 'Come with me, come ! ' . . . She would not hold out long ! She would certainly follow me. . . ." He knew it. Why did he not speak the right words ? Why did he not entreat her ? Why was he silent, as he sat at the piano and gently struck notes and chords. . . . ? Why ? . . . Then he felt her soft hand upon his head. His fingers lay heavy on the notes, some chord or other vibrated. He did not dare to turn round. She knows it, too, he felt. What does she know ? . . . Is it true, then . . . ? Yes . . . it is true. And he thought of the hour after the birth of his dead child—when he had sat by her bed and she had lain there in silence, with her looks turned towards the gloomy garden. . . . She had known it even then—earlier than he—that all was over. And he lifted his hands from the piano, took hers, which were still lying on his head, guided them to his cheeks, drew her to him till she was again quite close, and she slowly dropped down on to his knees. And he

began again, shyly: " Anna . . . perhaps . . . you could
manage to . . . Perhaps I too could manage for a few days'
more leave if I were to telegraph. Anna dear . . . just
listen. . . . It would be really so beautiful. . . ." A plan
came to him from the very depths of his consciousness.
If he really were to go travelling with her for some days,
and were to take the opportunity honestly to say to her,
" It must end, Anna, but the end of our love must be
beautiful like the beginning was. Not dim and gloomy like
these hours in your people's house. . . ." If I were honestly
to say that to her—somewhere in the country—would it
not be more worthy of her and mine—and our past happiness . . . ? And with this plan in his mind he grew more
insistent, bolder, almost passionate. . . . And his words
had the same ring again as they had had a long, long
time ago.

Sitting on his knees, with her arms around his neck, she
answered gently : " George, I am not—going to go through
it another time. . . ."

He already had a word upon his lips with which he
could have dissipated her alarm. But he kept it back,
for if put in so many words it would have simply meant
that while he was thinking of course of living again a few
hours of delight with her, he did not feel inclined to take
any responsibility upon himself. He felt it. All he need
say to avoid wounding her was this one thing : " You
belong to me for ever !—You really must have a child by
me—I'll fetch you at Christmas or Easter at the outside.
And we will never be parted from each other any more."
He felt the way in which she waited for these words with
one last hope, with a hope in whose realisation she had
herself ceased to believe. But he was silent. If he had
said aloud the words she was yearning for he would have
bound himself anew, and . . . . he now realised more deeply
than he had ever realised before that he wanted to be free.

She was still resting on his knees, with her cheek leaning

26

on his. They were silent for a long time and knew that this was the farewell. Finally George said resolutely: " Well, if you don't want to come with me, Anna, then I'll go straight back—to-morrow, and we'll see each other again in the spring. Until then there are only letters. Only in the event of my coming at Christmas if I can . . ."

She had got up and was leaning against the piano. " The boy's mad again," she said. " Isn't it really better if we don't see each other till after Easter ? "

" Why better ? "

" By then—everything will be so much clearer."

He tried to misunderstand her. " You mean about the contract ? "

" Yes. . . ."

" I must make up my mind in the next few weeks. The people want of course to know where they are. On the other hand, even if I did sign for three years, and other chances came along, they wouldn't keep me against my will. But up to the present it really seems to me that staying in that small town has been an extremely sound thing for me. I have never been able to work with such concentration as there. Haven't I written to you how I have often sat at my secretary after the theatre till three o'clock in the morning, and woken up fresh at eight o'clock after a sound sleep ? "

She gazed at him all the time with a look at once pained and reflective, which affected him like a look of doubt. Had she not once believed in him ! Had she not spoken those words of trust and tenderness to him in a twilight church : " I will pray to Heaven that you become a great artist "? He felt again as though she did not think anything like as much of him as in days gone by. He felt troubled and asked her uncertainly : " You'll allow me, of course, to send you my violin sonata as soon as it is finished ? You know I don't value anybody else's criticism as much as I do yours." And he thought : If I could only just keep her as a friend . . . or win her over again . . . as a friend . . . is it possible ?

She said : " You have also spoken to me about a few new fantasies you have written just for the pianoforte."

" Quite right ; but they are not yet quite ready. But there's another one which I . . . which I . . ." he himself found his hesitations foolish—" composed last summer by the lake where that poor girl was drowned, Heinrich's mistress you know, which you don't know yet either. Couldn't I . . . I'll play it to you quite gently ; would you like me to ? "

She nodded and shut the door. There, just behind him, she stood motionless as he began.

And he played. He played the little piece with all its passionate melancholy which he had composed by that lake of his, when Anna and the child had been completely forgotten. It was a great relief to him that he could play it to her. She must be bound to understand the message of these notes. It was impossible for her not to understand. He heard himself as it were speaking in the notes ; he felt as though it was only now that he understood himself. Farewell, my love, farewell. It was very beautiful. And now it is over . . . farewell, my love. . . . . We have lived through what was fated for both of us. And whatever the future may hold for me and for you we shall always mean something to each other which we can neither of us ever forget. And now my life goes another way. . . . And yours too. It must be over . . . I have loved you. I kiss your eyes. . . . I thank you, you kind, gentle, silent one. Farewell, my love . . . farewell. . . . The notes died away. He had not looked up from the keys while he was playing : he now turned slowly round. She stood behind him solemn and with lips which quivered slightly. He caught her hands and kissed them. " Anna, Anna . . ." he exclaimed. He felt as if his heart would break.

" Don't quite forget me," she said softly.

" I'll write to you as soon as I'm there again."

She nodded.

" And you'll write to me, too, Anna . . . everything . . . everything . . . you understand ? "

She nodded again.

" And . . . and . . . I'll see you again early to-morrow."

She shook her head. He wanted to make some reply as though he were astonished—as if it were really a matter of course that he should see her again before his departure. She lightly lifted her hand as though requesting him to be silent. He stood up, pressed her to him, kissed her mouth, which was cool and did not answer his kiss, and left the room. She stayed behind standing with limp arms and shut eyes. He hurried down the stairs. He felt down below in the street as though he must go up again—and say to her : " But it's all untrue ! That was not our goodbye. I really do love you. I belong to you. It can't be over. . . ."

But he felt that he ought not to. Not yet. Perhaps to-morrow. She would not escape him between this evening and to-morrow morning . . . and he rushed aimlessly about the empty streets as though in a slight delirium of grief and freedom. He was glad he had made no appointments with any one and could remain alone. He dined somewhere far off in an old low smoky inn in a silent corner while people from another world sat at the neighbouring tables, and it seemed to him that he was in a foreign town : lonely, a little proud of his loneliness and a little frightened of his pride.

The following day George was walking with Heinrich about noon through the avenues of the Dornbacher Park. An air which was heavy with thin clouds enveloped them, the sodden leaves crackled and slid underneath their feet, and through the shrubbery there glistened that very road on which they had gone the year before towards the reddish-yellow hill. The branches spread themselves out without stirring, as though oppressed by the distant sultriness of the greyish sun.

Heinrich was just describing the end of his drama, which had occurred to him yesterday. Ägidius had been landed on the island ready after his death-journey to undergo within seven days his foretold doom. The prince gives him his life. Ägidius does not take it and throws himself from the cliffs into the sea.

George was not satisfied: " Why must Ägidius die ? " He did not believe in it.

Heinrich could not understand the necessity for any explanation at all. " Why, how can he go on living ? " he exclaimed. " He was doomed to death. It was with his hand before his eyes that he lived the most splendid, the most glorious days that have ever been vouchsafed to man as the uncontrolled lord upon the ship, the lover of the Princess, the friend of the sages, singers and star-gazers, but always with the end before his eyes. All this richness would, so to speak, lose its point : why, his sublime and majestic expectation of his last minute would be bound to become transformed in Ägidius's memory into a ridiculous dupe's fear of death, if all this death-journey were to turn out in the end to be an empty joke. That's why he must die."

" Then you think it's true ? " asked George, with even greater doubt than before. " I can't help it—I don't."

" That doesn't matter," replied Heinrich. " If you thought it true now, things would be too easy for me. But it would have become true as soon as the last syllable of my piece is written. Or . . ." He did not go on speaking. They walked up a meadow, and soon the expanse of the familiar valley spread out at their feet. The Sommerhaidenweg gleamed on the hill-slope on their right, on the other side hard by the forest the yellow-painted inn was visible with its red wooden terraces, and not far off was the little house with the dark grey gable. The town could be descried in an uncertain haze, the plain floated still further towards the heights and far in the distance loomed the pale low drawn outlines of the mountains. They now had to cross a broad highway and at last a footpath took them down over the fields and meadows. Remote on either side slumbered the forest.

George felt a presentiment of the yearning with which in the years to come, perhaps on the very next day, he would miss this landscape which had now ceased being his home.

At last they stood in front of the little house with the gable which George had wanted to see one last time. The door and windows were boarded up ; battered by the weather, as though grown old before its time, it stood there and had no truck with the world.

" Well, so this is what is called saying goodbye," said George lightly. His look fell upon the clay figure in the middle of the faded flower-beds. " Funny," he said to Heinrich, " that I've always taken the blue boy for an angel. I mean I called him that, for I knew, of course, all the time what he looked like and that he was really a curly-headed boy with bare feet, tunic and girdle."

" You will swear a year from to-day," said Heinrich, " that the blue boy had wings."

George threw a glance up to the attic. He felt as though there existed a possibility of some one suddenly coming out on the balcony : perhaps Labinski who had paid him no visits since that dream ; or he himself, the George von Wergenthin of days gone by ; the George of that summer who had lived up there. Silly fancies. The balcony remained empty, the house was silent and the garden was deep asleep. George turned away disappointed. " Come," he said to Heinrich. They went and took the road to the Sommerhaidenweg.

" How warm it's grown ! " said Heinrich, took off his overcoat and threw it over his shoulder, as was his habit.

George felt a desolate and somewhat arid sense of remembrance. He turned to Heinrich: "I'd prefer to tell you straight away. The affair is over."

Heinrich threw him a quick side-glance and then nodded, not particularly surprised.

"But," added George, with a weak attempt at humour, "you are earnestly requested not to think of the angel boy."

Heinrich shook his head seriously. "Thank you. You can dedicate the fable of the blue boy to Nürnberger."

"He's turned out right, once again," said George.

"He always turns out right, my dear George. One can positively never be deceived if one mistrusts everything in the world, even one's own scepticism. Even if you had married Anna he would have turned out right . . . or at any rate you would have thought so. But at any rate I think . . . you don't mind my saying so, I suppose . . . it's sound that it's turned out like this."

"Sound? I've no doubt it is for me," replied George with intentional sharpness, as though he were very far from having any idea of sparing his conduct. "It was perhaps even a duty, in your sense of the term, Heinrich, which I owed to myself to bring it to an end."

"Then it was certainly equally your duty to Anna," said Heinrich.

"That remains to be seen. Who knows if I have not spoilt her life?"

"Her life? Do you still remember Leo Golowski saying about her that she was fated to finish up in respectable life? Do you think, George, that a marriage with you would have been particularly respectable? Anna was perhaps cut out to be your mistress—not your wife. Who knows if the fellow she is going to marry one day or other wouldn't really have every reason to be grateful to you if only men weren't so confoundedly silly? People only have pure memories when they have lived through something—this applies to women quite as much as men."

They walked further along the Sommerhaidenweg in the

direction of the town, which towered out of the grey haze, and approached the cemetery.

"Is there really any point," asked George hesitatingly, "in visiting the grave of a creature that has never lived?"

"Does your child lie there?"

George nodded. His child! How strange it always sounded! They walked along the brown wooden palings above which rose the gravestones and crosses, and then followed a low brick wall to the entrance. An attendant of whom they inquired showed them the way over the wide centre path which was planted with willows. There were rows of little oval plates, each one with two short prongs stuck into the ground, on little mounds like sandcastles, close to the planks in a fairly large plot of ground. The mound for which George was looking lay in the middle of the field. Dark red roses lay on it. George recognised them. His heart stood still. What a good thing, he thought, that we didn't meet each other! Did she hope to, I wonder?

"There where the roses are?" asked Heinrich.

George nodded.

They remained silent for a while. "Isn't it a fact," asked Heinrich, "that during the whole time you never once thought of the possibility of its ending like this?"

"Never? I don't quite know. All kinds of possibilities run through one's mind. But of course I never seriously thought of it. Besides, how could one?" He told Heinrich, and not for the first time, of how the Professor had explained the child's death. It had been an unfortunate accident through which one to two per cent. of unborn children were bound to perish. As to why this accident should have taken place in this particular case, that, of course, the Professor had not been able to explain. But was accident anything more than a word? Was not even that accident bound to have its cause?

Heinrich shrugged his shoulders. "Of course. . . . One

cause after the other and its final cause in the beginning of all things. We could of course prevent the happening of many so-called accidents if we had more perception, more knowledge and more power. Who knows if your child's death could not have been prevented at some moment or other ? "

" And perhaps it may have been in my own power," said George slowly.

" I don't understand. Was there any premonitory symptom or . . ."

George stood there staring fixedly at the little mound. " I'll ask you something, Heinrich, but don't laugh at me. Do you think it possible that an unborn child can die from one not longing for it to come, in the way one ought to— dying, as it were, of too little love ? "

Heinrich put his hand on his shoulder. " George, how does a sensible man like you manage to get hold of such metaphysical ideas ? "

" You can call it whatever you like, metaphysical or silly ; for some time past I haven't been able to shake off the thought that to some extent I bear the blame for it having ended like that."

" You ? "

" If I said a minute ago that I did not long for it enough I didn't express myself properly. The truth is this : that I had quite forgotten that little creature that was to have come into the world. In the last few weeks immediately before its birth, especially, I had absolutely forgotten it. I can't put it any differently. Of course I knew all the time what was going to happen, but it didn't concern me, as it were. I went on with my life without thinking of it. Not the whole time, but frequently, and particularly in the summer by the lake, my lake as you call it . . . then I was . . . Yes, when I was there I simply knew nothing about my going to have a child."

" I've heard all about it," said Heinrich, looking past him.

George looked at him. " You know what I mean then ? I was not only far away from the child, the unborn child, but from the mother too, and in so strange a way that with the best will in the world I can't describe it to you, can't even understand it myself to-day. And there are moments when I can't resist the thought that there must have been some connection between that forgetting and my child's death. Do you think anything like that so absolutely out of the question ? "

Heinrich's forehead was furrowed deeply. " Quite out of the question ? one can't go as far as that. The roots of things are often so deeply intertwined that we find it impossible to look right down to the bottom. Yes, perhaps there even are connections like that. But even if there are . . . they are not for you, George ! Even if such connections did exist they wouldn't count so far as you were concerned."

" Wouldn't count for me ? "

" The whole idea which you just tell me, well, it doesn't fit in with my conception of you. It doesn't come out of your soul. Not a bit of it. An idea of that kind would never have occurred to you your whole life long if you hadn't been intimate with a person of my type, and if it hadn't been your way sometimes not to think your own thoughts but those of men who were stronger—or even weaker than you are. And I assure you, whatever turn your life may have taken even down by that lake, your lake . . . our lake . . . you haven't incurred any so-called guilt. It might have been guilt in the case of some one else. But with a man like you whose character—you don't mind my saying this—is somewhat frivolous and a little unconscientious there would certainly be no sense of guilt. Shall I tell you something ? As a matter of fact you don't feel guilty about the child at all, but the discomfort which you feel only comes from your thinking yourself under an obligation to feel guilty. Look here, if I had gone through anything like your adventure I might perhaps have been guilty because I might possibly have felt myself guilty."

"Would you have been guilty in a case like mine, Heinrich?"

"No, perhaps I wouldn't. How can I know? You're probably now thinking of the fact that I recently drove a creature straight to her death and in spite of that felt, so to speak, quite guiltless."

"Yes, that's what I'm thinking of. And that's why I don't understand. . . ."

Heinrich shrugged his shoulders. "Yes. I felt quite guiltless. Somewhere or other in my soul and somewhere else, perhaps deeper down, I felt guilty. . . . And deeper down still, guiltless again. The only question is how deep we look down into ourselves. And when we have lit the lights in all the storeys, why, we are everything at the same time: guilty and guiltless, cowards and heroes, fools and wise men. 'We'—perhaps that's putting it rather too generally. In your case, for example, George, there are far less of these complications, at any rate when you're outside the influence of the atmosphere which I sometimes spread around you. That's why, too, you are better off than I am—much better off. My look-out is ghastly, you know. You surely must have noticed it before. What's the good to me of the lights burning in all my storeys? What's the good to me of my knowledge of human nature and my splendid intelligence? Nothing. . . . Less than nothing. As a matter of fact there's nothing I should like better, George, than that all the ghastly events of the last months had not happened, just like a bad dream. I swear to you, George, I would give my whole future and God knows what if I could make it undone. But if it were undone . . . then I should probably be quite as miserable as I am now."

His face became distorted as though he wanted to scream. But immediately afterwards he stood there again, stiff, motionless, pale, as though all his fire had gone out. And he said: "Believe me, George, there are moments when I envy the people with a so-called philosophy of life. As for me, whenever I want to have a decently ordered world I have always first got to create one for myself. That's rather a strain for any one who doesn't happen to be the Deity."

He sighed heavily. George left off answering him. He walked with him under the willows to the exit. He knew that there was no help for this man. It was fated that some time or other he should precipitate himself into the void from the top of a tower which he had circled up in spirals; and that would be the end of him. But George felt in good form and free. He made the resolve to use the three days which still belonged to him as sensibly as possible. The best thing to do was to be alone in some quiet beautiful country-side, to rest himself fully and recuperate for new work. He had taken the manuscript of the violin sonata with him to Vienna. He was thinking of finishing that before all others.

They crossed the doorway and stood in the street. George turned round, but the cemetery wall arrested his gaze. It was only after a few steps that he had a clear view of the valley. All he could do now was to guess where the little house with the grey gables was lying; it was no longer visible from here. Beyond the reddish-yellow hills which shut off the view of the landscape the sky sank down in the faint autumn light. A gentle farewell was taking place within George's soul of much happiness and much sorrow, the echoes of which he heard as it were in the valley which he was now leaving for a long time; and at the same time there was within his soul the greeting of days as yet unknown, which rang to his youth from out the wideness of the world.